# The Nyctalope
# Steps In

**IN THE SAME SERIES**

Jean de LA HIRE

# The Nyctalope
# Steps In

*With additional stories by*
Matthew Dennion, Emmanuel Gorlier,
Julien Heylbroeck, Paul Hugli,
Roman Leary, Randy Lofficier,
Stuart Shiffman and David L. Vineyard

Edited and translated by
Jean-Marc & Randy Lofficier

**BLACK COAT PRESS**

Visit our website at www.blackcoatpress.com

ISBN 978-1-61227-028-9. Printing. November 2011. Published by Black Coat Press, an imprint of Hollywood Com-
ics.com, LLC, P.O. Box 17270, Encino, CA 91416. All rights
reserved.
The stories and cha-
racters depicted in this anthology are entirely fictional. Printed
in the United States of America.

# TABLE OF CONTENTS

# Introduction

*L'Enfant Perdu* [*The Lost Child*, translated here as *The Nyctalope Steps In*, and reproduced with some of its original illustrations] was serialized from May 2 to July 12, 1942 in the weekly magazine *L'Actu*, published in Marseilles in non-occupied France. *L'Actu* was a pro-Vichy publication, which might explain why the novella was never subsequently reprinted, although other stories published in it at the same time, including some by Georges Simenon, the creator of Maigret, were.

The fact that the story was published in a pro-Vichy magazine was bound to impact the narrative—and it did—although La Hire was given, in some respects, a freer hand than many of his contemporaries. This is particularly true in Chapter One, which takes place in mid-June 1940, during the period of French history now known as the "Exodus."

A brief summary of the events of that year will help the reader contextualize the story: The German armies invaded France, Belgium and Luxembourg on May 10, 1940, going through Belgium and the Ardennes mountains in the North. The French Military High command had been relying on its heavily fortified Ligne Maginot in the East for its defense, believing that an attack from the North was all but impossible. They were, in this instance, sadly and famously wrong.

The German troops reached Paris on June 14 and France was forced to surrender on June 22, after losing 92,000 men and suffering 200,000 wounded in the battle. This "Second Armistice" led to the division of the country into a Northern France, occupied by the Germans, and the allegedly "free" France in the south, led by what became known as the Vichy régime because of the name of its capital.

The invasion of May 10 and the Germans' rapid advance triggered a massive exodus of the population of Northern

France towards the South. It is estimated that ten million people, nearly a quarter of the population of the country, fled on the roads, carrying whatever belongings they had, many without a fixed destination. To add to the tragedy, the convoys were attacked by the German airforce, which killed an estimated 100,000 civilians during the Exodus. The French government fled from Paris to Bordeaux on June 11, and, from there, eventually relocated to Morocco.

It is against that bleak and depressing background that *The Nyctalope Steps In* opens. The nature of the mission undertaken by Leo and his friend Gno Mitang is left unstated, as the Vichy publications were instructed to never refer to the battles between France and Germany. However, since there was no other enemy than Germany at the time, one supposes that Leo is somehow fighting the invaders; however, La Hire had no choice but to leave it unsaid.

To the extent that the Tripartite Pact, which became known as the Axis alliance, between Germany, Italy, and Japan, was only signed on September 27, 1940, it is possible that the Japanese Gno Mitang is still a "free agent," capable of helping Leo, even against the Germans.

The Exodus was a deep and lasting blow to Jean de la Hire. This patriotic man, who sincerely believed in the greatness of France, saw all that he held dear shattered in a flash. Some people fled, some joined the resistance movements at home or abroad, some collaborated with the enemy for ideological or pragmatic reasons, and finally, others genuinely tried to do the best they could to help protect or save whatever remained of their country. From his writings, we know that La Hire fell in that last category.

The tragedy of the Nyctalope is that, despite the troubled times, he still tries his best to be a hero, even if it means finding an accommodation with the Nazi occupiers. He succeeds in small missions, but, ultimately, and lacking the hindsight of history, he fails in the much larger one.

This is a situation that no hero from English or American popular fiction ever had to face. Had England or America been defeated and occupied, one might like to speculate which of its heroes might have been similarly compromised... Reprinting this story today, therefore, gives us a chance to better understand and appreciate the moral challenges of these dark times.

There is one aspect of *L'Enfant Perdu* which is somewhat unpleasant, perhaps even puzzling. The story uses Roms (or *Romanichels* in the original French) as stereotypical villains, reinforcing the abominable racist cliché of gypsies as child-stealers. This is rather surprising since, throughout his fiction, La Hire was sympathetic to the Roms' plight, having Leo live with them (under the alias of "Pedro del Campos") and joining forces together in *La Croix de sang*. It is possible that La Hire did this to kowtow to the racist ideologies of the Vichy regime, but if so, that is indeed disappointing.

Eight of the fourteen other stories collected in this volume are entirely new: *The Season of the Shark*, *The Lesson of Captain Danrit*, *The Hunters of Mars*, *The Nyctalope's New York Adventure*, *A Present for Hitler*, *Twilight*, *A Moment of Perfect Happiness* and *The Three Sisters*. The others have previously appeared in our anthology *Tales of the Shadowmen*. This collection comprise all of the Nyctalope stories published to date, along with those already reprinted in our earlier volume, *Enter the Nyctalope*.

The elaborate timeline by Emmanuel Gorlier which concludes this volume comes from *Nyctalope! L'Univers Extravagant de Jean de La Hire*, a book published by our sister French imprint Rivière Blanche about the Nyctalope "universe" and its creator.

Jean-Marc Lofficier

9

# L'ENFANT PERDU

## Jean de La Hire: *The Nyctalope Steps In*

### Chapter One
### *The Eye Witnesses*

A powerful car, bearing both front and the rear plates with the letters "CD," indicating that at least one of its occupants belonged to the Diplomatic Corps, was traveling from Paris to Orleans.

Built for high speed, it moved sedately, almost as if it was being driven by a tourist.

But how could it have gone any fastes in that month of June, 1940? After finally making its way through Etampes, past the rush of vehicles of all kinds that crowded the roads, carrying people, animals and furniture in a desperate exodus, it continued to encounter, at regular intervals, further groups of survivors that formed, separated and formed again once more.

The vehicle was a stark contrast to all the others that it struggled past on the road. There were no suitcases crammed inside; its roof carried no excess luggage, nor was it topped with mattresses, haphazardly tied by a network of ropes.

Only two passengers were inside, both smartly dressed. The man behind the wheel was a short, stocky Japanese, with a strong and flexible body, and a wise Buddha-like face. His companion was a Frenchman whose athletic vigor was hidden inside a deceptively slim, elegant silhouette. Only his eyes, two extraordinary eyes with amazing power, covered by dark glasses, could have attracted any attention, and betrayed his identity as being Leo Saint-Clair, better known as the Nyctalope, whose exciting adventures had been widely reported in the newspapers around the world.

His companion was none other than his trusted friend and confidante, Gno Mitang, the famous Japanese diplomat and personal advisor to the Mikado himself.

They were, obviously, not fleeing. They took part in the Exodus as observers, with a secret purpose known only known to themselves.

Passing one group of cars after another on the road, they inspected each vehicle, their faces reflecting more compassion than curiosity.

Yet, one of the cars held a special interest for them, judging from the fact that they scrutinized it for several minutes.

It was an open vehicle, driven by a young, athletic-looking woman, accompanied by a 12-year-old boy. On the back seat, the usual heap of suitcases betrayed the sad purpose of the journey, for which the elegant sports car was clearly not made.

It was the child's face which had attracted Leo Saint-Clair's and Gno Mitang's attention. It was difficult to imagine a friendlier and more graceful countenance, or one as vivacious. This golden-haired boy's mobile features radiated an already powerful intelligence, expressed through his extraordinary dark eyes, full of thoughts and dreams, occasionally sparkling with humor or the simple, pure joy of childhood. The rapid succession of expressions had baffled the two observers. One moment, it was childishly carefree, candid and cheerful, then it was suddenly superseded by the serious and reflective face of an adult.

"A strange face," murmured Gno Mitang.

"A strange child," corrected the Nyctalope. "One can't help but wonder what will become of him? Will he grow up to be a musical genius? A sublime poet? A philosopher? A scientist? He bears the mysterious mark of a genius on his forehead. I imagine that Mozart as a child, or the future Lord Byron, looked just like him."

"He might also be destined for a life of suffering," whispered the Japanese mysteriously.

"That, too," replied Saint-Clair thoughtfully.

They remained silent, having noticed that the young woman was now looking at them. There was concern in her gaze, perhaps even fear... They took pity on her and, reading his friend's thoughts, Gno Mitang stepped on the gas pedal and passed her vehicle.

The Nyctalope turned. He saw the young woman's face again becoming reassured, but at the same time, he saw an expression of great weariness, that moved him powerfully.

"That young woman is falling asleep behind the wheel," he said. "I wonder how many hours she has been driving without stopping... Her eyes are closing despite her will to stay awake. She should stop."

The boy, however, remained awake. He had pulled a small notebook from his pocket and was writing something in it with concentration. His expression was serious, almost alight with inspiration.

The gap separating the two cars was increasing by the second. Saint-Clair stopped being able to study their faces, and soon lost sight of the other vehicle. Other cars appeared, which the Japanese passed one after the other. The Nyctalope looked at their passengers distractedly, but none held his attention the way the young woman and the boy had. For too many hours, he had seen too many identical faces, pale, frightened, drawn with fatigue and anxiety. The image of the strange child, however, remained fixed in his mind...

They passed a caravan of gypsies, sordid, rickety, crowded with ragged brats, escorted by men with dark faces and colorful clothes. In the look that the Bohemians gave them, the Nyctalope and his friend were surprised to discover a sinister, disturbing flame. It was the look of a predator watching its prey; looters following a rout and waiting for their chance to strip bare those who fell behind.

But the road was still not deserted. Cars preceded or followed the caravan, which was continuing its slow progress, drawn by an emaciated horse. All the drivers of the other cars exhibited the same concern, the same desire to pass the caravan and move away as quickly as possible.

One car, however, appeared to be an exception, obstinately deciding to remain behind the pathetic equipage. It was a two-seater sports car with a single occupant; its trunk was full of suitcases and travel bags.

Many women and children were traveling on foot and falling behind; they had probably begged its driver to take them in. He could easily have carried two or three people. But his hard face and his evil look had discouraged the would-be supplicants. Hunched over the steering wheel, his shoulders hunmched up, his head down, the driver tried to conceal his face; it was the repulsive, ugly snout of a human hyena.

"That man certainly doesn't appear to be in a hurry," remarked Gno Mitang. "What pleasure can he get from breathing the dirt of that caravan?"

"He's just a looter of another kind," said Saint-Clair, whose keen eyes had had time to scan the character's face.

After they passed that final group of travelers, the Japanese's car sped up on the road. Towards the end of the day, they arrived at Orleans, taking the long avenue of Faubourg Bannier to go straight into the heart of the city, where Leo Saint-Clair had been asked to come on an important and mysterious mission.

The following day, returning to Paris along the same road, after passing the town of Cercottes, the Nyctalope and Gno Mitang were forced to slow down to avoid hitting a grotesque caravan which was preparing to leave the main highway to take one of the dirt roads that cut through the western portion of the Orleans forest.

Saint-Clair recognized it as the same one they had seen the day before.

"This is the wagon we saw yesterday," he pointed out.

"When it comes to speed, a tortoise would be faster," said the Japanese.

Just then, as if to contradict him, the gypsy who rode in front of the caravan whipped the horse. The vehicle sped up and soon disappeared into the trees.

"The route they follow is strange," said Gno. "If they intend to cross the Loire river, they're not on the right path."

"My guess is that they're trying to avoid the roadblocks around Orleans and the gendarmes," said Leo Saint-Clair. "Their papers are probably no more in order with the Law than their consciences. They're going to let the storm pass while hiding in these woods. They'll add poaching to their list of offenses."

The Nyctalope's car continued on its way, soon leaving Chevilly beyond. Shortly before La Croix Briquet, Gno Mitang had to slow down again to let another cortege of refugees pass by. Suddenly, cries for help aroused their attention. On the other side of the road, a young woman stood next to a parked car, and was asking the many haggard people who filed past her for help, but they all ignoring her cries.

Listening to her, the two men heard bits of sentences, chopped words broken by sobs and cries. But the line of sad, dazed faces that walked by the woman had been rendered indifferent to all but their own misfortunes by excessive fatigue and despair. They moved past, flowing like a heavy, dark tide, carried by its own weight that no wind, no ripple, can disturb.

"My child... A little boy..." said the woman. "Have you seen my child?"

The Nyctalope and Gno Mitang exchanged the same look of concern and compassion. They had recognized the woman and the car.

"It's the girl we saw yesterday!" murmured the Nyctalope. "The mother or the guardian of the little boy with the face of a genius!"

"But the boy is no longer with her," said Gno Mitang.

"Stop!" ordered Saint-Clair. "We need to question her and learn what has happened to cause such distress."

The flood of indifferent, dull people finished passing. One last car drove by, leaving the road empty. Opening the door, the Nyctalope jumped onto the road and walked across to talk to the woman. After parking their car, the Japanese followed him.

The woman, her arms tragically outstretched, called and gestured to them.

"Messieurs... Messieurs..." she cried in a shrill voice. "Have you seen a child, a handsome blond boy, bare-headed, with big dark eyes? He is wearing a little beige sport jacket, short brown pants and shoes of the same shade, but a little darker?..."

"Yes, Madame," said Saint-Clair seriously. "We saw him yesterday, on the road, in that car parked behind you."

"But what about today, Monsieur? He vanished last night, or at dawn, while I was asleep. I stopped the car last night. I was exhausted. I fell asleep at the wheel. Fearing an accident, I preferred to spend the night by the roadside. And, in the morning, Yves had disappeared..."

Her voice broke. The sentence ended in a whimper of pain.

"Is the child your son, Madame?" asked the Nyctalope.

"No, Monsieur, I'm only his guardian, but I love him as if I were his own mother—better than his mother. He is my life. He was entrusted to me on his deathbed by his grandfather, who was my benefactor. I swear..."

More sobbing interrupted her sentence.

"Calm yourself, Madame," advised the Nyctalope gently. "We understand your concern, but you must try to control yourself and tell us exactly what you think happened. Under what conditions did the child disappear? Could he have gone for a stroll while you slept? Gotten lost? Might he have been caught in one of these waves of evacuees who were drifting by? My friend and I are only too happy to help you, if we can. Let me introduce myself: my name is Leo Saint-Clair and this gentleman is his Excellency Gno Mitang, Japanese diplomat."

"Leo Saint-Clair! The Nyctalope!" she cried, while her eyes suddenly shone with a ray of hope. "Oh! Monsieur, you've been sent to me by Divine Providence! I've heard of you, of your superhuman powers, of your many exploits…"

"I am only a man, Madame," said Saint-Clair modestly, "but whatever I can do to help, I will be honored to do. First, we need to know more. You said that you don't know exactly when the boy left the car, nor the reason why?"

"That's right. It was because I was weak, foolish enough to give in to the exhaustion that nearly overwhelmed me. Now, I'm reduced to making the most elaborate guesses… I suppose there could be a simple explanation… Yves—Yves Marécourt is his name and I'm Lise Andrézieux—Yves could have grown tired of sitting for so long, and might have wanted to merely stretch his legs. The surrounding woods, the silvery moonlight could have lured him and caught his fancy… He is such an extraordinary child, so smart, so advanced, too much so perhaps… While trying to satisfy his curiosity and his desire to learn, he might have gotten lost... He's not just a dreamer, but already a researcher, an experimentalist… He has a prodigious imagination when it comes to science. I've always believed that he'll grow up to become a great scientist, a discoverer of the unknown, perhaps a new Louis Pasteur… If you only knew what he means to me and what dreams I have for his future—wonderful dreams… But such gifts are not without danger. Once inside these woods—if that's where he went— what discoveries might he have made? Where did his adventurous spirit take him? I fear the worst: an accident. But there are other possibilities. Retracing his steps, crossing the road, he might have been hit by a car… Injured, unconscious perhaps, he might have been picked up by the one who struck him and been taken to the next village to seek medical attention…

What should I do? I dare not leave this place in case he returns. I still hope to see him come back, running towards me, apologizing for the distress he unwittingly caused me, as he knows how to do so well…"

"These are only theories," interrupted Saint-Clair. "The first, an exploratory walk in the woods during which the child became lost, seems rather unlikely. I'm sure you've already gone and called for him…?"

"Of course!"

"Yves can't have gone so far that he wouldn't have heard you. As for the possibility of an accident, where the driver took the child away, if it's not entirely out of the question, it still strikes me as at least doubtful. The driver would have noticed your car parked beside the road. Logically, he would have come and woken you up to ask about the boy… It's true that we're living in traumatic and unusual times. Panic seems to have taken hold of the crowd and that could upset the balance and distort the judgment of even the soundest minds… On the other hand, I admit that, right now, I can't think of any other plausible explanation…"

The green eyes of Lise Andrézieux nevertheless detected a secret anguish hidden in the Nyctalope's face.

"Yves means so much to me!" she murmured. "I fear the worst."

She hesitated, seemingly afraid of blurting out ill-omened words, but finally felt reassured by the sagacious and penetrating glances of Leo Saint-Clair and Gno Mitang, full of compassion. She could read sincere concern on their faces. Now, what was needed was confidence.

"Yves isn't just a child prodigy," she said. "He is also worth ten million francs, bequeathed to him by his grandfather. As the child's guardian, I have the use of this fortune, and employ it to develop his gifts and foster his future. Of course, some could believe that I derive more personal benefit from it…"

Serious and thoughtful, the Nyctalope listened to the woman without responding, trying not to let her read his secret thoughts. That attitude eventually discouraged her, and her voice began to tremble. Desperate to be understood and share her secret fears, she let her last words expire on her lips.

"That fortune, you see... It's possible... I don't know what to think..."

The Japanese diplomat had gone to inspect the woman's car and its surroundings. Saint-Clair, from whom nothing escaped, had seen him bend down and pick up an object from the ground.

Gno Mitang returned and made an imperceptible sign to his friend, who immediately understood its meaning.

"Well, Madam, here is what we're going to do," he announced suddenly. "Assuming, as you yourself have suggested, that the child, injured or not, was taken by a motorist, we will follow that trail and try to catch the hypothetical car. Whatever the outcome of our investigation, we will return to inform you of its results."

He bowed and cut short Madame Andrézieux's expressions of gratitude. Ten seconds later, he and Gno Mitang were back in their car, again driving towards Orleans.

"Well?" Leo asked his friend. "What did you find?"

"Some kind of heavy vehicle—but not a car—was parked near that of Madame Andrézieux last night," explained the Japanese. "I found its tracks on the road. It then drove towards Orleans. And I also found this on the ground near the door of her car..."

He presented a notebook, the first page of which contained a name and address: *Yves Marécourt, Manoir de Folembray*. Its pages were filled with equations and chemical formulas. One unfinished last sentence, written in a hesitant hand, said: *Why is thewre the smell of chlo...*

The Nyctalope closed the notebook and pocketed it.

"Let's look for those gypsies whom we saw going into the Orleans forest," he suggested.

But several hours of fruitless searching proved the futility of their efforts.

"Let's go back," ordered Saint-Clair. "I have one more question for Madame Andrézieux.

But as they returned to the main highway, they saw two cars drive by at a breakneck speed, one of which seemed to be pursuing the other. Madame Andrézieux was driving the second car.

"Let's follow them!" cried the Nyctalope.

The pursuit took them to Orleans, which they crossed from one end to the other. As they arrived near the river front, they saw Madame Andrézieux's car take a bridge that crossed the Loire. Seconds later, the bridge exploded.

Horrified, the two friends saw the car and its driver sink into the river, amongst a rain of stones and debris from the explosion. The other car had disappeared.

"Now I'll never get the answer to the question I wanted to ask her," whispered Leo Saint-Clair, very pale.

## Chapter II
### *The Mysterious Farm*

Two years later, the Nyctalope and Gno Mitang had all but forgotten that adventure, so tragically cut short.

After the death of Madame Andrézieux, the human torrent that was carrying endless crowds of fugitives south of the river made it futile to continue searching. Where was the child worth ten million—the future genius? No one knew. The compassionate quest that had, until then, propelled the two men, had been brutally severed by the destruction of the bridge of Orleans. They still remembered the interest and curiosity that had been awakened in them by Yves Marécourt's small face, but that, too gradually faded away, replaced by more urgent concerns requiring their complete attention.

The mystery, if mystery there was, had lost its appeal with the disappearance of any element that might have enabled them to solve it.

"If he is still alive, the child will eventually be found," had murmured St. Clair, turning his back to the river. "Interest, if not affection, will guide the investigation that his family—if he has one—will not fail to undertake"

The Nyctalope was not being totally truthful when he uttered those words. For a long time, the regret at having been obliged to give up his efforts to locate the boy nagged at him in the deepest recesses of his soul.

*A new Louis Pasteur perhaps*, the child's guardian had said, a few hours before disappearing into the waters of the Loire.

Ah, if only she could have answered the question that Leo Saint-Clair wanted to ask her! Then, perhaps, as had happened so often in the past, he would have launched himself on a prodigious quest to find the missing boy.

But Fate itself seemed to have intervened, forever closing the lips of Madame Andrézieux. And then, he had been required elsewhere and the memory of the Lost Child had gradually faded.

Two years later, the Nyctalope and Gno Mitang found themselves occupied with very different concerns. Once again, Leo and his friend were driving along the road, this time in Southern France.

They had left Pau in the Japanese's powerful car, had ascended the valley of the Aspe and were on the winding road that leads from the Forges d'Abel towards Somport and the Spanish border.

It was the middle of a very hot summer and, around noon, they decided to stop and picnic by the side of the road in the shade of a clump of trees, a short distance from their car. They enjoyed a substantial lunch while feasting their eyes on the magnificent Pyrenean landscape.

Suddenly, abandoning his usual pose of apparent nonchalance, Gno Mitang straightened up.

"I think someone just got inside our car," he said, rushing towards the road.

"I can't believe someone would want to rob us," said Saint-Clair, following him. "The local people have a well-deserved reputation for honesty."

Still, he joined his friend, but, before they reached the vehicle, they saw a boy jump out and scamper away like a rabbit. He was holding under his arm, wrapped in a blanket, the few personal effects which he had found inside the vehicle.

"Where does that little bandit come from?" exclaimed the Nyctalope. "I bet he isn't from here!"

"I'll ask him when I catch him," said Gno Mitang, rushing in pursuit of the young thief.

Saint-Clair followed suit, but the child had good legs and quite a head start. Without letting go of his booty, he climbed the slopes at a pace that his adult pursuers could not match. Skirting a rocky overhang, which formed a promontory, he disappeared from both men.'s eyes

"We've got to catch up with him," said Saint-Clair, while continuing to run. "I don't know what he stole from us, but I left a portfolio with some sensitive documents in it inside the car."

They reached the base of the rock. Just then, they heard a tumult of voices over their heads. They were the voices of a man and that of a child, the first growling, the other whimpering. They fell suddenly silent.

A cautious head appeared over the edge of the cliff for a second then quickly withdrew. Saint-Clair and Gno Mitang had time to glimpse a swarthy face, two dark eyes and a mop of shiny black hair.

"The alarm has been given," murmured Saint-Clair. "But if our thief's lair is up there, he won't escape us."

Resuming their ascent, the two men circled around the rock and discovered a steep path which led them to the top.

Arriving on a plateau of bare rock, they noted with astonishment the presence of several low buildings which, together, probably made up a small farm.

Silence weighed heavily upon the scene; the area seemed deserted. Saint-Clair saw no livestock, although he assumed that whatever animals that shabby and dilapidated farm could afford had probably been taken to a pasture higher on the mountains. The children would be keeping an eye on them, with the help of a dog.

But what had become of the man, whose head Saint-Clair and Gno Mitang had seen—and the boy-thief whom they had followed? Both men were sure of having heard loud voices from the foot of the rock, then the cries of several children, who had been gathered and taken away with the use of threats and slaps. The Nyctalope imagined the scene. Had the entire family taken refuge inside one of the buildings? Were they waiting, perhaps in fear, for the arrival of the strangers, the victims of theft, who were probably ready to summon the gendarmes?

Leo Saint-Clair and Gno Mitang began to examine the buildings.

The Nyctalope's superhuman eyes recorded every detail, observed, noted, evaluated. It was an automatic exercise for him, an innate faculty, maximized beyond that of ordinary men. His eyes, having scrutinized the wall that the two friends were following, suddenly stopped. Leo's face reflected his powerfully aroused attention.

"Look," he murmured, half aloud.

Gno Mitang obediently looked.

The wall, which had been used for children's games, was smeared with black and white markings, made with fragments of charcoal and pieces of plaster.

Now, these markings did not show the usual mess of scribblings, looking like prehistoric relics or puerile graffiti, made by childish fingers poorly initiated into the mysteries of writing. The letters had been formed by a hand both practiced and quick. They followed each other, in uppercase, interspersed with brackets and algebraic signs, sometimes superposed, and separated by clearly-drawn lines.

Saint-Clair deciphered them, lingered, then silently solicited the Japanese's opinion.

"They look like equations," said Gno Mitang. "Or perhaps, chemical formulas?"

"They are indeed chemical formulas," confirmed Saint-Clair thoughtfully.

His face contracted by an effort of thought, or memory, and he remained silent for several seconds. Then, slowly, his right hand rummaged inside his pockets and he pulled out a small notebook.

"This reminds me of something," said Saint-Clair, opening it. "My friend, do you remember the child who disappeared on the road to Orleans during the Exodus? That notebook belonged to him; you found it near the car from which he was taken. I never could bring myself to get rid of it."

"Now I remember," recalled the diplomat. "The boy whose guardian perished in the explosion which tragically blew up the bridge. His name was Yves Marécourt. I believe you had, at one point, theorized that he might have been kidnapped by a gang of gypsies?"

"That swarthy fellow whose head we just saw might be gypsy," said Saint-Clair.

With a simple flicker of his eyes, Gno Mitang communicated that he shared his friend's opinion.

The Nyctalope leafed through the notebook, the pages of which contained numerous chemical formulas. He compared them with those written on the wall.

"The same hand could have written them both," he said.

Gno Mitang, impassive as always, was waiting for the Nyctalope to reach the inescapable conclusion.

"Yes, they are by the same hand," Saint-Clair finally said, replacing the notebook in his pocket. "You know, Gno, that I do not believe in chance, but only in a succession of events, comparable to forces in a mathematical formula, of which, therefore, one can calculate the resulting vector. We call this Fate. It follows its own laws, which no human, consciously or otherwise, can escape. Now, here's the second time that Fate presents us with the same problem. Don't you think that, this time, it is impossible to step aside and our duty is clear?"

The Japanese silently assented.

"The child whom we promised to find was here," Saint-Clair continued.

"He might still be."

"He clearly stayed here; these chemical formulas prove that."

"We should look for him," the diplomat suggested.

"Yes, but we need to thread carefully. We may have grasped only a tenuous strand of the web. We don't want to alarm or disturb those who may have an interest in breaking it."

The Japanese closed his eyes then immediately opened them, indicating that he agreed with Saint-Clair and would be appropriately cautious.

Leaving the wall, the Nyctalope walked around the corner of the building. Gno followed him. They found themselves facing a courtyard that separated a barn from the main building of the farm itself.

A door opened and a man appeared on the threshold. The Nyctalope recognized his swarthy face. This was the person they had glimpsed at the edge of the cliff.

The man's attitude was surly and gruff, like a wild beast more willing to bite and growl than to befriend a stranger.

"What are you doing here?" he growled. "This is not the highway, or even a public path which people have the right to take."

"We're looking for a boy who stole from us," said Saint-Clair, fixing the farmer with a steely gaze. "We know that he's found refuge here. If you don't give us back what he took from us, we'll return with the gendarmes. But we promise to be forgiving if you do."

The man bowed his head, but clenched his fists. He wanted to strike at those meddling visitors, but refrained, intimidated by the threat of the gendarmes.

He grunted, without looking up.

"If one of the boys took something from you, out of mischief, you'll get it back."

"Bring the children out," ordered Saint-Clair.

The farmer hesitated, glanced at him stubbornly, then, apparently subdued, he went back inside and quickly returned, holding a small package wrapped in brown paper.

"Is this your property?" he asked, hypocritically. "If so, you can have it back. The child intended no malice, but I will punish him anyway."

"I asked you to bring out the children. I wish to scold the thief in your presence," replied the Nyctalope firmly, taking the package.

Reluctantly, the farmer stepped over the threshold and called out:

"Come out, all of you, you little vermin!

A half-dozen little children, swarthy, wild-looking, dirty and ragged, came out of the farm, elbowing each other.

Saint-Clair and Gno Mitang exchanged a quick glance. Yves Marécourt was not among them.

"Is that your whole family?" asked the Nyctalope sternly.

"Yes," said the man, nodding.

"Tell me the truth. Do you have another child? An adopted boy, raised by you, found on the road during the Exodus for example?"

The face of the gypsy hardened. Did he expect this? It was impossible to tell. He immediately replied, feigning candor:

"What boy are you talking about? I've never been on the road. I'm just a poor farmer, who never leaves his mountain."

Without answering, the Nyctalope dragged the man to the wall where the young genius had scratched his chemical formulas.

"Who wrote this then?" Saint-Clair asked harshly.

Stubborn, surly, the man only shrugged his shoulders.

"One of them. My kids go to school. They think it's fun to scribble on the walls."

"The child who wrote this knows a lot more than your children," said the Nyctalope. "And these are not mere scribbles. I, too, know a lot more than you think. Why lie to me? Sooner or later, you will confess the truth—if not to me, to the

27

gendarmes. In your own interest. Perhaps it might interest you to know that the boy in question is a millionaire, and his family will pay a handsome reward to find him…"

The Nyctalope knew at once that he had hit bull's eye. The gypsy's eyes had lit the fires of greed. Obviously, he had not known the true value of the stolen child. The revelation left him speechless. At first, he appeared sorely tempted.

Saint– Clair followed the struggle on the man's face. He was calculating the chances and risks he might be taking if he spoke, and was trying to figure out how to best take advantage of the situation he had just discovered.

"A big reward, you say?" he repeated.

He was about to speak, to confess. The Nyctalope could feel the truth about to emerge. But, suddenly, the face of the gypsy changed His eyes became fixed, looking beyond Saint-Clair and Gno Mitang, at something or someone who had signaled to him. And then, his face closed up again.

Sensing the foreboding presence of a mysterious adversary, who alone could explain the farmer's sudden change of heart, Saint-Clair and the Japanese turned around, but they did not see anyone.

The farmer grinned.

"I'm sorry to disappoint you, gentlemen," he said defiantly, "but there is no such child here."

"There is and I will find him, and it will be much worse for you," retorted the Nyctalope, dryly.

He turned his back to the gypsy and invited Gno Mitang to follow him.

Saint-Clair understood that there was nothing more to be gained by remaining. The farmer was stubborn, having found a new assurance thanks to the mysterious foe whose presence the Nyctalope had sensed, but who could make himself as invisible as young Yves Marécourt.

The two friends walked down the slope.

"Are you giving up?" asked Gno Mitang.

"Of course not," replied the Nyctalope. "But for now, there's nothing more we can do. We'll return when these people are no longer on their guard.

"Obviously, we were being watched by someone," observed the Japanese.

Saint-Clair nodded but said nothing more. They were nearing the place where they had left their car... and also their interrupted lunch. The series of incidents that had occurred had killed their appetite. They contented themselves with gathering whatever was left of their picnic, putting it back into the basket and getting back into the car. The Nyctalope also returned the effects he had recovered from the gypsy to the trunk.

Afterwards, Gno Mitang took the wheel and asked for directions:

"Are we continuing towards the pass, and onward to Spain? Or are we turning around to go back to the valley?"

Before answering, Saint-Clair gave a final glance in the direction of the rocky promontory were the strange farm was located. His expression betrayed a certain reluctance to leave. He was visibly unhappy to go without finding the answer to the riddle of the lost child: why, and on whose account, had the gypsy kidnapped and held little Yves Marécourt, while remaining unaware of his fortune?

"Let's go back down to the valley," he finally decided. "The people in the next village might tell us more about the inhabitants of this farm."

Consequently, Gno Mitang, acceding to his friend's desire as always, was about to turn the car around, when, suddenly, they heard a cry.

Turning their heads in the direction of the cliff, whence the cry had come, they saw a human body spinning, falling and crashing to the bottom of a ravine, out of the sight of the two friends.

Gno Mitang stopped the car and Saint-Clair jumped out of the door. Both men ran to the place where the body had fallen. They had not exchanged a word, but the same question was on their lips: *Who was it?*

A man? A child? Because of the distance that separated them from the rock, and the rapidity of the fall, they had not been able to identify the victim. The same thought assaulted their minds: could their unplanned intervention have been the cause of a terrible, brutish crime, whose victim might be the child prodigy whom they were trying to save?

They were reassured when they reached the edge of the ravine. The size of the body lying there was that of a man, not a child. Carefully climbing down the rocks, they approached the twisted body.

Its limbs were broken, the skull cracked... The dead man was the farmer gypsy whom they had left half an hour before.

Was it an accident? Or a crime?

Suddenly, they heard another sound. They raised their heads. On the road bordering the ravine, a sports car passed, racing away, its driver barely glancing at them.

And both men, at the same moment, felt as if they recognized that car.

## Chapter III
### *Duel of Feints*

Neither Saint-Clair nor Gno Mitang had touched the gypsy's body. But the way his head had smashed against the rock during the fall, meant that there was no chance of survival. Still, the Nyctalope checked for a pulse.

"We'll get nothing more useful from this unfortunate man," he said. "Until we catch his killer, we won't know the reason for this crime."

"It seems clear enough to me," remarked the Japanese.

"Not entirely," said the Nyctalope. "We can, of course, use our imaginations to reconstruct the scene—what must have occurred after we left. Someone—perhaps the driver of that car we just saw go by—had been spying on us while we talked to the farmer. Foreseeing his possible betrayal, especially considering the lure of the reward that I was dangling before him, this individual, seeking to preserve his secret, first signaled to the farmer to order him say nothing. After our departure, a heated debate probably erupted between the two men, who must both be accomplices in the abduction of little Yves Marécourt. The gypsy, who had been kept unaware of the child's wealth, must have intended to take advantage of what I'd told him. The other, not caring to give in to the farmer's demands, got rid of him by throwing him over the edge of that cliff."

"All that is very plausible," approved Gno Mitang.

"But what is the murderer's interest in this case? And who is he? You remember, my friend, the car that Madame Andrézieux seemed to chasing shortly before her death?"

"Yes. It was a sports car," said the Japanese.

"Isn't it possible that Madame Andrézieux, concerned about the disappearance of her ward, might have recognized its driver and pursued him? I'm also reminded that we saw another sports car—possibly the same one—dawdling on the road behind a gypsy caravan the day we met with little Yves and his guardian..."

"And the car we just saw race down from above was also a sports car," remarked Gno Mitang.

"Yes. If that was the same car, the same person must be behind the wheel," said Leo Saint-Clair. "He should be found and identified. But he got away again. We must trust in Fate to again place us across his path. For now, if you don't mind, let's return to the farm. The murder might have been witnessed. The gypsy had his whole family up there, with many children... Maybe someone will decide to talk. Any information, any evidence we might collect, will be invaluable."

But once at the farm, despite looking everywhere and searching all the buildings, they found no one. Obviously unwilling or too terrified to talk, all the occupants, young and old, men, women and children, had taken flight, going into the mountains and, probably, across the Spanish border. There was a good chance they had already crossed it, putting more space between them and the object of their terror.

Had they taken little Yves Marécourt with them? This was the question that Saint-Clair asked himself. But he was suddenly distracted by a call from his Japanese friend.

"Come and see this!"

In a barn, under a layer of straw, Gno Mitang had discovered a large cement slab, the joints of which, free of dust and straw, showed that it had been recently raised. The Nyctalope and his friend set to work, raised it, and eventually gained access to a dark and damp cellar lit by only by a small, barred window.

This virtual tomb was empty, except for a small cot in a corner, standing on top of a wooden pallet, which suggested that it had been inhabited. Upon closer inspection, Saint-Clair found under the boards of the pallet a supply of chalk and charcoal. While examining the walls with his flashlight, he discovered the same signs and letters making up chemical formulas, which he had already noticed on one of the exterior walls of the farm. The conclusion was obvious: this cave had been used as a prison for Yves Marécourt.

Indeed, at the bottom of the groups of letters representing combinations of acids and bases, one could see in uppercase: *YM*.

"That's his signature," said the Nyctalopic. "The child wanted to leave a sign of his presence here, hoping that someone might discover it—and he was right."

"What do we do now?" asked the Japanese.

"Let's stop in the nearest town, Urdos," replied Saint-Clair. "Our first duty is to warn the gendarmes of the crime we witnessed. And it will give us the opportunity to investigate these strange farmers who kept that lost child—or should I say stolen child?—prisoner."

"Are you sure you want to mention the existence and the alleged kidnapping of Yves Marécourt?" said Gno Mitang. "It might only confuse the police and lead them to question the reasons for our presence here?"

"You're right. Let's keep that information to ourselves, at least until the gendarmes or we get hold of the murderer, or we find the child. Thank you, my friend, for reminding me of the need for discretion in this matter."

"You're very welcome, my dear Leo."

Less than thirty minutes later, Gno Mitang's fast car arrived in Urdos, where the two friends set out to find the gendarmerie.

"The nearest one is in Accous, the seat of the county," they were told.

"The telephone will alert them faster than we can by going there," replied the Nyctalope. Take us to the Mayor. We'll give him a statement and he can take care of things."

The kindly man who held the Mayoral post in the small village received the news with dismay and consternation. That a murder had been committed on the territory of his commune was the equivalent of a natural disaster! The whole village would be in an uproar. As far as he could recall, there had never been a murder committed in the peaceful valley. The very idea that he was going to have to telephone the police and be responsible for the initial investigation drove the poor man to the verge of tears. It took Saint-Clair and Gno Mitang a good quarter of an hour to explain to him what he had to do, and boost his confidence. The first thing, they said, was to report the suspicious sports car.

Afterwards, they were finally able to discuss their own, personal investigation. And this is what they learned regarding the mysterious occupants of the isolated farm:

Were they gypsies? Yes, it was quite possible they were... That was the impression they'd given when they'd arrived in the region, about two years before.

34

Saint-Clair noted the date, which coincided with the disappearance of young Marécourt.

Were they farmers? They had become so through their occupation of the old, dilapidated and abandoned farmhouse—owned or rented, no one knew, but the notary of the next town could probably tell them. In any case, they did not seem to be hard workers, and it was a miracle if they managed to live off their farm. But, they were not beggars either. They bought meat, wine, bread and vegetables, and plenty of spirits, in Forges d'Abel and Urdos, so they had money. They received postal orders, brought by the postman, from time to time.

Where did the money come from? The police would have to find out, if they were curious about it.

The family, as far as the villagers could tell, consisted of two men, one woman and a throng of children. The woman came alone to the village once in a while to buy supplies. The two men never came down and didn't they patronize the local café. If they had to celebrate something, they did it at home, behind closed doors. They were barely civilized. The children were as swarthy as the adults and ran off at full speed when the locals tried to talk to them. No one had ever seen a blond boy among them.

As for the sports car, pending a more detailed investigation by the gendarmes, the Mayor was quite certain that it had not crossed the village. The main road passed just in front of his door and he would surely have noticed.

Having noted all this information, Saint-Clair only had to sign his official statement, thank the Mayor and take his leave.

"I'm afraid that our investigation here is at a dead end," he said to his friend, as they were driving back to Pau. "We'll learn nothing more in the region. We have to seek the trail elsewhere…"

"But where?"

"At the child and his guardian's home—the Manoir de Folembray. The address is inside the book."

It was child's play for the Nyctalope to locate the Manor, located in a forest, near a village in the Aisne. But what he learned there hardly made the situation clearer.

He was referred to Maître Loureille, a local notary, responsible for overseeing the estate. Saint-Clair and Gno Mitang went to visit him.

"Certainly, Messieurs," said the notary, when asked, "I do know young Yves Marécourt, and his guardian, the charming Madame Andrézieux, but I haven't had any news of them since the Exodus. I'm sorry to learn what you've just told me. As for young Yves' family, I don't know if he has any. Apart from his grandfather, whose notary I was, I know of no other relatives. Of course, that does not mean that they don't exist…"

"They'll probably make themselves known when they learn of the death of Madame Andrézieux and the disappearance of Yves," said Saint-Clair. "Their self-interest, if not any affection they might feel for the boy, will surely motivate them to do so."

"I think so too."

"What was the legal situation of Madame Andrézieux vis-à-vis the fortune bequeathed to Yves Marécourt?"

"Just that of a guardian. According to the will of the testator, I was made the executor of his estate and accepted that responsibility, but I've confined myself to managing his fortune, which, as you know, is considerable. Madame Andrézieux, who had earned the confidence of the testator, received the income derived from my efforts, which I'm happy to say, she employed exclusively for the good of the child."

"So she was entitled to live off the proceeds?" asked the Nyctalope.

"Not at all. An entitlement is always attached to the person of the recipient and continues until his or her death. But in Madame Andrézieux's case, the enjoyment of her income would terminate upon the majority of her ward—or his death. Here is the exact passage of the testament: *Lise Andrézieux will receive all income generated by the Estate, and will dis-*

*pose of it according to the instructions I gave her. Her position, and the powers arising therefrom, will last only as long as she remains my grandson's legal guardian. At his majority, or in the event of premature termination of the guardianship, for any reason whatsoever, that position will expire. However, a reasonable annuity allowing her to live with dignity will henceforth be paid to Madame. Andrézieux."*

"Thank you, Maître. This proves that Madame Andrézieux had no interest whatsoever in disposing of her ward."

"Quite the contrary!"

"Indeed. We agree on that point, which is important. Since I intend, as I've told you, to find Yves, I have to know who may have had an interest in his disappearance. Let's proceed by elimination. We have now crossed out Madame Andrézieux. It seems to me that there are two possibilities. The author or instigator of the kidnapping may have a direct or indirect interest in removing the child. Or, given young Yves' wealth, we may be confronted with an American-style act of banditry, i.e.: the child was taken in order to extort the payment of a large ransom."

"I suppose that's a possibility..."

"Yes, but I don't find it very likely. If the kidnappers wanted to ransom the child, why haven't they tried to contact you? It's been two years and you haven't heard a peep... On the other hand, I ask myself, if the first hypothesis is true, why did the successor of the child not have him killed immediately? We have proof that Yves was still alive at that farm two years after the abduction..."

"Perhaps Madame Andrézieux's unexpected death had something to do with it?" observed Gno Mitang.

"True. Current events, too, may explain their inaction. I'm not however abandoning the first hypothesis, that of the intervention of a malicious heir. Can I ask you a favor, Maître Loureille?"

"Certainly, Monsieur Saint-Clair. What would you like me to do?"

"Could you place a classified advertisement in several newspapers saying something like: *Wanted: the heirs of young Yves Marécourt disappeared during the Exodus*. Coming from a notary, this will not appear suspicious. Someone is bound to see it and respond. Then, let me know who, in full confidence of course."

"Your reputation precedes you, Monsieur Saint-Clair. You have my trust and I assure you of my full cooperation."

"Thank you, Maître."

And the two friends left. Still, the Nyctalope remained anxious. The same questions, which he had outlined to the notary, continued to haunt him.

Why had Yves Marécourt been kidnapped? And why was his confinement being prolonged, without anyone trying to profit from it? What had been done to the child before and after the incident at the farm? What would happen to him now? The man who had killed the gypsy, whoever he was, had certainly not left the farm without resolving the fate of the child…

When asked, Gno Mitang agreed with his friend, but added a suggestion:

"If the murderer was the man we saw in the sports car, perhaps he took the boy with him?"

"I don't think so. He was clearly alone when we saw him. Also, he was driving towards the Forges d'Abel. If he had taken Yves with him, alive or dead, he would have been more likely to try to cross the Spanish border instead."

"Maybe he did."

"You're right, Gno. His departure towards the Forges might just have been a feint. Once he had seen us rush towards the ravine, he pretended to go in that direction, then he must have stopped and spied on us, watching our every movement. While we went back up to the farm, he backtracked and fled to Spain. He is a powerful and careful foe…"

"But I'm certain you'll get the best of him, my dear Saint-Clair."

"I hope so. But for now, the only thing we can do is wait for the outcome of the notary's advertisement."

But two days later, they received the following message from Maître Loureille:

*The advertisement that you suggested has become unnecessary. We have been forestalled. Read the attached text of an announcement that appeared this morning in several newspapers.*

The Nyctalope and Gno Mitang read:

*Anyone able to provide information about Madame Lise Andrézieux and young Yves Marécourt, her ward, 12 years-old, are invited to contact the Argos Agency, Boulevard Magenta, Paris. All expenses will be reimbursed. The persons in question left Folambray in June 1940 and were traveling by car on the road from Paris to Orleans.*

"Let's go and pay a visit to the Argos Agency," Saint-Clair decided.

When they entered the Agency's offices, which looked rather shabby, the Nyctalope and Gno Mitang were immediately certain that it was one of those shady private detective agencies that usually catered to questionable customers.

The director was a small man, sly and furtive, who jumped when Leo Saint-Clair announced his name.

"Saint-Clair? The Nyctalope? What an honor!" he stammered, wriggling and snapping the knuckles of his long and dirty fingers. "And you're here to provide me with information about...?"

"First, I want to the name and relationship of the person who is interested in the fate of the Marécourt boy," said the Nyctalope abruptly. "I personally witnessed the death of Madame Andrézieux and I do have fairly accurate information about the fate of young Yves Marécourt. What I have to tell you is important enough that I can only do so carefully and with certain assurances."

"Certainly... Certainly... I understand what you're saying," stammered the director, visibly worried. "If you were anyone else, Monsieur Saint-Clair, I would say that I am mandated to gather the evidence and judge its value first, but of course, I would never dream of saying that you. You are the Nyctalope. Besides, my client is a perfectly honorable man, and I don't think he'll mind at all if I refer you directly to him. His name is Monsieur Philogène Porcien. He told me he is the cousin of the Marécourt boy. Here is his address..."

"Tell him to expect my visit tomorrow," said Saint-Clair.

After exchanging a handshake, he left, followed by Gno Mitang.

"Naturally," said the Japanese, "you're not going to wait and you plan to see Monsieur Porcien immediately?

"Yes, but I also think that it might be interesting to monitor his actions after I've seen him and he believes I've truly left. I count on you to carry out a discreet surveillance."

## Chapter IV
### *The Eyes of a Tiger*

Leo Saint-Clair left the metro at the Alesia station, walked down the Avenue du Maine and turned into the Rue du Chateau, where Monsieur Philogène Porcien lived, according to the address the Director of the Argos Agency had given him.

After finding the number of the house he wanted, Saint-Clair climbed to the fourth floor and rang the bell. The door remained closed for several minutes until an ageless, ordinary maid opened it, staring at the visitor with empty eyes.

"May I see Monsieur Porcien?" asked the Nyctalope.

The maid let Saint-Clair into a dark, cramped hallway and left. She returned almost immediately.

"Monsieur is coming," she said.

Saint-Clair did not sit down, but instead went to the single window to look out. On the other side of the street, which, at that hour, was full of women with shopping bags, was a small hotel. Looking down, he saw a small, recognizable silhouette cross its threshold.

It was Gno Mitang, but a Gno Mitang unrecognizable under a disguise that had erased all his class and style.

The Nyctalope smiled and turned around. Monsieur Porcien had just arrived.

"What do you want, Monsieur?" he inquired.

Was this the same man who had been behind the wheel of the infamous sports car they had glimpsed in June 1940 on the Orleans road? The same car they had seen driving towards Somport shortly after the murder of the gypsy? It was possible, but not certain. Something baffled Saint-Clair, who was endowed with a powerful sense of physiognomy and an excellent memory for faces. It was the other man's eyes, which were now visible, but which bad been hidden behind driving goggles the first two times they had seen him.

*The eyes of a tiger*, thought Saint-Clair.

The Nyctalope introduced himself, but his name did not elicit any reaction from Monsieur Porcien.

"Why do I have the honor…?"

In a calm and perfectly neutral tone, Saint-Clair stated the reason for his visit:

"Monsieur, I have been sent to you by the Director of the Argos Agency, whom I went to see in response to an advertisement that he claimed you asked him to place. He felt that the information which I have in my possession should be brought and disclosed to you without delay.

"I see. And what do you have to tell me?" asked Monsieur Porcien blandly.

"I understand that you are looking for a lady, Madame Andrézieux, and a young boy named Yves Marécourt, who both disappeared during the Exodus?"

Monsieur Porcien raised his eyes towards Heaven and sighed deeply.

"I'm not the only one in France who's worried about a missing relative!" he replied in a long-suffering voice.

"So you're related to these two people?" said Saint-Clair.

"Only to the boy, yes, Monsieur. His grandfather was the uncle of my poor mother. Not a close relation perhaps, but I believe that the poor child has no other relative beside myself. It is, therefore, natural that I am concerned about his fate. As for Madame Andrézieux, we're not related, but I do know of her devotion to the family…"

"Then I can inform you of her death without it causing too much grief," said the Nyctalope.

The man with the tiger's eyes stared at him for a moment.

"Are you sure she's dead?"

"I witnessed it myself. She died in the explosion of the bridge of Orleans."

The eyes again became hooded. Monsieur Porcien heaved another sigh.

"The poor woman... What about young Yves?"

Watching the man closely, without seeming to, Saint-Clair said:

"I have every reason to believe that he was kidnapped by some gypsies. I found his trail recently, near the Spanish border. Do you know the Forges d'Abel?"

"No, Monsieur," replied Monsieur Porcien without hesitation.

"You've never been in that region... A fortnight ago, for instance?"

"I haven't left Paris for a month. My housekeeper will attest to it."

Saint-Clair tried to deal a decisive blow.

"Do you own a sports car?"

"Alas! I had one, but it was stolen at around the same time you mentioned. I reported it to the police. Is that all you had to tell me?"

"Yes, that's all."

"Thank you, Monsieur Saint-Clair. Might I ask you to inform Maître Loureille, notary at Folembray, of Madame Andrézieux's death?"

"I shall gladly do so," said Saint-Clair in his best poker face.

Then, the Nyctalope bowed before leaving.

"And on your end, if you learn something regarding the boy..."

"I shall not fail to let you know."

Saint-Clair heaved a sigh of relief. He was finally free from the presence of the heinous character. Once outside, he walked away purposefully without looking back, without checking the windows. Yet, on the fourth floor, a single hand raised a curtain. Two tigerish eyes full of hatred followed the Nyctalope.

Pretending he was unaware, Leo Saint-Clair disappeared at the end of the street, walking towards the bridge across the railway from Montparnasse Station.

At the end of the day, after returning to his house in the Rue du Commandeur, Leo Saint-Clair finally received the telephone call he had been expecting. The familiar voice he heard was that of Gno Mitang.

"Very well," said the Nyctalope, after listening to his friend's report. "Your observation post is good, right in front of the building we want to monitor—perfect. Yes, I noticed that hotel. I'll meet you tonight."

At the appointed hour, the two friends, installed near the window of their modest hotel room, exchanged their first impressions.

"I saw Monsieur Porcien," said Saint-Clair. I have the feeling that we were correct in our suspicions and are on the right track. His interest is obvious. If the Marécourt boy dies, and if he can somehow prove that he had nothing to do with his death, he stands to inherit ten million francs, as the child's only relative. He is one of the most abject and ferocious men I've ever met. His entire character is painted on his face. One thing surprises me, however; why did he wait two years without attempting anything against the boy's life. He had to have him in his power, since he arranged his kidnapping. I am so certain of it that I would bet my life on it."

"I'm sure we'll find an explanation for it eventually," said Gno Mitang.

"So am I."

"Did he suspect you?"

"He certainly is on his guard and has already skillfully prepared his alibi. But he's far too clever for his own good. The very speed with which he tried to meet my suspicions and defend himself, proves him guilty. He claims that his car was stolen shortly before the date of the gypsy's murder. He even reported it to the police. And he cites the testimony of his loyal and devoted maid to establish his presence in Paris at the exact time. I repeat: it is all too clever, and feels like a well-rehearsed story."

"He watched you leave, but has not left home since your visit," said the Japanese.

"Again, he's on his guard. He's going to try to lull our suspicions, but we won't give up. Sooner or later, he'll lead us to the child. You can relax now, my friend. I'll continue to watch his house. The night might be dark, but you know that darkness means nothing to me. Where did you leave your car?"

"In a nearby garage, Avenue du Maine. It's available to us at any time, day or night."

"Excellent! I'm sure we'll need it, but probably not immediately. Besides, I doubt that Porcien will venture out after curfew. Sleep. You can take over from me in the morning."

This program was faithfully followed for several days, during which nothing significant happened. Philogène Porcien did not put his nose outside and received no visits. Only his maid went out to buy food. When one of the hotel bellhops questioned the concierge of Porcien's house, the man said that their target had not received any mail recently. The riddle remained unsolved.

One morning, Gno woke Saint-Clair, who had just lain down.

"Finally something new. I've just watched one of the gypsy women that we see hanging around the streets of Paris enter Porcien's building. Could she be a messenger?"

"Since he killed one of their own, she might be delivering a message of vengeance... We need to know the purpose of her visit."

"Do you want me to go down and follow her when she comes out?"

"Yes, why not? It might prove useful. Meanwhile I'll continue to keep watch over Porcien."

The two friends parted. From his window, the Nyctalope saw the Japanese stroll away, but careful to not lose sight of the entrance to Porcien's building.

The gypsy woman came out soon after, and Gno Mitang followed her.

Then, following one of the hunches that made him the extraordinary individual he was, the Nyctalope rang the bellhop and asked him to fetch Gno's car from the garage and bring it to the hotel's entrance at once.

"I may need it soon," he said. "Pay the garage and keep the rest for you."

Richer by quite a few bank notes, the boy went running with great zeal, and discreetly followed the Nyctalope's instructions.

Installed behind the curtains, Leo Saint-Clair kept watch. Soon, Gno's car appeared and parked a few meters away from the hotel. The bellhop got out.

Meanwhile, a second car arrived and stopped exactly at the door of Porcien's building.

*He must have ordered it by phone*, thought the Nyctalope. *This is consistent with my predictions. The plot thickens.*

Indeed, it did not take long until the man with tiger eyes came outside. Without appearing to notice the other car, he dismissed the driver, took his place behind the wheel and started the engine.

Saint-Clair had just enough time to leave his room, run down the stairs and rush behind the wheel of their own car.

Porcien's car was already at the end of the street and turning into the Avenue du Maine, in the direction of the church of Montrouge. The Nyctalope strove to follow, while remaining at a sufficient distance so as not to be noticed.

He stood ready, his foot on the accelerator, to avert any eventuality of Porcien trying to escape.

But his target did not appear interested in doing so. Either Porcien didn't realize he was followed, or he believed he would be able to lose any pursuer any time he wished. In any event, he continued driving at a steady but reasonable pace.

*Is he trying to flee from the revenge of the gypsies? Or is he on his way to an appointment? Or perhaps he is being coerced into some kind of action?* wondered St. Clair. *If so, I have a chance of finding the gypsy woman and my friend Gno again at the end of that journey.*

Welcoming this perspective, he was still sorry that he and Gno had parted without any way of contacting each other, should it become necessary. He didn't even know which direction the Japanese had taken. If Gno, having lost the trail of the gypsy woman, or brought some important information, back to the hotel, he would find no instructions waiting for him there, and Saint-Clair berated himself for having left in such a hurry without making plans.

It was too late to entertain such regrets. He had to follow Porcien, who now required all of his concentration; Porcien remained the main character at the center of this drama, the one who held the key to solving the mystery.

*We seem to be taking the road to Orleans*, thought Saint-Clair after an hour. *Does he intend to retrace the fateful path of the abductors of Yves Marécourt?*

But in Etampes, Porcien, taking advantage of the passing of several trucks, suddenly increased his speed and disappeared from view.

The Nyctalope frowned. Was it a fortuitous incident, without premeditation or meaning? Or was it carefully anticipated and planned?

He hesitated a few seconds and rushed toward the exit for Etampes. Porcien's car was no match for Gno Mitang's. Putting his engine into a higher gear, Leo Saint-Clair knew that he could easily catch up with the other car if Porcien had simply wanted to get ahead. If, on the other hand, he did not see it after a few kilometers, having taken the precaution of jotting down the make and license number, he would backtrack and start look at the smaller roads which his target might have taken to escape him.

At first, he thought his fears had been unfounded, when, a few minutes, he saw a car in the distance that looked like Porcien's. Increasing his speed, he got closer to it and verified that it was indeed the case.

But he scarcely had the time to wonder why it had taken so little time to catch up, when a new incident occurred. The other car suddenly slowed down.

Suspecting a ruse, but unwilling to betray himself by stopping too, Saint-Clair forced himself to continue, only at a slower speed.

But the other car had parked across the road, blocking passage, forcing the Nyctalope to brake and stop barely two meters away.

Two men immediately got out. Neither of them was Monsieur Porcien, who also was no longer inside the car. Staring at it, Saint-Clair could clearly see that it was empty. He understood that Porcien had outsmarted him.

The two men approached his car and called out to him loudly.

"Why are you following us? Who are you? Come out now!"

Two revolvers were pointed at Saint-Clair who had no choice but to obey and step out.

He was immediately grabbed round the throat by one of the men, while the other one crushed him between two arms of steel.

"We'll teach you to be curious!" they sneered.

Meanwhile, sitting quietly in a cafe in Etampes, Monsieur Philogène Porcien was enjoying his lunch—and the success of his ruse.

It had all been very simple. Before leaving, he had called the unscrupulous Director of the Argos Agency.

"Hello! Porcien here! I am leaving to take care of you-know-what. But that damn Nyctalope is bound to follow me. If he does, I can kiss success good-bye—and you can forget the commission I've promised to pay you. So it's up to you to help me now. I'll make sure I arrive in Etampes at exactly 11:45 a.m. You must have a truck parked at the entrance of the Rue Saint-Jacques, and another at Rue Saint-Martin to slow down Saint-Clair. The first truck will provide me with cover to stop and get away. Then, have two of your most trusted men wait for me, ready to take my place in the car. I will give them my instructions before disappearing."

All had gone according to Porcien's wishes. Now he only waited to hear the result of his ruse. He had told the waiter that someone would be calling for him on the telephone.

The bell rang. He rushed into the cabin.

"Hello! Denis, here. Did you succeed?"

"Completely, boss. You can go ahead with no problem. The job's done. The guy won't bother you again."

"Excellent! May the Devil take the soul of the Nyctalope!"

And chuckling ominously, Monsieur Philogène Porcien returned to his interrupted lunch.

# Chapter V
## *A Dangerous Trail*

With the skill of a professional detective, Gno Mitang followed the gypsy woman to the Gare d'Austerlitz. He saw her approach a counter and purchase a ticket; then head for the departure platform.

Gno winced. This complicated matters. He now had to choose between abandoning the trail or leave Paris, without having time to notify the Nyctalope.

Another man might have hesitated, but working with Leo Saint-Clair had taught the Japanese the art of making quick decisions, sometimes adventurously, always intuitively.

Saint-Clair himself had instructed him to follow the woman. She was a messenger, but one connecting the gypsies and Philogène Porcien. She's either brought to him a message or an ultimatum. In any case, her destination was obvious. She was now going to report on her mission.

*I must continue to follow her,* concluded the Japanese. *She will take me to those who are holding Yves Marécourt prisoner. And perhaps Leo, tracking his own quarry, will meet me at the same destination.*

His reasoning was the same as the Nyctalope's when he had launched himself on his own pursuit.

In fact, the similarity of their situations, their decisions, and the risks they were running, was even more complete than Gno could have imagined. For, having purchased a ticket in turn, and having gotten in the same rail car as the gypsy woman, he noticed that the train was going towards Etampes.

Etampes! If the Japanese had had a premonition, or if he could have made a quick phone call to his friend, whose very life was in danger, perhaps he would have gotten off the train. But, like a hound running on a track, nose to the ground, indifferent to any call, Gno Mitang followed the gypsy, turning a deaf ear to the inner voices that might have warned him of the perils ahead. The train passed Etampes, Monerville, Anger-ville, Toury, Chateau Gaillard, and stopped at Artenay. The gypsy woman got off; so the Japanese did the same.

They left the station. Knowing he faced a cunning, mistrustful opponent, and not wanting to expose himself, Gno displayed as much finesse as he could to ensure that the woman would not become aware that she was being followed. She, on the other hand, was also obviously seeking to lose anyone trailing her. Gno kept his distance. Each of them could believe they had the upper hand in this game of hide and seek, and in truth, it was impossible to tell which had outsmarted the other.

Once they had left the village, and were walking down a lonely road, Gno saw an isolated inn ahead. He hid in a thicket which provided a convenient cover, while allowing him to watch his prey.

If the gypsy woman had turned around, she would have seen only the empty road, and concluded that the other traveler—if she had spotted him—was not following her after all and had arrived at his destination, one of the last houses of the village.

But she did not even do that. Carefree, she entered the inn. Another, older gypsy woman was waiting there, a meager snack on the table before her. The two exchanged a quick glance.

"You can talk. I'm alone," said the seated woman. "For now, no one can see us or hear us."

And the woman who had come on the train spoke and said simply:

"He will come."

Then, she left the inn, with a loaf of bread that the older woman had given her, to make it look as if she'd gone inside to beg.

She walked towards Chevilly, but Gno did not leave his thicket and did not follow her. He felt he would be better off concentrating on the older woman, who was clearly in charge. From his position, he was close enough to the inn that he could see through one of the windows and watch the gypsy seated at her table.

*This is exactly what I expected*, he thought. *The girl has made her report to her boss. It's this other woman I must now watch. It's only a matter of patience.*

And Gno Mitang needed plenty of patience. The hours passed. The gypsy woman did not leave the inn. The Japanese remained in hiding.

Finally, from the village, and probably from the station, Monsieur Philogène Porcien appeared.

He entered the inn. Gno Mitang moved closer. He had read on the face of the suspect, and in his hesitant attitude, a clear discomfort, which betrayed his fear.

This was an interesting clue. It confirmed one of the Nyctalope's hypotheses, namely, that Monsieur Porcien had not called for this meeting, and was not going to it without some concern. It meant he was not on the best of terms with the gypsies who had kidnapped Yves Marécourt, Madame Andrézieux's ward.

*After all, he killed one of them, and may legitimately fear their vengeance*, theorized Gno Mitang. But then, he thought: *But if that's the case, why is he taking the risk of coming here?*

Only one answer was possible: *He still needs them.*

The conversation promised to be very interesting. Yet, as eager he was to hear them, the Japanese did not try to enter the inn. He merely crossed the road quickly. At a distance sufficient to avoid being seen, he crept along the wall and crouched right under the window. The road was deserted, but the ratty clothes he was wearing would be enough—or so he hoped!— to make him look like a tramp taking a nap if he were to be spotted.

Philogène Porcien crossed the room and walked towards the table where the gypsy woman sat. She greeted him with a scornful laugh.

"There you are! You finally decided to come!" she said jeeringly.

Hiding his fear, which knotted his bowels, the man with the tiger eyes responded gruffly:

"Yes, I'm here. What do you want?"

"You didn't come all this way to ask me that. Another question burns on your lips. You want news of the child?"

"It's only natural. What have you done with him?"

"I'll tell you... when we reach an agreement. But first, let's deal with other things. You killed my husband."

Monsieur Porcien jumped back and, putting his hand inside his pocket, pulled out a gun.

"Is that why you asked me to come? Is this a trap? I warn you: I'm armed and I'm not going to let myself be slaughtered like a beast."

The gypsy woman shrugged.

"Don't worry! If my only intention was avenging Miarko, it would already be done. Look!"

A thin blade miraculously came out from under one of the folds of her multicolored skirt, flashed and flew through the air. It planted itself into the opposite wall from Monsieur Porcien, a mere millimeter away from the edge of a rustic earthenware plate hanging there. Thrown just as nimbly, another blade followed, then another and another, until the entire plate was surrounded by a ring of knives.

A final blade was thrown and stuck the plate right in the middle, causing it to shatter and the pieces to fall.

"You can reimburse the innkeeper for the plate," said the woman. "That was a demonstration. I have no rival in the art of knife-throwing. Do you think I would have left you enough time to use your gun? If I had wished, my first knife would have pierced your heart right where you stand. So stop trembling! I don't want your life. We have another account to settle than Miarko's death."

Monsieur Philogène Porcien was green with terror. His jaw trembled nervously and he tried in vain to stop the rattling of his teeth.

"What other account are you talking about?" he stammered.

"Don't play the fool," she retorted scornfully. "Do you think I don't know why you killed Miarko? It was because he had just heard from the lips of two strangers, who came to the farm, the boy's value. You had cleverly hidden that fact from us and only offered us a miserable sum of money for our services."

"I paid you very well for the service you rendered me, but I did intend to give you more later..."

"As little as possible, I'm sure. And you were afraid that the two strangers might have offered us more. You thought Miarko might betray you—that's why you killed him."

"Can you assure me that he wouldn't have done so?"

The black eyes of the gypsy woman flashed with anger.

"Yes, the clumsy oaf might have tried it," she admitted with a wicked voice. "Be he was much too stupid to manage this business alone. You swindled him the first time, when you paid him to kidnap the child—and the others would have gotten the best of him too. He was a brute, who never listened to anyone's advice. He only knew how to hit. He was violent, jealous and stupid—that's what he was. José and I were glad when you got rid of him. Without knowing it, you did us a great service."

"Who is José?" asked Philogène Porcien, perplexed.

The gypsy gave him a look that seemed to challenge the gods themselves.

"My lover. Now, thanks to you, I can proclaim it to all and no longer fear that Miarko would strangle or stab us in the night!"

"Your affairs are your business," cut Porcien, "but since you owe me a measure of gratitude, I think you shouldn't refuse to tell me what you've done with the child."

"He's safe and well kept. Now that we know his real worth, he's well treated. Don't worry; we won't let him wither away."

"That would suit me fine, in fact," grumbled Yves' evil cousin. "Listen, I have a proposal for you, something that could make you a fortune..."

But the gypsy woman seemed to not pay any attention this tempting speech. Her gaze was directed towards a mirror which reflected the window. And glued to one of the window panes was the face of Gno Mitang, whose eyes easily betrayed the interest he was taking in the scene.

The gypsy remained impassive, cold as ice, and her eyes returned to face Monsieur Philogène Porcien, her attitude seemingly wonderfully indifferent.

"Shut up," she said, barely moving her lips. "Someone's spying on us."

Monsieur Porcien turned as if stung by a fly. His gaze went first to the door, then to the window. But by now, the Japanese had gone.

"Idiot!" muttered the gypsy.

"I didn't see anyone," said Monsieur Porcien. "Why do you suppose someone would be spying on us? Besides, the door and the windows are shut. Even if there was someone, he couldn't have heard us."

"Let's not talk here anymore," said the gypsy. "Come with me! Our caravans are waiting for us not far away in the forest. We'd better continue our conversation there."

"As you wish," Monsieur Porcien replied, nodding.

Approaching the wall, the woman removed the knives, which had been planted there, and made them disappear beneath her clothes.

"Call the inn-keeper," she ordered, "and pay him for my meal and the broken plate. Don't be stingy. It wouldn't do for him to call the gendarmes. That wouldn't help your business."

Meekly, Monsieur Porcien went to the kitchen and did as he had been instructed. He then joined the gypsy outside on the road.

She had taken the lead without seeming to worry about the man whose face she had seen pressed against the window.

Gno Mitang had quickly returned to the thicket behind which he had carefully hidden earlier and was lying there in wait, crouched silently. He waited until Porcien and his accomplice had a good lead, and then he began to follow them, continuing to use the bushes and trees that lined the road for cover.

Arriving near the forest of Orleans, the couple entered it. It then became easier for the Japanese to tail them without being noticed.

Walking alongside the gypsy, Philogène Porcien was initially silent. But after a while, he could not stand it any longer and began to talk:

"Where are you taking me?" he asked. "Why did you insist on leaving that inn, where we could talk quietly? What are you afraid of?"

The gypsy smiled oddly.

"Are you sure you weren't being followed?" she questioned. "Could someone be interested in finding out what you and I had to discuss?"

"Quite the opposite, as a matter of fact," replied Porcien. "The two men who came to the farm somehow managed to find me, but they have lost your trail. And I took good care of at least one of them. He won't bother us anymore."

"But they were two of them."

"I'm sure the other one didn't follow me. I took precautions."

"Perhaps he preceded you. I saw an ugly snout watching us at that window, from outside. It's quite likely that he is still on our tail... No, don't look back! Don't give the impression that we've noticed his presence and that we're suspicious... Come here!" the woman suddenly said, with a gesture of appeal.

Another gypsy—a young man—jumped out from behind a tree and ran towards them. She whispered a few words in his ear, to which he replied with a nod.

Leaving him, the gypsy woman led Monsieur Porcien to the edge of a clearing and sat him down at the foot of a tree.

"Stay here!" she ordered.

She then listened intently. Deep inside the thicket of the forest, one could hear the slight rustling of branches coming ever closer. Despite all his skills and cautiousness, it was Gno

Mitant who, crawling through the bushes, was trying to get closer to the spot where he hoped to overhear Porcien and the woman's conversation.

A flame kindled in the gypsy woman's eyes. She smiled mysteriously. One of the trailers opened and the young gypsy came out, dragging behind him an iron chain that was attached to a huge black panther.

The gypsy woman nodded with satisfaction. She gave a whistle and said:

"Myrrha! Go!"

The young bohemian released the beast.

Immediately, the sound of running was heard in the thicket. Aware of the danger, and having realized what the woman's plan was, Gno Mitang had not waited to abandon his observation post and was beating a hasty retreat through the woods.

But would he succeed? The panther had sprung into the thicket with the speed of an arrow, traversed it, and disappeared into the depths of the forest.

Suddenly, there was a distant cry—the cry of an animal slain in the night. Monsieur Porcien couldn't repress a shiver.

"Myrrha caught up with him," said the gypsy woman, her eyes shining with savage joy. "We've got nothing to fear from that one now either."

"The other man was taken care of too," Philogène Porcien murmured, turning his eyes away from the dark forest in which an unspeakable drama had just played out. "There were two men at the farm. I settled the account of one of them. You took care of the other. We're safe now. But how are you going to catch your panther? If the locals see it, it's going to cause trouble. They'll organize a hunt and you'll be held responsible for the 'unfortunate accident' that cost the life of the all too curious friend of the late Leo Saint-Clair."

"Myrrha will return by herself when she's finished eating," said the gypsy, with a horrible smile. "Now, back to our business. What do you want me to do with the child and how much are you prepared to offer me?"

"That's what I'm proposing we discuss," replied Philogène Porcien, his eyes shining with a sinister glow.

## Chapter VI
### *The Little Martyr*

"Acrobats! Jugglers! Clowns!... Come see! They're coming!"

A band of children, shouting and clapping their hands, ran after the rather pitiful group of caravans that had just entered the village street. They were all excited by the arrival of this carnival. They expected a small circus tent to be set up soon, that would accommodate several performances which they might possibly attend—if seats were not too expensive.

They probably wouldn't be, because it was a rather tattered-looking circus that was passing through the village. It consisted of three emaciated horses, dragging their miserable trailers. As for the acrobats, jugglers and clowns, they had been recruited from among a dozen gypsies, men, women and children, who appeared and waved at the doors and windows of the trailers.

The caravan stopped in front of the church, and set up camp there.

This circus did not, in fact, have an actual tent. A circle of benches, surrounded by a canvas stretched on poles at ground level, was its only ring. Planted in the center, there was a pole supporting a metal circle, from which were suspended three acetylene lamps, to provide illumination.

While the men worked on setting up, the women, equipped with small Basque drums, were preparing to go around the village to announce the "grrreeeatest show."

"Dorr! Phoena!" called a gruff voice. "Dress up and take the Gimp with you."

That order, which couldn't be ignored, prompted two heads-with tussled hair to appear at the entrance of one of the trailers.

"We're ready!" shouted a copper-haired boy, accompanied by a ten-year-old girl. Her large black eyes already shone bright in her tender, soft face.

One after another, they jumped out of the trailer. As young Dorr had said, they were indeed ready, meaning that they both wore circus costumes. Standing tall over his sister, the fourteen-year-old Dorr was dressed as a small, white clown, with the classic pointed hat perched on top of his mop. Phoena wore a sequined dress, somewhat faded, making her a horse rider or a miniature ballerina.

Having come outside, they turned back towards the inside of the trailer and seemed to extract from it a pathetic little boy, dressed in the traditional tramp-like style of an Auguste clown.

A shabby, oversized coat, certainly found in a thrift store, wrapped the boy's thin body down to his feet.

The overlong sleeves, too large for the size of the tiny Auguste, seemed to hide only two stumps. Both his legs were trapped inside the single leg of a doctored pair of worn trousers, causing the little boy to stumble and fall as he tried to move. At any time, his balance had to be restored by his two companions. His eyes were beautiful and moving. However, the perpetually open mouth, frozen in an idiotic and painful grimace, gave his face a permanently bewildered expression.

Was the boy mute? Only inarticulate sounds came out of that mouth, which he could not close. Upon closer inspection, it appeared that an object placed inside prevented him from doing so.

Dragged brutally by Dorr, gently by Phoena, the boy hopped between them on his two shackled legs. To anyone thinking it just an act, such clumsiness would look amusing. Occasionally, incoherent syllables escaped from his open mouth, or rather almost incomprehensible sounds:

"Hi... Ha... Hou..."

When that happened, Dorr pinched him viciously, while tiny Phoena tried to calm him, stroking his hands under the sleeves of the coat.

Who could have guessed that what the boy was trying to say, to shout, to reveal to the audience was his name: Yves Marécourt!

For indeed, it was the ward of the late Madame Lise Andrézieux, now reduced to a miserable state and exposed to the ridicule of an unwitting public.

For two, long years, since the day of his abduction, the boy's life had been a long martyrdom. What a rude awakening he had had! Still under the influence of chloroform, which had been administered to him in the car, he had opened his eyes, and found himself lying on the floor of a trailer, tied up like a sausage.

Yves had wanted to scream, but a brutal hand had grasped his throat and stuffed his mouth with a strange gag, shaped like a pear. Made of soft iron, it fit inside the mouth without hurting his tongue, provided that he refrained from screaming or closing his jaws. He therefore had no choice but to remain quiet and keep his mouth half open, giving him a bewildered expression, not unlike that of a retarded child.

Subsequently, his kidnapper, the gypsy Miarko, had untied his legs, but had left his arms strapped in a tangle of belts and rags, turning them into two shapeless stumps, almost use-less.

To complete his work, Miarko had stained the boy's curls with mud, litter and dried leaves. A special application of skin dye had turned Yves the color of the other gypsy children from the caravan.

Thus disguised, the young captive was unrecognizable and could have been claimed at any time by a French Fagin.

The lost child—the stolen child—retained only scattered and often confused memories of the days that had followed his abduction. He wasn't mistreated and was reasonably well fed. When the gypsies were alone in the forest, away from prying eyes, they allowed him to have the use of his limbs and tongue. When, after some weeks of this half-wild existence, the caravan was finally able to cross the river Loire and was headed down to the Pyrenees, he was again gagged, immobilized and locked up inside a trailer.

It wasn't that, during that troubled period, Miarko had much to fear from public curiosity. Why would a single child have mattered in the constant flow of the lost and dispossessed, or even to the inhabitants of the villages they passed, where no one had eyes for a ragged band of gypsies? People had become inured to the spectacle of misery that marched across France.

Miarko was only obeying the instructions that he had received from Monsieur Philogène Porcien. His mission was to take his young prisoner to the destination that had been assigned, which was the dilapidated farm in the Pyrenees near the Spanish border.

Yves Marécourt only recovered his freedom on the day after the gypsies reached it and settled in.

They stayed for nearly two years, during which time the child continued to suffer, without understanding the reason why, the terrible circumstances of his new destiny.

A mind less dense than Miarko's would have probably wondered why the man responsible for the kidnapping desired to prolong, apparently unnecessarily, the child's barbaric captivity.

But Miarko did not have any curiosity. He didn't ask questions, and was simply happy to take advantage of the situation. Every month, he received the money orders sent by Monsieur Porcien and led the good life, lazy, reveling in his indolence. Undoubtedly, he wanted only one thing: that things should continue as they were.

Unaware of Yves Marécourt's real worth, he could not be surprised that his villainous cousin waited for so long without trying to take advantage of his capture.

In reality, the reasons that had prompted Philogène Porcien to commit his evil deed were not very clear, even to himself.

Maybe it was originally a simple act of vengeance against a young and rather distant relative, whose very existence had prevented him from getting his hands on an inheritance that he had expected and desperately wanted. Or revenge against the devoted and yet all too watchful guardian, Madame Andrézieux, whom he knew despised him.

At first, he had wanted to play a trick on her that would cause her great alarm and expose her as an unfit guardian. He had assumed that she would be held responsible for the disappearance of her ward and might even become a suspect in any subsequent investigation.

The best way to exploit the situation had not yet appeared to him.

It should also be noted that, during those two years, Monsieur Porcien had remained ignorant of the news of the tragic death of Madame Andrézieux, and that he dared not risk betraying himself by trying to find out what had happened to her.

It was during this period of enforced waiting that, slowly and mysteriously, his thoughts turned towards crime, and his mind was eventually made up much later, when he decided to go and visit the farm in person.

The picture of the life led by the boy during his captivity that the insightful Saint-Clair and his friend, Gno Mitang, had been able to imagine was quite accurate.

How many other young minds would have fallen prey to despair and madness if subjected to such an ordeal! But Yves Marécourt was made of sterner stuff. His strange and precocious genius saved him from despair, as well as from discouragement. Limited to only the resources of his memory and his innate gifts, which guided him on the road to science, he continued his studies. The inscriptions made in charcoal and plaster on the walls of the farm deciphered by Leo Saint-Clair were evidence of this.

Jealously guarded—like an interest-bearing bond—by Miarko and his wife, he enjoyed only a small measure of freedom. The other children were little savages who were as much his jailers and torturers as the adults. The single exception was little Phoena, who had instinctively befriended him and who protected him from the brutality of the older Dorr.

But then came the fateful day, when the visit of Saint-Clair and Gno Mitang, followed by the arrival of Monsieur Porcien, threw the farm in chaos.

Any foreigner was considered to be an enemy. The eventuality had been anticipated. As soon as the visitors had been spotted, at Miarko's command, José had taken young Yves into the woods.

They were soon joined by the other children, Dorr and Phoena leading them. Miarka came last, not shocked, but excited by the news she had to report.

Taking José aside, she whispered:

"Miarko's dead. The man from Paris threw him into a ravine. We must take refuge across the border quickly, otherwise they might accuse you of his death. But I also learned something else: we're rich!" She pointed at Yves and explained: "That brat is worth millions!"

His greed aroused, the gypsy was only too happy to obey Miarka. That same evening, taking smugglers' paths, the little band crossed into Spain and was taken in by another gypsy tribe, whom they had met on the road.

Eight days later, they returned to France, disguised as a small traveling circus.

But Miarka but was not amongst them. She and a few other women had gone straight to Paris.

Entrusted to the vigilance of José and Dorr, young Yves, forcibly enlisted in the troupe, reluctantly learned the art of being a clown.

Hopping about, hit by Dorr, comforted by small Phoena, the boy was forced to take part in the grotesque parade. Seemingly ugly and clumsy, he was the object of ridicule, provoking the laughter of children and the jeers of peasants.

If only he could have talked, cried, begged for mercy, and asked the crowd to find his "Mama Lise" and get her to come and rescue him!

But this wish was forced to remain inside him, unexpressed, except through the tragic look in his eyes, which the infamous makeup could not alter.

It was only after the humiliating parade that Yves, rid of the gag, but not of his clownish clothes, was able to empty his heart to Phoena.

"Can't you understand that I've hadenough of this life?" he confided to the girl. "Dorr's beatings and all the deprivations mean nothing to me. I carry inside myself a dream which gives me strength enough to withstand them and keep my faith in the future. You don't know about science, you poor girl. You don't understanding the meaning of the signs that I draw on the walls. One day, thanks to them, I will make some great discovery that will benefit all humanity... At least, that's still my hope. As I get older, I'll eventually grow strong enough to free me myself from Miarka's tyranny, Dorr's and even José's. Don't cry. That day, I'll take you with me and make you a beautiful city girl. I'm rich and I could pay dearly for my freedom, if they were ready to let me go."

"Why don't you tell them that?" asked Phoena.

The boy shook his head.

"Because I don't trust them," he replied. "Why did they take me from Mama Lise? It's probably because of my fortune. They're paid to keep me prisoner. Anything I might say would only serve to toughen the care with which they watch me. I've finally decided to escape. Today, I'ver had enough! I can no longer stand the role of clown to which they have condemned me."

"You're going to abandon me?" exclaimed the girl, her eyes filled with tears.

"Not for long, I promise you. Besides, you could run away with me. If I manage to put us under the protection of the gendarmes, and tell them what they did to me, Miarka, José and the others would certainly go to jail and the police would take me back to Mommy Lise, and you too. Don't be afraid, I'll never abandon you!"

"But how can you escape? They watch you day and night."

The boy was thinking.

"There's one chance I could take, if you wanted to help me," he said. "They're going to have another show tonight. There'll be spectators around the whole ring. Maybe there will be the Mayor, or the Constable among them... If, without being seen, you could remove that horrible gag from my mouth, I could rouse the public and ask for help. The authorities will want to hear what I have to say and those who keep me prisoner would be powerless to stop them. All the precautions they take to keep me silent show that they fear something like this. My accusations would be accurate and easy to prove, so they would take them seriously."

"You're my only friend and I love you," said Phoena. "To save you, I would risk being beaten—or even killed. If I can, I'll do what you ask me tonight."

"You won't be hurt," said Yves. "If I succeed, we won't be separated and the authorities will protect you, just like me, from the other gypsies. We only need to find a time when we're alone together before our entry into the ring. If not tonight, tomorrow or another day. We'll seize the first opportunity."

"I promise I'll do it," said the little girl gravely.

That night, their hearts pounding, the two children were waiting in the trailer, which served as backstage to put their plan into action.

Dorr was there, but because he was one of the acrobats, he would soon leave to perform his act. Yves felt hopeful.

Dressed in a dirty shirt and tights with red underpants, Dorr finished pomading his hair in front of a broken mirror. Considering himself ready at last, he finally left the trailer.

Yves and Phoena were left alone.

In his clown costume, the long sleeves of which hid his arms, his hands strapped into stumps, the boy had no freedom of movement, nor could he speak. Only his eyes implored the girl.

"It's time," they cried silently. "Keep your promise."

Trembling a little, but with a decisive look, Phoena approached him, stuck her fingers in his mouth and pulled out the odious gag.

"Thank you!" cried Yves. "I will never forget what you've done for me. Now I must act! We can'r waste any time. Listen. I'll rush into the ring and alert the public. I think the whole village is here. As soon as you hear me screaming, run out of the trailer and watch carefully. If I run towards someone, it'll be because I sensed that that person will protect us. So run towards him as well. Together, we'll be freed and protected. Do you understand?"

But, suddenly, instead of answering, the girl stepped back and ran to hide at the back of the trailer, behind a collection of rags hanging from a rope.

Surprised, Yves turned around.

The curtain that concealed the door had been raised. A woman entered.

Yves paled.

It was Miarka. Behind her, there was a stranger, someone dressed like a gentleman who had just finished climbing the few wooden steps that led inside the trailer.

"Come in," said the gypsy woman. "Here's the boy."

She pointed at Yves who stood there, mesmerized.

The visitor gazed at the boy for a long moment.

"You have certainly made him unrecognizable," he said finally.

A cruel flame burned in his tigerish eyes, chilling Yves with fright. But overcoming the feeling of discomfort that those inhuman eyes caused him, Yves rushed toward him.

"Monsieur," he cried, "have mercy on me! Protect me! Deliver me! My name is Yves Marécourt. These gypsies have stolen me from my guardian. Call the police! Please!"

Coldly, the visitor turned toward the gypsy.

"You claimed you'd rendered him all but mute," he uttered in a tone of discontent.

"He was," stammered Miarka. "Unless…"

Her eyes searched the interior of the trailer. Then, she rushed forward, pushed aside the curtain of rags, and violently pulled Phoena out of her hiding place.

"What did you do, you, little vermin? What do you have in your hand?"

It was Yves' gag that, unconsciously, Phoene was still holding. Miarka snatched it away and roared:

"You, little traitor! It's you who took it out? I'm going to kill you for that!"

A knife flashed from under her clothes. She held it, ready to strike, but Yves rushed over to her.

"Leave her alone! Don't kill her! I forced her to do it. If you want to kill someone, kill me instead!"

The visitor stepped forward. He whispered a few words in the ear of the gypsy, who calmed down immediately.

"You're right," she said. "I think that's a good plan".

Dropping, Phoena, more dead than alive, Miarka put her hand on Yves Marécourt's shoulder.

"That will depend on you," she pronounced.

Monsieur Porcien watched the scene, apparently unmoved, but a fierce hatred shone in his eyes.

Miarka kept her withered hand on the frail shoulders of the boy.

"You don't want me to kill Phoena, who deserves to die?" she uttered, staring into Yves' eyes. "You would rather suffer the punishment that I'd planned for her? So be it! Since you love her so much, I'll offer you a deal…"

"What kind of deal?" said the boy, suspicious.

"Why did Phoena remove the gag from your mouth?"

"Because I asked her to."

"Before you were gagged?"

" Obviously," acknowledged Yves with a shrug.

"So you were plotting this together for several hours," Miarka remarked, maliciously triumphant. "This little vermin betrayed us…"

The little boy tried to plead the cause of his ally, but in vain.

"Listen!" said Miarka. "Phoena will now pay for each one of your acts of disobedience, understood? It is she that I'll beat if you don't do what we say. It is she that I'll stab if you try to run away. From this moment, she will be watched by the entire family, just like you. And don't think that our vengeance couldn't reach her wherever she hides. Get it in your head that by running away or taking her with you, you'd be condemning her to death."

Yves did not answer. He bowed his head. Miarka's threat overwhelmed him.

"I'll put you to the test," the gypsy woman announced. "Open your mouth."

She was holding the gag that she had snatched from Phoena. She approached the young boy who stood there resigned.

"Very good," saids Miarka, stuffing the device back into Yves' mouth. "Now, you go and do your act just as if nothing had happened. Phoena will go with you. But watch out…"

She lifted the curtain from the entrance and called:

"Dorr! Come here! I need you... Here are Yves and Phoena. You'll take them into the ring to do their act. But take this knife too. If the boy does something stupid, like trying to alert the public, slice Phoena's throat at once. You understand me?

"Yes. I'll kill Phoena," said the boy savagely.

"That's not all. You have to watch her too. She's been in cahoots with him. So if she tries to stir up the public, don't hesitate to stab the boy. Did you hear me, Phoena?"

"Yes," groaned the girl, terrified.

"Wise kids," said Miarka, triumphant. "You can take them now, Dorr."

"Got it," said Dorr. "C'mon, kids!"

Dorr took the two children, locked Phoena, who retained the use of her limbs, in one trailer, and threw Yves Marécourt, like a bundle of dirty clothes, into another.

Despite being certain that the boy could neither stand up nor cry, because of the gag, Dorr gave two turns of the keys and sat whistling on the step ladder.

From his vantage point, he could watch the door of the second trailer, in which he had locked Phoena.

Inside, the little girl was sitting on a pile of rags and sobbing desperately.

Suddenly, she sat up, listening. His eyes looked up at a window in the left wall of the trailer.

Coming from outside, she could see a rectangle of light and distinctly hear the sound of a voice.

One of them was Miarka's and the other belonged to the newcomer, Monsieur Philogène Porcien.

The two voices were somewhat muffled; but, the conversation could be understood as clearly as if had taken place in the next room.

The girl's attention was caught by the mention of Yves' name, so she silently approached the wall and overturned an empty box upon which she climbed.

In this position, she could listen to everything, burning every word heard into her memory. But soon, the most intense terror gradually appeared on her face and in her eyes.

Freed from the presence of two children, Miarka and Monsieur Porcien had first glared at each other in silence.

They did not need to speak to understand one another. They shared the same natural ferocity, and an equal lack of scruples bound them together more tightly than the most explicit of contracts.

"So—what are we going to do with the boy?" said the gypsy at last.

"You know as much as I do now," said Porcien. "If the boy dies, I'll get the inheritance that has been denied to me."

"If he dies…" repeated Miarka slowly.

"But only in circumstances that cannot incriminate either of us," hastened to add the monster. "His death needs to be natural. I mean, it can't look like the result of a crime. The police would wonder who would profit from such a crime, and I would immediately become their prime suspect. Once they investiage me, they'll quickly find you…"

"And you'd lose the inheritance," said Miarka thoughtfully. "I understand perfectly. How much are we talking about?"

"Several million," said Porcien, whose eyes sparkled with cupidity. "At least, ten. Maybe even twenty. Anyway, there's more than enough for both of us…"

"How much would I get?"

"How much do you want?"

"I want an equal split," said the gypsy boldly. "My risk is just as great as yours, and my job far more demanding, because I expect that you're going to ask me to carry out your plan. And I don't need to guess what that is. You already said it: the child has to die."

"But only under the circumstances I've described."

"We'll discuss the details. But you can see how difficult my task is. So I'm not asking too much by wanting an equal share. Fifty-fifty. Do you agree?"

"Yes, I agree," replied Porcien, after a slight hesitation. "You're greedy, but I accept that if you do everything that you promise, you'll have earned your share." And quietly, the horrible man added: "Since we can't control disease, the boy must die a violent death. It has to look like an accident. A harsh blow of Fate. Do you understand?"

"Yes, of course," replied the gypsy, shrugging. "You're thinking of an accident that could be arranged beforehand... Something going wrong..."

"And that would happen right in front of an audience. That's essential to prevent suspicion."

"During one of our performances..."

She said no more, but had made a gesture to indicate that that she understood Philogène Porcien perfectly.

Nodding his head, he approved:

"Yes, during a public performance... Quite right," he murmured. "And the girl too. The accident will be two-fold. It will seem more natural and will divert suspicion away from your family. So we're in agreement. See you soon."

In the trailer next door, Phoena, terrified, stepped down from her box and backed away in fear.

"They want to kill my friend Yves," she moaned. "And me too. But I won't let them!... I won't!"

A week later, at nightfall, a poor-looking trailer arrived on the outskirts of Bordeaux and stopped in a vacant lot.

Inside, Miarka watched over Yves Marécourt, rendered silent by his gag and reduced to immobility by the straps which imprisoned his arms and chest.

Seated on a bundle of rags, Phoena wept silently.

Outside, Dorr was keeping watch and protected the occupants of the trailer from any intruders.

Later that evening, the door opened.

"This is the gentleman you were expecting," Dorr announced.

And he showed in Philogène Porcien, who wore a false beard that made him unrecognizable. Under his arm, he carried several packages which he laid on the floor of the trailer.

"Here's enough to make you all look nice and presentable," he said.

"So you found us an engagement?"

"Yes! A splendid one! And unexpected too! You start in two days at the World Circus with a sensational new act."

"I expected no less of you," said Miarka. "You'll have to give me some idea as to what kind of act we're supposed to perform."

"I had to pay a good price," said Porcien, "to buy the equipment and the right to continue doing the act under the name as its previous owner. It would have been impossible to get you the engagement without it. But now it's all confirmed. Starting tonight, you'll present to the public the most terrifying circus act ever, something called the 'sphere of death.' It's a metal ball that's launched from the top of the tent onto the rim of a giant, vertical wheel. An ingenious mechanism keeps the ball in contact with the rim, so that it makes a full circle before returning to its starting point, where it automatically locks. At that moment, there is a twist that tightens the throats of the public and even draws cries of horror from the most impressionable spectators. The sphere opens and two children, who'd been locked inside, appear to fall to the ground. In reality, they're held by invisible wires which stop them in mid-fall. They then seem to float gracefully through the air, sending kisses to the audience, before being slowly lowered to the sand of the ring, where they receive a storm of applause.

"I don't need to belabor the point. Tonight, and for several other performances, Dorr and Phoena will be inside the ball. Then, when it's clear to everyone that this is a perfectly safe act, you'll replace Dorr with my young cousin. On that night, the invisible wires, presumably worn out by friction, will break. And that will be the accident we need. Yves and Phoena will fall and crash onto the ring. It's a fifty foot fall; I don't think we need to be concerned that they'll survive it. As you can see, I've arranged for Phoena to share Yves' fate. First, we are thus assured of her silence and, second, it'll be harder to accuse you of having engineered an accident, when one of the victims is your own daughter."

"It's perfect," agreed Miarka coldly.

The following week, when everything had so far gone exactly to Monsieur Porcien's plan, Miarka decided to move on to the final act.

She did, however, make the mistake of whispering a few words to José, which caught the ear of the attentive Phoena.

*"Tonight is the night!"*

It was, therefore, in a mad state of anguish that the girl left for the night's performance. As for Yves Marécourt, rendered mute by the gag, he had no idea that the evening would be any different from any of the previous ones.

Once backstage at the circus, he let José drag him to the rafters of the tent, and the small gangway that gave access to the sphere of death, immobilized on the rim of the giant wheel.

José stood behind the boy. Suddenly, just as Miarka entered the ring, followed by Dorr and Phoena, the gypsy hit the back of Yves' head with a truncheon. Stunned, the boy immediately collapsed. José then grabbed his body and placed him, unconscious, inside the open sphere.

In the middle of the ring, the trio had stopped and was greeted by applause from spectators. Near the two young performers were two ropes that hung down from the rafters and which they would climb to reach the sphere above.

In response to the applause, Miarka and Dorr bowed, smiled and waved to the crowd.

But, in a box opposite the one where Monsieur Porcien sat, Leo Saint-Clair and his friend Gno Mitang also watched the show attentively.

There are several events to explain, which will enable the reader to better understand the respective positions of all the participants of this unfolding drama.

First, we return to June 28, when the Nyctalope was the victim of an aggression by Philogène Porcien's two henchmen.

Seized by the throat, grabbed by two powerful arms, Saint-Clair appeared to be helpless. He gave the impression that he had accepted his defeat and was giving up all resistance. Fooled by his attitude, more apparent than real, the two assailants felt triumphant and slightly eased their grips.

Suddenly, Saint-Clair acted. With a superhuman effort, he broke the hold of the arms that kept him prisoner. Then he stepped back three paces and faced his enemies. He sank to the ground, head first, performing a masterful somersault. Then his legs and feet arced through the air and violently struck his opponent's diaphragm.

The gangster collapsed, groaning. Immediately, Saint-Clair stood up, leapt upon him, and snatched the revolver that the man was still holding. He then hit the man with its butt, rendering him unconscious. The other gangster was taken by surprise, having barely had time to register the scene.

Saint-Clair shot twice, with his usual precision. His first shot broke the gangster's right wrist, the second lodged itself in his left forearm.

"Bull's eye," said the Nyctalope coldly. "You're finished. If you don't want the next shot through your head, you'll answer my questions... Who told you to attack me?"

"Some guy we met in Etampes, who gave us the car. After we'd taken care of you, we were to drive to Orleans and leave the car in a garage. He gave us the address. We're also supposed to report to him by phone."

"What number?"

"A restaurant in Etampes... I'm to ask for Denis."

The Nyctalope forced the two men, now manacled, into his car and quickly drove back to Etampes. His next moves were already clear in his mind.

First, he would entrust the two gangsters to the care of the local gendarmes. Then, he went to the post office and dialed the number that his prisoner had given him

"We're in Orleans," he lied brazenly, when he spoke to "Denis." "You can go ahead with no problem. The job's done. The guy won't bother you again."

The brief conversation ended, he went to lie in wait near the train station. His suspicions were justified. It wasn't long before Monsieur Porcien arrived. The Nyctalope saw him walk into the station, buy a ticket and go to the platform. He took the next train, traveling in the direction of Orleans.

After the train had left, Saint-Clair went to find the station master, identified himself and easily obtained the information he sought: Monsieur Porcien had purchased a ticket to Artenay.

*I have plenty of time to catch up with him*, he thought.

And while he was going to meet Porcien, he met Gno Mitang on the road.

When Miarka had ordered the release of her panther, Gno Mitang, lurking in the woods, was already on his guard. He had waited until the last second to not signal his position, but once the danger he faced had become clear, he had set off through the woods at full speed.

Just as he was beginning to feel the blast of the panther's fetid breath on his back, he heard a slight noise, a rustling of the branches and the hammering of the ground by four hoofed feet.

A deer had unexpectedly crossed their path!

The drama was brief. Gno Mitang heard the almost human death-cry that the poor beast uttered as it was attacked by the savage cat. There was a heavy fall, and the terrible sound of bones crushed between powerful jaws. The horrible feast had begun.

Certain that the panther would not abandon her meal to attack him, the Japanese slipped out of the woods and ran toward the road, where he was met by the Nyctalope a little later.

Having informed each other of their respective adventures, the two friends, comfortably installed in the car, drove to Orleans, where they spent the night.

The Nyctalope and Gno Mitang continued their investigation with renewed energy, but the gypsies had disappeared from the forest of Orleans and Monsieur Porcien seemed to have vanished off the face of the Earth. It was only several weeks later that one of the Nyctalope's contacts in Bordeaux called him to report that a caravan of gypsies, which might be the one he was looking for, had been spotted on the outskirts of that town.

Leo Saint-Clair and Gno Mitang immediately rushed down to Bordeaux. As they were driving through the city, chance, if not a premonition, drew their attention to a circus set up on one of the city's squares.

"Look!" said Gno Mitang suddenly, pointing at a man waiting in line to buy a ticket to the circus. "Don't you recognize that silhouette? It's Monsieur Porcien! What is he doing going to the circus? Maybe he has a stronger reason than merely wanting to be entertained. We should look into it."

"You're right," replied Saint-Clair thoughtfully.

His eyes followed Monsieur Porcien, who was just then standing in front of a huge poster advertizing a death-defying attraction. The flamboyant title proclaimed in huge letters:

*The Sphere of Death! Thrilling! Scary! Mysterious!*

The poster showed, at the top of a huge wheel, an open sphere and two children, a boy and a girl, falling down to their seeming deaths.

The eyes of the Nyctalope widened.

"This is it!" he murmured. "Gno, let's get box seats and watch Monsieur Porcien."

Installed in the box opposite to that of Philogène Porcien, determined not to lose sight of him, they were distractedly following the show, until they watched Miarka, Dorr and Phoena make their entrance into the ring.

Gno recognized Miarka at once, but not the children, whom he had never seen. But he couldn't help but notice the fear in the eyes of the little girl. He saw the tremor in her lips.

Suddenly, he shuddered.

"That little girl is making strange faces," said Leo Saint-Clair, also surprised by the movements of Phoena's lips.

"She is speaking," said Gno. "Calling for help. I can understand her words…"

By lip-reading, he repeated what little Phoena wanted to shout out:

"Up there! They're going to kill Yves! Yves is up there, with the wicked José! He's going to kill him! Help!"

Having understood more than enough, the Nyctalope jumped into the ring, followed by Gno, who snatched the rope from Dorr's hands and began to climb with such speed and agility that even Miarka, amazed, had no time to intervene.

But then, recognizing the Japanese, and guessing his intentions, she uttered a cry of rage, and grabbed one of the daggers hanging from her waist. She raised it in the air, ready to throw it at Gno Mitang.

However, two strong arms suddenly grabbed her, and prevented her from completing her deadly gesture. The Nyctalope had stepped in!

"Call the police!" he shouted to the audience. "I'm the Nyctalope! This woman is charged with two attempted murders, and the kidnapping and sequestration of a child!"

In his box, Monsieur Philogène Porcien had turned green with terror.

Meanwhile, Gno Mitang had climbed up to the rafters and reached the gangway leading to the sphere.

Phoena, just hoisted up by José, was just standing there, petrified with fear. The gypsy was preparing to shove her into the sphere, near the body of young Yves Marécourt, who was still unconscious.

Occupied by this sinister task, he had not paid attention to what was happening below in the ring.

He was therefore completely surprised when, raising his head, he saw Gno Mitang pointing a gun at him.

Terrified, José realized that the game was up and that his only chance to save his skin was to surrender.

He obeyed Gno Mitang's orders and reopened the sphere. He helped Phoena get out of the deadly object, and picked up Yves, who was still unconscious.

"Yves is your friend?" asked the Japanese to the girl. "The boy they wanted to kill?"

"Yes," Phoena said, her eyes full of hope and gratitude. "But you're going to stop them, aren't you?"

"It's already done," said Gno Mitang, smiling. "And all thanks to you, my brave little girl."

A few weeks later, back at the Manor of Folembray, Yves Marécourt, who seemed totally over his terrible adventure, was, for a few moments, playing the kind of games children of his age like to play. He was running merrily in the garden, pursued by Phoena, who was just as joyous as her young friend.

Three men watched the scene tenderly. They were Maître Loureille, the old notary of the late Monsieur Marécourt, the Nyctalope and Gno Mitang.

The two men had just been appointed by a family court as, respectively, the boy's new guardian and surrogate guardian.

"We did good work, my friend," said Leo Saint-Clair. "The rest is now in the hands of Fate. Time will tell if that child prodigy, miraculously rescued from death, will fulfill the hopes poor Lise Andrézieux had for him. Let's hope so. And speaking of fate, have you found out what will be those of Porcien and his accomplices?"

"Yes," replied the Japanese, "I've just learned that that Philogène Porcien was sentenced to death yesterday for the murder of Miarko. José and Miarka were both given life sentences and will remain in jail until the end of their days. As for that young rascal Dorr, he's been sent to a reform institution."

The Nyctalope nodded in approval.

*In pulp literature, there is a respectable tradition of heroes who span multiple generations: the Phantom, the Slayers, the Eternal Champion, to name but a few. In this introductory story, previously published in* Tales of the Shadowmen, *French author Emmanuel Gorlier delves into the Nyctalope's family tree and investigates whether Leo Saint-Clair might not have had some equally remarkable predecessors—and why...*

## Emmanuel Gorlier: *Fiat Lux!*

*Paris, 1639, 1641*

*Report prepared for the Watcher's Council by Quentin Travers, Chief Librarian, June 22, 1965.*

The following narrative has been translated and adapted from the diaries of Marquis Henri-Jean de Sainte Claire, who served as Lieutenant in the notorious Guard of Cardinal Armand du Plessis de Richelieu. Several events described therein might, at first glance, seem to stretch believability but I have attempted to make sense of them through logical extrapolations based on information already in our possession. This poem, allegedly composed by Cyrano de Bergerac, was found amongst the personal papers of Comte de Rochefort and, therefore, might not be authentic.

> « *Il convient de se dire, entre francs chevaliers,*
> *Tout le bien qu'on retire d'une histoire, versifiée*
> *Par une rouge Eminence à ce point inspirée,*
> *Que rien sur notre terre ne saurait l'égaler.*
> *La flamberge au vent froid met fin au long sursis,*
> *Et la face du faquin au fond du limon git.* »[1]

---

[1] It is proper to speak between gentle knights / Of all the good one thinks of a lyrical play / Penned by a crimson eminence so wonder-

It was on a cold winter morning in the year of Our Lord 1639 that one might have heard those verses declaimed loudly and clearly over the sounds of sword rattling against sword, if one found oneself in a lonely clearing in the woods lining the banks of the river Seine—in an area which, three centuries later, would become the location of the fabled Avenue des Champs-Elysées.

If fate had indeed brought a spectator to that muddy clearing, our bystander might have beheld the sight, familiar for the times, of two gentlemen engaged in a flamboyant duel. One was dressed in the dark red livery of the Cardinal's Guards; the other wore the proud uniform of the Cadets de Gascogne.

*« Mais enfin en baillant, je me suis éveillé.*
*A la fin de la pièce, aux vers si torturés,*
*Seuls les bras de Morphée avaient pu me sauver*
*Des affres de l'ennui où j'avais cru sombrer.*
*La flamberge au vent froid met fin au long sursis,*
*Et la face du butor au fond du limon git. »*[2]

These bold verses were being recited in a stentorian voice by the Cadet. Both combatants were of equal size and stature, and they each sported a thin mustache in the fashion of the times. The poet's face, however, was unique and truly remarkable. It was dominated by a nose that was so big and pointy that he himself had, occasionally, referred to it as a promontory.

Were our hypothetical spectator acquainted with Parisian society, he would have immediately recognized the notorious

---

fully inspired / That nothing in this world could ever be its equal. / The rapier in the cold morning quickly decides / And the oaf's face soon lies in the mud.

[2] But at long last I woke up yawning / At the end of that wretched play; / Only Morpheus' arms had saved me / From the deadly boredom engulfing me. / The rapier in the cold morning quickly decides / And the lout's face soon lies in the mud.

Savinien Hercule Cyrano de Bergerac, rightly feared as the deadliest swordsman in France, and equally famous for his fearless conduct. One might well have asked what insanity could have compelled his adversary to challenge such a man to a duel?

Cyrano's impromptu poem might have offered a clue: listening to it, one would have understood that the swordsman had, once again, publicly mocked Cardinal de Richelieu's literary aspirations, drawing inspiration, for reasons no one suspected, from the title of his most recent play, *Roxane*.

> « *Aujourd'hui, à l'épée, pour l'honneur d'un Duc,*
> *Afin de préserver toute gloire caduque,*
> *De Sainte Claire et moi allons nous rencontrer.*
> *Sur ce grand champ d'honneur, l'un de nous va tomber.*
> *La flamberge au vent froid met fin au long sursis,*
> *Et la face du cuistre au fond du limon git.* »[3]

That last stanza identified Cyrano's unfortunate opponent. Equally well-known throughout Paris for his bravery, he was none other than Marquis Henri-Jean de Sainte-Claire,[4] a man loyal beyond words to his master, who was obviously seeking retribution for Cyrano's insolence, despite the Cardinal's own edict forbidding duels.

Yet, despite Sainte-Claire's obvious talent with a sword, he could not prevail against Cyrano's superior skills. Soon, the issue of the duel was no longer in doubt. The Cadet de Gascogne easily blocked all of his opponent's thrusts, while he

---

[3] Today with my sword, for a Duke's honor, / In order to protect dubious glory, / Sainte-Claire and I shall meet / And on the battlefield one of us will fall. / The rapier in the cold morning quickly decides / And the boor's face soon lies in the mud.

[4] Historical records indicate that some members of the Sainte-Claire family later shortened their name to Saint-Clair during the French Revolution, when Louis-Jean de Sainte-Claire, a friend of the notorious Sir Percy Blakeney, helped saved numerous members of the French aristocracy from the blade of the guillotine.

himself managed to drive the tip of his rapier ever closer to Sainte-Claire's face. It was obvious that Cyrano, as was his wont, waited only to finish his poem before delivering the fatal strike.

The young Marquis, against almost all hope, nevertheless managed a skillful feint, parry and thrust that would surely have maimed Cyrano had he not been so light on his feet. In a bold counterstrike, the poet struck Sainte-Claire just above his left eye. The blow was so unexpected and the shock so violent that the Marquis fell face first on the ground—just as Cyrano's poem had predicted!

Sainte-Claire woke up four days later inside a dark bedroom in an inn that was patronized by the Cardinal's Guards. He heard someone come into the room.

"Rochefort—thank you for taking such good care of me," he said, recognizing his visitor at once.

"Henri! It's so dark in here! How could you tell it was me?... Well, who else would care for you, I suppose... I feared that Cyrano's blow might have left you blind, but it seems that, like the Duc de Guise and I, you're only condemned to wear an ugly scar on your face!"

"Please pour me a glass of wine! I see a jug and a glass on that table over there."

"How the Devil can you see in here! It's as dark as the Devil's bottom! Let me open the shutters first!"

Thus did Henri-Jean de Sainte-Claire become aware that Cyrano's sword had mysteriously affected his sense of sight. He was able to see in the dark as if it were daylight! He thought this new talent might prove very useful in the Cardinal's service...

Two years later, during a moonless night in December 1641, Sainte-Claire was back in the same fateful clearing where his duel with Cyrano, which had almost killed him, had instead ended up gifting him with his strange, new power. Wrapped inside a long, dark cloak, the Cardinal's Guard had been discreetly following a messenger dispatched by the Marquis Henri de Cinq-Mars.

The man had often turned back to check if he was being followed, but the darkness was too obscure for him to detect Sainte-Claire's presence—and unlike the Cardinal's man, Cinq-Mars' agent was not a nyctalope!

Sainte-Claire had been following the man since he had left his master's Parisian mansion. A few days earlier, Rochefort and he had been summoned by the Cardinal, who wished to entrust them with an important mission. When they had faced the man who had secretly ruled France for so many years from behind the scenes, they had found him pale and sickly. Yet, his eyes still carried within them the cold flame of his unbending will.

"Gentlemen," said Richelieu, "I have just obtained information about a plot against the Kingdom. Some of the ringleaders belong to the highest strata of our society and are even close to the King himself. One of them is the Marquis de Cinq-Mars, who owes me everything in life, and yet, it seems, hates me deeply. I do not know the details of the plot, but it is said to be bankrolled by Spain. We have been at war with King Philip IV for six years now; no doubt, he has found a more expedient way to bring our conflict to an end. Rochefort! Sainte-Claire! I trust you above all others. I want you to keep a close eye on Cinq-Mars and report anything suspicious to me at once."

Following their orders, the two Guards had kept a close watch on the Marquis' mansion, Rochefort by day, Sainte-Claire by night. That's how the latter had spotted the mysterious messenger dispatched in the depths of night and had followed him into the woods all the way to the banks of the Seine.

Cinq-Mars' envoy reached the clearing by the river. There, two men appeared to be waiting for him. They were wrapped in long, black cloaks which, nevertheless, did not hide the swords hanging from their belts. Sainte-Claire thought that they must be gentlemen of the nobility.

A stranger sight, however, was that of a small metal embarkation in the river, which looked like no boat Sainte-Claire had ever seen. It was smooth, grey and oval in shape, and was topped by a metal turret with a door large enough for one man.

Sainte-Claire watched the three men who, normally, would have been invisible to all in the darkness and listened eagerly to their exchange.

"Gentlemen, 'tis an ill wind that blows nobody any good," the Marquis' envoy said.

*Obviously a pre-arranged signal*, thought Sainte-Claire.

"The windmill doesn't care for the wind that's gone past," responded one of the two newcomers with a strong Spanish accent, making a courteous salute. "Do you have the draft of the new treaty?" he added, extending his hand.

At that moment, Sainte-Claire noticed something unusual about the Spaniard's hand: his fourth finger did not move and was bent at an unnatural angle. He looked at his companion and saw that his hand, too, presented the same, unusual characteristic.

Meanwhile, the Marquis' messenger had pulled a document from under his cloak and was handing it to the strange Spaniard.

"Here it is," he said. "My master asked me to tell you that it faithfully reflects our latest agreement, and your King should be pleased with the new territories conceded to Spain."

He then pulled back his hood and Sainte-Claire recognized François de Thou, Councillor at the Parliament and great friend of the Marquis de Cinq-Mars.

As the treaty changed hands, Sainte-Claire became concerned that such a damning proof of Cinq-Mars' guilt might be lost, so he pulled out his sword and jumped into the clearing, shouting:

"In the name of the King and the Cardinal, you are all under arrest!"

After a second during which they were struck by surprise, the three conspirators reacted—very differently.

François de Thou, his face contorted with fear, stepped back, trying to see who had sprung on them, already looking for a means of escape.

One of the two Spaniards seized the treaty and jumped aboard the metal boat. The other pulled what looked like a strange hand-held metallic weapon from beneath his cloak and peered through the darkness, trying to find his opponent.

With a swift turn of his blade, Saint-Claire disarmed him, causing the gun to fall on the grass, and stabbed him through the neck. Then something truly extraordinary happened: As soon as his foe's body touched the ground, it was surrounded by a reddish glow and disappeared, leaving only a scattering of ashes behind!

It was now Sainte-Claire's turn to be awestruck on the spot.

François de Thou took advantage of the Cardinal's man's shock to vanish into the woods, running as fast as his portly legs would carry him.

Meanwhile, the third man, the one with the treaty, had reached the door in the turret of the strange metal ship. Sainte-Claire was too far to catch him. He saw the strange gun lying on the ground, grabbed it, pointed it at the fugitive and pressed the knob on its side.

The gun made a strange high-pitched sound and the Spaniard's body became also enveloped by a red glow before it, too, disappeared. Then, the metal ship began to vibrate and disintegrate. The Seine waters bubbled up and, after a few seconds, nothing was left of the incident, except some thin grey smoke which floated above the water before the wind blew it away.

Sainte-Claire looked at the supernatural gun in his hand. "Even the treaty is gone," he muttered dejectedly. Then, he threw the accursed object in the river and went home to write his report.

*Report prepared for the Watcher's Council by Quentin Travers, Chief Librarian, June 22, 1965 (cont'd).*

Sainte-Claire's diary does not contain any more information about this strange affair, the next section being devoted to his dalliance with a young lady-in-waiting from the Court, which offers little or no interest as far as we are concerned.

A few months later, Cardinal de Richelieu was able to lay his hands on written proof of Cinq-Mars' treacherous exchange with King Philip IV of Spain, a conspiracy which also implicated the King's own brother. On September 12, 1642, Cinq-Mars and de Thou were beheaded in Lyon. It is not impossible that Sainte-Claire took some further part in those events.

The strange facts related in his diary are, as far as I have been able to ascertain, not mentioned anywhere in any other chronicles of the times. The identity of the two strange persons posing as Spaniards remains unknown. It is possible that they were Invaders from another world, who, upon seeing their plot foiled, left, never to return. It is highly unlikely that we will ever learn the truth about this matter.

As for the remarkable powers exhibited by Marquis Henri-Jean de Sainte-Claire, it is tempting to juxtapose this information with what we know is contained in the papyrus written by Greek historian Manetho preserved in our Library.

Manetho relates that, during the reign of Pharaoh Akhenaton in 1360 BC., the High Priest of Aton, Merira, created a special caste of sacred warriors to spread the faith of Aton and defend the values of light and justice throughout Egypt. The leader of that caste, one special warrior, was endowed by the Sun God with a special power which enabled him to see in the darkness as if it were light. As we know, Manetho went on to mostly detail the story of Akhenaton's death and how the Pharaoh was buried in the Chamber of Horus located beneath the Great Pyramid, but he also noted that this warrior had the ability to transfer his power to his descendents in order for them to keep defending the values of Aton in times of great need.

Might Marquis Henri-Jean de Sainte Claire have been a descendent of this great warrior whose name has been lost in history? Certainly, the fact that his descendent, Leo Saint-Clair, a.k.a. the Nyctalope, was endowed with the same power and fought a great number of foes threatening the stability of our world leads us to speculate: as there has been a line of Slayers since time immemorial, can there also have been a line of Nyctalopes?

*Emmanuel Gorlier is also the author of* Nyctalope! L'Univers
Extravagant de Jean de La Hire, *a companion book about La
Hire and his universe, from which we have excerpted and
translated the chronology appended to this volume. This story,
published in* Les Compagnons de L'Ombre—*the French version of* Tales of the Shadowmen *published by our sister imprint Rivière Blanche—is a sequel to* Fiat Lux! *and expands
upon the Nyctalope's mythological origins, while clearing the
way for his triumphant return in the 1950s...*

## Emmanuel Gorlier: *The Three Sisters*

*A long, long time ago...*

Silence. Darkness. Suddenly, the Sun appeared over the horizon, lighting a vast, desolate landscape of rocks and dust with
its harsh light. A man stood, resting on the edge of a small crater, unconcerned by the vacuum of space, lost in thought. He
wore flamboyant clothes and white boots adorned with purple
ribbons. He shook his fawn-colored gloves, which swung
more slowly because of the gravity that was six times less than
that of Earth, and a double spiral of multicolored stones appeared, rotating upon themselves quickly. They were Ioun
stones which he had found on a distant white dwarf star. Each
had its own unique power—one of which being that they allowed him to move unimpeded on the inhospitable surface of
the Moon.

After a long moment of hesitation, the Magician took a
small, wooden box from one of the many pockets of his elegant lemon-yellow shirt. He opened it gently. Inside were
three compartments; two were empty while the third was occupied by another Ioun stone of a shimmering color. He removed the crystal from the box with an overly cautious gesture and lifted it to the sky. A thought crossed his mind:

*Rialto, my friend, thanks to this stone you will surpass yourself! The first stone, which you deposited on the Sun, will transmit its stellar energy to this stone, here, on the Moon, which in turn will rebroadcast it to its sister stone on Earth, and that will cause an explosion like nothing anyone has ever seen! Ha! Ha! It will be just as I swore: I won't have to use even a hint of magic to destroy that bothersome mountain! It will be eradicated entirely due to a natural phenomenon! It is not for nothing that I am known as Rialto the Marvelous—the most powerful magician of our times! In fact, in my opinion, limiting this phrase to a specific time period is highly inaccurate, but still... When I meet my fellow magicians of the Dying Earth, no one will think of searching this far back in time to discover my trick! Now, the only thing that remains for me to do is to bury the stone and place a minor dust elemental over it, set to disperse on the day of our meeting. The planetary conjunction that will place the three stones in perfect alignment will do the rest!*

Using a small silver shovel, Rialto dug a tiny hole into which he deposited the stone. He then poured the contents of a multicolored vial over it. A powder spread over the hole as if it were animated with a life of its own and quickly covered the excavation.

Rialto smiled, made a few strange passes with his hands and vanished abruptly.

*One hundred thousand years later...*

The small crater on the Moon was still there, unchanged. Suddenly, a meteor crossed the ink-dark sky and hit the lunar surface a few yards from where the Ioun stone was buried. The silent shock had the power of a small atomic bomb. The dust elemental vanished. The stone had been born at the center of a star and easily withstood the tremendous heat of the explosion. Now, it sat alone, undisturbed, at the center of a very large crater. Nothing prevented it from being in alignment with its solar sister when the Moon was down, and the crater was bathed in sunlight.

As for the third stone, despite Rialto's best intentions, it had been discovered on Earth by the necromancers of the dark kingdom of Acheron, who had divined its weird energy broadcasting powers and had buried it in a long-forgotten underground cave where it lay hidden for millennia. But all the elements were potentially in place for what Rialto had only intended as a practical joke to be turnred into a major threat to Mankind, for if the third stone ever came to be discovered and was exposed to moonlight at the wrong time...

*Egypt, 14th Century BC,*
*during the Reign of Pharaoh Akhenaton...*

The dark, underground passage was suddenly lit up by the distant light of a torch. A light step sounded and a young woman appeared, her beautiful face was illuminated by some secret joy. She wore a long, hooded cloak and carried a small canvas bag over her left arm. After a hundred yards, she stopped before a massive wooden door and knocked gently. A few moments later, the door opened silently, revealing the weathered face of a powerful-looking man.

"Hecate! At last! Do you have the stone?"

The girl entered the room. The man closed the door behind her, after casting a worried glance at the corridor. Hecate opened the bag and pulled out a milky, oval stone with a dark spot that glowed with an inner light.

"Amon be praised!" exclaimed the man. "The Egg of Set! After all these years, we finally have the means to destroy the Heretic!"

"Don't talk so loudly, Imhotep! We could still be overheard."

"Pah! We're in a temple that Akhenaton has struck with a curse! His minions are not likely to be wandering about..." Then, with a sibilant voice, he continued: "Thanks to the power of this stone, we can repay the wicked! Are you sure you can use it according to the legends?"

"Thanks to the old Stygian scrolls you gave me, I was able to discover where the stone was hidden. It was hard, but I found the entrance to the Black Pyramid. It was protected by many traps, as if those who had buried it there feared that someone might someday remove it. It had been hidden there for tens of centuries! This is probably what allowed me to succeed, for few things can withstand the passage of time and most of the traps had rotted away or disintegrated into dust. Finally, I reached the center of the pyramid. The Egg was on an altar. Behind it there was a solemn warning making a final attempt to warn any tomb robber, threatening appalling devastation, the fall of kingdoms, the sinking of continents, and above all, warning that it should never be exposed to the light of the Moon! Well, we have been warned! I think I can control its frightful power and turn it against the accursed Pharaoh."

"And now, we will be able to restore the worship of the true gods! Thanks to the treasure of the Temple of Amon your reward will be without compare!"

"The important thing is for me to keep the Egg and, with your help, to find the information necessary to use it to its fullest potential in the archives of the Temple of Aton."

"Upon the Pharaoh's death, you will have access to all the documents you want."

"Very well. Then I shall strike during the next official ceremony."

"It will not be hard to get close to the throne. We have many secret supporters, even amongst the Pharaoh's relatives. Since he separated from Queen Nefertiti, his power has weakened. His only allies are Smenkhkare, his son-in-law, and Tutankhaton, his only son who is but nine."

"Not true! Don't forget Merira, the High Priest of Aton! He will try to stop us—if he can!"

"I do not forget him, but could he know that we're about to strike?"

The next day, Merira stood before the sacred altar, facing the rising sun, chanting a prayer to the divine star, the first-rays of which were bathing the temple in golden light. With a sweeping gesture, he poured a powder on the red hot coals that burned in a gold tripod. A dark cloud immediately filled the air. Under the rays of the sun, the cloud began to change colors and offer fleeting glimpses of scenes and images: a large, milky stone hidden inside a temple, a young woman grabbing it and, later, meeting someone in a forbidden temple of Amon, then the ceremony of the Rising Sun in the presence of the Pharaoh... Suddenly, a great flame lit up the cloud, which vanished. The vision was over. Resplendent in the light of the Sun, Merira stood tall, deeply puzzled. The large statue of Aton then began to glow. The gold disk that crowned its face shone with an eerie gleam. The god himself appeared to react to the strange prophecy.

A few days later, just before sunrise, the temple was still in darkness, but already the light of dawn eclipsed that of the stars and the Moon. The amphitheater outside was filled with dignitaries in full ceremonial dress, standing respectfully between the massive columns. Around the temple entrance, a crowd had gathered. On a dais, separated from the worshippers by a line of soldiers, the High Priest Merira stood, his arms raised, his eyes fixed upon the horizon, waiting. Behind him, his face drawn and tired, was the Pharaoh Akhenaton, the instigator of the mystical cult of Aton. For many long months, he had been plagued by an unknown disease. Perhaps today, he would welcome the god—and the cure for his condition. His young wife and his son, Tutankhaton, stood at his side. Slightly below, a young priest of Aton was scrutinizing the crowd with his unusually piercing eyes. He stared into each and every man, despite the ambient darkness.

Lost at the back of the crowd, her face hidden behind a veil that showed only her eyes, Hecate moved unobtrusively towards the dais, hiding a shiny object in the palm of her hand.

Suddenly, a murmur rippled through the assembly; the sun had just appeared in the East. The High Priest began a long incantation. Quickly, the light began to fill the temple. But the Moon was still very close to the position of the star, and had not yet faded completely...

Taking advantage of the general distraction, Hecate quietly took out the Egg of Set. The sun, rising majestically in the middle of the sky, was drawing every eye in its direction. Every eye? No, for the young priest was continuing his careful monitoring of the crowd and had just noticed the young woman's strange behavior. Immediately, he beckoned to the Captain of the Guard, who seemed to expect his signal, and gestured to indicate that they should apprehend her. In turn, the officer made a sign to his men and they plunged into the crowd, trying to surround their prey.

At that moment, a ray of light coming from the stone on the Sun bounced to its sister on the Moon and rushed towards the third stone on Earth. As it made contact, the Egg of Set seemed to catch fire and emitted a powerful ray of light that shone on the backs of the dignitaries standing in front of the young woman. Instantly, their clothes were set ablaze amidst their cries of surprise, then pain. Their very skin began to darken, crackle and char. Within seconds, several people were burned to death, utterly consumed, and the fire began to spread.

The crowd shouted in panic, "Aton, have mercy!" "Fire!" "Help!" Struck by a beam of light, one of the temple columns collapsed noisily, killing more people.

The soldiers tried to approach Hecate, or get between her and the Pharaoh in order to shield him with their bodies. The young priest also tried to intervene, but, like the guards, he was blocked by the panicked crowd rushing forward to escape the devastation.

Making a sweeping, circular motion, Hecate swept away most of the guards. The survivors gazed in horror with eyes full of resignation. How could they escape the wrath of Aton?

A smile on her lips, Hecate now raised her hand in order to burn away the last remaining obstacles between her and the accursed Akhenaton. The last guard collapsed, burned to a cinder. She screamed in excitement:

"Die, Pharaoh, die!"

She leveled the Egg of Set at the monarch, but suddenly, the ray disappeared![5]

During these dramatic events, unnoticed by anyone, another singular spectacle had unfolded in the sky. Gradually, a portion of the sun had disappeared! First, it was only a small crescent at the place where the moon had faded; then, that crescent grew slowly until it filled the entire orb. Soon, night again fell on the Temple!

Anyone who might have watched the faces of the main characters in this drama would certainly have been surprised. The Pharaoh's face was illuminated by mystical ecstasy; his god, after threatening to kill him, had then saved him! The High Priest Merira thanked the god for having answered his prayers. As for Hecate, her eyes were wide open under the effect of a profound surprise, which, gradually, gave way to terror.

The young priest whose eyes were so piercing did not seem bothered at all by the darkness. Stepping over the many corpses barring his way, he boldly marched towards the woman. Then, and only then, could he have been identified as the one whom Merira has named the "Eyes of Aton," upon whom the god had conferred the power to walk through the darkness as if it were full daylight in order to defend the values of justice held dear by the Solar God!

The Eyes of Aton, hidden by the darkness, but not hampered by it, reached Hecate and forced her hand open, causing her to release the stone before she could even attempt to fight. Immediately, he took off his cloak and wrapped the stone in it. It was too dangerous to remain out a minute longer. Mean-

---

[5] Eclipse of May 14, 1337 BC.

while, the sorceress retreated cautiously and tried to flee under cover of darkness. But she could not escape the Eyes of Aton!

At that moment, light began to return and the darkness again faded. The Sun was back! Realizing that she was about to be captured, Hecate plunged her hand under her dressed to grab a powerful magical talisman that she had taken with her. But before she could use it, Merira, who had assessed the situation, pointed his finger at her and said in a loud voice:

"By Horus, stay!"

Instantly, the sorceress froze.

The High Priest repeated: "By Horus, stay!" three times. Hecate fell to her knees. The High Priest with his imperious air then proclaimed:

"Let your name be no more!" and pointed towards the desert.

The sorceress got up and, with a haunted look, began to walk unsteadily towards the empty expanse of dunes. After a few minutes, she disappeared over the horizon.

Merira then cast a glance around. He saw many charred bodies, the Pharaoh dazed on the dais, the Queen and her son trembled in a corner… He looked up and exclaimed:

"O mighty Aton! Through your divine intervention, we have won the day! However, our Lord is still weak and the future of thy worship is not assured. I will do my best to preserve his health, but this infernal stone must not again fall into the wrong hands. With your blessing, I will entrust it to the Eyes of Aton who will guard it and use it only for the triumph of Good. And after him, his descendants will do the same, for what happened today can never be allowed to happen again."

*1642, The South of France near Banyuls.*

The coach was traveling at a gallop through the night. Inside were a richly dressed man and woman. From time to time, the man looked out of the window to check that they were not followed. Finally, he turned to his companion and said:

"It seems we've managed to escape!"

"What's more important is that we're close to our destination," she replied.

"What fancy caused you to seduce that Marquis? Yes, it kept him busy, at least for a while, but it didn't prevent the failure of Cinq-Mars' conspiracy, nor his execution."

She looked up at him, frowning in anger:

"He was a dangerous man who had to be watched! He killed two of our own in Paris and, somehow, even destroyed our submarine! A mere human! Unthinkable! But don't think I took any pleasure in seducing him! Even though we failed, he had to be kept in check."

"You may well be right," replied her companion, sighing. "Still, he seemed to be besotted with you. I fear he guessed your true nature and now will want revenge!"

"Come on," she said, smiling. "We're almost at our spaceship. After that, he can no longer harm us."

She ruffled her hair with her delicate hand, the pinky of which was oddly stiff.

Soon, the coach left the main road to enter a narrow path and, a few minutes later, arrived in a clearing, at the center which was a craft that would someday be described as a "flying saucer."

Several men dressed in silver jumpsuits approached the coach, brandishing shiny metal tubes that projected beams of light. Soon, they recognized the two new arrivals.

"At last!" said one of the men. "We were beginning to worry! We must hurry. It will soon be dawn."

During this conversation, a man, entirely dressed in black, jumped from beneath the rear of the coach where he had been hiding. He did not seem bothered in any way by the surrounding darkness. He was Henri-Jean de Sainte-Claire, lieutenant in the Guards of Cardinal de Richelieu. After a duel with the famous poet and swordsman Cyrano de Bergerac, he had acquired the mysterious power to see in the dark.

For several days, he had been discreetly following the couple while they ran. He had discovered that she, whom he thought was the love of his life was, in reality, one of these mysterious Invaders who had been behind Cinq-Mars' nefarious plot. The creatures looked like men, but sported a stiff pinky and disappeared with a red glare when they were killed. Sainte-Claire had discovered their existence by chance during a mission and, since then, sought only to thwart and destroy them whenever possible...

Now, it seemed that he had finally found their "metal fortress." At dawn, he would destroy it, using an ancient family relic that was supposed to be unspeakably powerful.

As the night began to fade and the sky grew lighter, the men in the silver jumpsuits finished stowing inside their metal crafts various objects, the nature of which he could not fathom. Meanwhile, the two travelers changed into jumpsuits as well. Afterward, they all went inside the ship. A metal door closed behind them and became indistinguishable from the surface of the craft. After a few moments, a strange noise sounded and the metal ship suddenly lit up with a bright light.

Sainte-Claire pulled a milky stone out of a bag just as the sun appeared on the horizon. Meanwhile, in the clearing, the metal ship suddenly rose from the ground and began to move away at great speed.

Suddenly, a ray of light came from the Sun, bounced to the Moon, and then to the stone Sainte-Claire held firmly, before hitting the spacecraft.

Within seconds, the saucer became red-hot, then white, then began to melt, before finally exploding. The force was so strong that it knocked Sainte-Claire off his feet. He inadvertently let go of the stone which whirled around through the air, its deadly beam burning and wreaking havoc on the surrounding hills, destroying everything in its path.

Eventually, the stone rolled on the grass and again became inert. The Marquis hesitantly took it. It was cold, almost icy, to the touch. He buried it back inside the pouch, looking at the devastation all around him. His face was white as a sheet. He stood there for a long time absolutely still, trying to recover his composure.

Then, finally, he muttered: "This... thing is too danger-ous. In the wrong hands, it could destroy the world. One way or another, I've got to end that threat!"

*1657, A forest near Paris.*

It was almost midnight when Henri-Jean de Sainte-Claire ar-rived in the clearing. The full Moon lit the scene with a plea-sant silvery light. He opened his bag and pulled out a strange leather harness to which were attached numerous small bottles containing a clear liquid. He put it on, thinking:

*I have duplicated the harness described by that dreamer, Cyrano. I hope he really journeyed to the Moon and that it wasn't another of his poetic flights of fancy. I had enough trouble getting the dew and also that strange metal powder which he didn't mention in his book, but which was clearly described in his notes. I must hope it will be enough to take me to the Moon where I have business to conduct.*

No sooner had Sainte-Claire donned the harness that he felt lighter and his feet began to leave the ground. *It works!* He thought. *Incredible! Sacré Savinien!*

Beneath his feet, the Earth was now moving away in-creasingly faster. Above him, the lunar circle became bigger and bigger. He flew, as he had planned, towards the Moon. Soon, he began to distinguish the details of the lunar surface. Up close, it looked like an Eden. Lush vegetation covering a wonderful land, populated by animals living in peace and freedom, herbivore alongside carnivore without fear or risk of being eaten. Henri-Jean could not believe it! Once again, Cy-rano's account had been correct.

In the midst of that Eden stood a tall tree, and upon it, a fruit-shaped gem shone like a thousand candles. Henri-Jean landed near the tree, extended his hand and plucked the fruit. No sooner had he touched the gem that the landscape around him changed abruptly. The Moon was now a barren surface, empty and desolate. He could not help thinking: *And all this from just having tried to pick a fruit in this garden...*

In reality, the second Ioun stone was creating illusions reflecting the thoughts of the untrained minds that approached it. It was that power that had deceived Cyrano as well as Sainte-Claire.

Protected from the lack of atmosphere by the stone, Henri-Jean took the second stone to the Dark Side of the Moon. There, he knew, the three sisters could no longer be in alignment, since the Moon always shows the same side to the Earth.

While Sainte-Claire returned to Earth using the power of the Earth stone, he thought he had eliminated the threat of the "Three Sisters" forever. But was it really the case?

*February 2, 1958. Morocco.*

The desert stretched out of sight. The heat was oppressive. Apart from a great, big rock, there was nothing but sand and rubble. On the left, a long dune shimmered in the air because of the glare of the sun.

Suddenly, a black spot appeared at the top of the dune, and slowly grew larger until it was possible to distinguish that it was a man riding a camel. He was dressed in Western-style clothes, with riding breeches and a leather jacket belted at the waist. He wore a turban on his head and a Browning revolver on his belt. He had the look of a warrior about him. A bag hung on the saddle of his mount.

Viewed more closely, as he alighted at the rock, he was not very tall, but had an athletic build. He looked around attentively. Any observer would have had trouble concealing their surprise at his singular gaze; his eyes were like those of a nocturnal bird, large and yellow in color.

He stopped near the rock. He put his hand in a small cavity inside it, seemingly looking for something. He must have found it, because suddenly, he pushed hard and, with a great creaking sound, a large double door, more than five feet high, opened in the desert floor. Beneath was a vast dark cavern.

The man stepped inside, going down a flight of wooden steps, staring at a place that he had obviously not seen for many years. The cavern was cool and he took off his turban. It was then possible to identify the visitor as Leo Saint-Clair, a.k.a. The Nyctalope. He barely looked a day older than forty, even though his exploits had been chronicled for over sixty years.

With his powers, he did not need any light, artificial or otherwise, to examine the contents of the secret cave, even though it was pitch dark. It had once been a secret military base of the French Colonial Empire, long abandoned and forgotten. In addition to the type of equipment one logically expected to find in such a place, such as military bunks, tables, metal cabinets, gun racks, wireless facilities, and piles of cash and fake passports, Leo recognized a number of strange machines. On the left was the prototype of the Flying Machine Gun invented by his friend, Captain Cazal, which could have won the war for France if only.... On the right was a Martian tripod, partially disassembled, and behind it, a crate of radium-powered weapons from Helium. In the middle of the cave was a metallic rocket-shaped craft which still seemed in good condition. It was the *OLB -1*, the ship designed by Professor Olbans, with which he had explored the vagabond planet, Rhea....

For a brief moment, Leo thought fondly of the Professor's niece, Veronique, who had once been his wife...

Then, shaking his head, he went inside to examine the spacecraft and came out a few minutes later smiling. He headed to the armament section of the cavern and quickly located a strange weapon stored in a metal cabinet. It was a recreation of Engineer Korrides' Lightning Projector, the construction of which he had himself supervised.

"Excellent," said Leo, talking to himself. "I'll mount it on the rocket and will be on my way."

He was glad to have had the forethought of setting up this secret base with a few friends from the CID, in 1939, when war had seemed all but inevitable.

After the tedious and delicate work of mounting the Projector on the rocket and setting up a system for firing it from the control panel inside, the Nyctalope sat in the cockpit, thinking: *It reminds me of my youth when I helped my father in his research. Had he not been murdered, my life would have been so different! Ah! Sadi Khan! Without your despicable deeds, the Nyctalope would not have been born...but then again, I might still be in jail...*

Leo remembered what had happened barely six months earlier when he had decided to surrender himself to the French authorities. The rain had been falling non-stop at the airport of Le Bourget. As soon as he had landed, he had been arrested and handcuffed. The Press was there and the scene was intermittently illuminated by flashes from the journalists' cameras. The next day, the newspapers read: *After ten years on the run, the Nyctalope surrenders! The Nyctalope in prison! Like many collaborators before him, Leo Saint-Clair, condemned to a ten-year-sentence in absentia in February 1947, will finally pay his debt to society. The former adventurer was taken in handcuffs to the Prison de la Santé where....*

A few hours later, after a routine interview, Leo had asked to speak to an officer of the Deuxième Bureau about some "an urgent matter concerning National Defense."

After being left alone in a cell for two hours, he had been taken to a large room with only three chairs and, a large oak table upon which were a desk lamp and a folder.

Two of the chairs were occupied: one by a man of strong build, with a thick body and a wrestler's head, the other by a tall, lanky man with crew cut blond hair and the square face of a Breton, who smoked a pipe. Both had stood up as the Nyctalope had entered the room and had offered him their hands to shake, which surprised Leo a little.

"*Bonjour, mon Commandant*," had said the "wrestler," giving Leo the rank to which he was entitled. "My name is Geo Paquet of the Direction de la Surveillance du Territoire."

"And I am Lieutenant Roger Noël of the Service National d'Information Fonctionelle," had said the Breton. I believe you told Commissaire Ferret during your interview that you wanted to see someone from the Intelligence services regarding an 'an urgent matter concerning National Defense?'"

"That is correct," had replied Leo.

"Then, please, sit down," had said Paquet.

The Nyctalope had taken the empty chair and had sat. As was his method, Paquet had immediately launched himself into the heart of the matter.

"You are aware that the Russians are about to send up a second Sputnik?"

"How could I not know it?" had replied Leo. "All of the world's secret services have been following the news. But do *you* know that, in reality, the Soviets plan to launch *two* satellites simultaneously?"

Paquet and Noel had looked at each other with a puzzled air. The former's unspoken question had been answered by the latter's slight negative shake of the head.

"Are you sure of your facts, Monsieur Saint-Clair?" Noel had asked. "Our agents are among the best in the world, and yet we know nothing of this."

"May I suggest, Lieutenant, that you contact some of your colleagues in the OSS...?"

Stung by the Nyctalope's slightly superior smile, Geo Paquet, who was known in France by the nickname of the "Gorilla," had jumped up and left the room saying: "I'll be right back."

Forty-five minutes later, the door had opened violently. The Gorilla had returned. His face was red and congested. He immediately shouted at the Nyctalope: "How did you hear that?"

Without losing his composure, Leo had replied:

"Did the Americans tell you *why* the Russians are sending two satellites?"

For once in his life, Paquet had remained speechless. The Nyctalope continued:

"Now that I have proved my skills to you, let me tell you everything I know, because you'll soon need my help. The reason why the Soviets plan to launch a second satellite, equipped with powerful deflectors is because…"

And then, the Nyctalope had told Geo Paquet and Roger Noel how, sixty years ago, Sadi Khan, had stolen not only the plans of the Radiant Z, his father's greatest invention, but also—and this had not been immediately discovered at the time—the diary of one of his ancestors, the Marquis Henri-Jean de Sainte-Claire, and a strange stone that never left his father's desk.

Leo had read that diary when he was a child. It talked of a stone with fearsome powers, and a trip to the Moon! The metal powder that Cyrano had mixed with dew was attracted by our satellite like a magnet. Later, Leo guessed that it was a variant of the Z-4 substance discovered by Professor Olbans, which had allowed him to travel to Rhea.

The Nyctalope had, unfortunately, never managed to find Sadi Khan, who, later, had joined Lenin and taken part in the October Revolution.

Things might have remained as they were, if Leo hadn't learned by accident, thanks to a contact within the OSS, a distant cousin, Hubert Bonisseur de la Bath, that Stalin had gotten his hands on the stone, found amongst the effects of Sadi Khan, and intended to get the second stone from the Moon!

When the first *beep beep* of Sputnik resounded through the skies, everything had become clear. The Soviets planned to go to the Moon, and there was nothing the West could do to stop them!

The OSS had learned that the Russians were about to launch a secret satellite codenamed SK-1—for Sadi Khan—which had been the last clue Leo needed to confirm his guess—at the same time as Sputnik 2. SK-1 was to be equipped with reflective panels and circle the Moon.

Leo had guessed that the Russians were trying to put the Moon Stone in alignment with the Earth Stone, which was in their possession, using mirrors. But what could he do to stop them? It was then that he decided to surrender to the authorities, preferring to trust France rather than the U.S., embroiled in a shameful "witch hunt," to support him in what he planned to do...

After finishing his story, the Nyctalope had concluded:

"...Now you know everything. Let me make you an offer. I propose to take action to solve this problem on behalf of France, but secretly, to avoid any incidents, diplomatic or otherwise... in exchange for a full pardon, of course."

"This could be arranged," had said Noel, pulling on his pipe.

"What do you propose to do?" had asked the Gorilla

"That will be my own business. Grant me a full pardon and I will end the Soviet threat forever. This offer is non-negotiable."

Paquet had looked at Leo Saint-Clair with respect, then said:

"I'll go and talk to the Boss."

"And I to SNIF," had said Noel.

Everything had followed logically. The French were eager to demonstrate to their powerful American ally that they, too, could still play a decisive role in major international crises.

The two Sputniks were launched on November 3, 1957. On November 15, French President Rene Coty pardoned Leo Saint-Clair in light of the great services he had rendered to his country.

The time had come for the Nyctalope to fulfill his part of the agreement!

Emerging from his thoughts, Leo pressed a switch on the control panel. A launch pad opened, pushing away the desert sands. Then, the rocket rose into the sky.

Very quickly, it left Earth's atmosphere and approached the secret Soviet satellite launched three months earlier. The SK-1 had deployed its solar reflectors and was positioned in an orbit enabling it to reflect a ray from the far side of the Moon to Siberia.

Leo triggered Korrides' Lightning Projector. The artificial satellite blew up in an explosion muffled by the silence of space. He smiled and thought: *I finally have my revenge, Sadi Khan--although it isn't the one I was hoping for!*

Then the ship headed for the dark side of the Moon and landed at the place indicated by the ancient diary of Henri-Jean de Sainte-Claire.

After donning a protective suit, Leo exited the rocket and picked up the Ioun Stone. Then he returned to the ship and landed a few minutes later in the Sea of Tranquility, on the other side of the Moon. He then reexited the rocket and buried the stone in moon dust.

*No one will find it here*, he thought.

He took off and returned to Morocco.

But, in orbit, an American Explorer satellite launched on January 31, 1958, had observed his actions...

*July 20, 1969, Sea of Tranquility on the Moon*

American astronaut Neil Armstrong left the LEM and set foot on the Moon.

"...One small step for man, one giant leap for mankind," he said.

*The Nyctalope does not appear in this story by young French writer Julien Heylbroeck. Instead, it features the Hictaner, the water-breathing anti-hero created by Fulbert, the mad scientist in* L'Homme qui peut vivre dans l'eau. *At the end of that novel, the Hictaner retires with his wife to Tahiti to live in peace. However, in* The Nyctalope on Mars, *La Hire later informs us, rather casually, that the couple died in a hurricane, leaving behind their baby daughter, who was then adopted by the Saint-Clair family. Julien's story provides more details about the Hictaner's demise...*

## Julien Heylbroeck: *The Season of the Shark*

*Tahiti, 1895*

The ship docked smoothly. The ropes were tied around the posts and, gradually, the noisy, motley crowd emptied out of the boat, shoving its way over the rickety gangplank. Caged birds chattered; children ran and shouted. Behind them, a massive shadow stood quitly, waiting for the rush to end. When calm had returned, it moved into the light. It was a broad-shouldered man, wearing a black cloak that covered his entire body.

The Hictaner—for it was he—had reached his destination. Time was of the essence. His body kept mutating and he could not abandon his quest until he had found his creators—his torturers. Remembering those two odious scientists, he ground his teeth. They were massive and hooked—the fangs of a shark that had replaced his human dentition. The grafts that had transformed his body were rapidly changing it into something at the crossroads of two species. He was becoming a man-shark, an aberration, a scientific monster abhorred by nature itself, and abandoned by its creators. It was probably a side effect of the massive exposure to radium that had been

108

meant to counter any tissue rejection during the grafting process.

With the aid of a cane, the Hictaner made his way over the gangplank and crossed the harbor in haste, pushing away a few *vahines* who were trying to sell him slices of fresh pineapple.

He was sweating profusely because of the heavy, thick, humid atmosphere. He soon found the harbor master and, removing his stovepipe hat and wiping his forehead, he asked:

"May I have a minute of your time, Monsieur? I am Inspector Charbonneau. I have been sent by the French Government to investigate the mysterious disappearances of several young women on this island…"

He showed an old, yellowed police card, hoping that that false identity would allow him to glean some useful information. With his imposing stature, the Hictaner easily dominated the harbor master, who was secretly impressed, but felt the need to speak in burly tones to assert his authority.

The interview was brief. The Hictaner got the address of a supposed witness. However, the harbor master had warned him that the man was an artist, a little crazy and addicted to alcohol and *pakalolo*.

The Hictaner went up a dirt road to the address in question and eventually reached the house where the artist lived. It certainly had known better days. It was overgrown with creepers and damp. That once elegant colonial mansion now suffered from the ravages of time and was a shadow of its once luxurious splendor. On the porch was a small man with thick hair and wild eyes bent over an easel, a crutch at his side. His skin was dotted with the tiny craters characteristic of the pox. Looking up at the visitor leaning on his cane, the artist gave a little smile and his eyes flashed.

"Ah-ha! A cripple, just like me!"

He put down his brush on a table strewn with dried crusts of paint.

The Hictaner did not have the heart to lie to him.

"I'm investigating the recent disappearances of twelve young local women. The harbor master told me to talk to you. He thought you may have witnessed one of the kidnappings."

"That damned fool didn't believe me when I told him what I saw. Mind you, I don't know if I believed it myself…"

The artist got up with some difficulty and the help of his crutch. He then disappeared inside the house and returned a few moments later with a pipe, a tobacco pouch and some matches. He stuffed the pipe, lit it and inhaled a few puffs of the strong-smelling tobacco.

"I seem to have forgotten my manners," he said. "Sit back, grab a glass… (he pointed at a bottle filled with a yellow liquid) This is a ginger liqueur, unlike anything you've ever tasted. Call me Paul. What's your name?"

"Guy Oman. I've lived in Tahiti for a short while. I heard of the disappearances of young women in Papeete. I think I know who's behind it. But first, I need to hear what you have to say."

"You think you know who is behind it? I fear you're mistaken, Monsieur!"

The painter looked at the Hictaner with an air of suspicion mingled with curiosity. It was not altogether surprising since his face had an abnormally pale complexion which only highlighted his two, inky black, almond-shaped eyes, covered with a sort of white film. Monsieur Paul had originally thought he was dealing with a blind man, and the stranger's cane had bolstered that impression, but now he realized that his visitor's sight was not impaired. The stranger's lower jaw was unusually square, almost as if it had been reshaped by a cartoonist, and his teeth were white and very sharp. There was something odd about the man, something animalistic. However, the painter attributed his impressions to the drugs he had been taking for months.

"I say you're mistaken, because the criminal is not human, Monsieur. God in Heaven, it is a monster! Let me tell you in detail what I saw—no, let me show you!"

The painter angrily rifled through a portfolio of drawings. Between two tawny sketches depicting women in the Tahitian countryside, he found a few crumpled papers adorned with several gray silhouettes. He handed those sheets to the visitor.

"Look! I was on a small hill a few miles from Papeete. From there, one has an unobstructed view of the sea. I was working on a new composition, a lovely sunset scene with a beautiful *vahine* in the foreground, lasciviously eating a tropical fruit, when my eyes were attracted by a shape in the waves. At first, I thought it was a dolphin. But upon closer inspection, I saw that it was almost human! It was one of those creatures that I sketched here... (the painter used the stem of his pipe to tap at the paper that the Hictaner held in his gloved hand) It was gray, with long, deformed arms, hideous... Something between man and fish. There were three of them. One carried something on its shoulders, something big—like a body... A ray of light suddenly created a reflection on a frothy peak of water and a second later, there was nothing. Not even a residual wave as evidence of their presence. Nothing... Sometimes, I think I was hallucinating..."

With a sigh of relief, the Hictaner took off his coat and his hat. Underneath, he wore the same wetsuit that his creators had once made for him, except that it was now patched and missing scales. Still, it allowed him to move through water at fantastic speeds.

He spat one of his last few remaining human teeth into the grass and entered the sea, feeling instantly soothed by the cool liquid. His gills greedily swallowed the water, beating in rhythm with the man-shark's breathing. He was back in his element—the same element that had caused his downfall, but that he couldn't live without. Once again in possession of all the agility and strength that left him as soon as he set foot on land, the Hictaner quickly dived toward the sandy bottom, avoiding several coral reefs. His intention was to explore the maritime area that Paul, the painter, had told him about.

After a few minutes of fast swimming to loosen his muscles, he decided to follow the coast line. Near a rocky point, his attention was drawn to the hull of a ship. He approached it, carried by his fervor, his scaly suit slicing the water silently. It was a merchant ship, the *Queen of Sumatra*, flying the Canadian flag,. There was no sign of activity aboard. The vessel was anchored.

Climbing along the anchor chain, the Hictaner quietly stepped onto the bridge to take a closer look. There was nobody in sight. Yet, the ship was not abandoned; it showed signs of recent occupation and it was missing one lifeboat. Her crew must have gone ashore. Without missing a beat, the man-shark walked to the main cabin. Its door was locked, but it was a simple lock and did not resist long.

Inside, the cabin was just like the rest of the ship: old, but sturdy and in good condition. One felt that that ship had sailed the seven seas and even explored waters long forgotten or ignored. On a table, there were a few maps, including one of Tahiti, and some old books bound in leather. The Hictaner opened one, taking care to wipe his hands in order to leave no trace. He did not understand the language in which it was written: a myriad of tiny, incomprehensible characters positioned around strange and disturbing illustrations. These showed the same creatures that the painter had seen: hunchbacked fish-men with monstrously thick lips and enormous bulging eyes. Around them, there were drawings of strange pentacles, skulls and knives.

The man-shark closed the book, feeling very uncomfortable. A few years ago, he had been the victim of two mad scientists, willing to sacrifice many innocent lives in order to accomplish their megalomaniacal ideals. But these illustrations were even more repulsive than those men; they were the very negation of the ideals of humanity. Something extremely ancient, savage, ruthless and cold oozed from those pages. The Hictaner felt he had to identify the owner of the ship.

Quietly, he returned to the bridge, plunged back into the waters without a stir, and swam towards the coast.

Back at the harbor, the Hictaner again played the part of "Inspector Charbonneau" and, once more, the harbor master was impressed by the authority of the official from the *Métropole*. He identified the owner of the ship as Tobias Marsh, from the town of Innsmouth, in Massachusetts. The worthy sea-faring merchant of forty had just acquired a dilapidated colonial mansion on the island that he planned to renovate. So far, every transaction had been conducted through an emissary, a solicitor's clerk, and Captain Marsh had not yet introduced himself. The harbor master said, while rubbing his belly as if trying to lend more gravitas to his words, that Captain Marsh would no doubt be a welcome addition to the island's small community of *notables*, especially given his impressive fortune, certainly more welcome than that mad painter, he added, his voice dripping with contempt.

The sun was about set on the island, turning the sky dark-red in color. Leaning on his cane, he Hictaner found his way to a hotel. His back hurt after the afternoon and only underlined his increasing difficulties in moving on land. He had lost another tooth after meeting with the harbor master. His right arm was getting increasingly stiff. Time was definitely against him. Soon, he wouldn't be able to walk and would be forced to abandon his quest. He would have to leave his beloved Moisette, and his young daughter Christiane, who would grow up fatherless. It broke his heart. But before he got to that point, he wanted revenge.

Tobias Marsh... The name meant nothing to him. There was no connection with Fulbert and Oxus. No traces of the Mad Monk and his associate. Yet, these disappearances, the strange semi-aquatic creatures seen in the water, everything pointed to some new experiment by these two lunatics. However, dabbling in the occult was not their specialty... What role had Captain Marsh and his mysterious books played in this affair?

The man-shark had trouble falling to sleep. The air was heavy, his lungs burned. He tossed and turned under the mosquito net, crumpling his sheets, sweating, growing restless, feeling pain all over his body. He also hurt because he needed to feed. A dull hunger twisted his guts. He dreamed of greedily shredding flesh and bone, then swallowing ravenously...

He finally decided to get up. There were still a few hours before dawn. If he wanted to invade Marsh's house surreptitiously, this was the best time to do it.

The house overlooked a small cliff, giving it an impregnable view over the ocean. It was almost a ruin. The roof was torn off and one of the wings had partially collapsed, probably during a tropical storm. Vegetation had invaded the building. A *mapé* tree had deployed its immense trunk right in the middle of the entrance, pushing away the door frame and the walls. This house was clearly uninhabitable. It would have been easier to destroy it and rebuild a new one. There seemed to be nothing left to save. The Hictaner approached quietly. While the house appeared empty, he had noticed the presence of recent footprints...

The lobby was filled with dead leaves, too damp to beneath under his steps, forming a putrefying, sweet-smelling carpet. His presence disturbed the tranquility of a few bats which flew away in spiraling panic. The footprints led the Hictaner to a door that seemed to access the cellars. Behind it, a spiral staircase descended into the murky depths. It seemed to have no end. The steps were rough, having been cut directly into the stone. A few torches hanging on the wall were almost burnt out, giving off a pale glimmer and witness to a recent visit. It was more than enough for the Hictaner. His eyes had developed the ability to see in complete darkness, almost like those of a cat—or a shark. That's what allowed him to notice the strange murals etched along the staircase. It depicted creatures half-fish, half-frog, dancing and praying, and the carvings were in a language that resembled Aramaic.

After several minutes of descent, as he almost reached the bottom of the stairs, the Hictaner heard the weak sound of an electromagnetic field. It was one of the new powers that he had recently acquired. That meant that there were people not far away. The man-shark hid behind a pillar decorated with more bas-reliefs and observed.

He had arrived in a great, vaulted room full of wooden crates. He heard the sound of water which told him that the cave opened out onto the sea, at the foot of the cliff. He advanced cautiously between the crates. He had set aside his cane and instead had grabbed a long hunting knife with a serrated blade. The air was filled with the smell of the ocean, the mud saturated with the unpleasant scent of rotten fish--and death.

He eventually reached the center of the cavern. At last, he saw the ocean and a small bathyscaphe anchored to a pier. The man-shark found the source of the disturbance in the electromagnetic field which he had detected earlier: there were three women, obviously pregnant, whose bodies were laid on tables, chained and shackled, their swollen bellies heaving painfully. One of them looked dead. On the wall, strange machines hissing steam gave off powerful, crackling arcs of energy, illuminating the dark cavern with a fleeting glow.

A little further away, there was a cage with thick bars. The Hictaner approached it. Indistinct shapes shrank back, uttering weird little cries: they were the same humpbacked creatures that the painter had mentioned. There were half a dozen of them, all similar, with large heads, drooping mouths with wattles, scaly skin and bulging eyes, on top of twisted bodies, inhuman and yet humanoid. Around their necks, the creatures wore a kind of mechanical apparatus fitted with different colored bulbs. Their webbed hands waved frantically, trying to repel the Hictaner or, perhaps, protecting themselves. They gave off an odor that disturbed the man-shark; it was at once repulsive and appealing.

Behind him, one of the shackled women moaned softly. Turning around, the Hictaner saw that, at the far end of the cave, a halo of light was signaling that approach of another visitor. Silently, he crept behind a massive machine that hummed.

Two men arrived. The Hictaner quickly identified the magisterial and slightly disapproving timbre of the voice of one of them. It belonged to Fulbert, the Mad Monk, his creator. A shiver went up his spine; too many painful memories were tied to that voice. His hand gripped the handle of his knife. The other voice seemed to carry some barely repressed anger; he didn't recognize it. The two men moved into his line of sight. He recognized Fulbert's robe-clad silhouette. The other man was burly and wore a sailor's jacket.

"Fulbert, I don't know what you've done here, but I don't like it," said the other man. "This wasn't the nature of our agreement. This temple has to be ready for the ceremony!"

"But, Tobias..."

"Captain Marsh," interrupted the other man, abruptly.

"Captain Marsh," said Fulbert, "what I propose is not a mere mystical ceremony, but to use science to build our empire. All the oceans of the world will be ours!" Fulbert stretched his hand, as if to embrace an imaginary globe. "We'll control all the trade routes to India, China, the Americas! No ship will be able to travel without our permission. We'll be masters of the seven seas!"

"I do not desire economic power, nor do I care about your plans to achieve it. I worship Dagon. I am a member of his Esoteric Order. My family has been totally devoted to Him for two generations. Your attempt to establish a maritime monopoly has nothing to do with the rehabilitation of this temple. I have been financing the founding of a new chapter of our cult here, not the start of a trade war!"

The two men had reached the part of the cavern where the tables, the crates and the cages were. Marsh took off his hat, his eyes wide with surprise at beholding such a spectacle. Completely ignoring the women prisoners, he approached the cage. After scrutinizing the creatures trapped inside, he turned around, his face flushed with anger, and looked darkly at Fulbert.

"How dare you!" the Captain exclaimed. "The Children of Dagon! You're a monster! An impious blasphemer!"

Fulbert could no longer contain his anger.

"You pathetic cultist! Can't you see beyond the tip of the nose of your heathen god—an ordinary man-fish! I created a man-fish once, and he was a lot more effective and useful than your underwater monkeys! I had to fit them with control boxes because they're so primitive and stupid! And this would be my army? An army composed of a bunch of degenerate humanoids with the brains of tuna fish!"

Captain Marsh seethed in anger. He did not reply to the Monk. Instead, removing his jacket, he pulled out a small knife. Fulbert quickly stepped back but then realized that the other man was ignoring him. Marsh began chanting in an incomprehensible, unknown language, with chopped syllables and disturbing rhythms. This immediately calmed the creatures in the cage. Fulbert, jeering, shouted:

"Stop your singing, you second-rate zealot! You're not impressing me at all!"

But Marsh only continued to recite the prayers of another age. Raising his knife, he planted it without hesitation in his right arm, twisting it into the wound. He was so focused on his litany that his face barely registered a grimace of pain.

The Hictaner shuddered. He looked at the cage. The creatures, which until now had been agitated, suddenly became unnaturally calm. They seemed to be waiting. The smell of blood hit his nostrils. It flowed along the arms of the Captain and spread toward the edge of the pier. When the first drop of blood fell into the water, a shock wave ran through its cold and dark surface. The ocean began to stir, first with small waves and then gradually with more powerful ones which shook the bathyscaphe.

"*Iä ! Iä ! Cthulhu fhtagn ! Ph'nglui mglw'nafh Cthulhu R'lhel wgah-nagl fhtagn !* Come, Father Dagon! Come and avenge thy children for this infamy! Come, I beseech thee, O Father!"

Tobias Marsh was using witchcraft. The Hictaner did not know exactly what for, but it felt dangerous. He stood up to try to stop him.

Fulbert, initially awe-struck, responded quickly when he saw his former servant emerge from behind one of his machines. He guessed why the Hictaner was there. Ignoring Marsh, he launched himself at the cage and opened it. The creatures, surprised, did not stir. The Monk then grabbed a small box and pressed a few buttons. Immediately, a small red light flashed on the metal necklaces clamped around the creatures' necks. The Children of the Deep shook and fell upon the Hictaner *en masse*.

The battle was fierce. The Hictaner was overwhelmed, surrounded on all sides by a half-dozen Deep Ones. They tried to seize him, but he overcame each of their attempts with fierce savagery. One creature threw a pale arm over his face, apparently trying to strangle him. The Hictaner bit powerfully though the gray-green flesh. His teeth penetrated deeply, tearing away the muscle. His mouth filled with dark blood that was thick and cold. The creature screamed and tried to free his arm. The Hictaner spat the flesh out. His mouth—his jaws— were dripping with blood, his fangs gleamed. There was glimmer of defiant madness in his eyes. He threw himself upon the nearest Deep One and tore out its throat with a single bite.

But the others were not afraid of him. They continued in their attempts to overwhelm him through sheer numbers—and they nearly succeeded! The Hictaner had killed three more Deep Ones, but the others managed to immobilize him against the ground, pressing against his neck and mouth. He tried to bite into whatever came close to his jaws, but without success. The hand that still held his knife was similarly immobilized by a large webbed foot. One of the Deep Ones approached, holding a heavy stone. He raised it above the skull of the man-shark, preparing to crush it like an egg. It looked like the end.

Suddenly, a powerful earthquake shook the cavern, making the support pillars tremble. One of them collapsed, split in half by a large crack. Pieces of the ceiling crashed to the ground. A boulder fell onto the bathyscaphe, sending it to the bottom of the ocean in seconds. Dust was everywhere. On the ceiling, cracks began to appear, then merged into a larger crack that spread out like a spider's web. A huge wave rolled into the cavern, sweeping away the creatures and freeing the Hictaner.

Fulbert realized that the cavern was going to collapse, and tried to reach the open sea in a small boat tied to the pier. Marsh continued his horrible incantations, his face twitching and his eyes rolled back into his head. Blocks of stone fell around him but he ignored them. The Monk now understood the true power of the Captain and blamed himself for having underestimated him, but it was too late.

Now rid of the Deep Ones, the Hictaner stood with difficulty. His swollen face reflected the savagery of the fishmen's attack. He saw Fulbert trying to climb into the boat; an operation that was made difficult because the surface of the water was now crisscrossed by large waves, and thick blocks of stone fell into the water, creating additional turmoil. The Hictaner ran towards his erstwhile torturer. Fulbert saw him and became even more frantic. Now in the boat, he tried to untie the ropes that still held it moored at the pier. The man-shark did not have time to reach the Mad Monk. A huge wave suddenly lifted the boat and flung it against a stone pillar, smashing it and its occupant. Fulbert's body fell heavily to the ground, disjointed, surrounded by wood debris.

A creature began emerging from the water. He looked like a Deep One, but much more massive. His grinning face was that of a monstrous shark with teeth protruding from its jaws, but its appearance was much more savage. His bulging black eyes expressed such wickedness, such hatred, that the Hictaner cringed. The monster was more than two meters high. His squat limbs lacked agility, but endowed him with formidable power.

Dagon paid no attention to the Hictaner. He swept the bulky crates away as if they were nothing but empty cardboard boxes, uttering a hoarse cry. They smashed against the wall, scattering various mechanical parts across the floor. Marsh uttered a cry of joy. His knife still planted in his arm, he knelt down before the giant sea monster.

"You came, Father Dagon! Praised be Your Name! See the evils of Men! See how they have defiled thy children. Take umbrage at their impudence. Avenge yourself!"

The monster, oozing, seemed to look around. His gaze took in everything, coldly analyzing the situation. Noticing the Children of the Deep with their neck collars, he raised his head and let out a roar of rage that shook the very foundations of the cavern.

"Father, thy temple has been desecrated," continued Marsh. "This crime must not go unpunished! Ravage this island! Destroy the humans to repay their arrogance!"

Dagon bent forward to take a closer look at—and smell—his summoner. The Captain had closed his eyes, blissfully happy, basking in the aura of his god. The breath escaping from the jaws of the monster made his hair flow back. After a moment, the creature let out another roar and turned around. Dagon was preparing to return to the sea to do his worshipper's bidding.

During this silent exchange, the Hictaner had posted himself between Dagon and the ocean. He could not let this monster destroy the island. Suddenly, the man-fish stopped and looked down at the man-shark from his domineering size. His eyes expressed an undecipherable emotion. But when he saw that his opponent did not intend to let him pass, Dagon closed his scaly fists and rushed at him.

The shock of the confrontation sent the Hictaner flying into the water, half-stunned. Dagon followed him mere seconds later. Scarcely had they entered the ocean than the cavern collapsed entirely. Massive rocks crashed into the water, creating huge waves, barely slowing down as they sank. A stalactite grazed the Hictaner, narrowly missing impaling him. He swam toward Dagon without losing his sense of purpose.

Around him, the ocean was choppy. A cyclone was ravaging the surface of the island, probably created by the invocation of the sea-god.

The man-fish moved through the water like a snake, undulating his massive body with grace and speed. He quickly caught up with Dagon and planted his teeth into his side. The monster turned around to grab his assailant. His massive jaws grabbed the Hictaner's left arm, breaking it like a twig. The Hictaner fought the pain that threatened to overwhelm him and clamped his teeth further. He had to stop Dagon, to prevent him from ravaging the island. He would save the people of Papeete—Moisette, his wife, and his dear daughter, Christiane. With his remaining arm, he repeatedly stabbed Dagon's abdomen. Black blood escaped from the monster's wound and began to permeate the surrounding sea. Finally, kicking and bellowing, the monster managed to free himself, leaving a large chunk of his flesh in the process. He turned around and watched the Hictaner as a predator looks at its prey.

The Hictaner kept his left arm close to his body. His gills breathed the water in and out, creating a crown of bubbles around him. He pointed his knife at Dagon, barring his way to the port.

After a moment, during which the sea-god examined the man-shark with an expression of cold cruelty, he rushed toward the Hictaner. The latter tried to dodge the blow but Dagon was faster and stronger. The man-shark was caught at the waist. With a snap of his cyclopean mouth, Dagon crushed his pelvis. The Hictaner spat a thick cloud of blood and nearly fainted. But he still had enough energy to bite the monster's throat, his teeth sinking as far as possible into the flesh, using his jaws as a saw to slash and cut his foe's muscles.

Dagon, shaken by spasms of pain, fell onto a rock to try to get rid of the Hictaner. He was losing blood at an alarming rate now. The Hictaner collided head-on with the rock. He broke his jaw and was forced to release the monster's throat.

He waited for the coup-de-grace but it never came. His opponent had been too severely injured to continue the fight. He saw Dagon swim away, back to his hellish lair, leaving a bloody trail behind him.

On the surface of the island, the hurricane seemed to fall apart with a last, few violent gusts, then vanished. The Hictaner let himself sink to the sandy bottom of the ocean. Blood was pouring from his gills. He knew his time had come. He leaned against a rock. When death took him, he had one final thought for his wife and his daughter. A reddish bubble burst from his mouth and climbed slowly toward the surface of the sea. It burst in the light of dawn, leaving only a small ephemeral halo, soon swept away by the spray.

Gauguin's sketches of the Children of the Deep were never found.

*La Hire often mentioned the Nyctalope's heroic feats during World War I, and, without giving any details about the various missions that he undertook. The purpose of this story by Emmanuel Gorlier is to flesh out Leo's war-time conduct, as well as to provide an explanation for the fact that the Nyctalope appears to be estranged from his oldest son, Pierre, who is never mentioned again in the series after* Les Mystères de Lyon. *"Captain Danrit" was the nom-de-plume of real-life science fiction writer, politician and war hero Emile Driant, who features prominently in this tale...*

## Emmanuel Gorlier: *The Lesson of Captain Danrit*

On a sunny day in December 1930, the Nyctalope was reading a large, profusely illustrated book in the library of his castle at Blingy, near Versailles.

He seemed to enjoy what he was reading. His eyes became sometimes lost in the distance, as if the book reminded him of long-lost memories half-buried in his mind. The small twitches that occasionally appeared on his face conveyed the impression that such memories were not of the best times of his life.

His concentration was such that he did not hear his oldest son, Pierre, enter the room. The boy was surprised to discover his father totally engrossed in what appeared to be the first volume of a trilogy of popular novels.

While reading, Leo Saint-Clair murmured: "Captain Danrit... Colonel Driant... It's amazing how correct you were... I can almost smell the battlefield..."

At that moment, Leo looked up and saw his son. It pulled him out of his reverie.

"Oh, it's you, Pierre..." he said. "You were here all the time?"

"Yes, father. I was watching you. With some surprise, I might add..."

"Why? I was reading this book, written by one of my oldest friends, which I bought two days ago at a charity auction."

The Nyctalope handed the book to his son, who took it and read the title:

"*The War of Tomorrow*, by Captain Danrit. I don't know. What's it all about?"

"It is a novel of scientific anticipation. Captain Danrit was the nom-de-plume of Lieutenant-Colonel Driant, who wrote many books describing futuristic wars. This one is the tale of a major conflict between France and its allies and Germany..."

"You mean, the Great War of 1914-18...?"

"Not exactly! He wrote that book in 1892. I'd never read it before today, and I've been struck by how prophetic he was in anticipating so many of the technical innovations that really happened during the Great War..."

"You said he was one of your oldest friends?"

"I was exaggerating a little. As a matter of fact, I only met Colonel Driant once, briefly during that war. But I must admit that it was an encounter I will never forget..."

Pierre sat opposite his father and begged him to share his reminiscences. It was a rare privilege, for, like many veterans of the Great War, Leo Saint-Clair did not often like to remember those tumultuous years during which he had lost so many of his friends.

"Since you ask me, and we have time before lunch, I'll tell you about our meeting and the events surrounding it that are still classified as military secrets. I would, however, ask you not to repeat any of this, especially not to your German student friends when you go back to school after the holidays."

"Of course, father. You can trust me."

"Very well. It happened on February 20, 1916. Until then, I had been mainly engaged on different battlefields. However, a few weeks before, I'd been contacted by a Colonel Lumen who wanted to strengthen his intelligence service. He thought that, given my background and my power to see in the dark, I might be more useful for certain highly sensitive missions. Subsequently, my detachment would become permanent. But, in early 1916, it was still only as series of one-off missions to test my military potential...

"That evening, I was walking under the cover of dark with a courier who was to take me close to the front lines where the 56th and 59th battalions commanded by Lieutenant-colonel Driant were garrisoned. The night was quiet, and nothing would have caused you to think that we were only a few miles away from the enemy lines. After crossing a checkpoint, we approached a wooden barracks located behind a row of sand bags at the edge of the Bois de Caures. Several lines of deep trenches scarred the landscape. Only the points of bayonets could be seen gleaming in the darkness.

"At that moment, an older man came out of the command post. From the five bars on his jacket, I saw that he had the rank of Lieutenant Colonel.

"– Colonel Driant? I asked

"He nodded. I greeted him by saying:

"– Captain Saint-Clair at your service, Monsieur.

"He smiled slightly and replied:

"At ease, Monsieur. I'm on a short patrol. Join me and tell me to what I owe the pleasure of your visit.

"First in silence, we walked slowly towards the trench that was the nearest to the German lines. It was occupied by few soldiers. After a couple of minutes, I finally decided to speak:

"– Is it quiet here?

"– Yes, although the small size of our garrison worries me a little. We're only two battalions and if we're attacked, our position won't be easy to defend. Has the High Command sent you?

"– Yes Monsieur. I'm on a delicate mission... but since sound carries in the night...

"– ...And the enemy is close. I understand. Let's get back to the post. In any event, I've finished here.

"We quickly returned to the main building, went inside and sat down around a rustic table.

"– So—your mission? he inquired at last.

"– As you know, we use air power to detect enemy movement. Sadly, we don't have enough planes and monitoring is sometimes incomplete, but, it is an advantage...

"– Yes, I have always believed that the new technologies should be applied to our conflict, but please continue...

"– There seems to be no movement of enemy troops in this sector. Yet, during the last two weeks, we've lost several aircraft in the area, which is rather surprising since nothing seems to be happening around here. I was sent to investigate and do a quick recon behind enemy lines...

"– Captain Saint-Clair, I don't want to discourage you, but you have no chance of crossing enemy lines without being detected. In daylight, it's totally impossible, and at night, while they won't see you, you won't be able to see them either and...

"– May I use your binoculars? I asked.

"– Of course, he replied. But it's too dark. They'll be useless.

"I took the binoculars and described the surrounding countryside. Even though everything was shrouded in darkness, the enemy lines appeared to me clearly. They were located on the side of a hill that faced the French lines. The top of that hill was crowned by a small wood which blocked the view. There were many sentinels, but I could tell that none would be able to prevent my passage, especially at night with an overcast sky and heavy clouds announcing rain, or possible snow considering how cold it was.

"At that point, Colonel Driant looked at me with curiosity and said:

"– Captain Saint-Clair... ...The Nyctalope... I'm beginning to understand...

"We used the next two hours to determine the best approach to avoid possible encounters and evaluate the various obstacles set up by the Germans. In fact, the last fifty meters would be the most dangerous of all, and I would have to act very carefully...

"At 22:00, I left the trenches and made my way to the enemy lines as quickly as I could, stooping in order to escape detection. I used my night vision to avoid any area likely to make noise or cause me trouble. When I arrived near the German trench, I began to crawl, trying to stay as far away as possible from the sentinels. They were evenly spaced, just as on the French side, which made my job easier. I entered the enemy trench and as I was about to climb out, my foot hit a metal object hidden in a mud puddle. A clear sound was heard.

"A watchman said in German:

"– Who goes there?

"I responded in the same language:

"– Don't worry it's me. I'm coming.

"I walked slowly toward him just as if I was as handicapped as he was by the absence of light. The trench was lit only by a small lantern behind me which prevented him from seeing me clearly because of the back light. At the last moment, when he managed to light a lighter, he realized that I wore a French uniform, but before he could say a word or to use his weapon, I paralyzed him with a quick jujutsu choke. I had to leave hastily.

"I left the trench on the side controlled by the Germans and headed for the woods that blocked the horizon.

"The wooded area was relatively sparse at that point and ended rather abruptly on the other side of the hill. Once out of the woods, I had to be alert for any possible encounters, but my nyctalopic powers once again gave me a huge advantage. After crossing several fields, I came to what looked like a makeshift airfield.

"Hidden behind a bush, I watched the airfield and understand why we had lost several aircraft. Along a dirt track were twenty Albatross B-II biplanes, all equipped with Parabellum machine guns. That could only mean one thing: the Germans had secretly created a squad of large and powerfully-armed aircraft.

"My mission appeared to have ended with the discovery of that new German secret weapon. However, I decided to continue my exploration because the concentration of so many airplanes in this specific place still seemed odd to me. Why station this formidable air force here, where nothing important was happening?

"I discreetly walked around the airfield and came across a small ammunition depot with a snoozing sentinel. It was of no interest. I circled it and came in sight of a large, deserted agricultural area. Obviously, I had seen everything there was to see. Puzzled, I was about to retrace my steps when I heard the distinct sound of a swear word muttered in German. I turned quickly but saw no one. It was quite bizarre. I slowly walked into the field and, again, heard people speaking in German but saw nothing. I then headed towards the voices. All of a sudden, I found myself inside a huge military camp: thousands, tens of thousands of men and equipment were all there, waiting! I stepped back, and the camp disappeared. I stepped forward again, and it reappeared! Everything then became clear to me: the camp was cloaked from sight by some unknown process. I quickly glanced around and noticed a strange little tent out of which poked an antenna that gave off a dull and continuous hum. It was difficult to draw near it without being detected. I had started to make a circular motion to approach it from the back when two senior German officers came out of the tent. They spoke loudly and I recognized the voice that had guided me to this point.

"– Will you bet that within a month, we shall be marching under the Arc-de-Triomphe in Paris? The German Colonel laughed loudly.

"His companion replied mockingly:

"– I do not like making bets in a situation like this! You're certain to win. With that prototype cloaking device Herr Doktor Krueger built for us, we made our entire Fifth Army invisible and we'll unleash it tomorrow upon our dumbfounded enemies. Even if they were warned, they could not stop us now!

"Hearing those words, the final details of the German plan fell into place in my mind. I now understood that the planes were there to prevent the French air force from randomly bombing the field and uncovering the cloaked army. I had to act quickly and decisively if I wanted France to retain a chance to win the war.

"I left the tent and the cloaked area, walking quickly toward the ammunition depot. The sentinel was still half-asleep and I neutralized him without any difficulty. Inside, I made a rapid inventory of what was stored there. At first, I could not find anything directly useful: guns, ammunition, more guns, machine guns... I was going to give up when I saw a box of grenades. I hurriedly took a few. Then I returned across the field to the tent containing the cloaking device. With a quick gesture, I threw two grenades through the canvas door.

"A huge explosion tore the air... and suddenly the Fifth German Army reappeared!

"I did not stay to appreciate the confusion that followed. Instead, I quickly ran towards the wood. I made a wide detour to avoid the German trench, now brightly lit since the soldiers had been awakened by the explosion. A few miles away, using darkness as a cover, I was able to cross the enemy lines and return to our side.

"Once I was back at the command post, I saw Lieutenant-Colonel Driant waiting for me. He saw me, smiled and said:

"– So, it ended with a fireworks display after all!

"– Unfortunately, it's not over, Monsieur. The entire Fifth German Army is ready to attack on the other side of these woods!

"Colonel Driant paled. He had only two battalions with him. I added:

"– I'll radio High Command, but I think our situation is critical, since we need at least two more days to line up sufficient forces to contain such an opponent. But I might be overly pessimistic. Let me report and see what they say.

"While the radio officer tried to contact High Command, I watched Colonel Driant, who sat on a stone bench. His pale face reflected his strong emotions. First, he expressed deep grief. I could almost read his mind. He probably thought that, for over forty years, he had waited for a rematch of the 1870 Franco-Prussian War. At the age of 58, at the beginning of this war, he had not hesitated to leave his safe political seat to put on a soldier's uniform once more. Now he was at the right place at the right time—but could he afford to act? Could he afford not to?

"Against all odds, his features suddenly shifted. I saw a new resolution appear in his eyes. Now that I read his book *The War of Tomorrow*, I finally understand what he thought at that moment.

"It was then he realized that he was, in fact, not entirely without resources. He had the two battalions under his command. He had previously theorized that it was vital to delay the enemy, to stop the clock as it were, in order to allow the rest of the main forces to regroup to the rear. The time had come to test the reality of his theories. He was in no mood to write one of his futuristic novels, but he had to act as if he was living in one, as he had once advocated, even if it cost him dearly.

"Meanwhile, on the other end of the radio, the voice of High Command responded that they did not see how they could gather enough troops to contain such a mass of German forces. They needed at least 36 hours.

"Colonel Driant got up and walked towards me. He said:

"– Tell them that they will have them!

"After a few seconds of silence, High Command gave the order to contain the enemy at all costs. At the same time, I received my own orders to return to my regiment at once.

"I turned to Colonel Driant and prepared to salute him as protocol demanded, but he shook my hand and said:

"– Go, Monsieur Saint-Clair. France cannot thank you enough for what you did tonight. But I cannot linger. I must organize our defense...."

"We parted after we shook hands. As I walked away, I heard him give the first order:

"– Sergeant! A double-ration of spirits for everyone. The men will need it.

"It was four o'clock in the morning. The rest is history.

"The next morning, February 21, 1916, at 7:15 a.m., the Fifth German Army went on the attack. A deluge of steel and gas shells fell on the French positions all day. In late afternoon, they launched their first assault. The first French positions were quickly taken. But at the Bois des Caures, Driant's men bent but did not break. After a strategic retreat and despite a rain of shells that had lasted all night and yet another attack after that, they still held their position on the morning of February 22.

"Once the snow began to fall, the Germans resumed their offensive. In full force, the 18th Corps of the Fifth Army attacked the survivors of the two French battalions. One by one, each of their positions was taken. The 59th French Battalion was virtually annihilated. Its last, few survivors continued to defend their positions while falling back behind the trees. Gradually, Driant and his men were surrounded.

"At 16:00, thirty-six hours after my departure, Lieutenant-Colonel Driant ordered a retreat towards Beaumont. He was amongst the last to leave the battlefield with only a few trusted men at his side.

"But he was struck by a rifle bullet to the head, which killed him instantly.

"His sacrifice, however, was not in vain. With the time he had managed to gain, the French army had the opportunity to regroup, according to the strategy he had once developed in his writing, and they were able to stop the German attack during what we now call the Battle of Verdun."

The Nyctalope's voice broke with emotion at the memories of those times.

"Now, you understand why I do not lightly recount my memories of that war, because they remind me too much of my missing comrades. But enough talk! It's getting late, and Sylvie is waiting for us to have lunch…"

Pierre noticed that his father's last sentence had been uttered in a playful tone that rang falsely to his ears.

After his father had left the room, he remained silent for a moment, reflecting on what the Nyctalope had just told him. Lost in thought, he too left the library slowly.

Several years later, on the morning of July 23, 1940, a ship ran aground on the English coast. On board was Pierre Saint-Clair who had come to join General de Gaulle's Free France forces. In recent weeks, he had long reflected on what his conduct should be. Should he, like his father, consider that all was lost and stand in the shadow of Marshal Petain and rebuild a new France upon questionable foundations, or retreat now and to return to fight on another day when the allied forces would be reconstituted?

In making his choice, the haunting memories of a distant story that his father had once told him played a vital role. Pierre had obviously not forgotten the lesson of Captain Danrit.

*One of the most intriguing loose ends left by La Hire is the un-
explained fate of the French Martian colony established at the
end of* The Nyctalope on Mars. *Subsequent books do mention
it a couple of times, then it just disappears from the series,
never to be referred to again. This story, by Matthew Dennion,
and the next story by Roman Leary, tackle the problem with a
clever mixture of originality and emotion. We open on Mars
during one of Leo's return trips near the end of the Great
War...*

## Matthew Dennion: *The Hunters of Mars*

*Helium, 1917*

Leo Saint-Clair sat in the transport to Helium and, as always,
his mind was dominated by two thoughts: his motherless
children here on Mars, and the Great War raging at home on
Earth.

Leo loved his children and his country, and both needed
him more than ever now. The only problem was, they were
literally worlds apart. He silently ran through his decision in
his head again. It had been safer to leave his children here on
Mars, away from the horrors taking place on Earth. As much
as he wanted to, he couldn't stay with them; people needed
him too much on Earth. He knew that his physical skills and
knowledge of battle tactics were necessary on the battlefield,
and his presence there was crucial for the troops' morale. He
was more than just a soldier and an adventurer—he was the
Nyctalope! He was a symbol of France, the super-man the
other soldiers looked to... His very presence instilled confidence in those around him. He was needed on Earth to inspire
the Allies to win the war—and the war needed to be won in
order for him to be reunited with his children.

Leo leaned his head back against the wall of the transport. He sighed and mused that this was an opportunity to take a bold step toward ending the horror of the Great War. He had been personally requested to assist in a morbid situation by John Carter, the famous Warlord of Mars.

As Warlord, Carter was in control of some of the most advanced weaponry in the Solar System. With this in mind, when Carter had requested his help to investigate a series of bizarre murders, the Nyctalope knew he couldn't turn him down.

The people of Barsoom were historically non-trusting. Prior to Carter's arrival and ascent to power, the red planet was marred by constant war between various races. Carter's actions had convinced these people who had battled for centuries to unite against common enemies. Later, he had even persuade the other on the far reaches of Mars, such as the Sorns and the Hither people, to join their forces to his and drive off an invading force of Cephales from Mars. They had fled to Earth, where, after crushing the armies of England, they had been wiped out by the many strains of bacteria they had encountered there. The surviving members of that loathsome species had returned to Mars. Leo could vividly remember how he and Oxus had fought them together to protect the newly-established French colony.

It was not until after the defeat of the Cephales that they had learned of the existence of other races on Mars, such as the Tharks and the Red Men of Helium. The technology the latter possessed stunned even Oxus. Despite Carter's willingness to share their technology with the colony, many of the Elders of Mars did not trust the humans.

Until now, the technology had only been coveted for the advancement of the colony. Oxus, in particular, believed that the radium used by the people of Helium could not only double the power and speed of his ships, for trips back and forth to Earth, but might even revive an ancient capsule he discovered in one of the nearby Martian ruins. The secrets held by that ship could literally advance the speed of space travel by light years. More importantly, the weapons possessed by Carter could end the Great War in a manner of months.

Leo envisioned a fleet of massive, heavily armed sky ships flying over Germany, raining exploding radium bullets down on its soldiers. A smile crept across the adventurer's grim face as he pictured his country's flag flying high on the masts of those ships as the Germans surrendered. All of this was within his grasp. The people of Mars judged men by their actions and their prowess in battle. An Earthman could win them over—Carter was proof of that. Leo nodded to himself. He was sure that if he could assist Carter in this matter, his actions would give the Warlord the leverage he would need to convince the Elders to share their technology with Oxus. With that, the Great War would soon be over. With that, Leo could hold his children in his embrace again.

The ship slowed to a stop and Leo Saint Clair cleared his mind as the transport docked.

The Nyctalope stepped off the transport and on to the landing dock at the Royal Tower in Helium. The cool Martian wind blew red dust into his enhanced eyes as he looked down the long runway to a group who approached him.

Just by looking at them, he knew exactly who they were. In the back of the group was a massive green man with four arms and menacing tusks protruding from his jaw. He was a member of the race know as the Tharks. The majestic figure took long strides with confidence and power that proclaimed he was a warrior born. The Nyctalope realized this majestic figure was none other than Barsoom's most honored son, the mighty Tars Tarkas.

Just in front of him, a woman pushed back her hair to reveal one of the most beautiful faces the Nyctalope had ever seen. Her perfectly shaped body had a red hue to it that only made her more appealing, while her traditional Martian attire left just enough to imagination. Had she not been Dejah Thoris, Princess of Helium, and, more importantly, the wife of the man next to her, the Nyctalope would have attempted to woo her to his will.

To call her husband a mere man was to do him no justice—he was truly a legend. He stood slightly over six feet tall and had the build of a world class athlete. Dressed in the meager garbs of a warrior of Helium, his chiseled muscles gave him the appearance of a barbarian warrior. The man's face was rugged and bespoke the look of person who had been through countless battles. This was John Carter, Warlord of Mars.

The Nyctalope had been briefed by French Intelligence before returning to Mars. John Carter was a legend on Earth as well. His age was unknown. He was reported to have fought in the American Civil War, but couldn't remember his life before that. Even now, he hardly looked a day over thirty! The belief on Earth was that he may have suffered from some kind of amnesia prior to the Civil War, and that his stay on Mars may have slowed the aging process. Outlandish report mentioned a warrior of similar appearance showing up in ancient Phoenicia, as well as a 13th century "Outlaw from Torn." The Nyctalope wrote off these reports as far-fetched folklore.

What was known was that Carter had somehow been transported to Mars—or Barsoom as the natives called it—and had risen from slave to Warlord in the span of only a few years. He was not just warlord of one race, but had forged several warring races into a single alliance. In effect, he was to Mars what Arthur had been to England, but what he had accomplished had been on a near global scale. Carter was also reported to be a master swordsman, horseback rider, and marksman.

As the group reached him, Leo bowed and said: "Honored emissaries of Helium, I am at your service!"

The group returned the bow as Dejah Thoris spoke: "Leo-Saint-Clair, it is you who honor us, with your presence!"

The Nyctalope quickly made a mental note to be aware of the Barsoomian custom of addressing a person by his full name.

"I am Dejah Thoris, this mighty Thark is Tars Tarkas!" she continued. (The Thark grunted and nodded his head.) "May I also introduce my husband, John Carter, Warlord of Mars!"

Carter extended his hand and the Nyctalope replied in kind: "It is truly an honor to meet a warrior the caliber of one such as yourself, John Carter."

"Please Leo-Saint-Clair, your own prowess far exceeds mine, if only half of what I heard about you is true. However, we are presently in dire need of your skills as a detective. I fear we may have a serial murderer on our hands." Carter's face became grim. "We have had a series of bizarre murders in Helium, and in the nearby abandoned city the Tharks occupy. Strangely, all of the victims were warriors in the prime of their lives. To slay someone in a duel of honor in Helium is rare, but not unheard of. Tharks slaying other Tharks is far from unusual, as that is how in their culture, one advances his status. Yet, in all of the slayings, no one has come forth to claim a duel of honor, or the status or belongings of the slain Tharks."

They had now entered the palace. The Nyctalope attempted to learn more about the circumstances of the crimes.

"What of the slayings themselves? You seem to think they're all connected... Do they have similar wounds in common?"

John Carter looked off into the distance. "Yes, but to describe them as mere wounds hardly conveys what's been done to the victims. It's more like mutilations." Carter sighed. "We have left the latest bodies as we found them. Perhaps you should see for yourself."

John Carter looked at the Nyctalope. "The room has remained undisturbed and as we found it," he said. "No one has stepped in it since the bodies were found. I must warn you: it is a gruesome sight."

The door to the training room swung open. Even the hardened Nyctalope had to turn his head from the stench that came rushing through the doors. John Carter walked in first, followed by Tars Tarkas, and the Nyctalope.

Leo surveyed the room. It was large, about 40 meters longs, 30 meters high, and 25 meters wide. Its center was largely empty, as it was meant for the training and sparring of warriors. The walls were adorned with weapons of various kinds. The floor and the ceiling, however, drew the most attention. They were awash in blood.

The Nyctalope could not help but step in it and leave tracks across the floor. From the ceiling, suspended upside down, were the bodies of two men who had been training when they were attacked. As the Nyctalope walked through the room, he could see that both men had been decapitated, and the red color of their bodies which he had initially thought to be their skins, was in reality nothing but blood and muscle—as both bodies had been totally skinned.

He looked away and rubbed his fingers across his chin, taking a moment to compose himself. He thought that even the notorious Ripper murders in London were nothing compared to what he now beheld.

The Nyctalope asked that the bodies be taken down. He then started examining the walls of the training room. As he slowly walked around, his keen eyes searched every centimeter of the place, looking for information.

After circling the room, he came to back to John Carter and Tars Tarkas.

"I can tell you that the men hanging there were caught completely off guard," he said. "Moreover, they were both dead before either one of them could react."

The Nyctalope led the others to the left wall of the room.

"See here, this dark discoloration on the wall... It's a burn, not a smudge." John Carter and Tars Tarkas eyed the spot in question. "Strangely, there is no projectile in the wall, nor are there signs of ricochet to another point in the room..."

Leo walked over to the bodies and stopped at the nearest corpse. A cursory exam put the picture of how this man had perished together in his mind. He pointed to the gaping hole in the man's chest.

"That hole was cauterized instantly," he said. "Then, whatever hit him blew out his back and hit the wall over there. It was almost as if he was killed by a ball of fire."

He looked at the second man in question and focused on the man's muscle tissue.

"This man's body is even more confusing. His flesh shows a fine pattern of cuts throughout his body as if a net had been thrown over him and then used to slice him to ribbons. The manner in which it was done is unorthodox as well..." Leo pointed to the man's chest. "Look: small shards of steel are embedded in the chest. I also found small shards of the same steel on the floor over there..."

He led the group to a section of wall with some blood splattered in a distinct pattern.

"This wall has small holes in it, which appear to form a circular pattern. As impossible as it sounds, I believe that a net of some kind was thrown over this man, then it attached itself to the wall and constricted, slicing into his flesh. The odd thing is that, looking at the shards in the man's chest and on the floor, I'm sure that he'd managed to get his sword between him and the net. Still, in the end, the net sliced through the sword as well as the man..."

Tars Tarkas growled: "What manner of creature could have done this?"

The Nyctalope looked back at the bodies to see if he might have missed anything. After further examination, he turned to the other two. "Over the span of how many nights have these murders occurred?"

John Carter closed his eyes. "Four of the past six nights. The first two murders took place in the city of the Tharks three nights ago. A day went by with nothing, then there was a murder in Helium, and this double murder yesterday."

The Nyctalope shook his head. "Sadly, I fear this will not be the last murder."

The Nyctalope awoke to find a frantic Dejah Thoris in his bed room.

"Leo Saint-Clair! Something has attacked Tars Tarkas! Please come with me at once!"

Dejah Thoris raced through the palace with the Nyctalope close on her heels. As they ran through the hallways, Leo was once more struck by her beauty, but he quickly pushed the thought to the back of his mind.

They came upon the room that was Tars Tarkas palace dwelling, and saw the massive warrior being carried out on a stretcher. He was bleeding and unconscious; his lower right arm had been nearly cut in half. Inside, Kantos Kan and several other Martians were gathered around the dead bodies of two palace guards that lay on the floor.

Dejah Thoris ran over to embrace her husband while the Nyctalope crouched down examined the bodies. When he had finished, he stood up and found John Carter standing next to him.

"John Carter what happened?" he inquired. "Is Tars Tarkas in stable condition?"

"Tars Tarkas will heal with time; his wound is serious but his arm can be repaired. It seems that he was returning to his quarters when something attacked him. Several guards heard the commotion in the hallway. Two went to assist Tars Tarkas, while another alerted me. I ran back to find the two guards dead and Tars Tarkas battling a phantom! He fought valiantly, but nothing was there. I saw his arm nearly cut into two as something invisible struck him in the head. I sprang to his aid and crashed into something. Whatever it was made some kind of a clicking sound, like a rock being used to sharpen a knife, and jumped out the window." John Carter grabbed the Nyctalope by the shoulders and spoke in hurried voice. "My friend, what manner of being is this? The creature is invisible and capable of killing our mightiest warriors."

"I have a hypothesis of what we might be dealing with," said Leo. "The bodies of these guards were killed in a much quicker fashion than those victims which were put on display earlier. This one was clearly shot with the same cauterizing weapon we saw utilized on the warriors in the training room. The second guard has double puncture wounds through his heart. He was killed with a twin-bladed instrument, like a pitch fork."

"Walk with me back to my chambers and explain the matter, please, Leo-Saint-Clair," said Carter. "I do not wish to discuss the situation in front of such a crowd as has gathered here."

Kantos Kan and a small group of Carter's trusted allies walked back toward his chamber, along with the Nyctalope and the Princess.

As they came to an empty hallway, the Nyctalope voiced his thoughts:

"To allay any fears, I do not think that our murderer was a phantom or an evil spirit. However, what I believe him to be may be even more fearsome. With further evidence from the latest victims, I can be certain of only one thing: our attacker is not from any of the known species on Barsoom. Not only does he not seem to operate under the ethical codes of the Tharks, the Sorns, the Hross, the Hither People, or any other known race, but his weapons are clearly beyond the scope of Barsoomian technology. No Martian species has been able to develop weapons able to cut through steel like paper, or use camouflage that renders them invisible."

The Nyctalope took a deep breath as the group kept walking. "It is my belief that the creature we seek is of alien origin to Barsoom," he said at last.

Dejah Thoris questioned, "If that is so, why then did the creature attack us in such a brutal way? Why did he not try to make contact with us? Is he the vanguard of an invasion?"

The Nyctalope shook his head. "His method of operation does not imply that he is looking to invade Barsoom. I think he is here on a hunting trip."

John Carter's face took on puzzled look "A hunting trip?"

"Yes. Based on the method he is using to mutilate the bodies of his victims, I believe this to be the case. The skinning of the bodies and removal of their heads is akin to what a hunter on Earth would do to a fox or a stag. I think he is collecting trophies. I also feel he is now going for the big game, so to speak. He started out with Thark and Helium warriors; now, he has made a run on Tars Tarkas, one of the most renowned warriors on the planet…"

The group turned a corner and saw a large, spear-like weapon sticking into John Carter's chamber door. The Nyctalope turned to Carter:

"I think he has just set his sights on the biggest prize on Barsoom."

Dejah Thoris began to weep and threw her arms around her husband.

John Carter, Leo, and a small squad of a half-dozen guards had set up in the desert as per the Nyctalope's instructions.

Carter, himself, rode out into the desert shortly before sunset, armed with only a sword. He was purposely making a spectacle of himself to ensure the creature would follow. Shortly after that, the Nyctalope and the guards headed in the opposite direction into the desert. They then double-backed under cover of dark.

The Nyctalope instructed the guards to lie close to ground behind a hill in sight of Carter, while he positioned himself at the bottom of another hill, roughly a hundred meters from them.

As the sky slowly lost it light, the Nyctalope pitied the guards. He knew what fate held in store for them. Hunting big game operated under the same principles in any circumstances. Saint-Clair was well versed in the techniques of Quatermain and Roxton. One of the main concerns about hunting a lion or an elephant who was the leader of his group was the other animals under his protection. If you wanted the head beast, you had to make sure the other animals were either scared off—or dead.

This thought no sooner ran through the Nyctalope's mind that three burst of blue light rained down on the guards, burning them to cinders. However, their unwitting sacrifice had allowed the Nyctalope to see where the shots were coming from. Even with his enhanced vision, he did not so much see a being as a distortion against the desert.

He drew his pistol and fired. His first shot hit the distortion, causing electrical sparks to run across it. The sparks faded as the distortion morphed into a humanoid being. The creature was large and powerfully built, with a yellow gray skin. It had some kind of armor around its shoulders and appeared to have a helmet protecting its face. Tightly woven hair protruded from its head, dangling down to its shoulders. In its hand was a massive spear, identical to the one embedded in Carter's chamber door. The Nyctalope mused that whatever this Predator was, he was neither from Mars, nor Earth.

The Predator snarled and turned toward the Nyctalope. A small cylinder attached to its shoulder adjusted itself. Leo jumped as soon as he saw the cylinder snap into motion. The area where he had been standing exploded in a bright flash. As the ground burned, Carter flexed his legs and leapt the thirty meters between him and the alien. As he landed, the Warlord swung his sword at the rotating cannon and severed it from the creature's shoulder armor. In a backhand swing, Carter brought his sword across the monster's face, cutting his helmet in two. The Predator kicked Carter in the midsection, sending him tumbling head over heels.

The Nyctalope drew his pistol, only to have some kind of spinning blade slice the barrel off the weapon as he held it. He looked up to see the creature remove what was left of his mask. The beast threw the mask to the ground, revealing a terrifying face. A mandible-like maw opened as the Predator held his spear above his head and screamed. The Nyctalope drew his rapier and a large knife as he ran up the hill toward the monster. The creature swung his blade towards Leo's head. The Nyctalope ducked the blow and drove his rapier into the

Predator's torso. The sword pierced through its rib cage and protruded from the alien's back.

The Predator howled in pain. The Nyctalope heard what sounded like a sword being unsheathed, and his stomach was lacerated as the creature dealt him a backhand blow. The Nyctalope tumbled away to see two long blades extending from the monster's gauntlet. He watched in awe as the Predator pulled the rapier from his rib cage, seemingly unfazed by the wound.

John Carter screamed in fury as he sprang back on the creature. The Predator turned around just in time to block an overhead strike from the Warlord's sword. The two dueled for several seconds before Carter was able to dodge the monster's spear and bring his sword up across the creature's body. Glowing, blue-green blood showered Carter as he moved in for the kill. He raised his sword to strike when the monster drove his spear into the Warlord's shoulder.

Carter fell back in pain as the Nyctalope sprang on the injured alien. Rolling under a thrust from the gauntlet's blades, the Nyctalope sliced into the creature's hip. Momentum carried Leo behind the monster and, quickly, he thrust his knife into the base of the alien's spine.

The Predator fell to his knees. The Nyctalope grabbed him by the hair, placed his knife under the alien's chin, and slit its throat. The creature gargled in its own blood as John Carter walked over to the Nyctalope.

Carter looked down. "A fitting end to a beast who has killed so many," he said. The two men turned toward the creature as a beeping sound emanated from one of its gauntlets. The Predator laughed once before expiring.

The Nyctalope examined the gauntlet to see obscure red lines and symbols that seemed to be decreasing in number. Startled, he grabbed Carter.

"We have to get away from here now!" he exclaimed.

They began to leap across the desert as the low gravity of Mars allowed the two to cover a greater distance than they would have running. Not too far away, the two warriors could see one of the incubation chambers the Tharks used to hatch their eggs. They reached it and crouched behind it as the horizon behind them cascaded with a bright blue light, followed by a massive shockwave. The shockwave raced across the planet...

As the energy burst reached its farthest point, it touched an ancient space capsule in a long-dead city...

A strange high-pitched whine awoke John Carter. Regaining his senses, he saw the Nyctalope unconscious on the ground. He awoke the adventurer and helped him to his feet as the high-pitched whine continued.

"What's that sound?" he asked.

The two followed it to the demolished incubation chamber. In the dirt, amongst the bodies of its brethren, writhed a baby Thark. John Carter reached down and picked up the screaming infant.

The Nyctalope peered down at the pathetic creature. "Will he live?" he inquired.

Carter raised his eyes to the sky "I do not know, my friend, but he is responsible for saving our lives, and the fact that he still lives is a testament to his strength. I will take him to Sola; she is a skilled healer and a gifted caregiver. If he reaches adulthood with only a portion of the strength he now possesses, he will prove a proud addition to the Thark warriors of Barsoom. For his sake, we must make haste in our return to Helium"

The Nyctalope entered the throne room of Helium to see John Carter and Dejah Thoris waiting for him. Next to them stood the proud Tars Tarkas, his arm in a sling. As Leo approached, Carter stepped forward and extended his hand.

"All of Helium owes you a debt of gratitude, Leo-Saint-Clair. Without your efforts, many more would have perished. If ever you need assistance, John Carter and the warriors of Helium will be at your beck and call."

"Thank you, John Carter. However, access to your radium weapons and fliers would be a far greater benefit to my allies, both on Earth and Barsoom, than anything else you could offer."

"They are yours, my friend. You have proved yourself beyond any doubt. From this day forward, all on Barsoom shall revere and honor the name of the Nyctalope. Several of our flyers and warship are yours to take to your colony. An ample supply of radium and fire arms will be placed in these transports."

Leo shook hands with Carter once more.

"You honor me, my friend. You cannot fathom how many lives your gesture of gratitude may save."

Leo turned, bowed, and kissed the hand of the Princess. once more letting his imagination have his way with her. He then turned and bowed to Tars Tarkas, who nodded in return. Then, the Nyctalope strode away from the throne room.

Oxus and Leo's children were waiting at the colony as he arrived on the warship.

"Papa, Papa!" The boys shouted as they ran to embrace their father.

Leo held them tight, thinking he would soon return well-armed to Earth and bring an end to the Great War. But, for the first time, a strange feeling came over him. He looked down at his boys, his artificial heart swelling with love for them, but in the back of his mind, he saw them as something different from him. That strange feeling persisted as Oxus shook his hand.

"Excellent work, Leo. Excellent work! The technology you have returned with will advance us here and propel the war effort back home," said the old scientist, smiling.

"But that's not all Leo. There was some amazingly powerful blast in the desert. We could only see a cloud from here, but it sent a strange pulse across the land. It reached us, Leo—us and the ancient capsule! Whatever that blast was, it brought a spark of life to the craft. With the radium you've brought back, I'm sure we can restore it to full power. Who knows what secrets it possesses?"

Leo vigorously shook his head to clear his mind. His boys clung to his legs and his friend stood beside him. He knew these people meant more to him than any other people in existence, and yet, he felt that they were different from him. Leo felt that they were somehow *other*...

*After Matthew Dennion's previous story set the stage, Roman Leary's tale details the tragic events that led to the demise of the Martian colony. It also chronicles the Nyctalope's adventures after World War II, begun with* The Heart of a Man *reprinted in* Enter the Nyctalope. *The Nicholas Flynn character seen in this short story was introduced by Roman in* The Evils Against Which We Strive *published in* Tales of the Shadowmen 4.

## Roman Leary: *The Children of Heracles*

*California, 1949*

The desert night was cold and quiet; the only sounds the traveler could hear were the steady click of his boot heels on the dusty pavement, and the insistent whisper of the Mojave wind.

The traveler was not dressed for cold weather. His jeans and leather jacket provided scant protection for his lean and muscular frame, but he felt no discomfort. The chill night air was far preferable to the infernal heat of the day, when the land was transformed into an open-air crucible. It was during those times that he took his rest, sleeping under a small tent that protected him from the burning rays of the Sun.

He carried the tent—along with toiletries, a generous supply of water, a few changes of clothes, and some meager portions of food—in a rucksack strapped to his back. Beneath his left arm, concealed in a holster he had designed himself, was a Browning automatic. Near the pistol, strapped securely to his side, was a passage wallet containing money and documentation for a variety of false identities.

He sometimes wondered why he bothered with the documents. Though an exile, he was not wanted for any crimes and he certainly had no fear of the authorities. In his former life—a life of wealth and privilege and high adventure—he had enjoyed fame and took great pleasure in being recognized. He would walk down a street and smile when he heard people whisper: "*Is that Leo Saint-Clair? No, it can't be him. Wait, I believe it is! The Nyctalope, himself!*"

He would sometimes turn and smile or wink, inwardly laughing at their startled reactions.

"Bon Dieu! *His ears must be as sharp as his eyes! The eyes, is it true what they say about them? That he can see even in pitch darkness?*"

"I can," the Nyctalope said aloud, speaking to no one but the shades of his imagination. "I can see through the darkness as if it were day."

"*And your heart? Is it really made of plastic and steel, and powered by magnets?*"

The Nyctalope chuckled. It was a sound as dry and parched as the sands that surrounded him. "Oh, yes," he said. "It's practically indestructible."

"*Amazing! You are the most extraordinary man in France! If only we had more men like you!*"

Leo smiled sadly up at the stars, their lights as cold and distant as the faded affections of his countrymen. The whispers would be very different if he were to appear on a Paris street today.

"*Is that Leo Saint-Clair? No, it can't be him. That traitor wouldn't dare show his face around here! That collaborator! That Nazi lap-dog!*"

Leo winced. There had been a time, not so very long ago, when he would have defended himself against these calumnies. But no matter how vigorous or logical his arguments were, the shades were never satisfied. They were uniform and intractable in their condemnation, and after a while, he simply gave up. To Hell with them. He could live with their hate. He had lived with worse.

He was shaking his head, as if physically casting off these ruminations, when he saw something that brought him up short. About a kilometer ahead of him, a man was staggering through the darkness. He weaved and stumbled along the road, his arms stretched stiff at 45 degree angles from his sides.

*A drunkard*, Leo thought. *What the Devil is he doing out here?* He remembered a sign he had seen earlier in the night: CARMELITA 10 MI. THE CITY BY THE "C"

Leo sighed. If that's where the man was from, then the fellow had wandered at least four kilometers into the desert. If Leo didn't help him, he might die of exposure before he could find his way back. Even as he considered this, he heard the sound of an approaching engine. He glanced over his shoulder and saw a pair of headlights racing toward him in the distance.

*Perhaps I can flag this person down*, he thought. *Get them to give the man a ride back to the town. I'll even offer to pay them for their trouble.*

He nodded to himself. It was a good solution, neat and simple. His mind made up, he slipped off his rucksack and began to jog toward the drunkard. If nothing else, he could prevent the poor sod from stepping into the path of the car.

Twenty-six hours before the Nyctalope saw him barreling through the Mojave in a rented Plymouth sedan, the Professor had been enjoying a rare evening of unfettered luxury. He was wrapped in satin sheets, reclining on feather pillows, and savoring a fine claret while perusing a copy of Shakespeare's sonnets that had been with him since his college days. As he paused in his reading to take a sip of the dark red Bordeaux, he smiled at the thought of what his colleagues in London would say if they could see him in such a state.

*"Is that Bernard Quatermass? No, it can't be him. Our Quatermass is a Spartan, not some decadent layabout!"*

"Oh, it's me, all right" Quatermass chuckled. "Just a part of me that's seldom seen." In fact, Quatermass did feel a bit guilty. The Biltmore Hotel in Los Angeles was far removed from his usual accommodations, and certainly not something he would have selected on his own, but Karnes had made the arrangements and refused to listen to any of his objections:

*"For Heaven's sake, Quatermass! Live a little before you die!"*

*"But the cost, Steve! Surely the California Science Institute can't afford to…"*

*"Hang the cost! You're the most respected rocket scientist in Britain! The Institute is honored that you're willing to speak here and wants to make your trip as pleasant as possible."*

*"Oh, well. I suppose it would be churlish to refuse."*

*"It certainly would! I'll drop all the information you'll need in the post this afternoon. I'll look forward to hearing your lectures."*

The talks had been remarkably well-received and Quatermass had been surprised to find himself (inadvertently, of course) enjoying his first real vacation in years. There was one more presentation scheduled for the following evening, followed by the long journey home on the next day. Goodbye room service and California sunshine. He wouldn't really mind leaving it behind for the more familiar trappings of drizzling rain and London fog, but he couldn't deny that a small part of himself had fallen in love with the congenial atmosphere of the American West Coast.

His wistful thoughts were interrupted by the ringing of the telephone. He sat up and answered it, and was startled by the familiar voice at the end of the line: "Professor, this is Jeff Stuart."

"Jeff!" Quatermass exclaimed. "Good Heavens! How are you, lad? Are you here in Los Angeles? I suppose Karnes told you where I was staying."

"I haven't spoken to Steve in years," Stuart replied. "Listen, I don't mean to be rude, but I'm afraid I have to be very direct. I need your help with something, and I can't really discuss it with you over the phone. Can we meet?"

"Well, I have a rather full schedule tomorrow but I suppose I can arrange for something around lunchtime if you know of a convenient place to…"

"I can't do that, Professor. I'm about 150 miles northeast of you in a small town called Carmelita. It's absolutely vital that you come here as quickly as possible."

Quatermass scowled. "Now see here, Jeff. This all rather peremptory, don't you think? I don't see how you can expect me to..."

"Professor, it's a Code Prometheus."

Quatermass fell silent, absorbing the implications. Keeping his voice calm and even, he asked: "How did you become involved?"

"I'm working with a recently formed agency, the Office of Scientific Investigation. Three days ago, we received a call from a doctor who had been referred to us by the people at Fort Ord. He was trying to get someone to check out an object that had been unearthed here in the local copper mine. I was sent to check it out and...well..."

"How large is it?" Quatermass asked.

"Two adults could fit inside of it with room to spare."

"Inside? Have you...?

"Yes."

"How did...?

"Please," Stuart said firmly, "don't ask me to say more. Will you come?"

"Yes. How do I get there?"

Quatermass spent the rest of the night and the following day striving to think of anything but Stuart and his impossible find. He did a fair job of it, delivering his final lecture with a relaxed aplomb that belied the tension he felt in every nerve. A Code Prometheus! Stuart would never have used the phrase unless he was absolutely certain, and the man was no fool. He had worked with Jeff during the War, and knew that he was earnest, meticulous, and devoid of imagination.

*No doubt I can take him at his word*, Quatermass thought as he raced through the desolate landscape. *If he's wrong, then he's been gulled by the most elaborate hoax of the century. But if he's right...*

Quatermass cried out and slammed his foot hard on the brake. A man had fallen from the darkness into the glare of his headlights, rolling across the road directly in front of him. He twisted the wheel and the car slid sideways, tires screaming against the asphalt. Quatermass, teeth clenched and knuckles white, felt time expand into a small eternity as he slid past the man in the road, missing his head by inches. The car continued to skid until it had completed a full 180-degree circuit, the headlights now pointing back toward Los Angeles, the inert form of the man still bathed in their harsh glare.

Quatermass leapt from the car and ran to the man he had nearly killed. "Are you all right?" he shouted. He knelt beside the man, who appeared to be unconscious. He was uncertain what, if any, injuries the fellow had sustained, and was reluctant to touch him for that reason. Still, he had to at least check for a pulse. He gently lifted the man's wrist, and was startled when his arm was suddenly clasped in a grip of iron. The man's eyes snapped open, and for a moment Quatermass could have sworn they were burning with an unnatural glow.

"Get down," the man rasped, and he snatched Quatermass to the ground. Quatermass fell hard, and before he could recover enough to even make a noise of protest, he was treated to the shocking sight of what he would later identify as a barrel cactus whistling through the air just inches from his face. Astonished, he lifted his head and saw a snarling young man in gray coveralls step into the glow of the headlights. His eyes were wide and glazed with stupor—or madness—and his arms were stretched stiff from his sides. He stopped, lifted his arms upward, and Quatermass saw shapes move in the air behind him.

*What in the name of...?*

The shapes floated into the light and became more distinct. They were cacti, 20, 30, perhaps even more, uprooted from the desert sands and hovering impossibly about this wild-eyed youth.

Quatermass watched in horrified fascination as the youth made a gesture, and the floating cacti rolled forward until they resembled nothing so much as a fleet of missiles, aimed directly at him.

"Get inside the car," said the stranger. "Now!"

Quatermass jumped to his feet as the first of the cacti came rocketing toward him. For a moment, he dared to hope he would reach safety without being hit, but his hopes vanished in an explosion of agony as one of the cacti slammed into his side. It buried its spines into his flesh and the impact sent him rolling across the sand.

Nearly blinded by the pain, the Professor managed to recover himself enough to scramble into the car. "Come on!" he shouted, holding the door open for his presumptive ally. The fellow was behind him, but he shocked Quatermass by kicking the door closed from outside.

"Stay down!" the man commanded, and the Professor obeyed. There was a series of staccato thumps accompanied by the sound of cracking glass as the cacti rained down on the sedan. Then there was a moment of silence, and suddenly the car began to tremble.

Quatermass risked a look through the window and saw the young man reach forward and raise his arms. The car began to lift accordingly.

*Telekinesis*, the Professor thought, his mind racing. *It's the only explanation! This has to be related to Jeff's find. I have to get to that town!*

The sedan was now about four feet from the ground. What was the young man planning to do? It hardly mattered. The car had swiftly gone from being a shelter to a death-trap, and Quatermass had no choice except to run for it. He turned to the opposite door. As his hand closed around the handle, he saw the form of the stranger running toward the car. The man jumped, landed on the hood of the floating car, and propelled himself forward through the air in an arc that terminated with his fist smashing into the face of the crazed young man.

The young man fell to the ground and the car immediately followed suit, landing with a spine-jarring crash that sent a fresh wave of agony through the Professor's wounded side.

Willing himself to ignore the pain, Quatermass opened the door and cried out to his rescuer: "Well done! Is he unconscious?"

As if in reply, the young man came to his feet. He did not rise as a normal man would, but simply floated upright, as if lifted by invisible hands.

The other man reached into his coat and drew a pistol. "Please don't make me kill you," he said. "Why don't you talk to me? Why you are attacking us?"

The young man sneered, then gasped. His hands went to his chest and he dropped to his knees. He wobbled there for a second, then fell forward, burying his face in the sand.

"What just happened?" Quatermass shouted. "Did you shoot him?"

The man was kneeling by the prostrate form of their attacker. "I did not," he said without turning, "but he is certainly dead."

"Do you know him?" Quatermass asked.

"I have never seen him before." The man looked at him, and Quatermass saw that his senses had not been deceived: The man's eyes gleamed softly in the darkness.

"Your wound looks serious," he said, and Quatermass came to a sudden awareness of the blood drenching his side. He tried to pull his coat open but a flash of pain made him stop.

"I'll live," the Professor said, "but I need medical attention. There is a town near here called Carmelita. Can you drive me there?"

"Yes," said the man, and he rose and walked to the car.

"Wait," Quatermass said. "What about him? We can't just leave him here!"

"We can and we will. There is nothing more we can do for him."

"But...to simply leave him for the vultures...It's indecent!"

"Don't be ridiculous," was the terse reply. "You saw what he could do. Can you explain it? What if his body is har-

155

boring some strange disease or parasite? We could be exposing ourselves to deadly danger by merely touching him."

The Professor nodded, conceding the point.

"What is your name?" the man asked.

"Quatermass. Bernard Quatermass"

"Listen to me, Mr. Quatermass. You are in shock and you are losing blood. Your concern for this fellow does you credit, but you should be thinking of yourself right now."

The man reached out and touched the back of the Professor's neck, and his pain was suddenly and dramatically reduced. Quatermass gasped in surprise. "What did you just do?"

"No miracle cure, I'm afraid. The pain will be back soon enough, but you should have at least an hour with it considerably numbed."

"Who are you?"

"My name is Leo," he said. He stepped to the front of the car and slipped behind the driver's seat. He turned to face Quatermass.

"After I get you to a doctor, I will either send someone for that man, or I will come back for him myself. Do you believe me?"

"Yes."

"Excellent."

Leo started the car and the engine roared to life. "Been a while," he said, mostly to himself, and Quatermass thought he heard a smile in the man's voice.

A moment later all that remained of them was the echo of screeching tires.

The first that they saw of the place was a distant crimson glow, and a cloud of smoke that obscured the stars. By the time they passed the WELCOME TO CARMELITA sign, the smoke had become tangible and caustic, and the glow had expanded into several raging fires that appeared to be consuming about a third of the town.

The light from the flames illuminated a hellish landscape strewn with shattered glass, wrecked automobiles, and the twisted, broken bodies of men, women, and children.

Leo stopped the car. For a moment, neither of the men spoke. They simply regarded the carnage in a stunned, almost reverent, silence.

Leo heard a peculiar scraping sound, and realized it was his teeth grinding together. He forced his mouth to open and, ignoring the stench of the smoke, took a deep, calming breath. What had he stumbled onto? Worse, why did it seem some-how…familiar?

*It's not the first scene of horror I've encountered,* he thought. *The important thing is to keep a clear head, formu-late a plan, remember to focus…remember to…*

Something began to scratch at the back of his mind.

*There is something I need to remember.*

A flash of red suddenly bloomed before his eyes, accom-panied by…

(*let them stay buried*)

…a skull-splitting burst of pain. He cried out, clutching his head. Then, as quickly as it struck, the pain vanished. He felt a firm hand on his shoulder and turned to face the alarmed gaze of Professor Quatermass.

"I'm all right," Leo said, gently pushing the hand away.

"I don't believe you," Quatermass flatly stated. "Who is it that should stay buried?"

"What?"

"You whispered that, just now. You said to let them…"

"Forget it. That was just some foolish babbling."

"If it's relevant to what's happened here…"

"I said to forget it," Leo said sharply. "This conversation is a waste of time. We need to find survivors, if there are any. In a situation like this it is absolutely imperative that we…"

"GET OUT OF THE CAR."

Startled, both men turned to see a group of heavily armed men in military uniforms. Their faces were covered in gas

157

masks. One of them was holding a megaphone before his concealed face.

"GET OUT OF THE CAR IMMEDIATELY. IF YOU DO NOT COMPLY WE WILL BE FORCED TO OPEN FIRE."

Leo and Quatermass opened their doors and slowly stepped out, hands raised.

"Echo Team checking in with two prisoners," Leo heard the lead soldier say. He was addressing a burly man with the stripes of a master sergeant on his sleeve.

They were standing atop the concrete steps leading to the doors of the town hall. Four men, including the sergeant, had been waiting to greet them. The NCO was the only one not wearing a mask.

The hall was an impressive building; three stories with tall windows and a line of Doric columns at its entrance. According to the sign by the door, it also contained the courthouse and the jail. It was in the center of the ruined city, but had apparently managed to escape the destruction that had been visited upon most of the town. Electric lights still burned in its windows.

"Are you the person in command?" Quatermass asked. He spoke with force and confidence, but Leo could see that his injuries were getting to him. The Professor was pale and shaking. Rivulets of perspiration streamed down his face like tears.

"I'm Master Sergeant Vincenzo of the 821st Civil Affairs Battalion, United States Army," the burly man said. His tone was neutral, almost business-like. Leo half-expected him to extend a hand in greeting. Instead, he took a bundle of papers from the lead soldier.

"Their identification," the soldier said. "This one's an Englishman. The other one…Well, see for yourself. He was also carrying a Browning."

Vincenzo glanced at the papers. "Bernard Quatermass?" he said, addressing the Professor.

"Yes, yes, of the British Experimental Rocket Group," Quatermass snapped. "Please, I must speak to your commanding officer immediately!"

"You'll get your chance." The sergeant turned to Leo. "Looks like you've got a lot of names," he said. "Any of them correct?"

Leo shrugged.

"This man saved my life," Quatermass said. "I insist he be treated with courtesy and respect!"

"Really?" Vincenzo said. "How did he manage to do that?"

Quatermass and Leo exchanged a look.

Vincenzo nodded. "I figured as much." He looked at the leader of Echo Team. "Tyler, get them to the cells. It doesn't matter if they stay together." He pointed at Quatermass. "Ask Captain Flynn to check this man out as soon as possible."

"Yes, Master Sergeant," the soldier replied, and he ushered Leo and Quatermass into the building.

Vincenzo shook his head as he watched the door close.

*A Brit rocket scientist and some hardcase with about eight different names*, he mused. *How are these guys tied up in all this?*

He desperately wanted to question the prisoners himself. Although he had managed to maintain a façade of professional detachment, inside he was burning to solve the mystery of Carmelita's overnight destruction. He was certain that he could put the pieces together if he were given half a chance. He had always had a knack for...

His eyes narrowed. "Johnson," he said.

The soldier closest to him stepped away from the column he been standing beside. "Yes, Master Sergeant?"

"Weren't there four of our trucks parked across the street?"

"I...think so."

"Where'd the fifth one come from?"

They looked at the truck in question for a silent moment. "Stay here," Vincenzo said. "It's probably nothing, but I just want to be sure…"

He drew his sidearm and descended the steps. He was crossing the street when a dapper, middle-aged man stepped gracefully out of the back of the truck. Vincenzo immediately snapped into a firing position. "Halt!" he shouted. "Place your hands behind your head!"

"Oh, Good Heavens," the man said. His low, smooth voice was laced with a hint of irritation. "You're making a complete fool of yourself. Lower that weapon at once."

Vincenzo, to his own amazement, did so without question. Inside his mind, a rebellious voice began to rage: *What the Hell are you doing? Raise that pistol! Call out for assistance!*

"Come here," the man said. "I like to look into a man's eyes when I am speaking to him."

*Don't do it! He's done something to you! Can't you feel it? It like he's hypnoti—*

The voice was abruptly cut off, and was replaced by a strangely pleasant white noise. Vincenzo was suddenly filled with a profound sense of inner peace. Why would he not want to do what this man said? It seemed so…natural.

He holstered his automatic, advanced until he was directly before the man, and stood at attention. The man was of average build and height, but he carried himself with an aloof confidence that made him seem much taller. His dark, handsome features were framed by a neatly-trimmed beard which gave him a slightly diabolical air.

No, not diabolical. He was trustworthy…paternal…*masterful*…

"Please allow me to introduce myself," the man said. "My name is…" He trailed off, thoughtfully tapping his chin. "Lord," he said at length, "Agent Lord of the FBI. And you are…?"

Vincenzo cheerfully gave him the same information he had shared with Leo and Quatermass.

"And what, pray tell, are you doing here, Master Sergeant?"

"We were on a training exercise at Camp Hunter Liggett when we received emergency orders from Fort Ord to isolate and secure this community, sir"

"Why? What happened here?"

"We're not certain yet, sir. We've only been on the scene for a few hours. It appears that part of the population...well...it seems that they went insane. The few survivors that we have taken into custody are all giving confused and conflicting accounts of what occurred."

"Have you formed any theories?"

"Me, personally, sir?"

"Of course."

Vincenzo blushed. He felt honored that such a man would be interested in his opinion. "I'm reluctant to speculate with so little information," he said. "I can tell you that there has been talk about something that was unearthed at a nearby mine. One of the survivors said they'd accidentally freed a demon."

"Do you think that's possible?" Lord asked.

"I think it's a lot of nonsense."

Lord chuckled. "You are right to be skeptical," he said. "Pay no heed to carping Cassandras and their wild tales! Stick to the facts, that's what I always say."

Vincenzo nodded in enthusiastic agreement. He harbored dreams of a career in journalism after his time in the Army was done, and he made a silent promise to himself to always remember this sage advice.

"Well, go on," Lord said, his expression both expectant and encouraging.

"There isn't anything more to tell, sir," Vincenzo said. He was ashamed that he had so little to offer. He lowered his eyes.

"Oh, come now, Top," Lord said brightly, and Vincenzo's heart sang at hearing the familiar nickname for men of his rank. "There's no need to be so downcast. As you have said, you've only just arrived here. I'm certain that working together we can get to the bottom of this mystery."

"I don't doubt it, sir, now that you're here."

Lord beamed. "That's the spirit! Now, kindly introduce me to your commanding officer. I think it's past time he and I became acquainted."

The jail was in the basement of the courthouse. Leo and Quatermass were led through the narrow passage between the cells by a pair of young soldiers. Tyler walked behind them, a gun at the ready.

Leo found the place to be fairly clean and well-lit, but it reeked of antiseptic covering a stench of misery and fear. The cells were full to bursting with men and women who were portraits of abject despair. They were, for the most part, clothed in tatters, their faces streaked with blood and dirt. A pall of eerie silence, broken only by muffled whimpers, hung over them all.

Quatermass was making grumbling noises about the inhumanity of it all, but he was being generally cooperative until he suddenly erupted in fury.

"Children!" he shouted. "Locked up like animals! This is an outrage!"

Leo followed his gaze and found himself looking into the eyes, red and swollen from weeping, of a little girl. She was sitting on a cot clutching a boy, younger than herself, who had fallen asleep in her arms.

The scratching in Leo's mind intensified into clawing, the desperate efforts of some beast raging not to be freed, but to burrow deeper into the darkness. Leo braced himself, expecting another burst of pain, but instead what he felt was an inexplicable wave of sadness. Unconsciously, he stepped toward the cell containing the children, but was halted by a command from Tyler: "Eyes front," he said. "Keep moving forward."

Leo reluctantly obeyed, but his way was blocked by Quatermass. "By Heaven, we'll not move another step until you…"

"Stop it," Leo said quietly. "This isn't the time."

Quatermass glowered at him, and then nodded. "Of course," he said. "One should choose one's battles carefully."

"I'm glad you think so," Tyler said. "Now get moving before I lose my patience."

They were escorted to the last cell on the left, the only one which wasn't already occupied.

"Captain Flynn will be along shortly," Tyler said as locked them in. "He'll get you patched up. He's a doctor."

"And he approves of this? Treating these people like criminals? Like cattle?"

Tyler sighed. He was a young man, but in that moment he seemed far older. "Listen, pal," he said. "We don't like this anymore than you do. We're just trying to get a handle on this thing. You should get off of your high horse."

Quatermass seemed to soften at this, but he didn't reply. Tyler gestured for his men to follow and he retreated down the passage. Leo looked after him for a moment, then turned his attention to the adjacent cell.

Standing at the door, gripping the bars in enormous hands, was one of the biggest men he had ever seen. He estimated the fellow to be almost 2 meters and 110 kilos of solid muscle. He was dressed in dirty coveralls that were identical to the ones worn by the killer in the desert. He stared back at Leo with a look of bemused indifference. Leo acknowledged him with a nod, which the man returned.

Behind the big man, lying in one of the bunks, was the shape of another, somewhat smaller man. This fellow forced himself up and squinted at Leo through bleary eyes, which suddenly widened in amazement.

"Professor," he said, his voice a papery whisper. "Is that you, sir?"

"Jeff!" said Quatermass, pressing himself against the bars. "Jeff Stuart, thank God! What's happened in this place?"

"It was…" Stuart coughed and cleared his throat. His head was tightly wrapped in a bandage and Leo could see specks of red where the blood had seeped through. "It was the…artifact. I'm not sure that I should discuss…"

Quatermass rolled his eyes. "Jeff, we don't have time to be circumspect. Please speak plainly. Was there something in the vessel? Something that caused all this destruction?"

*Artifact?* Leo thought. *Vessel?*

Stuart's eyes moved back and forth from the big man to Leo, and he appeared to come to a decision. "All right," he said. "It hardly matters now. We—that is, me and a team of miners—we doubled the power to the shaft where the ship was discovered. We were trying to drill open what appeared to be a sealed compartment. Suddenly, the surface we were working at just…crumbled away." He fell into another fit of coughing.

Quatermass impatiently waited for him to recover himself. "And what did you see?"

"The pilots," Stuart replied, his parched voice laden with awe and horror. "They looked like locusts, about three feet long I should say. Their bodies began to decay as soon as the air hit them."

"Oh, Christ," Leo said. It was not an oath but an appeal. "Oh, dear Lord, no."

The others turned to him, surprised. He locked eyes with Stuart. "The power started to drain, didn't it?" Leo asked him. "The lights began to flicker, and then you heard the roaring, didn't you?"

Stuart gawked at him. "Yes," he said. "The miners broke and ran, and a second later so did I. I barely remember making to the surface, but then…"

"But then it was too late to stop it," Leo finished. "Tell the truth: Did it affect you?"

"No, but there were others…"

"What in God's name are you two on about?" Quatermass growled.

Leo ignored him. "How long did the effect last?" he asked Stuart.

"I can't be sure. Once I was on the surface, I only had time to make it to a phone and call OSI before I was attacked. I was trying to tell Forbes what was happening when one of the miners threw a hammer....no....he didn't throw it...he *sent* it..."

"Don't focus on that," Leo said. "I need to know what stopped the process. Something had to, or some of these soldiers would be affected. Can you tell me what did that?"

"I'm glad to see you're up and about, Doctor Stuart," someone said. The men turned to see a pale, red-haired officer dressed in fatigues and toting a medical bag. He was accompanied by two soldiers Leo had not seen before. "I'm Captain Flynn," the officer said with a friendly smile, "but I'd rather you called me Doctor."

One of the soldiers unlocked Leo's cell and Flynn walked straight to Quatermass, whom he gently pushed to one of the bunks. "Don't let me stop you fellows," he said as he examined the Professor's wounds. "Just keep talking as if I weren't here. It sounds like a fascinating conversation."

Leo half-admired the man's nonchalant approach, but he didn't have the patience for games. He turned back to Jeff and said: "Well, you heard him. Let's keep going. Can you answer my question?"

Stuart shook his head and shrugged. "I'm sorry, but all I can remember is being found by a team of soldiers and brought here."

"I think I know what stopped it," the big man interjected, breaking his silence. "I think it was me."

"How?" Leo asked.

"I wrecked the generator feeding power to the exploration shaft. There were bolts of electricity flashing out of it like lightning and it seemed to be drawing power off everything at the site. I didn't know what else to do but go at it with a sledge hammer."

Leo smiled. "The Gordian knot approach," he said.

"I don't know what that is," the man said. "But I know that roaring I was hearing stopped."

"Did the people who were affected immediately return to normal?" Leo asked. There was hope in his voice, which was crushed as he watched the big man slowly shake his head.

"Whatever it was, it had gotten too deep into them. They started to…they started to die…drop like flies. But not before they'd done one hell of a lot of damage."

"That may explain some of my findings," Flynn said without looking up from his ministrations. "I've already examined three subjects whose hearts burst within their chests. I've never seen anything like it before. It's really pretty amazing."

Leo thought Flynn was pretty amazing himself. He sounded as if he were talking about an interesting new variation on the common cold.

"There, now," the doctor said to Quatermass as he finished dressing his wounds. "It wasn't as bad as it looked. You should be yourself again no time."

"I don't anticipate being myself for quite some time to come," Quatermass said with a scowl. "Wait, what's in that syringe? Don't you dare—ouch! Confound you! What the Hell did you just… "

"Just something to help you rest. You'll thank me for it later."

"I sincerely doubt that," Quatermass growled, his voice already growing thick. Struggling mightily against the sedative, he turned his heavy eyes to Leo. "What is your connection with this horror? How do you…know so much…about it?"

"I've seen something like it before," Leo said.

"Where?" the Professor asked.

"You wouldn't believe me if I told you."

Quatermass tried to respond, but merely collapsed into the bunk with a sigh.

"What about me?" Flynn asked. He stepped out of the cell and closed the door. He dismissed the soldiers and turned to Leo. "I think you would be surprised at what I am prepared to believe," the doctor said. "When the OSI called Fort Ord, we were immediately sent here to investigate, but there was nothing to prepare us for what we've found. On the surface, it looks like an epidemic of insanity, followed by wholesale slaughter and mass suicide."

"On the surface…" Leo said.

"Yes," Flynn said, "but there's obviously a lot more to it than that. We're aware of Dr. Stuart's extraordinary find—his OSI friends were very forthcoming—but its relationship with these events is unclear to say the least. I would be very grateful if you would share with me what you know."

"There's only one thing I can share with you that matters," Leo said. He pointed at Stuart. "The thing that this man was examining is incredibly dangerous and must be destroyed as soon as possible."

Flynn shook his head. "You know that's not going to happen. There are scientists on the way here right now who simply cannot wait to get into the bottom of that mine. We might be able to stall them, but we can't blow up their prize. Not unless you give me something to work with…"

Leo sighed. "All right," he said, "The object in the mine is a rocket-ship from Mars. If that ship is exposed to an electrical power source, it will release an energy wave that affects the minds of certain people exposed to it."

"Certain people," Flynn said, "but not everyone. Why is that?"

Leo clenched his teeth. "There's no way to explain it that doesn't sound completely absurd. Can't you just take my word that the damn thing needs to…to…" Leo closed his eyes. The clawing had begun again and the pain was building like the prelude to a volcanic eruption. "It needs to stay buried," he whispered. "Look at what it's done, at what it can do. Look at all the blood…"

"I believe you," Flynn said, and Leo opened his eyes to meet the doctor's level gaze.

"Do you?" Leo said, incredulous.

"Yes, but I need more information if I'm going to…"

"No!" Leo said. "If all of this death won't convince you fools, then how can anything I say make a difference!" He turned his back to Flynn and braced himself against the far wall. He took several deep breaths and the pain began to recede. After a moment, he glanced over his shoulder, but Doctor Flynn was gone.

The military occupation of the town of Carmelita had been hastily code-named "Operation Lockdown," which Lord thought was accurate, if not particularly original.

The commanding officer was one Lt. Col. Jack Evans, a tough but amiable man's man in the classic mold. Lord was delighted, though not surprised, to find the Colonel almost as pliant and eager to please as Vincenzo. Contrary to the views of his many detractors, Lord was actually quite fond of military types. He felt that their rigorous discipline predisposed them to the sort of blind obedience that he valued in subordinates. There were, of course, always a few stubborn exceptions, but they tended to be individuals who had been trained in dealing with a person of his uniquely persuasive qualities.

"I hope you find those reports helpful, sir," Evans said, interrupting Lord's musings. Lord, mildly annoyed, glanced up from the papers he had been perusing. Evans and Vincenzo were seated across from him in high-backed chairs of wine-red leather. Lord himself was comfortably ensconced behind an expansive desk that had apparently belonged to a judge, now presumably deceased.

"Please do not speak unless you are spoken to, Colonel," he said. He saw the man's jaw clench and took it as a warning. It was a sign that a part of him was chafing under Lord's authority, and that was no good at all. He stared deeply into Evans's eyes and said: "This report is clear, succinct, and does you great credit. I consider it a pleasure to be working with an officer of such obvious intelligence."

Evans blinked. "Why…um…thank you very much, sir."

"No need to thank me," Lord continued. "I am sure that a man of your wisdom and insight understands that the only way this operation will be a success is if you do exactly as I say without question. Any resistance to my will would result in a complete disaster. Do you understand?"

There was a nagging, pestilential doubt lurking behind Evans's eyes. Lord saw it and focused on it. "Do you understand?" he repeated.

The doubt withered, died, and Evans was his. "I understand completely," the Colonel said. "You can depend on me and my men, sir."

"Excellent," Lord said. "Now, according to what you've written, the first man on the scene, this Doctor Stuart of the OSI, was convinced that the object at the mine was of extraterrestrial origin and that it was responsible for this outbreak of violence."

"That is correct, sir."

"Has he been thoroughly questioned?"

"Not by me. He's been fading in and out of consciousness since he was picked up."

"I want to speak to him as soon as he is fit for interrogation."

"Yes, sir."

Lord dropped the report on the desk. "It also says that you are awaiting further authorization before attempting to approach the object yourself."

"Yes, sir" Evans affirmed. "Considering what's already occurred, I think that extreme caution…"

Lord cut him off with a wave of his hand. "I am giving you that authorization right now. I want every available man dispatched to the mine and applying their full efforts to the excavation of that object. I'll be expecting regular reports on their progress."

Evans flinched. "Certainly, sir, but what if the men fall under the influence of whatever it was that affected…"

"Oh, don't be concerned about that. As soon as access to the object has been restored, tell the men to withdraw to a safe distance and inform me immediately. I will come to the scene and take command personally. I have some very specific ideas about what took place here and I am certain that I can handle whatever we may find."

Evans stood up and saluted. "I'll start the operation at once, sir," he said, and marched out of the office.

"Would you like me to join him, sir?" Vincenzo asked.

Lord considered it, then nodded. "Be careful, Top," he said to the Master Sergeant. "I would hate to lose you. You're a very useful minion."

Vincenzo swelled with pride. It wasn't every day that one received such praise.

"May I escort you out?" Lord asked. "I have to retrieve something from my...vehicle."

"It would be an honor, sir"

"I know."

Flynn was exiting the stairwell on the floor where Lt. Col. Evans, his commanding officer, had set up HQ, when he was met with a surprising sight.

Stepping out of the judge's office that Evans had commandeered was Vincenzo and a sharp-dressed civilian with a jutting chin and confident stride that said, *power*, or, lacking that, *arrogance*. Something told Flynn to hang back, and long years of practice at listening to helpful *somethings* kept him behind the corner as a hidden observer. Flynn was astonished when, just as the men were about to step into the elevator at the far end of the hall, the civilian reached over and absent-mindedly gave Vincenzo a pat on the head. Knowing Top fairly well, Flynn braced himself for the inevitable explosion, but instead Vincenzo...blushed.

The elevator door had been closed for several seconds before Flynn recovered from the shock enough to propel himself forward into the office. He had hoped Evans might be present and ready with an explanation for the bizarre scene, but the room was empty. Flynn glanced around and his eye fell on a blackboard in the corner of the room. It was covered with small, neat handwriting that he was certain had not been there when he met with Evans briefly an hour or so before. Flynn walked over to the board and read:

*ANALOGOUS EVENTS – RELATED? UNRELATED?*

*1968. Piedmont, Arizona. Extraterrestrial microbe*

*1973. Evans City, Pennsylvania. Biological weapon*

*1982. Snowfield, California. Intelligence(?); possibly amoeboid; shoggoth?*

*1995. Desperation, Nevada. Intelligence; Tak? Tak=Sutekh? Unlikely*

*Most Likely: Arizona incident; so-called "Andromeda Strain" variant. Could be very useful*

Beneath this last, the writer had whimsically added a doodle of a smiley face. Flynn stared at words. Their meaning was both obvious and electrifying: He was looking at a time-line of events that hadn't yet taken place. He was tempted to dismiss it as insanity, but he had learned long ago that what many would deem impossible was, to certain people, merely commonplace.

Many years before, when he was a small boy living in Hell's Kitchen, Flynn had met two such persons. One was a grim avenger who called himself the Shadow. The other was the man who had inspired Flynn to become a doctor; a brilliant and flamboyant man who called himself Sâr Dubnotal.

Suddenly, Lord opened the door and was intensely displeased to find the young officer studying his notes. "Who are you and what are doing here?" Lord demanded. He was surprised when the fellow snapped about and, in a smooth but lightning-fast motion, drew his sidearm and brought it to bear on Lord's head.

"I'd like to ask you the same question," Flynn said. Despite his aggressive stance, his voice was calm, even friendly.

Lord scanned the man's uniform for his name and rank, found them, and smiled warmly. "Captain Flynn," he said, "there's no need to be so hostile. I'm Agent Lord of the FBI. I've assumed control of this operation."

"I hope you'll forgive me if I wait to hear that from the Colonel himself."

"I assure you," Lord said, staring at Flynn intently, "that you can take my word for it."

"No doubt, but for the time being could you please keep your hands where I can see them?"

Lord scowled. "Captain, before this charade goes any further, I think I should define the terms of our relationship: I am the Master, and you will obey me."

Flynn blinked a few times, and burst out laughing. "I heard you feds could be cocky, but this is really the limit. You're the 'Master?' Give me a break!"

Lord chuckled and shrugged and decided that Flynn would not leave the room alive. He had encountered humans before who could resist his influence, but never someone who didn't seem to feel it at all. It was entirely too dangerous, and infuriating, to be countenanced.

"I'll admit that was a bit over the top," Lord said. "Perhaps we can start over again. Would you like to see my identification?" He began reaching inside of his coat. Concealed there was a device called a Tissue Compression Eliminator, a weapon with which he could treat Flynn to a swift but agonizing death.

"If you move that hand another inch, I'll blow your brains out," Flynn said.

Lord, silently cursing, raised his hand. "Captain, I must warn you that when I report your behavior to Colonel Evans, he will no doubt…"

"Colonel Evans would never have ceded command to a civilian authority without informing every senior officer on site. Who are you really?"

Lord sighed. "Oh, very well. I am actually a traveler through space and time. I came here in the hopes of securing whatever caused the destruction of this community for myself. I believe that it could be a very useful weapon."

Lord gave Flynn a genuine smile. He so seldom had occasion to tell the plain truth that the found the experience refreshing in its novelty. He calmly waited for the Captain to start his inevitable sputtering protests of disbelief. To his surprise, Flynn merely looked thoughtful.

"I wonder what the Doctor would make of all this," Flynn said softly.

Lord suddenly felt nauseous. "The Doctor?" he said. "Doctor who?"

"Oh, no one you would know."

"Don't be so sure," Lord said. He found himself glancing around nervously. *Damn the man!* he thought. *It would be just like him to show up now! Must he dog my steps everywhere I go?*

His agitation did not go unnoticed by Flynn. "What's got you so worried all of a sudden?"

"I'm not worried about a thing! Tell me, is the Doctor here? If he is, I would certainly like to see him. We happen to be old friends."

Flynn lowered the pistol slightly. "I don't think we're talking about the same man."

Lord believed they were. "Tall fellow?" he said. "White hair? Bit of a dandy?"

Flynn smiled, and the pistol fell a little lower. "That *does* sound like him. Although I don't know about the hair. He was always wearing a turban."

*A turban?* Lord thought. *How gauche!* Truly there was no limit to the Doctor's affectations. No doubt this impertinent twit was one of his so-called "companions." Well, Lord would soon be rid of him. If the fellow would just let that pistol drop a little more…

"Unfortunately, I haven't seen the Doctor since I was just a little boy," Flynn said, "but I would give just about anything to have him here now."

"As would I," Lord said, his hand inching toward his pocket.

"I wonder if that's true. He didn't seem like the sort of man who would associate with guys trolling time and space for weapons from Mars."

"Mars?" Lord said. "Why do you say that?"

173

"There's a man in the cells who claims that there's a space-ship from Mars in the bottom of the mine."

"That can't be right. It would be impossible for…"

"For what?" Flynn prodded.

Lord, intrigued by this new wrinkle, temporarily forgot his murderous impulses. "Can you take me to this man? I would very much like to speak to him."

"Why not?" Flynn said. "You're going to a cell anyway."

Leo sat cross-legged on the floor of the cell. His eyes were closed, his breathing slow and rhythmic, his focus turning ever inward. The clawing had faded, becoming more weak and tentative.

The storm was coming. He could sense it. He had been overtaken by it once before, many years ago, but it wouldn't happen again. *I'm ready for you this time*, he thought. *I know how to fight you, how to resist you. I won't let you use me again.*

"Open your eyes, my good man," someone said. "You and I need to talk."

Leo, masking his anger, looked up to see an imperious little man glaring down at him. He was surprised to note that the man was being held at gunpoint by Flynn.

"Do I know you?" Leo asked

"Call me Lord. Why did you say the object in the mine was a ship from Mars?"

"Because it is."

"How would you know?"

"I've said all I'm going to say. Please leave me alone."

Lord clenched his teeth, and Leo suddenly felt as if his skull were enclosed in a hand of iron. "You most certainly have *not* said all you are going to," the man sneered. "In fact, you are going to tell me everything I want to know. Isn't that right, my good man?"

The hand squeezed. The fingers punched through the bone and into the brain beneath. The tip of each finger sprouted 1000 writhing tentacles that snaked through his mind, encircling his will, binding it to that of the man called Lord.

"Isn't that *right*?"

The tentacles pulled themselves taut, and Leo became a puppet. "What...do you want...to know?" he said in a halting voice. He fought against every word, but his tongue refused to obey.

"Again, why did you say it was from Mars?"

"I saw one there."

"That's ridiculous. Admit that you're lying!"

"No! I lived there! I had a wife...children...There was an entire colony! Oxus and the others...they discovered some ruins near the settlement. There was a ship there. Oxus believed it had been built to travel to the Earth. He translated some documents that were found at the site. He said that the Ancient Martians were...that they were..."

"Go on."

"They were experimenting on humans. Trying to affect how human life would evolve. He said that, if he were right, it could mean that a portion of the human race carried a Martian strain in their genetic code."

"He sounds like a very imaginative fellow. What became of him?"

"He was killed."

"How?"

"He thought that it would be possible to reactivate the devices on the ship...learn their secrets. But when he tried...the ship took on a life of its own. It released an energy wave that...that..."

"Stop stammering! What did it do?"

"It awakened the Martian strain! It was some sort of race memory. Everyone who carried the taint inside them was driven to kill everyone who didn't."

"An ethnic cleansing."

"Yes, and they manifested abilities that gave them the power to do it."

"Abilities?"

"Yes, yes, mental powers...telekinesis. In the end, it was too much for those affected. Their hearts began to burst, but not before they had killed...they killed..."

"Why is there no record of these events?"

"There is, but it was passed off as an exaggeration of one my adventures. I went back to Mars years later and personally destroyed every trace of the colony...razed it to the ground...I didn't want anyone to ever know the truth..."

"Why not? What are you not telling me?"

"No...please...I can't..."

*"What are you not telling me?"*

Leo cried out and clutched his head. Some of the tentacles in his brain began to burn white hot. They lashed about, and then plunged down, down, down into the depths of Leo's mind, melting their way through every barrier, every defense. They came to the thing, the thing that had been burrowing so fiercely into the safety of the darkness. It redoubled its efforts to escape, digging furiously but to no avail. The tentacles leapt forward, ensnared it, and dragged it wet and red and screaming into the light.

"That's enough," Flynn said.

Lord gave him a fiery glance. "Why don't you let me be the judge of that?"

"I've given you too much of a free hand already. What did you do to him? Some kind of hypnosis?"

Lord was about to answer when he was cut off by a moan from the cell. The two men turned to see Leo, his features twisted into a rictus of agony, tears streaming down his face. His mouth worked, and a choked whisper escaped from his lips.

"What?" Lord said, impatiently. "What are you saying? Speak up!"

"I killed them," Leo gasped.

"Whom did you kill?"

*"The children."*

Flynn felt the blood drain from his face. He suddenly became aware of how quiet it was in the jail. All of the other prisoners were silent as stones. He knew they couldn't see what was happening, but they could hear. He felt as if they were all standing beside him, crowding at his shoulder, staring down at this piteous man. From the corner of his eye he saw Stuart, awake now, and a giant of a man who looked back at him accusingly. *Why don't you stop this?* he seemed to be saying.

"It took control of me," Leo continued. "It took over my mind and I...joined in the slaughter. Then I found the children. When I looked at them, all I could see was...that they were *other*. They were not of the *hive*."

"You don't have to talk about this anymore," Flynn said. "You've told us everything we need to know."

"They held up their hands," Leo said, his voice rising. "They cried out to me! Papa, no! Papa, please don't hurt us! *Papa! Papa! Papa!*"

He threw back his head, his body shaking as if battered by tidal waves of grief. "My little ones," he cried. "Oh, God, I'm so sorry. I loved you so much. I...loved...you...so..."

His hands covered his face, and for a terrible moment Flynn thought the man might claw out his own eyes. But he merely held them there, quietly weeping.

"Heracles cursed by Hera," Lord muttered. "Oh well..." He turned to Flynn. "It appears you were right. He has given us everything. We need to get to a radio immediately."

Flynn opened his mouth to ask why, but didn't bother. He already knew the answer. "You've sent everyone to the mine, haven't you?"

"I think it would an excellent idea to recall them. Wouldn't you agree?"

Then they heard the roaring. The cells erupted with screams. Entreaties to God and cries of "not again!" began to fill the air.

"Has someone restored power at the mine?" Stuart was shouting. "For God's sake, shut it off!"

"I really don't think there's any time for that," Lord said. He looked at Flynn. "We need to make good our escape before any of your fellow soldiers…" He fell silent and cocked his head, listening to a crackle of gunfire, followed by a series of explosions. Lord shook his head ruefully. "Too late," he said. "It would seem that some of the men have gotten in touch with their Martian heritage."

"Thanks to you," Flynn snarled. Lord's only reply was an infuriating smirk. Flynn, overcome with anger, made the fatal mistake of stepping within Lord's reach, thus giving him the opportunity he had been waiting for. He lunged forward and smashed the palm of his hand into Flynn's jaw even as his other hand deftly plucked the pistol from his grip.

Flynn's vision went black for the briefest of instants, then he found himself looking up from the floor into the barrel of his own gun.

"Goodbye, Captain," Lord said pleasantly, and then he disappeared into an explosion of dust and metal. Flynn, thoroughly confused but glad to be alive, rose to his knees to see Lord lying unconscious under a cell door which had been blown off its hinges.

The shouting in the cells reached a fever pitch of hysteria. *It's one of them! Get us out of here! Get us out!*

"Professor!" Stuart yelled. Flynn turned and saw Quatermass walking toward him through the billowing clouds of dust. His eyes were glazed and his jaw was slack.

*He's in the grip of it*, Flynn thought. *He'll kill everyone here if I don't stop him!* He saw the gun lying where Lord had dropped it. He leapt for it, but it suddenly flew out of his reach. Hanging in the air, it turned and pointed itself at his head…and was snatched away by an intervening hand even as it fired, sending a bullet harmlessly into the wall.

For a fraction of a second, Flynn was able to look into the burning eyes of the man who had saved him. "Thanks," he said to Leo.

The Nyctalope did not reply. He turned and violently slammed Quatermass into the back of the cell. "Who are you?" he thundered, his face only inches from the Professor's. "Tell me your name!"

Debris from the shattered entrance to the cell began to rise from the floor and fly through the air at Leo. Pieces of stone, wood, and metal smashed into his back and head, but he refused to let go.

"If you don't fight it now, it's going to kill you! Fight it, damn you! You're not an insect in a hive! You're a man! Fight it! Tell me your name!"

Blood began to run from lacerations in Leo's scalp, dripping into his eyes. He was being stoned like St. Stephen, but he refused to let go.

"*Tell me your name!*"

"I...I...am...Bernard...Quatermass..."

"*Say it again!*"

"I am...Bernard Quatermass of...of the British Experimental Rocket Group!"

"*Again!*"

"I am Professor Bernard Quatermass, and I am...I am a man!"

"Yes," Leo said. "Yes, you are."

The stone and metal rain suddenly stopped. Quatermass fell forward, but Leo caught him and guided him to a bunk.

"Dear God," Quatermass whispered. "It was horrible. I saw myself as..."

"I know what you saw, and how you felt," Leo said, "but it is over now."

The Professor's eyes widened. He looked around in a sudden panic. "Oh, no! Was anyone hurt? Did I...?"

"No," Leo said. "You will not have to live with that."

A shadow fell over them and they turned to see Flynn. "Is he going to be all right?"

"As well as can be expected," Leo replied.

"What do we do now? Should I let everyone go? I can hear the gunfire getting closer."

Leo listened for a moment to the cries of the hysterical survivors. He thought of the two children, the boy and the girl. Would they be able to escape before the deranged soldiers caught them? "No," he said, "they're safer here." He looked at the opposite cell. "Stuart, can you get me to that mine? Show me the way to that damned ship?"

The scientist nodded.

Leo turned to Flynn. "Do you have any explosives?"

Before the Captain could answer, the giant in Stuart's cell spoke up. "There's dynamite at the mine."

"How much?"

"More than enough for what you have in mind."

Leo nodded. "What's your name, my friend?"

"They call me Big John."

"They have a knack for understatement." He looked at Flynn. "Let them out," he said. "They're both coming with me. With any luck, some of your unaffected comrades will have escaped and will be heading back here."

"But what if..."

"Stop wasting time!"

They commandeered a "deuce-and-a-half"—a big 6X6 GMC troop carrier—which roared through the streets like a prehistoric beast, smashing with impunity through any obstacles they couldn't avoid. Leo was driving, with Stuart sandwiched uncomfortably between him and Big John.

"How far to the mine?" Leo asked.

"We should be there in about five minutes," Big John said. "Just stay on this main road, then you'll turn left in a couple of miles."

They passed a jeep that was racing in the opposite direction. Leo thought he recognized Vincenzo at the wheel. A moment later, two more trucks went by them.

"Those men," Stuart said, "the ones we just passed, do you think they're under the influence of..."

"No," Leo said. "If they were, they would be on foot."

There was a brief silence, then Stuart asked: "How are you resisting it?"

"With great difficulty."

Leo hit the brakes and the men slammed forward into the dash. A line of soldiers was standing across the road. They were staggering forward in a clumsy but deliberate march, their arms stretched stiff at their side.

Leo muttered a curse and pressed the accelerator, leaving the road and plunging into the rock-strewn sands of the desert.

"Why didn't you just go through them?" John asked.

"I have enough blood on my hands," Leo said. "I don't want any more, at least not tonight."

John nodded and pointed at a dim, flickering illumination in the middle distance. "Keep this thing pointed at that light," he said. "That's the mine."

The light flickered out. "What just happened?" Stuart asked.

"The generators are probably blown," John said.

"No more power," Stuart said. "That's a good thing, right?"

"It depends," John said. "If you think you can shimmy down 300 feet of elevator cable in pitch dark to get to Main Level Two, then it's great! That's not even considering getting down the winze to the drift exploration, which is where we need to set the charges."

They closed the distance to their destination without further conversation. The ride over the rough terrain was difficult, but Leo was a skillful driver and they arrived quickly. It took John only a few minutes to gather the explosives and lead them to the lift entrance.

"I could only find one helmet that didn't have the lamp blown out," John said. He held out his hand. "Well, gents, this is where we part ways."

"What do you mean?" Stuart asked. "We're going with you!"

"Like Hell you are," John said. "I know you've been down there before, Stuart, but you had more than just a safety lamp for illumination." He tapped the helmet. "If this light goes out, then what? You won't be able to find your own ass, much less an exit."

"I could do it," Leo said.

John shook his head. "How? Can you see in the dark?"

Leo smiled.

"Forget it, pal," John said, not unkindly. "This is a one-way trip, and I'm the only one here qualified to take it. Don't lose any sleep over me. I've always known that one day I was gonna die in a mine."

"Maybe so, but not today," Leo said, and he ended the argument with an uppercut to John's jaw that actually lifted the big man off his feet before he went crashing to the ground.

Leo turned to Stuart. "I need you to tell me exactly how to find my way through these tunnels to the ship."

Stuart did so, even drawing a map in the dust with his finger. Leo studied it for a moment, asked a couple of questions, and then amazed Stuart by gently lifting John as if he weighed no more than a child. Leo carried the big man back to the truck and then tossed Stuart the keys.

"Get back to the jail and help Flynn," Leo told him. "I can take care of this."

Stuart nodded. "One thing," he said.

"What?" Leo asked.

"Unless they can somehow shake it off, everyone affected by the energy wave dies from heart failure."

"That's appears to be the case."

"Then how did you survive when it took you over on Mars?"

The Nyctalope sighed. "It would seem my heart can survive anything," he said, and he disappeared into the darkness of the mine.

Lord was awakened by the sound of the explosions. They were little more than a rumble of distant thunder, but he was close enough to consciousness that they finished bringing him around.

He blinked a few times. He was surrounded by complete darkness, manacled securely in a reasonably comfortable chair. His first thoughts were of the Doctor. Was he here after all? Had the pompous dolt captured him at last?

He rattled the chains, testing their strength. As if in response to this, a door opened and a blade of light sliced into the room, temporarily blinding him.

A shadow stepped into the door and said, "Welcome back to the land of the living."

Lord recognized the voice. "Hello, Captain Flynn," he said. "Tell me: are we currently under a state of siege?"

"I'm sure you'll be glad to know," Flynn replied, "that Colonel Evans returned safely, along with most of the unaffected men. We were able to defend this building from the others—the ones who fell under the Martian influence—until they...well...until they began to die of their own accord."

"Excellent," Lord said. "The crisis has passed! I suppose it would be too much to ask for you to release me immediately?"

"That depends on you," Flynn said, closing the door and plunging the room back into darkness.

Lord was intrigued. "Do I take it that you're about to make some sort of proposition?"

"You are correct," said Flynn's disembodied voice.

"Pray, do go on," Lord said.

"I don't know if you heard those explosions a moment ago, but it would seem that the man you tortured has succeeded in destroying, or at least burying, the Martian ship. I think it would be best for everyone if it stayed under the ground forever."

"And you believe I can help you with that?"

"I certainly do," Flynn said. He was a little closer now, and Lord was surprised that he had not heard footsteps. "I have seen that you're a man with, shall we say, *influence*. I think you can help me persuade the necessary people that this was a natural disaster brought on by...oh, I don't know...maybe a cloud of toxic gas released from the Earth by digging at the mine?"

"What of the OSI?" Lord asked. "Doctor Stuart has already told them a far different story."

"Stuart wasn't thinking clearly. He was suffering from hallucinations, delusions brought on by exposure to the gas."

Lord chuckled. "No one will believe that fairy tale."

"They will if it's the finding of the Colonel's official report, backed up by the scientific expertise of Professor Quatermass, and the testimony of *every single survivor*."

Lord gave a derisive snort. "My dear Captain, you can't honestly expect me to hypnotize everyone here! Do you have any idea how long that would take?"

"If what you told me earlier is true," Flynn said, "time is the one thing you've got plenty of."

"Very witty," Lord said. "What are you offering me to go along with this absurd scheme?"

"Your freedom," Flynn said. He was almost at Lord's ear. Lord was startled. How could Flynn get so close without him hearing his approach? "I've been thinking about it," Flynn continued, "and I've decided there's really only two ways to deal with you. One is to let you go. If you cooperate, I give you my word I will do exactly that."

"And the other?" Lord said.

He heard a loud click, and felt cold metal press against his temple.

"Do you really have to ask?" Flynn said.

He awakened just before dawn. His eyes fluttered open in time to see the last of the stars fading into the emptiness of the daylight desert sky.

*Still alive*, he thought. *I guess God isn't finished with me yet.*

Slowly, painfully, he rose to his feet and dusted himself off. He surveyed the destruction he had wrought with satisfaction. He had made a good job of it. He only hoped that it would last.

He saw the Sun peeking over the horizon; brilliant bands of orange, yellow and red heralding its arrival. He stood silent and perfectly still as he watched it rise. As the rays washed over him, bathing him in the early morning warmth, he allowed himself to think of things and people that he had not allowed himself to think of for a long, long time. Images danced before his eyes; faithful friends, laughing children.

*I am sorry for denying your memory*, he thought. *I will not do it anymore. I will keep you with me, in my heart, until the day it finally stops beating.*

Then the Nyctalope took a deep breath of the bracing Mojave air, and began to walk toward the light.

*We now turn to the 1920s with a story whose heroine is none other than the Phantom Angel—in reality, Sleeping Beauty awakened by Doc Ardan in the 1920s (see* The Reluctant Princess *in* Tales of the Shadowmen 4). *As was the case with* The Season of the Shark, *the Nyctalope is only peripherally involved in this tale, which is about his future wife, Sylvie MacDhul...*

## Randy Lofficier: *The English Gentleman's Ball*

*Paris, The 1920s*

Once upon a time, she had been called Beauty and had slept for a thousand years. But ever since being awoken, not by a handsome prince, but by a dashing scientist, she was used to being referred to as "The Phantom Angel."

This new, modern world in which she found herself pleased her most of the time. Certainly she realized that the role of women had undergone a drastic change from when she had last been awake in a time of darkness and ignorance.

As the Phantom Angel, she was free to do as she pleased. Go where she desired. Dress as the mood took her. The world was far from a paradise, but it was a vast improvement on what she had known before, even if she had been a princess in those days.

But Angel was not satisfied with her adventures of derring-do; she felt that there should be more to her life on some level, but could not quite put her finger on what that might be. Part of it was the awareness that she was still privileged in comparison to many in this brave new world. Poverty, ignorance and darkness were still out there, but the rich pretended not to see the ugliness in the corner.

Because of her own past, Angel was particularly aware that the lot of women and children still needed great improvement. She knew that she could not save them all, but hoped that she could at least aid a few individuals. Thus she kept her ears open for cases where she could intervene.

Her sources in the Secret Society of Adventurers told her that a Gregor Mac Dhul, a wealthy man with a daughter, had lost his wife in childbirth. He had hired a housekeeper to look after the child, and in the course of time, this woman, Simone Desroches, had become his new wife. What he didn't know was that Simone was in reality the notorious masked criminal known as Belphegor. She had targeted the industrialist to gain access to his fortune.

Because Gregor Mac Dhul traveled frequently, his new wife was often left alone with his daughter, Sylvie. But Simone was not a good mother, nor even a kind woman, and treated the girl as little more than a servant.

To keep Sylvie from telling her father of her treatment, Simone told her young charge that she would kill the Professor if ever he heard a word of the truth.

The Phantom Angel decided that this would be her next "project;" to save Sylvie from her evil stepmother and allow her to step out into the sunlight once again.

Angel tracked down the mansion where Sylvie practically had to clean the cinders from the fireplace in order to earn a meal while her father was away. It was clear that Simone ruled with an iron hand.

The woman once known as Beauty decided to use her contacts to gain an introduction to the household and to see the situation first hand. Because of Simone's desire to flaunt her wealth, it proved an easy task to be invited one afternoon for tea.

Once there, it was clear that the rumors about Sylvie's treatment were accurate. The 17-year-old girl was forced to wait on Simone and Angel, and was barely introduced as "my wretched stepdaughter" before being dismissed back to the kitchens to scrub out pots and pans. Poor Sylvie dared a pleading gaze at Angel, as if begging her for help.

The Phantom Angel was quickly able to turn the conversation to the subject of a lavish ball that was soon to be held by a visiting English aristocrat who had taken up temporary residence in a *hôtel particulier* in the fashionable *Marais* district of Paris. Word had it that his family was eager for him to wed, and had sent him to France to find a suitable candidate; thus all of Paris–the part that counted, at least–had been invited.

Simone was clearly interested in this new "opportunity" to enhance her own wealth. It was obvious to Angel that the evil stepmother was suddenly aware that she had a powerful trump card in Sylvie; for although she treated the girl as a scullery maid, underneath the hand-me-down clothes and ashes was a stunning beauty.

Clearly wanting to get rid of her visitor so that she could further her plot, Simone suddenly claimed a headache and called Sylvie to show her visitor out. Taking advantage of the short time they were able to spend alone, the Phantom Angel whispered: "Don't worry, I'm here to help. Think of me as your fairy Godmother!"

Our heroine was satisfied with the turning of events and began her own plot to save her new-found friend from the clutches of the evil woman who controlled her. Indeed, she immediately went to the very same *hôtel* and knocked at the entrance, where a truly British Gentleman's Gentleman opened the door with great courtesy.

"Are you Monsieur Jeeves?" she asked.

"Indeed I am, Madam," he replied.

"Then it is you I am here to see."

The door closed behind her.

The night of the grand ball arrived, and Simone had worked hard on Sylvie to make sure that the "prize" was secured by her and no other. The young girl looked nothing like a scullery maid and could have been a fairy princess in her exquisite gown and jewels. But her eyes were still sad and she had the air of a rabbit in the snare of a hunter in her manner.

The Phantom Angel, of course, was also at the ball. She nodded towards Sylvie and received a nod of acknowledgment from that most distinguished of valets, Jeeves. What she knew from him, and what no one else present realized, was that Bertram Wilberforce Wooster, the aristocrat in question, had no intention of marrying anyone at the ball, no matter what his family desired. However, as always, he was up for a good time, and the Phantom Angel's plot as recounted to him by his "man" Jeeves sounded as if it would be the highlight of his Parisian visit.

As the evening wore on, the wheels began to turn. Belphegor tried her best to put Sylvie into Bertie's path, but each time something was contrived to interfere. The evil stepmother became more and more frustrated as she had visions of the Woosters' fortune slipping ever farther away. Each time her plot failed she reached for another glass of champagne. Soon it was clear that she was more than a little drunk and she was having trouble controlling her temper. She grabbed hold of Sylvie's arm, her scarlet claws leaving marks on the porcelain flesh and hissed, "Get over there and dance with that man or you'll be sorry!"

That was the moment for the plan to reach its climax. Standing directly behind Simone had been her husband, Gregor Mac Dhul, whom she had been told was on business far, far away. The Phantom Angel had flown her plane to fetch him and Jeeves and Wooster had sequestered him in the house, making sure that each time his wife had threatened or abused his daughter during the evening, he had been in a perfect position to observe her.

"That's enough, Simone!" Gregor cried in anger. "It's clear you're not the woman you pretended to be and it's over. You'll not get another penny from me and you will never come near me or my daughter again!"

Belphegor stared at him in drunken astonishment, then turned to see the Phantom Angel, Jeeves and Wooster watching her in triumph.

Sylvie ran into her father's arms and began to cry tears of happiness as she realized that she was at least free of the evil woman who had ruled her life so cruelly.

Angel turned to her allies, "Gentlemen, you've done a fine thing tonight. I'm afraid, Mr. Wooster, that if word of this gets out, you're reputation as a drone may be damaged forever."

"No fear of that, Madam," said Jeeves. "Mr. Wooster knows precisely how to tell a story so that he is able to continue in his life of pointless pleasure."

"What ho, Jeeves," said Bertie.

And they all lived happily ever after.

*There is nothing like a good Egyptian yarn to evoke images of pyramids, animal-headed gods, tombs hidden in the desert and ancient curses... Following in the footsteps of Talbot Mundy, Sax Rohmer and others, and echoing some of the revelations contained in Emmanuel Gorlier's tales* Fiat Lux! *and* The Three Sisters, *Paul Hugli takes us back to the 1920s—the Nyctalope's greatest era—and the magical land of the Pharaohs in...*

## Paul Hugli: *Death to the Heretic!*

*Egypt, October 1929*

*He's fond of enigmas, of conundrums, of hieroglyphs...*
Edgar Allen Poe
*The Murders in the Rue Morgue*

Ra's Solar Barge had barely begun its journey from the East to the West and, already, the heat was oppressive. Yet that was expected at 8 a.m. just a score miles south of Cairo. Removing his broad-beamed straw hat, Bruce Wayne fanned his face, hoping to cool himself, to shoo away the sandy dust which had caked his sweaty face. He stared at his manic driver, Alfred Pennyworth, man-servant, guardian and oldest friend. The butler was taking the ride all in stride, dressed in an *abayyah*, cloth face mask, goggles and aviator cap. The 1907 Daimler bumped and groaned as it traversed a barely utilitarian desert road. Having spent time in Egypt during the Great War, he knew the proper attire for surviving a motorized jaunt through the desert in an open touring motor-car, although Bruce doubted Alfred had driven such a sporty motor-car during the War to End All Wars.

"Long ways from Gotham, eh, Alfred?" Bruce said, a bit green around the gills, replacing his hat, covering his now dusty jet-black hair, wishing he had listened to his friend: a blue-blazer and white trousers were not proper attire for the open desert. The straw hat was acceptable, but a *kuffryah* was more practical. Next time he would listen to Alfred

Maybe...

"Yes, Master Bruce, a long way from Gotham. A long way from anywhere... civilized, if I may say so," remarked Alfred, as he skirted the motorcar around a flock of sheep and goats without slowing one iota. "It was kind of Mrs. Emerson to loan us his Daimler."

"Yes, kind," Bruce echoed unconvincingly. He had given up trying to read the Cairo daily about reported incidents of "fire-stick robberies" having set it aside to get a better grip on the dashboard—and his nerves. He swore to himself: *When I get back to Gotham, I'm going to sell my Stutz, Ballot, Grand Prix, Hotchkiss, Indian, and DKW, and get a Model A—no a Model T.* His need for speed was sated, thanks to Alfred. Ford used to brag that you could get a Model T in any color—as long as that color was black. *Yes, a black motorcar... nice and safe.*

His thoughts were interrupted when the Daimler hit a pot-hole and bounced. A "Sorry, Sir," from Alfred did nothing for Bruce's nerves.

They came to a rise, and Alfred stopped. In the morning haze—almost mirage-inducing—was the splendor of the Sakkara plain, stretching out before them, majestically littered with ancient burial ruins of rulers and couriers of Egypt's Old Kingdom, dominated by the Step Pyramid of King Djoser, over 4500-years-old, consisting of a series of unequal mastabas stacked atop one another, the world's first large stone structure ever built.

Shifting the Daimler back into gear, Alfred followed the dusty trail into the Saqqara plain and passed the mastabas of brick-sized stones and stone slab ceilings. Bruce pointed out an encampment of tents. Alfred nodded and slowed the motorcar to a reasonable speed, skirting around workers carrying dirt and stone in baskets upon their heads, avoiding scattering geese and chickens, and down-shifting to a safe and successful halt just a few meters from the largest tent, which Bruce surmised was the dig's headquarters.

Exiting the Daimler, the Gothamites adjusted themselves to Terra Firma. Bruce used his hat to swipe the dust from his suit as Alfred removed his scarf and goggles, placing them in his up-turned helmet before tucking it under his arm.

About to make a remark, Bruce was interrupted when a *kuffryah*-covered head popped up out an ancient walkway buried beneath the ground and said: "Thomas?"

"No," Bruce said as the lanky man climbed out of the tunnel.

"Of course, your father, ah…"

"Yes," said Bruce, his face a blank mask.

"Then you must be Bruce," the blue-eyed man said, offering him his hand. "I was sorry to hear of your parents' death. You father was quite generous in funding my research."

"Yes, Doctor Jones. And Wayne Enterprises will continue to contribute to you excavations."

"As long as I get results?" he said with a crooked smile.

Allowing himself a reflective smile Bruce said: "Dr. Jones… Henry, if I may… I read your proposal…"

"Indiana," he interrupted.

"Excuse me…"

"I prefer 'Indiana' or 'Indy.' Dr. Henry Jones *is* my father's name. We are two different persons."

"No doubt, er, Indiana. As I was saying, I read your proposal. A search for the tomb of the legendary—I believe you wrote 'mythical'—Imhotep…" Bruce said with a sweep of his hand, indicating the entire burial complex around them, "the vizier and chief architect of the Djoser Pyramid. If I recall, correctly, he became the patron saint of scribes in Greece, while other cultures consider him the world's first physician. Quite an achievement for one man."

"Yes, indeed," Jones concurred, absently brushing the dust from his *galabeeyah*. "People have fanciful goals and beliefs, searching the world, hoping to verify myths: Noah's Ark, the Ark of the Covenant... or like my father, right now in Alexandria, pouring over Coptic records, believing they will lead him to—of all things!—the Silver Chalice of Christ. As I said: fanciful."

"And you are being more factual, searching for Imhotep's Tomb?"

"Actually," Indy smiled, "that and his Ibis Stick. Empowered by Thoth, himself, it is said."

"Empowered to do what?"

"According to legend, the Stick possesses the power to levitate gigantic building stones, like those used here and later at Gizah... that the wane could create city-wide force-fields, and cause images to appear and disappear at will."

"I see. Nothing fanciful."

"No," Indy answered with a straight face.

"Master Bruce," Alfred voice filtered into Bruce's consciousness before the latter could ask a follow-up question relating to Jones' quest, and turned to his friend, who added: "If you are not presently occupied, I have a gentleman who wishes to meet you."

"I shall be there momentarily," Bruce said, turning back to Indy to say they would talk later.

Entering the excavation's main tent, he spotted Alfred standing next to a tall, handsome man, with a timeless quality about him. "Master Bruce, may I introduce you to Monsieur Leo Saint-Clair."

"It's an honor, Monsieur," Bruce said in stilted schoolbook French.

Saint-Clair smiled, wondering again why Americans always felt it necessary to tell a person they are honored to merely meet him? He shrugged it off; he should be used to it by now.

"Leo and I have been chatting-up old times, and I am at liberty to inform you of his true identity and work," Alfred stated as he poured tea. The three men had settled in canvas camp chairs. The butler filled his employer in on some of his adventures during the Great War, dealing with a score of espionage missions with the Frenchman. Bruce was amazed, but not surprised.

The whole time, he studied Saint-Clair: medium-height, quite broad-shouldered and thick-chested, a handsome man with striking, penetrating greenish-blue eyes which reminded him of the almost hypnotic eyes of a pilot named Allard he had met once. Bruce had to break his glance; the man seemed to have the ability to force his personality on others...

"Are you aware of a Doctor Hugo Strange," Saint-Clair began, after a sip of tea, "formerly employed by Wayne Enterprises? And a Professor William Omaha McElroy, who is funded through the Wayne Foundation's Oriental Studies Museum?"

"Yes, of course," Bruce replied cautiously. Even before reaching his majority—and inheriting 51% of the vast Wayne holdings—he has tried to keep current with the running of the vast empire. With the help of advisors and, of course, Alfred Pennyworth.

Wayne Enterprises, in conjunction with Wentworth Works, sponsored Hugo Strange's experimental research into the practical applications of "concentrated light," based on work theorized by Nikola Tesla. The goal: a polyphase system to power and direct an elevated monorail through Gotham City. By the end of the project's first year, the outlook had been promising. Yet, clandestinely, Strange had adapted the polyphase system into a primitive "ray gun"—like something out of *Amazing Stories*—and embarked on a crime spree. He was eventually defeated and imprisoned, but his invention and research papers had been destroyed in the process.

"Yes," Bruce repeated, studying the Frenchman: there was something about his eyes... something he couldn't put his finger on... "Yet, how does Strange tie-in with Professor McElroy? Sure, he's a little eccentric..."

McElroy had recently been referred as the "Tut Nut," due to his almost fanaticism over the Boy King—especially since Howard Carter's discovery of the almost intact tomb of Tutankhamun seven year before—and total antipathy toward his predecessor, King Akhenaten, the "Heretic." A dreamer or a madman, Akhenaten had erected his capital city half-way between Memphis and Thebes, and upset the *ma'at* (The Divine Order of Things) by elevating his personal God, the formally obscure solar disc Aten, to the One and Only, outlawing the worship of *all* other gods and goddesses. And the Glory which was Egypt was in jeopardy. The "renegade" king was disposed of, Tutankhamun was elevated to Pharaoh, and the priesthood was restored. Alas, the damage was done and—except for the reigns of Seti I and Ramses II forty years later—Egyptian known-world domination had ebbed, soon to be over-run by a succession of foreign powers.

This much Bruce had learned from reading abstracts from papers presented to Wayne's Oriental Studies Museum, and also that—even though he felt antipathy toward the "heretic"—McElroy was preparing to resume digging at Tell el Amarna, looking for evidence that Tutankhamun had resided there before becoming king and returning the capital to Thebes. Bruce believed that the professor was a professional, and that he put his science before his personal beliefs.

Leo Saint-Clair listened, nodding, noting a slight hesitancy when the young American mentioned Howard Carter. A look from Alfred confirmed the Frenchman's thoughts of Bruce's parents' relationship with the Carter dig and their...

"In fact," Bruce said, "my next planned stop is Amarna. I still don't see how Professor McElroy figures in your scheme of thing... with Dr. Strange."

Leo smiled at the American's naiveté, his inability to connect the dots. He had found that most, if not all, opinionated intellectuals are blinded by their own brilliance, failing to see any other interpretation or even consider other facts, even to the point of falsification and open hostility to any opposition. And the Frenchman's file on McElroy had been getting thicker by the day, especially his rants since the opening of the Boy King's tomb, and his questionable activities. This young man Wayne didn't realize how much in the dark he was… as blind as a bat…

"You will not find Professor McElroy at Amarna, nor anywhere near," Leo said matter-of-factly.

"What?" Bruce said incredulously. "But I received a cable from him… just before we set sail from America."

"Perhaps…"

"A forgery?" Alfred offered.

"Or a ruse," the Frenchman replied.

"But why?" Bruce was confused.

"To deceive you. To make you believe he was going to the dig, so you wouldn't become suspicious of his actions. He didn't figure on your trip to Egypt."

"Why? What's he hiding?"

"For one thing, we believe he's trafficking in illegal antiquities. Most notably, a suspicious group of pillow-shaped clay tablets from the razed administration office of King Akhenaten at Amarna have appeared on the market. Also, a brown quartzite bust of Nefertiti… not as fine as the limestone bust in the Berlin Museum, but valuable, nevertheless. Your McElroy has been raising a great deal of money."

"For what? He never struck me as a greedy man. Oh, of course, in a scholarly way… always promoting himself. For the fame. But never for financial gain."

"It's always about money," Leo said to Bruce, a young man who never had to worry about where his next meal—or million—would come from; in fact, the whole Tut-mania and talk of a curse was nothing more than greed. "In answer to your question, I believe that McElroy has been trafficking in antiquities to finance the construction of a polyphase weapon based on Dr. Strange's designs. That, in some manner, he has obtained copies of Strange's supposedly destroyed blueprints."

Bruce's head was swimming. "You believe McElroy has perfected Strange's device, and that he's using it here, in Egypt?"

"There has been *fahddling*—rumors—of 'fire-sticks' in the outlining villages, of the Fire of the Prophet."

"Yes," Bruce said with a glance at Alfred, who just lightly traced the edge of his mustache. "On the way out here, I saw a mention of this in the newspaper. An Anubis Gang, if I'm not mistaken… Strange's polyphase device?"

"It would appear." Leo paused for a sip of tea. "And we have a lead."

"I want in," Bruce said without thought.

Getting a glance from Leo, Alfred said: "Just as I told you: If you tell Master Bruce the whole story, he will want to take part."

"So you did."

They made plans.

Sipping tea, Bruce watched the Great War veterans discuss old times, old adventures. Yet, he couldn't help thinking that, at the turn of the last century, the British (especially under Admiral Horatio Nelson at the misnomer "Battle of the Nile") had defeated Napoleon's forces. Not too far from where Bruce sat, a treaty was signed, in which the 167 French *Savants* were forced to cede to the British their collection of antiquities, including the Rosetta Stone; though the British had showed some magnanimity: they had allowed the French to keep their animal collection and plant pressings.

The world has come a long way, but in other ways, it was drifting apart…

Ra's Solar Barge had settled in the West long ago as the trio made their way pass the Giant Sphinx, beyond the Great Pyramid of Khufu, and in amongst the tombs of pre-Empire Egypt. Leo Saint-Clair and Bruce Wayne were dressed entirely in black, and as point-guard was Indiana Jones, dressed in tan slacks, bomber jack and brown fedora. Coiled on his belt was a bull-whip; holstered on his hip a Welby Mark VI .455 pistol.

"You appear prepared, Indy," Bruce whispered, nodding at Indy's bull-whip and pistol.

"I was a boy scout."

"I never had the time."

Indy nodded. "Plus, the tomb might have snakes. I hate snakes."

"I feel the same about bats."

"Great, kid. Snakes and bats just love dark, warm places. Like tombs." He shrugged. "We're OK on scorpions, right?"

Though Bruce hated being called "kid," he had to grin at Indy's obviously sardonic remark and turned his attention to Saint-Clair, who led in only the ambient light of a waxing moon, without the benefit of a map or of an electric torch (almost as if he could see in the dark), appearing to know where he was going, even if he and Indy were constantly tripping over every tiny rock or stone in their path.

Perhaps what Alfred had told Bruce was true. He was The Nyctalope, the champion of the French Republic and its waning Colonial powers. The reality of the man was fantastic enough, but then, there were the rumors that he could see in the dark, that he had an artificial heart, was perhaps immortal... Yet, the man leading them looked no more than 30, at the most, and, save for his uncanny eyes and obvious strength, there was nothing to suggest he was any sort of *ubermensch*. No doubt, like Lawrence of Arabia, there was some exaggeration at play. The public did love to embody its mystery men with almost superhuman abilities, and no doubt Saint-Clair used that to his advantage. Then, again, Alfred himself had been known to exaggerate, especially over late-night milk and cookies in the kitchen when his master was younger.

"We're here," Saint-Clair said *sotto*, coming to a stop. His intrepid companions managed not to bump into him.

"You sure?" Indy asked, studying the structure as best as he could in the dim light. It was an offering niche with a statue of the deceased. "Doesn't look like much. In fact, it looks just like all the others we've passed."

Without comment, the Frenchman pushed against a stone slab and it swung inward on silent hinges, revealing nothing. Just blackness. Or so it seemed to the Americans. The Nyctalope's eyes adjusted to shifting shadows, the lights and darks and grays, searching the heat emulations for any hidden traps, literal pit-falls. His intelligence had been accurate: there were none.

Satisfied it was safe to proceed, Leo motioned for his companions to follow, switching on a mini-torch to lead the way.

"Let us proceed… vigilantly," he said.

The passageway was of claustrophobic granite. Yet, the two older men proceeded unfettered as if it was a walk in the park. *Perhaps it was, to them*, Bruce thought. Fortunately, his fear of enclosed space was cured some years back, after a fall into a cave on the manor's back lot. He noted that there were no bats here, or snakes… with probably put Indy at ease.

The Nyctalope's eyes detected heat registers and followed them south, which brought him to a chamber, the interior naked light flickering on the passageway's stone walls. He motioned for his companions to halt. A quick glance revealed a long, rectangular altar, piled high with a cornucopia of electrical and mechanical parts, dominating the chamber. Also he saw the backs of three burnoosed men hunched over what appeared to be a set of blue-prints. Turning to warn his companions, he realized it was too late, even before Indy whispered: "What do you see?"

The answer to his question was obvious when the three burnoosed men turned and ran at the intruders, screaming: "*W'Allah*! *Ferenghi*!" [By God! Foreigners!]

The *ferenghi* reacted.

Quickly, Leo stepped to the side and brought down his hand against a man's carotid, dropping him to his knees. Bruce was backed up against a wall, his fists balled at his sides, trying to remember everything boxing champ Ted Grant had taught him in the sparring ring. His fist shot out, landing a haymaker across his attacker's jaw. But the man did not go down. He just grinned at the young American, trying to shake the sting from his bruised knuckles. Gloves were preferable to bare knuckles, but he had to make due with what God had given him. Still shaking his fist as the man grinned and inched forward in a hunch, Bruce forcefully brought up his steel-toed booth and rammed it into his attacker's jaw, sending him into a back flip.

Indy was making headway with his attacker until Bruce's henchman slammed into the back of the archeologist's opponent, propelling both men into Jones, sending them all to the hard stone floor, in a snarl of arms and legs. In the entanglement, a hoodlum got the upper-hand on Indy, grabbing his Mark VI and waving it from one intruder to the next. When he turned to make his escape, a *crack!* echoed through the chamber and the tip of Indy's bull-whip lashed around the man's ankles, crashing him to the floor, dragging the struggling man toward him.

"Here, kid, hold this," Indy said, retrieving his pistol and handing it to Bruce, who wasn't sure what to do with it. Indy hauled the man to his feet and stared into his eyes. "I don't like your looks." Then landed a haymaker across the captive's jaw. As he fell unconscious to the stone floor, Indy shook his pained fist. "Ouch! That hurts."

""I could've told you that," Bruce said, grinning.

"Thanks, kid," Indy replied without conviction.

The three burnoosed goons were bounded and gagged; later to be picked up by the proper authorities.

"Hey, kid," Indy said, removing the tarp off an object on the altar, "remember what we said about snakes and bats?" Bruce nodded as Indy continued: "Well, here's the scorpion. I wonder if it has a sting."

"I would say, yes," Saint-Clair said, studying the three-foot long pewter sculpture of a scorpion, with eight-segmented and flexible legs ending in semi-circular claws, which when brought together formed four in-lined lens-holders of diminishing sizes. "No doubt a prototype for a polyphase device. Too bulky for practical use."

"Why the scorpion motif?" Bruce asked, "It seems rather bulky… impractical."

"Who can truly understand the working of the criminal mind?" Saint-Clair said, adding: "Criminals are a superstitious and cowardly lot."

"Perhaps to strike fear into the hearts of men?" Bruce offered.

"I think I'll stick to this," Indy opined, patting his Welby.

"Obviously," the Frenchman continued, pointing, "when the claws are brought together and the lens in place, an energy harvester is created."

"Like the Ark of the Covenant is alleged to have been?" Indy asked as he dusted away the dirt and soot from the wall hieroglyphs, studying them.

"Yes, but impractical," the Nyctalope stated as he unrolled a set of blue-prints. "Now, this is more practical. It explains the 'fire-stick' rumors."

Gracing over his shoulder at the blue-prints, Indiana Jones decided they had no archeological value and went back to the wall. But Bruce was interested in the schematics. He had studied many just like these as he had busied himself over the last few years with the workings of the varied Wayne enterprises, including trying to grasp the scientific implications of a myriad of details. He listened as Saint-Clair indicated the drawing of a long tube, with two trailing wires, labeled "R" (red) and "W" (white) to a bulky metal "nap-sack." A cutaway of the "nap-sack" revealed a series of vacuum tubes, wires and piezoelectric quartz arranged in a zigzag configuration. Flipping through a few more blue-prints, the Frenchman said: "Yes, this design is a polyphase arrangement of noncentrally symmetric crystals."

"And this," Bruce said, jabbing a finger on the diagram, "is based on the work of Dr. Hugo Strange? It doesn't look the same."

"No. It's been adapted, adjusted from linear oscillation. It's an energy harvester similar to the one employed by the Martians, except that those manipulated heat, while this instrument converts mechanical stress into a potential current of electroplasmicized concentrated energy."

"A ray-gun?" Bruce asked, which got Indy's attention.

"A crude analogy, yet correct."

Saint-Clair returned to studying the blue-prints, while Bruce turned to a tap on his shoulder. Indy asked: "Did he say Martians?"

Bruce smiled. "I think he was referring to *The War of the Worlds*. That these 'fire-sticks' or 'ray-guns' are different than the ones in Wells' novel."

"Good. Because I don't want to wake up 30 years from now and find out the Earth has become the playground for space aliens."

"Perhaps they will be benign."

"More likely some super-race with powers and abilities beyond those of mortal men."

"No such thing," Bruce stated plainly, turning back to the altar as the Frenchman ran his finger under the lip of the slab top, an amused look on his face in relation to the Americans' talk of Martians.

Indy returned to studying the tomb's walls, running his fingers along a groove, noting dust and plaster falling away. Removing a knife from his pocket, he opened it, inserted the blade into the cracks and wiggled it back and forth, mostly chipping away ancient dust and plaster. After a bit of work, he was able to dislodge the a two-foot long dried mud-brick, hoping some treasure was hidden behind it—perhaps the Lost Treasure of Khufu.

"Ooophs," Indy said as the brick fell, shattering on the stone floor, alerting Bruce and Saint-Clair, who watched as their colleague bent down, and noted a collection of brownish bones. "What the ...?"

"Frogs," Saint-Clair said, "probably *Bufo regularis*, the common African frog. Thousands of their remains have been found in the ruins of the tombs in this necropolis."

"But blood makes poor mortar," Indy said, shifting through the remains with his forefinger.

"True," Saint-Clair agreed, "but when you had a tight time-table, you just dug in the Nile mud and mixed your mortar with whatever was available."

"So, there *are* skeletons in the old man's closet?"

Saint-Clair remained silent as he turned back to the slab, clicking a button on the underside of the slab. It slid open, revealing a hidden compartment in the base of the altar. On a bed of excelsior were three working models of the polyphase tube devices amongst a dozen six-inch long duo-tapered crystals.

"The polyphase devices," Saint-Clair stated.

"Polyphasers?" Bruce pondered.

"Or, simply, phasers," Indy two-cented.

Bruce was antsy—all but twirling his thumbs—sitting in the relatively posh suite at the Sheperard's Hotel, waiting for information—any information!—dealing with their mid-night jaunt two days ago. Saint-Clair had told him to hold tight, while Indy had added: "Just wait, kid. Don't get cocky." But that was easier said than done. The residue of the adrenaline rush was only now subsiding. It was a feeling like none other. He doubted if he would want to make a career of adrenaline-rushes. Yet, when a resolution was too slow, action was called for…

No, that wasn't for him…

….too much night work.

Yet… the waiting….

He picked up his letter of introduction to the Egyptian Minister of Antiquities, written by a colleague of his late father, a Doctor Francis Ardan. But it all became a blur; he couldn't concentrate on the actual reason he was in Egypt: to visit various digs sponsored by the Wayne Foundation's

Oriental Studies Museum and to scope out a few sites—the Gizah Pyramids, Deir de Medina, Luxor, Karnak, the Valley of the Kings, and points in between—the itinerary for the Grand Prize Winner of the Foundation's "See the Pyramids Along the Nile" contest celebrating the opening of a new wing to the OSM.

Just being in Egypt had taken a great deal of courage on Bruce's part. Seven years ago, he had been there with his parents, right after Howard Carter had revealed the "wonderful things" contained within the tomb of Tutankhamun. As wealthy Patrons of the Arts, his parents had toured the cramped chambers of the Boy King. Bruce was denied entrance. Carter explained that he was too young—just passed his 13th birthday—even though many of the *fellahin*, the workers, were barely out of their nappies themselves. What happened a few months later still sent a chill up his spine…

Yet he wouldn't—couldn't—just sit around and wait for something to happen; he had to get out in the world and hopefully make it happen. Was that being cocky?

"I'm going out, Alfred." Bruce decided. "Sit by the telephone… in case we get a call."

"Very well, Sir," Alfred replied, helping the young man into the jacket of his European white silk business suit, dusting off his broad shoulders with a whiskbroom. "Mustn't have you appear untidy in public."

"Yes, Alfred. Though I doubt my shoulders will be clean once I step outside the hotel," he said, pulling on his cuffs,

"Alas…"

Bruce eschewed the easy walk to the Red Light District, proceeding to the Khan el Khakili, dodging the hectic traffic of motorcars, camels and mules, carts, and carriages of various shapes and sizes. The smog and stink of dung blended soothingly with the pleasant aroma of freshly-baked bread, which greeted him from all directions as he strolled through the *souk*, causally stopping here-and-there to take in the multitudes of shops selling fabrics and rugs, *autika*, drinks and fruits, geese and ducks. Historic mosques, facades and fountains surrounded the young American, the enormousness of it all made it difficult to concentrate.

A few steps further down the mall, Bruce picked up a cat figurine of the goddess Bastet when he felt a tug on his sleeve. Turning he saw a raggedly boy's face as dirty as his linens, who he figures was just asking—begging?—for *baksheesh*.

"Many pardons, *sahib*, you are Master Wayne?" the boy said politely. Bruce nodded and the boy handed him a note. Unfolding the note Bruce read:

*Mr. Wayne,*

*You were not at the hotel so I sent this runner to find you and deliver this message. We have found a clue to the problem facing us. Meet us in the Abbasia Quarter. The boy will lead you.*

*Dr. Jones.*

"Lead away," Bruce said with a sweep of his hand. Tucking the note in his pocket, he followed the boy weaving in and out, ducking under, almost losing him here and there, but managed to keep up, even though something was nagging in the back of his brain. What was in the Abbasia Quarter indeed? Only military barracks and an insane asylum, if he remembered his *Baedeker* guide correctly. Like Arkham back home?

While in his thoughts, Bruce lost the boy and stopped, looked around. Then the boy popped up and waved. "Over here, *sahib*. This way."

Rounding the corner he found himself in a long, narrow alley way—or was it a street? Alone. The boy was nowhere in sight. The hairs on the back of his neck began to tingle. That was what had been bugging him: he had been set up, sent on a wild goose chase, but by whom? And why?

Turning back Bruce froze.

Blocking the entry to the street were two large men, muscles upon muscles, dressed in priest kilts, sandals and colorful papier-mâché masks: hawk-headed Horus and ibis-headed Thoth. Each hefted an apparently hollow six-foot long tube, attached to wires leading to a metal case on the backs.

But—of more direct importance to Bruce—the tubes were aimed at him.

It had been a trap. The note from Indy, a fake. If truly from Indiana Jones, it would've be addressed to "kid," nor "Mr. Wayne," and signed "Indy," not Dr. Jones. First, the false telegram from Professor McElroy before leaving Gotham, and now…

Too late…

Turning round, Bruce dashed down the alley, weaving to and fro, stopping and starting as best he could through the narrowness, as beams of concentrated light flashed, tearing chunk of debris from the mud-brick walls, vaporizing the chips into exploding dust, to rain down upon the fleeing American.

Zig… Zag…

His legs pumped. His muscles burned up lactic acid, fatiguing them. Breathing came fast, in huffs and puffs. Primitive instincts had reacted to the influx of adrenaline, and he unconsciously took the "L" passageway.

A mistake. It was a dead end…

All that flashed through his mind as he turned, his back to the wall, was Indy's reprimand: *Don't get cocky, kid!* And this was way pass being cocky…

His feet spread. His fist balled. He waited tensely as the two "demi-gods" leisurely walked towards him. They had been playing with him like a cat with a mouse, knowing his prey was trapped, just waiting to be tortured to death. And they just stood there, holding out their power-sticks. What had Indy called them? Polyphasers? No: *phasers*. That tidbit helped him not at all as the ends of the tubes neared him. Should he charge them? Try his best to make Ted Grant proud? Then, suddenly, Horus and Thoth stopped and parted like the Red Sea, allowing a jackal-headed Anubis to step between them, his phaser tube held aloft like Moses' staff. He stepped forward.

Bruce held his ground.

"Well, if it isn't Young Master Bruce," Anubis said, his sarcasm evident as it echoed in the hollow of the mask.

"What's your game, Professor McElroy?" Bruce bravely and boldly said.

"No games."

"But dressing up like a tin-plated god? Why? You had prestige. You were in charge of the Amarna dig. You were…"

"…Nothing!" Anubis/McElroy exclaimed, stamping a gold-gilded sandal on the stone path. "People laughed behind my back! Hell, they laughed to my face!" Bruce knew this was accurate, to a degree, and he understood some of the Professor's anguish, but not his fanaticism: his anti-Akhenaten rants, allowing not a quarter for opposing views. His "my way or the highway" obsession had cracked him. Bruce could see that now. "But…"

"No buts, Mr. Wayne. I will determine what is to be done. And that is the complete annihilation of Akhetaten… of Tel el Amarna."

"It's already in ruins." Bruce tried to reason with this… madman.

"Not completely…yet," McElroy's voiced boomed from beneath the mask.

"What do you mean? Can't we reason…?"

"Shut up!" Bruce could hear Elroy breathing beneath the mask as he continued: "You and your meddling friends have already cost me dearly, robbing me of my only supply of back-up crystals. But not to worry… much. Ha!" He waved his phaser tube. "I can always get more dough… more crystals…"

*So, we did get his back-up supply of crystals*, Bruce thought. Not that that did him any good in his present predicament. Aloud, he tried calmly to ask: "And what do you want with me?"

"Well, I expect you to die, Mr. Wayne."

With that, Anubis drew a pistol from beneath his kilt and fired. A noisome gas sprayed out, engulfing the young American, dropping him coughing to his knees. Before losing full consciousness, he heard Elroy laugh: "But not just yet."

Bats. It had to be bats! These were Bruce's first conscious thought when awakening from the knock-out gas from Professor McElroy's pistol.

Bats.

They seemed to have been his constant companions since childhood. And here the flying mammals—these "overgrown mice"—hung overhead as Bruce's meandering thoughts were suddenly interrupted by the full realization of his predicament, like being rapped on the knuckles by the teacher's ruler when she caught you daydreaming. Not that it had ever happened to him. Not the Kid Genius. The Boy Wonder. Bruce Wayne.

*Yeah, sure...*

His wrists were bound together, the joining leather strap hung over a hook driven into the stone wall above his head, the toes of his boots barely scraping the limestone floor of the cold, damp, swarthy chamber, illuminated by only a burning torch in a sconce. The only sound was that of a ticking clock.

A ticking clock?

The flickering flame's light revealed the clock: the hour hand was near 12 as the second hand sweep past it and the minute hand jumped a notch towards denotation time. High noon? High midnight? The clock mechanism was attached to a blasting cap wired to a small stick of dynamite atop a large wooden barrow, with fading red letter: $NH_4NO_3$. Fertilizer, ammonium nitrate. With the added phosphorus and nitrogen in the bat guano when ignited the tomb would go up like Krakatoa...

*Tick...Tock...Tick...Tock...*

"Monsieur Saint-Clair... Leo," Alfred said anguishly into the telephone, "I am worried about Master Bruce..."

"Did you manage to plant...," Saint-Clair said, his last words indecipherable due to the poor connection.

"Yes," Alfred replied, guessing the answer to the Nyctalope's unheard question.

"Fine. Then, don't worry, Pennyworth. We'll find him."

"I'm coming with you."

209

"Of course."

The minute hand clicked nearer 12 as the second hand continued to sweep.

Breathing in deeply and slowly, Bruce pressed his shoulders against the damp stone wall, bracing himself, willing his legs up to a "L" with the wall. His hands gripped around the hook nailed into the wall, his biceps bulging. Steadily, he commanded his stressed, spasmodic, oxygen-starved muscles to perform beyond impossibility as his legs inched higher, until the toes of his boots where over his head.

He allowed himself a brief second rest...

*Tick...*

...then, with all his fortitude, the toes of his boots pushed up and off the wall. The leather strap binding him wiggled, pushed up...

*Tock...*

...and off the hook. He came crashing down.

*Tick... Tock... Tick...*

Though dazed, Bruce managed to stumble to his feet and rush towards the barrel of nitrate, grabbing for the clock, and tripped...

An elderly—but spry—couple, dressed for the desert heat, walked around a couple huge boulders, a destination in mind.

"It has been a while since we visited *his* tomb," she said.

"Yes," he said, his voice booming. "It's about time we paid our respects, though one wonders where the old boy *himself* may be."

"An enigma in his own time, and still remains one."

"You and your romantic novels."

Stumbling over a discarded piece of masonry Bruce managed to catch himself before falling. He closed his eyes and inhaled and exhaled a couple time, calming himself, and finally...

*Tick... Toc—*

...grabbed the clock and ripped it from the blasting cap in mid-tock. The explosion had been averted. Sinking to the cool stone floor, Bruce stared at the clock in his shaking hand. He had 15 seconds to spare. Hardly exciting...

Then the flickering torch went out.

"We're here," the lady archeologist said to her husband, from under her parasol.

"Let's see if anyone's home," the man said with his tra-demarked riotous laugh, flicking on his electric torch.

Then—as if in direct action to the light—a thundering bawl of high-pitch screeches pieced the air.

A dozen... a score... a hundred bats shot out of a hole in the hill. Flying, flapping at the archeologists, forcing them to duck, to hold their hats down, to protect their hair. When they looked up they saw a... mirage? A scene from Dante's *Inferno*? No... it was real.

The last of the bats had flown the coop and a man stepped out, his clothes in tatters, his hand groping, finding the side of the tomb's entrance for support. He looked up, smiled.

"Hello, Professor and Mrs. Emerson," he said.

"Ramses... Walter...?" Amelia Peabody Emerson gasped, thinking Bruce was her son.

"Good Gad, Peabody," Radcliffe Emerson exclaimed, calling his wife by her maiden name as he was wont to do.

"This is Akhenaten's tomb?" Bruce asked, rubbing his bruised wrists, brushing bat-ticks off his shoulders. Bruce had read Emerson's definitive work on the subject: *Excavation at the City of Akhetaten*.

"Yes, my boy," replied Emerson, slapping the young man on the back, almost wounding Bruce further. "Yes, in-deed."

As the Emersons and Bruce trudged through the arid, barren and crack-potted wasteland towards the ruins of Akhe-taten—el Amarna—the American filled them in on the activi-ties of Professor McElroy--"crackpot" was the kindest thing Emerson had to say about his fellow colleague—the Anubis

Gang, the bomb and his escape from the former tomb of King Akhenaten.

When the light had flickered out, he had followed the fleeing bats through the tomb complex as they were activated by the blowing of his Galton or Dog Whistle. The supersonic sound had driven them... "batty," as Peabody joked.

Coming out of the desert, they walked along the ledge running in front of the series of tombs hewed into the cliff wall for the wealthy and courtier of the ancient capital of the 18th Dynasty's so-called "heretic."

Passing one tomb, Bruce saw a man and he froze. Then he chided himself. It was only his own reflection in two highly-polished dressing mirrors, each six-foot tall and three wide, set on bass rollers. Emerson explained he used the mirrors as light sources while working in the tombs, to eliminate the damage caused by the pollutants released by magnesium flares and common fire torches, which further contributed to the deterioration of already fragile artworks. Bruce learned, also, that even human breathing could harm the delicate balance of ancient pigments. Though, these days, archeologists used flashlights and portable battery-powered lanterns, the Emersons still had a fond preference for the old methods, the ones used when they had first met and fell in love.

At the bottom of the ramp leading down from the cliff tombs, they settled under the shade of a canvas umbrella, where Amelia tended to Bruce scraps and scratches, after a drop or two of "medicinal" brandy from the flask attached to her "belt of tools." Bruce admired her belt, how utilitarian it was with its many items: sewing kit, pen and paper, first-aid kit, and other practice items needed on a dig.

As Amelia mumbled something about "another ruined shirt" and made use of cotton swabs, iodine and more traditional alcohol to treat Bruce's wounds, he explained about his adventures during the last three days. The Emersons were especially rattled to learn of McElroy's poaching from the Amarna dig; they believed the past belongs to the present... to Egypt.

Neither of the Emersons mentioned the death of Bruce's parents—seven years back—but since then the Emersons and the Wayne Foundation had been in constant communications, both on a personal and an academic basis, there was no need to go over old ground. Emerson has always "hmph'ed" at the notion of the "Curse of King Tut," claiming that it had nothing to do with his parent's death by a street thug, within months of the Waynes tour of Tut's tomb; that Carter, himself, the Emersons and scores of others were still among the living. That there was no inscribed curse on the entrance to Tut's tomb, but a piece of fiction created by a popular romance novelist: "The kind Peabody reads," he added slyly. Amelia "shushed" her husband, ever if it was true. Bruce, himself, didn't believe in the Curse of King Tut either. Yet...

The mending done, Bruce and the Emersons settled in under the umbrella for tea and scones, perhaps a couple whiskey sours...

*Sizzzzzzzzzzzzzzzzzzzzzzzzzzzzzzzzzzzzzzzz*

The ground at their feet erupted, turning to dusty powder as a ruby-red beam ripped a long, razor-thin trench across the desert floor.

"Hell and Damnation!" Emerson exclaimed, jumping to his feet, knocking over the table in the process.

But ever the "Greatest Egyptologist Who Ever Lived"—in Peabody unbiased opinion—Emerson had to pause, to stop haltingly in his tracks, his face red with anger, his ham-sized fists balled antsily at his waist as he stared at the scene before him.

Anubis stood there like a monolith; his right hand outstretched, gripping the seemingly hollow-tube—the phaser—the business end pointed at Bruce and the Emersons. On either side of him, properly attired in costumes and masked, were Thoth, Horus, Seth and Sobek, each wielding a phaser and power pack.

"I am the Judge," Anubis declared, "and you have all been found guilty of heresy."

"Good Gad," Emerson exclaimed. "Is that you, McElroy? Why the costume? This isn't All Hallow Eve!"

"It *is* the end of October," Peabody offered.

"Hmph," was her husband's reply as he ventured a foot forward. A sizzling swatch across the ground had him rethinking his action.

"Have you nothing better to do than act the fool, Professor?" Bruce chimed in, standing his own ground.

"I thought I might find you here," Anubis/McElroy spat out, "since the destruction of the Heretic's tomb failed realization. I should've killed you before."

Then, a rumbling noise saturated the air. Everyone turned and saw what appeared to be a *simoon*, a desert sand twister, coming straight at them. Closer and faster it came... the dust dissipating... frittering away to reveal:

"That's my Daimler," Emerson huffed out. "And a maniac is driving it!"

The "maniac" was Alfred Pennyworth, decked out in his "touring gear," trying his best to keep the wheels on the ground as Indiana Jones stood haphazardly on the back seat, trying to level his Welby at one—at any!—of the demigods. He quickly gave up, holstering the pistol, grabbing his bull-whip.

The recovered demi-gods swung into action, their phaser-tubes buzzing, zapping, streaming beams of lights flashing through the air like an angry Zeus, but without the accuracy of that god, coming close but missing the zig-zagging Daimler.

The Nyctalope, wearing shaded goggles, stood balanced in the passenger seat, waiting, squaring himself. Then he leapt across the span, plowing into the bodies of Thoth and Horus, crashing them all to the hard dirt in a jumbo of electronics and humanity.

Indy's bull-whip lashed out, wrapping it around Seth's phaser-tube, yanking it out of the hood's hands, sparks flying, as Alfred swerved. Then, a lucky blast of energy hit, evaporating the left front tire, crashing the motorcar to a screeching, dusty halt, jettisoning a unbalanced Indy jetting into the arms of an unsuspecting Seth.

Anubis turned his attention back to his equally stunned captives just in time to see Emerson about to make a jump at him. "None of that, Emerson!"

Stepping back, Emerson snaked a comforting arm around his wife's shoulder, holding her close, though she was itching to bash the Lord of the Underworld wannabe over the head with her parasol, but it had fallen somewhere in the shuffle. Only at a five-foot stature and her Golden Years, Amelia Peabody was a formidable foe… given the right situation and her trusty parasol. Her husband was ever more formidable, given the edge. Yet, now, the phaser-tube was pointed menacingly at them there was little they could do… but bide their time.

In the confusion, Bruce Wayne had disappeared. Anubis almost laughed. He'd always figure Young Wayne a coward at heart. All talk, all hot air. Alas, with all his money Wayne could be anything, anyone he wanted to be.

"Hey, Jackal-Head," a voice bellowed, almost echoing.

Anubis head jerked up, to the source of the voice. High on the ledge fronting the tombs, before one stood Bruce Wayne akimbo. Anubis hissed: "Wayne… you fool… you coward! You think you can escape my wrath… your destiny! By running away?"

"If you want me, you're going to have to come up here," the Gothamite yelled back tauntingly.

Laughter echoed from the hollow of Anubis' Jackal mask. "You fool! I don't have to come up there!" Almost nonchalantly he leveled his phaser-tube at Bruce. "I failed the first time to bury you alive. Another heretic… another Criminal of Akhetaten. This time I will not fail!"

And without further fanfare the megalomaniac fired his weapon at Bruce. A razor-thin ruby-red beam of highly-intense photo-electromagnetism zapped out…

…and almost instantaneously an identical ruby-red razor-thin beam issued from the tomb, sizzling into Anubis' phaser tube, frying, exploding in his hand. In a cry of agony the former demi-god stared at his fried hand, unbelieving, disbelieving.

"How...?" he mumbled.

Emerson answered with a right cross across McElroy's chin, sending his former colleague to his knees; which was fortunate for McElroy because Peabody had found her parasol and had it raised about her head, ready for action.

From the tomb's ledge, Bruce briefly scanned the scene before scrambling down and across the ancient ruins.

Saint-Clair and Indy had been backed into each other as Seth and Horus approached them from either side, their phaser-tube inching toward them. There was no room to use the bull-whip. With their backs together, the Frenchman and the American acted as if they had practiced gymnastic routines together for years as the Nyctalope hooked his elbows into those of Indy and bent forcefully forward, propelling the archeologist up and over the menacing Seth, landing flat on his feet, his whip lashing out, wrapping around the neck of the demi-god, yanking him off his feet. While Saint-Clair, from his bent position, swept a leg around, toppling Horus.

Alfred had scooped up a fallen phaser-tube, twirling it, then stepping forward toward Sobek with an: *en garde!* He stepped forward, lunged, his tube "sword" crashing against his foe's equally unpowered tube with the sounding ring of metal against metal, the *ting* echoing through the air. Parley after parley, the butler countered his opponent and then went on the offensive, wracking Sobek across the knees, crumbling him to the ground. Alfred stepped back. Waited. As Sobek began to rise, Alfred lunged in for the "kill," dropping to one knee, planting the end of the tube into the man's stomach and the other in the ground, pulling backward, lifting up Anubis' hench-god, yanking, tossing him over his shoulder, to crash into the back of Thoth, sending them both into a thud on the ground.

Bruce had rejoined the Emersons and was looking down at the defeated, pitiful McElroy, moaning in agonizing pain. A glance at the Emersons told him they were OK, though Bruce wondered why, after the haymaker punch he had delivered to McElroy's chin, Radcliffe Emerson wasn't tending to bruised knuckles.

"How...?" McElroy mumbled though he pain.

"Something I learned from Houdini," Bruce grinned. "It was done with mirrors."

"The mirrors in the tomb!" Emerson exclaimed, slamming his knee. "Good Gad, Lad! Good work! My boy, Ramses, couldn't have done better."

Bruce acknowledged the praise, then explained. Once McElroy had turned his back on him, he had dashed up to the tomb and swiftly arranged the two tall mirrors at the correct angle, just as if performing a physics experiment at the university. Standing back a half-meter from the left-hand mirror Bruce was reflected into the right-hand mirror, egging on McElroy, giving the illusion that that was where he was standing. When the beam had been fired at that spot, at the "illusory" Bruce, it had hit the first mirror, reflected to the other, then turned back to its original source: McElroy's phaser tube.

Emerson yanked his horrified "colleague" to his feet, shaking him, not caring a wit about the man's injuries, considering the harm he might have caused Amelia. At a loss for words—definitely not a common occurrence for the "Father of Curses"—Emerson shoved McElroy into the waiting hands of Leo Saint-Clair and Indiana Jones, as Alfred finished tying-up the fallen once-but-not future demi-gods.

McElroy hissed: "You haven't heard the last of Professor William Omaha McElroy! No! No! You will—you all will! Bow down to my royal feet! No, you have not heard the last of... King Tut!"

"Hmph," Emerson huffed out.

"I couldn't have said it better," Bruce Wayne said.

"Indeed, my boy," Emerson said, slapping the American on the back and came away with a small metallic rectangle. "What's this?"

"Not a bat-mite, I hope."

"Your post, Sir," Alfred said, setting a silver tray on the desk where Bruce Wayne was trying to put together the finishing touches on the mundane details of his business, here, in Egypt; his *Baedeker* guide book-marked at various entries and fold-out maps. He noticed that, with the mail, was a glass of a clear liquid, ice-floating in the effervescence; he wasn't about to ask Alfred where he obtained the ice cubes.

"What is it?" Bruce asked, picking up the glass.

"A new product, from the States, called Seven-Up."

Bruce tasted the lemony-lime soda, liked it. "This would go well with bourbon."

"I wouldn't know, Sir," Alfred said with the slightest hint of a smile at the corner of his mouth. "With the Prohibition and all."

Bruce grinned and tried to return to his chore, but the adventures of the last three days still jabbed at him. The rush of adrenaline, the "fright, flight or fight" complex, had evaporated. He wondered if he'd ever feel that rush in just that way ever again. Probably not. Just boardrooms and meetings: migraines and ulcers. Plus such adrenaline rushes required too much night work…

Still he considered the people he had met. The Nyctalope had provided Alfred with a tracking device—the "bat-mite" which he had planted on his Master when he had "brushed-off" his shoulders before Bruce went into the Cairo street.

Professor McElroy had been turned over to the Egyptians for questioning in relation to the stolen artifacts; then the "Tut-Nut" would probably be deported to America, for "rehabilitation" at Arkham Asylum.

Dr. Henry "Indiana" Jones, Jr. had decided to leave the Saqqara dig, having received information about the location of something known as the Cross of Coronado, an artifact he has been searching for since he was a youth.

The Emersons continued their vacation at Tel el Amarna, celebrating at the place they had first meet 40 years earlier. Though Radcliffe Emerson was a tad "peeved" at Alfred and Bruce in connection to his damaged Daimler, he promised that he and Peabody would be on hand to help promote the Wayne Foundation's "See the Pyramids Along the Nile" contest tour.

Bruce willed himself back to the task at hand, glancing through the various pieces of mail, all indicating the various subsidiaries of Wayne Enterprises were financially sound, and looking forward to a prosperous new decade.

There was a knock at the door. Alfred answered the call and then appeared before Bruce with another silver tray, a single telegram rested upon it. "A telegram from home, Sir."

"Thank you, Alfred." Opening the telegram he noted it was dated the day before—October 29, 1929—from his CFO. It read:

*Return home, immediately. Stop. The stock market has crashed. Stop.*

Bruce reread the cable, shrugged and set it aside. Probably just a minor dip in the market, a glitch. The man was constantly over-reacting, creating worse-case scenarios, horror stories out of the most mundane of Wall Street indicators.

Out of the corner of his eye, beneath the window, he saw some movement. A little gray and black mouse. The mouse stopped, seemingly startled by Bruce, then ambled away. Bruce smiled. Perhaps the mice—the meek—would inherit the Earth. But, if so, they were going to need some help... A protector...

Suddenly, his mind flashed back to the tomb, to the bats. Were not bats and mice cousins?

Bats... An omen?

Naw.

*Stuart Shiffman, who penned the comical "The Milkman Cometh" in Volume 5 of Tales of the Shadowmen, offers a new and amusing take—almost a spoof—of the Nyctalope in New York, behaving like a fish out of water, interfacing with the murky world of Law & Order in the 1930s in...*

## Stuart Shiffman: *The Nyctalope's New York Adventure*

*New York, 1934*

> "And these questions, the unknown, the invisible,
> all these problems—how interesting they are!
> And the mystery—so amusing!"
> Jules Claretie, *L'accusateur* (1897).

The commercial airship *Cyclone III* flew high above the dark waters of the Atlantic Ocean. It had left the aerodrome of Le Bourget outside Paris in the early misty morning after custom control as well as the Lloyd's inspectors' check-through. Representatives from the Compagnie Transatlantique Aérienne let out a collective breath. They appreciated passengers taking their liners rather than the German Zeppelin Company's better known *luftschiffs* from Friedrichshafen. French airship companies had no problem obtaining helium from American suppliers, unlike the Germans who had to make do with the more dangerous and combustible hydrogen.

Leo Saint-Clair was not a small man found his first-class compartment confining. It was especially tiny when compared to first-class accommodations in a surface liner. His "gentleman's gentleman" was sharing a second-class compartment with an American, and he blanched to think of what that must be like. As an antidote to the tight space, he strolled up to the fire-shielded smoking lounge.

The lounge was spacious and featured a wide bar; the whole space was decorated in the latest Art Moderne style in shades of silver, blue and black. There was a large Lucite sculpture designed by Erte and molded by Lalique that dominated the space.

"Impressive, isn't it," asked a man in French, coming in after him. "The expansive view of all creation and a top notch drinking station, eh?" He was tall, immaculately clad in a regimental-style tie in dark orange and blue and a charcoal-gray suit. His most noticeable characteristic was his face, his flat cheeks and aristocratic nose firmly molded and almost mask-like in its composure. He was smooth-shaven and had a quiet, dignified expression. The gentleman carried a rolled-up copy of the Paris edition of the *Herald Tribune* under one arm. On his hand, he wore a fire opal ring known as a girasol.

"How can they have such a massive bar here?" responded Saint-Clair in wonder. "That looks to be mahogany!"

"I was told by the purser," said the other man, who introduced himself as businessman Henry Arnaud of Chicago, "that it is, in fact, aluminum, redressed and painted to resemble stained mahogany grain. The rest of the furniture of the lounge is also built on aluminum frames."

"Ah, I should have guessed as much," said Saint-Clair. "I had suspected some kind of balsa laminate. My name is Leo Saint-Clair, by the way." He held out a hand.

"I've heard of you, Monsieur; you're the man they called the Nyctalope aren't you?" asked Renaud.

They walked into the lounge and took stools, bolted in place, at the bar. Giving orders to the waiter (gin and tonic for Arnaud, tonic water for Saint-Clair), they soon found a number of points of agreement on international politics and crime—and this despite Saint-Clair's rather conservative views. On modern art and music, the Nyctalope showed a preference for the classic form of *Le Jazz Hot*. Although an admirer of the talents of Josephine Baker in Paris, he was shocked by her cultivation of nudity and loose living. Arnaud was an aficionado of the new American big band swing and especially artists like Bix Beiderbecke and Benny Goodman.

"What's taking you to New York?" finally asked Arnaud.

"Besides a large silver gas-bag?" Saint-Clair noticed that Arnaud had taken the barest sip from his cocktail. Was the businessman also trying to minimize diminution of his alertness? He slipped his cigarette case from his breast pocket and offered a *gauloise* to his new acquaintance.

Arnaud demurred, insisting that he preferred his own Turkish tobacco.

"Excuse me, gentlemen," said a voice in American English of no fixed or familiar accent, coming from a large well-dressed but neckless man who had waddled up holding a whiskey and soda. His hair was barely a suggestion on top of his head. "Am I right to think that you are the French adventurer known as the Nyctalope?" He pronounced it "nicht-a-loop."

"Certainly one of us is," quipped Arnaud, his eyes glued to Saint-Clair. How would he handle his international celebrity?

"Yes," Saint-Clair replied slowly. "I am sometimes known by that sobriquet."

"Wonderful! I'm Ivor Llewellyn, head of Superba-Llewellyn Pictures in California. I'd love to sit down with you and work out a deal to put your adventures on the big silver screen! If you're willing, we might even have you star in them yourself. That'd be a super-colossal attraction and be sure to get seats filled! Teamed with our own star, Lotus Blossom, you would be an incomparable hit. Maybe we could write in an underwater love scene!"

"I fear that you're confusing me with the *Hictaner*. I doubt very much, Monsieur Llewellyn, that my name means very much to the average American."

"Well, not as much since the talkies came in. They hurt the movie import business for French pictures, but we used to get all the silent serials based on your adventures and on those of Judex! I think that we still have the American remake rights to remake to some of them."

"They were all unauthorized, Monsieur. You will find that there might be some legal complication were you to use such materials." Saint-Clair had dealt severely with the French film-makers who had had the audacity to use his life as fodder for their films and, each time, his lawyers had wrung substantial settlements from them. Arnaud seemed amused at Saint-Clair's discomfort.

"You haven't already signed with anyone else, Mr. Nyctalope? I wouldn't put it past those *momzers*, Schnellenhamer of Perfecto-Zizzbaum, F. X. Weinberg of Metropolis Pictures, or the Boy Wonder Jacques Butcher of Magna to peach you at the post!" The mogul waved his flipper with its large unlit Havana cigar to emphasize his bullet points.

"No, I have not signed with any other film company."

"Mr. Nyctalope, please avoid simooms, earthquakes, and other Acts of God, and hurry back as quick as you can once you do decide to sign with Superba-Llewellyn!"

"Mr. Llewellyn," inserted Arnaud, "I think that you can be reassured that M. Saint-Clair has not signed away any rights to his life and adventures, and I'm sure that he'll be in touch the moment he decides to do so."

"Oh." The mogul seems non-plussed. He pulled out a handkerchief to mop his forehead. Perhaps he had never had this experience before, a celebrity who had no interest in being taken up by Hollywood. "Oh," he said again. "Well, thanks for your time at least, and it's an honor to meet you, sir."

Ivor Llewellyn handed Saint-Clair two calling cards: "My New York office and my personal number back in Hollywood." He nodded to them both and ambled quietly away.

"If not to get into the movies," drawled Arnaud, "what brings you to Baghdad-on-the-Subways?" He liked Saint-Clair, who projected a dazzling fascination that could feel. Was this an aspect of his hypnotic powers or just the consequence of the great self-confidence of a true hero? he wondered.

"The official reason was an invitation from Dr. Orestes Preson, Curator of Fossil Mammals at the Bradley Institute of Paleontology and Natural History..."

"...on Central Park West," interjected Arnaud.

"We met years ago, during one of my explorations in Central Asia, and he wants me to inaugurate a new series of lectures sponsored by the Institute. Preson is one of those rare men who combine a mastery of science with the type of literary touch that converts research into bestsellers. The lectures are being underwritten by his publishers." He took a sip of his sparkling tonic water.

"And the *unofficial* reason?" Arnaud's face was friendly, but it was like being stared down by a hawk.

"Some time ago, a friend of mine, Judge Coméliau, an investigating magistrate, received a jaunty little death trap in the post in the form of a tear-gas-trapped packet of gourmet sausage. He was in the midst of an investigation at the time of a cosmopolitan criminal calling himself Zigomar."

"After the hooded criminal mastermind of 20 years ago?"

"Yes, the King of Thieves himself. Presumably this new Zigomar wants to capitalize on his namesake's notorious and mystique to control his own sinister phalanxes. How many times did the policeman Broquet think he had slain the original? But this new Zigomar is a modern criminal, with diversified interests and international scope..." Saint-Clair finished his glass of tonic water and put it aside. He looked at Arnaud and concentrated his hypnotic powers. His eyed shifted colors subtly. "Who are you really? You are no mere businessman."

"I suspect that you will get a headache concentrating like that, my friend," said Arnaud. "You can't compel me to speak like that. I am but a shadow..."

The commercial airships used Naval Air Station at Lakehurst, New Jersey, for their landings. Some had had high hopes for the mooring mast proposed for Manhattan skyscrapers like the Empire State Building, but the city's updrafts made them unworkable. The passengers viewed Bartholdi's statue of Liberty along with the fine collection of steel towers as the French airship followed its route north along the Hudson River. Eventually, it struck east, high over the steel arch of Hell Gate Bridge, over the "Hell Gate" itself to Long Island Sound and its destination. Far below were the gothic towers at each end of the bridge, standing 220 feet high.

The French line had shunned the New Jersey facility and preferred to use the new North Beach Airport on Flushing Bay. The mooring masts and their cluster of floating blue and silver dirigibles looked to one driver at the taxi stand like one of cartoonist Jay Irving's comical blimp-like Cops in *Collier's Weekly*.

There was a taxi waiting for Henry Arnaud outside the Embarkation Building, a worn but shining Model A Ford with a rapidly ticking taximeter and engine that might have needed a tune-up. He knew the waiting driver well: Moe Shrevnitz.

Arnaud signaled with a wave of his hand. Shrevnitz's cab wheeled from across the street. It had trim lines with a more streamlined look than previous models, looking more modern with the grille pushed forward and made more prominent by de-emphasized and more-integrated fenders.

"We're dropping M. Saint-Clair at the Churchill," he instructed Shrevnitz as the two men entered the vehicle. "You know where that is."

Moe Shrevnitz shook his head subtly and hunched his leather jacketed shoulders.

It proved to be a quick trip into Manhattan through Long Island City and onto the 59th Street Bridge over the East River. Saint-Clair seemed to hear a cheery little ditty from the vibration of the metal roadbed as they drove over the river.

"I am starting on a journey tomorrow," said the Shadow, in Arnaud's tones. "I have some private business to transact. A friend of mine may look after you—a gentleman named Lamont Cranston. Should he visit you, you may speak to him as

confidentially as you would to me. I'll leave you with his telephone number in case of an emergency. And of course, I will
arrange for this cab and driver to be available to you." Shrevnitz looked nonplussed at this.

"Very kind of you and Mr. Shrevnitz" said the Nyctalope.

The immense and impressive Churchill Hotel occupied the
whole block from 49th to 50th streets, and Madison to Park
Avenues. It had two towers, 42 stories, and 1850 rooms. In the
main lobby was an 8-sided bronze clock made in 1893 for the
original hotel by Goldsmith's of London. It was the height of
luxury by New York standards.

*It's a rather nice hostelry*, thought Saint-Clair. A un-
iformed Field Marshal came forward with a detachment of
well-drilled bell boys in their monkey suits to open the cab
door and receive the Frenchman's luggage. With a wave of
thank you to Arnaud, the Nyctalope entered the lobby.

A tall thirty-ish man with the manner of an amused grandee, a vibrant tan, and blue buccaneer eyes stood before the
registration counter. He was immaculately dressed in a navy
double-breasted suit and had his black hair brushed back. He
seemed to having a dispute with the manager.

"There should be a suite," said the grandee in a posh
trans-Atlantic accent, "under the name of Sebastian Tombs.
My pyramid of leather goods is waiting along with my companion, and I'd like to move them out from vulgar gaze."

The manager seemed relieved to finish with him and
move onto the radiant Saint-Clair, who went into the Presiden-
tial Suite.

"Have I ever spoken to you, Archie," asked Nero Wolfe,
"of Monsieur Anatole?"

I gave myself a few moments to mull over the question.
He had seated his seventh of a ton firmly behind his massive
desk, his yellow tie and shirting flashing forth from his dark
suit. He had just descended after his morning up in the plant

room, working with the orchids. At one elbow on the desk blotter, sat a new copy of Dr. H. Orestes Preson's *The Trumpets of the Forests: The Rise and Fall of the World's Mastodonts and Elephants*.

"He's one of those fancy French chefs who lives and works in what amounts to private practice for Thomas Travers and his wife. Travers is a Brit, who made his pile Out East somewhere. Their usual residence is in Worcestershire but they brought him over and keep him at the Churchill."

Wolfe was examining the three-foot globe made by Gouchard in the corner of the office, and contemplating a location in the British Isles.

"Mr. and Mrs. Travers are said to have come to New York in order to unload the periodical edited by his wife on some unsuspecting publisher in Garden City," I said. "He customarily renders the magazine's title as *Madame's Nightshirt*, but that's not much improvement over the real title of *Milady's Boudoir*."

"Pfui! Don't act like a witling," said Wolfe. "Archie, I will not rise to your bait. M. Anatole, if he practiced his art at some restaurant or hotel, would deserve to be regarded as one of the supreme creators of Gallic cuisine. In this world, as I have said, there are a few great chefs, a sprinkling of good ones, and a pestiferous host of bad ones. Anatole is a great one and should be counted among the Fifteen Masters. His *Rognons des Montagnes* and *Selle d'Agneau à la Grècque*, among other signature dishes, are supposed to be beyond compare. He is said to make Fritz's culinary feats seem the merest roadhouse fry-up…"

I sat down at my desk and swiveled back to him.

"That seems unlikely. What's the deal about Anatole and Travers anyway?" I asked.

"A spectacular meal by Anatole is part of the contract offered us by Dahlia Travers. She wishes to see me soon in order to explain the matter further. The honor to be invited to a meal prepared by Monsieur Anatole, for whatever reason, is not to be belittled."

"So," I said, "this is on the order of excitement of your getting the recipe for *saucisse minuit* from Jacques Berin?"

"Very close to that sublime pleasure, Archie. It is a very tempting a remuneration, but this agency does not lower itself to retrieving antique silver cow creamers, even when they are Georgian and highly collectible."

The telephone rang and I went to answer it.

"Goodwin?" said the hurried and authoritative voice before I could even say hello, "this is Cramer. I'm sending your boss an important package."

"It's Inspector Cramer, he's sending us a gift," I told Wolfe in an aside. I could hear Cramer's cigar-chomping through the receiver. "Good afternoon, Inspector. What's new on the Rialto?"

"It's an important Frenchie who was passed along to me by my superiors," Cramer growled. "He needs the type of help that comes easier to Wolfe than New York's Finest. Stebbins is escorting him over and then he is all yours."

"A client is on the way," I signaled to the great detective, signaling cash in a hand signal. This was unusual as New York's Finest seldom referred someone to us. The inspector gave me a few more details: the famous European hero trying to find the criminal behind a murderous assault of his friend, a French investigating judge, room at the Churchill, special handling.

"...And make sure that Wolfe knows that I don't want this to come back and bite me in the posterior!" He rang off.

I recited the conversation from memory in detail for Wolfe.

"The *Nyctalope*?" mused Wolfe. "This case may have elements of interest. Give me your notebook, Archie." I handed it over and he wrote swiftly on a page. "This is the number for Colonel Dubois of the Deuxième Bureau in Paris. I will need to speak with him as soon as possible, preferably before Sgt. Stebbins arrives with the Monsieur Saint-Clair. Also give Saul Panzer a call to come in as soon as possible."

I immediately sat down at my desk with the telephone and did this, starting with Saul since I knew that would be a quick connection. He agreed to be over within 15 minutes.

It took a little maneuvering with my high school French to get past Colonel Dubois's protective perimeter, but once he heard Wolfe's name, he emitted a broadcast of Gallic syllables that overwhelmed my knowledge of the language. I passed him back to Wolfe, and distracted myself by updating the plant room books. I heard the name of "avocat Prosper Lepicq" in clear, but that was all.

I was brought back to the world by Wolfe replacing the receiver. "Satisfactory! Have Saul come in when he arrives, Archie."

The doorbell rang. I presumed that it was Saul, but peeked around the curtain just in case. There was no one there, but parked across the street there was a Ford taxi cab with a driver, a small man in a leather cap and sporting a big beezer, who looked close enough to Saul Panzer without actually being him. I knew it was not Saul because I could see him walking swiftly up West 35th Street, so I opened the door for him and escorted him to the office.

I paused outside the office where I could hear voices murmuring within. I knocked, there was a pause of a few beats, and Wolfe called out "Enter, Archie!"

I brought Saul in for his marching orders. No one was in there with Wolfe and the telephone was on my desk.

"Archie," Wolfe said, "there will be a guest in the alcove by the peephole. Make sure that it is prepared properly for our guest." I left the office to allow Wolfe to give Saul his instructions in privacy and to get the secret panel opened. I pulled over a bar stool in front of it.

Saul was on his way out when I returned to the office.

"So what should I know or do I just sit back and enjoy the show?" I asked, taking my seat.

The doorbell rang. I hurried over to the door and opened it to reveal Detective Sgt. Purley Stebbins, NYPD, and an enormously well-built cliff of a man, a veritable New Jersey Palisades example of humanity.

"He's all yours now, Goodwin," Stebbins growled. "Do me a favor; keep him from doing another Brodie!" I presumed that this cryptic comment would be explained. Stebbins retreated down the brownstone's brown sandstone stoop back to the curb where a taxi, a new yellow Checker from Sunshine Cab Company, waited for him. He seemed a bit anxious to leave the vicinity of our row house.

His companion, the slab of man, entered our humble home. He was well over six feet tall with a massively perfect physique and shoulders that a naval biplane could land on. His features were what I usually think of as Gallic, but like a clean-shaven Gaulish chieftain.

"You are not Monsieur Nero Wolfe?" he said in a loud whisper, clutching me by the arm.

"If you're here to consult Mr. Wolfe, Monsieur Saint-Clair, you'd better come along with me. I'm Archie Goodwin, Mr. Wolfe's assistant." I took his black wool overcoat, fedora, gloves and walking stick and lead him into the office. Wolfe rose to greet him from behind his desk. I slipped away to Fritz Brenner in the kitchen. Fritz was chopping herbs on the block. I explained to him that hot and cold liquids and pastry would be required in the office, and then slipped back to stand next to the globe.

The Frenchman was still taking in the office geography, rotating and surveying the sets of book shelves, the Persian rug, the framed Holbein reproductions, the globe, an engraving of Brillat-Savarin, the picture of the waterfall and finishing with the framed portrait of Sherlock Holmes above my desk.

"Welcome, Monsieur Saint-Clair," said Wolfe in French. He speaks a number of European languages while I only have my English and a modicum of high school French as it is spoken in Chillicothe, Ohio. I hope that it would be adequate to the task at hand.

"Ah, you know me already?" said the Frenchman.

"Do not bother with such flummery, my dear sir. You were already famous before the Great War and your face was documented in many newspaper photographs and newsreel reportage." Wolfe wagged his finger at Saint-Clair.

The Nyctalope was more of a Wagnerian hero type than I had expected, and it was not a surprise to learn that he was a pretty famous fellow on the other side of the pond. His eyes were a little off with a greenish-yellow cast. He was obviously the type of man equally at home in an elegant ballroom and striding across mountains in Africa or central Asia in boots and jodhpurs. I sat him in the red chair and took my own seat at my desk with notebook in hand. He didn't beat around the bush.

"I need help, Mr. Wolfe," he began. Saint-Clair told us of the murderous "Death by Sausage" attack on his friend, Investigating Magistrate Coméliau, and of the shadowy underworld figure using the identity of the legendary Zigomar.

"I received a tip from a friend in the *Sûreté* that this putative new Zigomar had left his new gang in Paris to come to New York. I want to find him and bring him back to France for justice."

Wolfe pursed his lips in thought.

"You obviously are not going through the usual official channels for capture of wanted criminals," he mused, "or else, there would be legitimate charges and an official request for extradition."

"There is circumstantial data, but not enough for criminal charges of to be filed; my friend the magistrate is slowly recovering from the attack."

"Surely, he must have been involved with other investigations of criminal organizations. What made you so sure that this Zigomar II was responsible?" Wolfe asked. "Might any other gang leader have a personal vendetta against Judge Coméliau?"

"This was very personal, Mr. Wolfe."

"What happened when you went to meet Inspector Cramer, Monsieur Saint-Clair?" Wolfe asked.

"I never got there for the appointment, I'm afraid."

Saint-Clair explained that he had gone down to the Churchill's sumptuous lobby after breakfasting in his room, expecting to find the little taxi driver Shrevnitz waiting. Instead, he was met by two men in well-tailored suits and worn-soled shoes that pointed to either policemen or nightclub bouncers.

" 'We're here to take you to Inspector Cramer,' explained the bigger of the two with a flash of a billfold too fast to see. I was willing to accept them in the beginning, remembering that New York is a true melting pot. They escorted me out via a back way—for security, they said—to a waiting panel delivery truck. The interior was lined in benches and we had a long uncomfortable ride amidst the noises of Manhattan traffic until we disembarked in the courtyard of a huge brick building which worn signs identified as the Panther-Pilsner brewery…'"

"Ah," I said, "the quintessential mysterious ride with dubious companions to the equally mysterious lair of the Panther. They've switched back to proper beer production since the end of Prohibition."

"Behave yourself, Archie," said Wolfe, "and let our guest continue."

"Thank you, Mr. Wolfe. I quickly realized that they were not police but rather criminals working for someone whom they referred to as The Big Fellow…"

I noticed now that Saint-Clair had switched to English and I was to learn later that he spoke half a dozen European languages and that my attempts at French pronunciation had been excruciating for him.

Saint-Clair had eavesdropped on his escorts and discovered that they were Harry the Horse, Little Isadore and the driver was nicknamed Spanish John. I nodded to myself; they were a trio of independent operators for hire from Brownsville.

"It was a long echoing space within the brewery, with the smell of ancient malt and hops, barely illuminated by a few bare bulbs." The thugs were strangely genteel with him, indi-

232

cating his path further into what must have been the thickest darkness to them.

The Nyctalope had smiled. The darkness hid no terrors for him.

"They didn't know, gentlemen, that I had powers of sight in the darkness. Soon they were stumbling around while I made my way to a steel stairway to the upper levels." In his chest, he felt the resonance of the steel frameworks and brewing vats with the magnetic fields of the electro-magnets of his artificial heart. It was disquieting. Saint-Clair had never felt anything like it even in the Hertzian radio-planes that he had ridden to Mars or on the Eiffel Tower. "I heard my captors stumbling about until a doorway opened, flooding the space with light and the yells of the three men. They'd spotted me and I barely stayed away of them while I found the door to the roof."

He barricaded the steel roof door with a wooden chair and ran to the edge below the water tank. Below were the streets and tenements, offices and factories, of Lower Manhattan.

"I heard the crash of the smashed wooden chair and leapt for the next building before I could think. I skidded on the tarpaper of the next roof and turned to look. I could see my pursuers hesitate. Harry the Horse fired twice with a pistol, and then leapt after me."

The next building's roof was a story shorter and he ran down the steel access ladder until he could jump again. The taller building after that only gave him a bedroom window to access. The young lady there had been very gracious.

"Finally, I was running down the street, through back alleyways and private back gardens, draped with drying laundry, with the occasional accompaniment of gunfire."

Wolfe had his eyes closed throughout this, his lips pursing in and out. To anyone else, it would appear that he had fallen asleep, but I knew that his analysis continued with all extraneous distractions excluded.

"Suddenly, I saw that I had turned onto Centre Street and I could see the white dome of the Beaux-Arts palace where Inspector Cramer was supposed to be waiting for me. The men were still in pursuit, so I had to run away from Police Head-quarters and onto the pedestrian walkway of a great bridge."

"The Brooklyn Bridge," I wrote in my notebook, "and 240 Centre Street." This was quite a tour that the Nyctalope had gotten. I was surprised that he had missed Chinatown and Greenwich Village! That "white city" pile at 240 Centre Street had been designed "to impress both the officer and the prison-er with the majesty of the law." It certainly had always im-pressed me—especially that amazing lobby. The structure had housed the headquarters of the New York Police Department from 1909 to the present, replacing an older building nearby on Mulberry Street. When the NYPD had shifted to Centre Street, all the gun shops, cop saloons, and police reporters had followed suit.

"I ran up the boardwalk of the pedestrian way onto the bridge," explained Saint-Clair, "heading for the great Gothic stone tower supports. The three boys from Brooklyn were still on my tail despite it all."

Fritz entered with a silver tray holding a coffee pot, creamer and cups, a glass of milk, an empty glass and two bot-tle of Remmers beer and a dish of his small apple tarts, placing it on my desk. I poured for Saint-Clair and took the glass of ice-cold milk for myself. The beer was Wolfe's and he looked please to open one and pour it out.

"I ran up the main bridge cable using the guide wires to steady me," Saint-Clair continued after a sip of his coffee, holding the cup in both hands as if to absorb its warmth. "I'm not sure now what I thought I was going to do because I was not about planning to climb to the summit of the tower. There was a crowd gathering below on the walkway and the flow of traffic over the bridge stopped."

"No New Yorker can resist a free show," I diagnosed.

"The view from up there was extraordinary, gentlemen. Up and down on either side of New York the bright sun-lit water lay rippling, while to the south it merged into the great bay and disappeared toward the sea. All up and down the harbor, the shipping, piers and buildings were crystal-clear and the flotilla of ships and ferries in motion. The streets of both Brooklyn and New York were full of multitudes of people."

"Archie, do you recall that stanza of Hart Crane's poem *To Brooklyn Bridge*?"

Of course I did, reciting it to myself: "*Out of some subway scuttle, cell or loft/A bedlamite speeds to thy parapets,/Tilting there momently, shrill shirt ballooning,/A jest falls from the speechless caravan.*"

The cops and the City don't keep track of suicide attempts or other jumpers from New York City's bridges, so the actual number is not known. One beat cop told me that the hardest part of patrolling the bridges wasn't dealing with the would-be jumper, but the crowds that would gather and yell to egg the person into jumping.

So the Nyctalope jumped from some 200 or 250 feet above the East River.

I didn't envy him the experience. Once upon a time, the waterways around Manhattan and the 53-year-old bridge had been the home of frolicking dolphins and seals. Two and three quarters centuries of human and industrial effluvia had changed that. And the East River is ridiculously cold as it is just a tidal strait connecting Upper New York Bay and Long Island Sound. The East River can be dangerous to people who fall in or attempt to swim in it, with water moving as fast as four knots, a speed that can push even strong swimmers out to sea.

"I descended rapidly and tried to shape my body to the perfect diving form to minimize my impact on the water surface." Saint-Clair paused. "I really don't remember hitting the water. The next thing that I remember is sitting on a police launch covered in blankets while indigo-clad policemen ranted about someone named Steve Brodie. Who's Steve Brodie?"

"Back In 1886," I explained, "a barkeeper named Steve Brodie claimed that he jumped off the bridge to win a bet with a bar-owner pal, and whether he really did it or not, Brodie became a New York legend and vaudeville celebrity. He even operated a Bowery saloon-museum dedicated to his feat. George Raft played him in the movie *The Bowery*."

"At least that is explained," said the Nyctalope. "The police wanted to send me to your Bellevue Hospital for observation, but I was recognized and they brought me to Centre Street instead. Finally, Commissioner Wainwright Barth took me to Inspector Cramer."

"The circle is complete," said Wolfe. "And now the inspector has kindly given you to us. Wasn't he able to help you?"

"Inspector Cramer had me checked by a doctor at Headquarters. He also got me a drink at a bistro across from the police building… there is a tunnel that connects the two."

"I'd call Headquarters a ginmill myself," I commented, "but they do serve food. They unbricked that tunnel after the repeal of Prohibition."

The telephone rang again and I took it. It was Cramer again and he was on the way over.

"Archie, enough of these digressions!" Wolfe gave me a glare. "Monsieur Saint-Clair, Mr. Goodwin and I are not bounty hunters. We are private detectives. I entrap criminals, and find evidence for the state to imprison or kill them. I do not hesitate to charge large fees for this service. However, we can do none of this without the straw and clay to make the bricks. I do not know what kind of private inquiry agents operate in France, if this is what you expect of us."

"I was told that you were a genius, Monsieur."

Wolfe sat back into his chair and fussed at the perfect knot of his yellow tie.

"We should like to help you, Monsieur Saint-Clair," he said, after a moment's contemplation, "but there is nothing with which to help. And I will not be stampeded."

I was thinking of the state of the checking account. I hoped that more than a meal was at stake here. An idea occurred to me.

"This Zigomar..." I began.

"An odious man!" interrupted the Frenchman. I agreed, since that's a classification in which most gangland kingpins, fascists and other authoritarians belong.

"It is time to come to the point, Monsieur Saint-Clair," said Wolfe, "I must let you know that I have spoken with Colonel Dubois of your Military Intelligence."

The Nyctalope looked stricken.

"Then, you know the full story?"

"I wish that someone would tell me," I said. Apparently Wolfe had reserved this for his star turn.

"The colonel had full information about the case through your attorney, Maître Lepicq. Your friend Magistrate Coméliau was not the only person affected; he had the mildest dose and is expected to have a full recovery. His secretary—one of your many girl-friends, Monsieur Saint-Clair—was sadly the real victims of the sausage gas attack. It was analogous to a milder form of chlorine gas. Monsieur Coméliau only got a merest whiff while his secretary and cook were severely exposed, and the latter has, in fact, died. You may be a great hero, Monsieur, but you are the prince of witlings and an unspeakable ass for running off across the Atlantic in search of a wraith without clues or authority while your girl-friend lies in the hospital and may not survive!"

"I could not handle the situation," whispered the Nyctalope, his strange eyes filling with tears. "I could not see her so small and in pain. I needed to be active, to strike back at the enemy who had done this. That is what I do, take the battle to my opponent."

"You are an Agent of Atropos, Monsieur Saint-Clair!" said Nero Wolfe, coming to his feet. "Heroes like you rush out expecting the universe to violate causality and produce coincidences to lead you to a resolution. The problem is that this works for men like you as in this abortive kidnapping incident. I, on the other hand, have a liking for causality and sequence which allows us to pretend that we live in a puzzling but logically constructed reality..."

The doorbell rang again.

"I know that you were devastated by the death of your first wife, and all your relationships since then have been, shall we say, less than happy. I am not an alienist, Monsieur, but I can see that what happened to Judge Coméliau's secretary triggered some kind of unfortunate emotional reaction in you..."

I heard Fritz scurry along the hallway to answer it.

"Inspector Cramer and some gentlemen here to see you," announced Fritz, entering some time later. "They say that they are expected." Wolfe asked him to show them in.

Inspector Cramer stomped in, the first of a parade that included District Attorney William Skinner and his assistant, Anthony Quinn. Athletic with slicked back dark hair, Quinn looked like a guy who spent a lot of his spare time at the Racket Club working on the exercise machines. I directed them to a variety of chairs drawn in front of our desks, introducing Skinner and Quinn to our guest. Fritz took their coats and hats to the front room.

"This isn't my show," growled Cramer. "You tell'em, Skinner!"

"Monsieur Saint-Clair," began the District Attorney in his deep bass after clearing his throat, "we are asking you to return to Paris."

"He can't go home yet; he hasn't been officially greeted by Grover Whalen yet."

"Cut it, Goodwin," snapped Cramer, "now is not the time for that nonsense." He supported his weary head on one fist and bent towards Skinner again.

"We're here to pass on requests from the French Consul-General and the Ministry of Foreign Affairs that you go home. Your dear friend, President Alexandre Prillant, is quite worried about you. "

"But what about Zigomar and the Big Fellow?" asked a plaintive Saint-Clair.

"The last Big Fellow was William Valcross," explained Skinner. "He was remanded into the custody of Inspector Fernack several years ago, and later executed by electric chair."

"We checked the Panther Brewery and there is no clue to who was using it," said Cramer. "There is no evidence that this new Zigomar has come to New York and so nothing to follow up. If we could find the Harry the Horse, it might be different…"

"Your girl-friend needs you; France needs you, Monsieur Saint-Clair," stated Nero Wolfe. "I'm sure that Dr. Preson will understand cancelling the lecture."

The Nyctalope sighed, then gave a sharp nod of the head and got up on his feet. Fritz brought his things back to him. Saint-Clair bowed to me and Wolfe and followed the others to the door. Once we heard the door close, Wolfe turned to me.

"Saul should be back soon, Archie. I sent him myself to examine the brewery to look for clues. I have the greatest respect for Inspector Cramer and his police methods, but more faith in Saul's acuity. While we are waiting, you can bring in the watcher in the alcove."

I heard Wolfe reciting to himself from *Macbeth* as I left the office:

*"Canst thou not minister to a mind diseased;*
*Pluck from the memory of a rooted sorrow;*
*Raze out the written troubles of the brain;*
*And with some sweet oblivious antidote*
*Cleanse the stuff'd bosom of that perilous stuff*
*Which weighs upon the heart?"*

There was a man in the alcove, swathed in a black cape with scarlet lining, a wide-brimmed black hat and scarf that only revealed burning eyes and a prominent aquiline nose. He seemed to coalesce out of the shadows.

"He'll see you now, so follow me."

I brought the mystery man into the office and gave him the red leather chair.

"You have handled this well, Nero Wolfe. You have a fine way," said the dark man in sepulchral tones, "of marshalling all the data and resources."

"Thank you," replied Wolfe. "I do not have as many sources and agents as you do, but can still assemble my players."

"The Nyctalope never remembered meeting you before?" This from the mystery man startled me; Wolfe had known the Frenchman before?

"No, he did not recognize me as the slim detective he met in Cairo over ten years ago."

"You were operating then as Augustus Fennec in North Africa, as I recall."

Wolfed laced his hands over his belly and smiled to himself. His eyes caught mine to say that he still had enough mysteries of his own in the shadows of his past.

*The role played by the Nyctalope during World War II, and his collaboration with the Nazis, was briefly evoked in* Marguerite *and, retroactively, the subject of Roman Leary's* The Heart of a Man. *Emmanuel Gorlier, however, tackles the issue head-on and brings Leo Saint-Clair into the heart of the Nazi Empire for a desperate adventure with some rather remarkable associates...*

## Emmanuel Gorlier: *A Present for Hitler*

*Berlin, 1941*

Comfortably seated in the back of the Mercedes, the Nyctalope gazed with curiosity at the Berlin nightlife. On eother side of the street, buildings were decorated with long, red flags marked with the black swastika. Unlike in Paris, which was subject to strict curfew rules, the capital of the Third Reich seemed joyful and full of life. Preceded by two motorcyclists in Nazi uniform, the official limousine drove him to his ap-pointment.

The affair had begun a few weeks earlier at the Paris Opera Garnier while Leo was attending the premiere of *Aida* with his friend, Nina Boucher. During the intermission, he was ap-proached by a senior SS officer. The grimness of his black uniform contrasted with the more colorful dress of the reve-lers. Leo had been surprised to recognize his former foe Otto Von Kubitz, whom he had fought in Morocco in 1934. The SS came towards him with a smile and a glass of champagne in hand.

With a slight snap of his heels, Colonel Von Kubitz had saluted the Nyctalope:

"Monsieur Saint-Clair, I am pleased to meet you again. Truthfully, I came here tonight in the hope of seeing you..."

"Colonel, the pleasure is all mine The occasion is more relaxed than the last time we saw each other."

"Indeed! Are you enjoying the performance? I know you're a connoisseur."

"I've been an opera buff since the Great War. But, if you were looking for me, maybe we should discuss what brought you here before the end of the intermission…?"

The colonel glanced at Nina Boucher. The Nyctalope understood and said:

"Nina, would you mind if the colonel and I left you for a few minutes to fetch some champagne?"

" Of course not, darling," replied Nina cheerfully. "I'll wait for you here."

As they approached the bar, the colonel whispered in the Nyctalope's ears:

"I have a service to ask. A friend of mine would dearly like to meet you, to make you an offer… I assure you that it will not in any way compromise your principles…"

The Nyctalope remained silent for a moment, standing in line at the bar. He stared at his former enemy with his penetrating gaze.

"Who is your friend?"

"It's Reichsmarschall Herman Göring. He's waiting for you in Berlin…"

Three weeks later, the Nyctalope stepped out of the car, followed by Colonel Von Kubitz, and entered the building where his meeting with the Reichsmarschall was to take place. They were saluted by the guards as they made their way through a maze of corridors, their progress punctuated by a seemingly endless series of resounding "Heil Hitlers." Finally, they crossed a monumental threshold and entered a large room decorated with precious artworks looted from all the museums of Europe. There, the Nyctalope saw three men seated around a conference table.

The Reichsmarschall was the central figure of the trio. The former Luftwaffe ace was now just a fat man, bloated due to his excessive consumption of morphine, a drug he had begun to use to relieve his injuries after the Munich Beer Hall Putsch. Göring wore a white uniform.

To his right sat a man of medium build wearing the uniform of commander in the SS; to his left was a colossus wearing the uniform of a captain in the Bersaglieri corps of the Italian army.

A few steps from the table, Von Kubitz bowed and saluted the Reichsmarschall in the Nazi fashion; the three men returned his salute. The Nyctalope merely nodded.

Göring spoke in German:

"Please sit down. I'm eager to tell you about a project that has been dear to my heart ever since our victorious troops conquered Bolshevik Russia. But first, the introductions..." He pointed with his head at the Italian giant. "This is Captain Maciste of the Bersaglieri dispatched by Benito Mussolini himself." Then, to the SS commander. "And this is Herr Doktor Merkwürdigliebe,[6] a Knight of the Swastika." Turning towards the two men, he concluded. "And, Gentlemen, this is Leo St. Clair, the Nyctalope."

He continued:

"The three of you make up the ideal of human achievement: Captain Maciste, strength; Doktor Merkwürdigliebe, intelligence; and you, Herr Saint-Clair, spirit. The best of man in its three components, as defined by the Greek philosophers, is achieved through you. You must have asked yourselves why I wanted to meet you. I am now going to tell you and I hope that you will decide to help me with this rather special mission...

"As you might know, on April 5, 1242, the Bishop of the Teutonic Knights, Hermann von Dorpat, was defeated during the so-called Battle of the Frozen Lake by Alexander Nevsky, as he was about to deliver Russia from its Orthodox heresy. The Knights were moving towards an inevitable victory when, pursuing the pitiful Russian army on Lake Peipsi, the ice

---

[6] Strangelove.

243

broke beneath their feet, causing most of them to be swallowed by the icy waters and die. During that battle, the Knights' Standard was lost. For centuries, historians believed that it, too, had been swallowed by the lake's dark waters. But recently, when our troops conquered the Soviet Union, we discovered an ancient manuscript in the library of a monastery that had been converted into a collective farm. Once translated from medieval Russian, that document explained that the Standard had been recovered by the Russians after the battle. To celebrate their victory, it was kept in a shrine supposed to embody the supremacy of the Slavic Race over the Aryan Race. Alexander Nevsky was a mystic and, as you know, he was later canonized by the Prelates of the Orthodox Church. They have since protected the shrine with devices meant to repel any invader and which have successfully defeated all would-be looters throughout the centuries.

"In fact, once we had control of the area in question, about a hundred kilometers from Moscow, we sent an SS company to reclaim the Standard, but only a few made it back alive, deeply traumatized.

"Although it might seem childish, I would like to present the Standard to my beloved Führer as a gift. It would also damage the morale of our Bolshevik enemies. The mission that I would like you to undertake is to enter the shrine and return with the Standard of the Teutonic Knights. What say you?"

The Doctor replied immediately:

"Reichsmarschall, it will be done according to your will!"

Göring then turned to his other two allies, awaiting their responses. Maciste spoke first:

"I'm ready to retrieve an object which rightfully belongs to Germany."

Göring then looked at the Nyctalope who said:

"The same goes for me."

The Reichsmarschall's face brightened.

"Excellent! Von Kubitz, please call for some champagne! We must celebrate! I'll present the Standard to the Führer for his birthday. Doctor, tell our friends about how you plan to get there…"

"We have developed a new type of rocket-powered plane that we plan to use to strike deep inside England and, by turning them into bombs, reduce London to a heap of ashes. One of our prototypes can be piloted and can carry three passengers. We'll use it to reach Moscow in three hours."

Only five hours later, towards midnight, three men descended from a flying object resembling an airplane, but without a propeller, and fitted with small, straight wings. Its main feature was a large reactor placed on his back. They had landed at a small, makeshift airstrip prepared in a few hours by the engineering and military genius of the Wehrmacht. Quickly, they embarked in a tank-like vehicle that had been waiting for them and traveled straight north, towards the location of the no longer secret shrine once built by Alexander Nevsky.

The countryside was gloomy, consisting of low hills with sparse vegetation. There were no birds, no animals in sight. The eerie silence was broken only by the sounds of their vehicle on the muddy road.

Saint-Clair was driving. Sitting next to him, reading a map, the SS doctor tried to give him directions. Maciste sat at the back, where there was enough room for him to move his corpulent body.

"I think we should be coming to a road on the left..." said the doctor, looking at his map.

Suddenly, thanks to his preternatural vision, the Nyctalope caught a metallic gleam flashing briefly from behind the chaos of rocks and boulders on the right side of the road.

He swerved at once as a hail of bullets fell on the vehicle.

It was an ambush! Hidden behind the rocks, a dozen Soviet soldiers opened fire on the three men. Because of the Nyctalope's quick reflexes, none of the bullets had harmed them. But the engine wasn't as lucky! Smoke was coming out from under the hood. Then, the vehicle's right track locked, causing it to abruptly turn 90-degrees then stop.

Leo could no longer steer. His two companions were flattened on their seats in order to escape their enemies' fire.

The SS doctor then pulled three metal spheres from a small bag he had been carrying.

"Deadly 'eggs' from my friend Korridès," he said.

He flung one towards the Soviets. When it touched the ground, a cloud of green smoke filled the air and enveloped their opponents, who began to scream—briefly. A minute later, the gas had dissipated.

"I'll take care of the survivors," the SS said softly, unholstering his Luger and leaving the vehicle.

The Nyctalope and Maciste followed more slowly. They arrived at the scene as they heard the first shots.

*That Merkwürdigliebe has no mercy, killing helpless men in cold blood*, thought the Nyctalope.

Examining one of the Russian soldiers, Leo realized that it was a woman, paralyzed by the gas. Looking up, he saw that Maciste, a little further away, had made the same discovery. Their opponents had been a patrol from the women's section of the Red Army.

He heard a loud noise that sounded as if the Italian had crushed the skull of his victim under the cover of darkness, but, thanks to his particular vision, the Nyctalope saw that Maciste had not hit the female soldier but rather a stone near her head, which had shattered under the blow. So he, too, would not strike a defenseless enemy either! With a quick movement of the hand, Leo pressed the nerve centers of the young woman before him, giving her the appearance of death. His companion looked at him, with a glimmer of understanding in his eyes. Apparently, he knew a lot about the ancient martial arts of the Orient. But Maciste said nothing and continued the pretense.

After repeating their deceit on several more occasions, the two men returned to their vehicle. The SS doctor was wiping his boots, which were covered with blood. The idea that his companions could show compassion for their enemies had not crossed his mind. He opened the hood and examined the engine.

"We'll have to continue on foot," he said. "But we're almost there!"

They took bags containing equipment and supplies and headed for the shrine. After a few hours walking through the hills, they stopped at dawn for a quick breakfast.

"We shouldn't be very far from our goal now," said the doctor. "I'm surprised, in fact, that we haven't reached it yet. I'll walk a little further ahead to check if the Shrine is just around that turn."

He got up, took a torch and walked away. Leo and Maciste remained silent for a few minutes, watching the first rays of the sun.

"You did not kill those Russians," said the Italian suddenly.

"Neither did you," replied the Nyctalope.

Maciste looked surprised, then smiled.

"Ah! I forgot about your superhuman vision! I think we're involved in some rather murky business. This story about a long-lost Standard seems suspicious to me…"

"Maybe, but then, what is the real goal of all this?"

"Goal, yes… I ask myself how someone like me could be associated with men like that Nazi doctor, and I wonder… I was persuaded by Gabriele d'Annunzio to help unify Italy and restore it to its rightful place in Europe, but how did I go from there to killing soldiers who only seek to defend their country and catering to the whims of a tyrant? Many of my compatriots must now ask themselves the same question…"

"I share your views," said the Nyctalope. "We should remain vigilant in case things don't go as they should."

At this point, the Nazi doctor returned looking very excited.

"I found the entrance to the Shrine. Come quickly! I'm eager to get inside!"

The two men stood up. They took the equipment and followed the doctor who led them outside the entrance to a cave that opened at the bottom of a hill.

The doctor directed the beam of his flashlight into the crevice, but the light stopped abruptly at the threshold.

"It is said that no light can penetrate the Holy Shrine," quoted Merkwürdigliebe. "We have reached our goal. Monsieur Saint-Clair, can you see through the darkness?"

For the Nyctalope, darkness did not exist.

"Yes. Put your hand on my shoulder and I'll lead you!"

One after the other, the doctor and Maciste followed Leo into the cave. It was spacious. On his left, the Nyctalope saw a corridor leading away diagonally. After a cautious glance, he followed the narrow passage. A few meters further, the corridor widened, revealing a gaping pit in the center. The Nyctalope cautiously walked around it, still directing his companions. He glanced at the pit and saw, ten feet below, several skeletons piled up and a fresh corpse wearing a German uniform.

After crossing a stone bridge with no railings, they came to a point where the underground passage split into two. Leo noticed that the floor of one of the corridors was covered with a thin layer of copper wires, so he took the other direction. They emerged into a vast room the floor of which was strewn with round copper plates. Near each of them were skeletons or corpses showing deep burns that could only have been caused by a high voltage electricity discharge. Leo slowly walked around each of the booby traps.

While proceeding cautiously, the Nyctalope came to the conclusion that Alexander Nevsky could not have created such elaborate defenses. It required a level of technology far beyond that of the 13th century. A hypothesis began to take form in his mind...

They reached the end of the room. Before them, there was another corridor, about ten meters long, leading to another cave. The Nyctalope looked carefully and saw a small metal sphere at the end of the corridor.

After some hesitation, he stepped forward, drawing his revolver. But after two meters, he began to feel a sort of mental pressure. He heard his companions moan. His brain was being subjected to a violent psychic attack. He had to draw on all his knowledge of the occult sciences in order to block the psychic assault. He then raised his arm and fired his Luger at the metal sphere. Once the first bullet hit it, the psychic invasion ceased. Leo shook his head to regain his composure. Behind him, his two companions were acting as if they were shell-shocked. He understood why the Nazis who had penetrated into the Shrine had gone mad. Without his years of training with the great Tibetan masters, he too would have gone mad—or worse.

They eventually reached the end of the corridor without any further attacks and entered a room with a large stone portal on the opposite wall. A gigantic swastika was carved on it. As they stepped inside the room, the doctor's flashlight mysteriously again came to life.

They approached the swastika. The Nyctalope thought: *This is the missing element: the symbol of Thule. The ancient civilization which inspired the Knights of the Swastika, the mystical branch of the Nazi party. This is probably the real reason for this mission.* He looked at the ground in front of the portal and saw a banner decorated with black designs. So there really *was* a Standard of the Teutonic Knights!.

Without bothering to look at it, Dr. Merkwürdigliebe walked to the swastika, as if hypnotized. At the center of the cross was inlaid a cartouche filled with Kabbalistic symbols.

"I know these symbols," he murmured. "Their precise meaning is obscure... But if I place them in the right order, taking into account the works of Kepler and Dr. Omega..."

Lost in his thoughts, he no longer paid any attention to his two companions who were watching him skeptically.

The Nazi doctor then began to press the symbols in a specific order. A metallic sound was heard and the swastika suddenly protruded from the stone wall. Dr. Merkwürdigliebe turned towards Maciste

"Turn the cross to the left!" he ordered.

Maciste, after a look at the Nyctalope, grabbed the cross and slowly turned it as instructed. The effort required must have been enormous because even the giant began to sweat. The cross yielded slowly and, gradually, the portal swung open, revealing a brightly-lit secret room.

It was filled with futuristic machines whose purposes seemed mysterious. The three men entered and separated, each looking randomly at one device or another: metal consoles, glass bells, huge light tubes, slabs of plastic floating in the air. Some of these things appeared to have been designed according to non-Euclidean geometry and just looking at them induced a sense of dizziness in the observer.

The Nyctalope discreetly watched Dr. Merkwürdigliebe. After several minutes, he hesitantly went to a column-shaped artifact covered with complex equipment. The column was supplied with power by massive red cables. Out of it came a metal helmet, before which was a control panel. Oddly, ten human skulls were attached to the machine, as if they were part of its design. While the Nazi doctor was busy examining the control panel, the Nyctalope searched his memories, feeling that he had seen such a device once before, a long time ago...

At that moment, Dr. Merkwürdigliebe pulled out a transparent helmet and placed it on his head. He then looked at his companions with a strange expression. The Nyctalope understood they faced great, imminent danger.

A glass helmet, human skulls in a strange machine... Suddenly, he remembered... *The teledyname!* This was none other than a more sophisticated version of the device built by is old enemy Lucifer, which he had first seen at his Castle of Schwarzrock! With this device, it was possible to control the minds of all men everywhere. That was going to be Göring's present to Adolf Hitler!

Because of the teledyname, Merkwürdigliebe was already untouchable. The Nazi doctor's eyes became more and more exalted. He was about to smite them both.

The Nyctalope looked up. He noticed the red power cables at the same time than the doctor's hand went to press the single switch that would trigger the teledyname.

"Maciste! Destroy those cables!" shouted Leo.

Everything depended on the reaction time of the Italian hero. He had only seconds to act. But moving like greased lightning. Maciste turned around and, in one, smooth movement, took his Bersagliere helmet and threw it like a disk at the power cables. The gesture was absolutely perfect, as if it had been done by an ancient Olympic athlete or a demi-god. *Perhaps*, thought the Nyctalope, *he wasn't just named Maciste but he really was the legendary eternal defender of the oppressed.*

The helmet struck the cable with a force like no other. Nothing could have withstood such an impact. The shock triggered an explosion that short-circuited the teledyname. Metal fragments of shrapnel size were projected throughout the room. A block of metal shattered the legs of Merkwürdigliebe who was thrown to the ground like a disarticulated doll.

A fire began to spread rapidly. The Nyctalope realized that he would not be able to reach the Nazi doctor. He told Maciste:

"Let's go! It's all going to blow!"

They ran towards the exit. The Nazi doctor looked at them with vengeance in his eyes. He pulled his Luger and took aim. But another explosion sent a large splinter of metal flying, cutting off the arm that held the weapon.

As they were exiting the secret room, the Nyctalope picked up the Teutonic Knights Standard.

"It might come in a handy later," he said. "Let's run!"

A few minutes later, the two men had reached the exit and left the Shrine while a series of new explosions echoed behind them. From afar, they saw a plume of black smoke coming out of the cave.

"The last Outpost of Thule is destroyed. The world is safe," said the Nyctalope.

"The memory of centuries has returned," said Maciste. "I now know who I truly am and why I stayed so long in this century... Today, I have performed the last of the tasks that had required my presence in this time. I can now leave and resume my deathless sleep, only to wake up when my presence will again be required. However, I share your concern about the world. The Nazi threat appears in full swing, triumphant everywhere..."

The Nyctalope remained silent for a moment. It had begun to snow. A snowflake fell upon his nose.

"The game isn't over yet," he said. "Winter is approaching. Other conquerors have seen their hopes utterly annihilated in the snowy wastes of Russia. Maybe bringing this Standard back to Berlin will compel Hitler to try the same thing. Goodbye Maciste. Maybe we shall meet again."

The two men arrived at the fork in the road. The Nyctalope went south, Maciste north.

A few days later, a German division en route for Moscow, which had strayed into the hills, discovered the mutilated body of an SS officer. Both his legs were crushed and he had one arm missing. He seemed to have suffered a severe mental shock and was delirious. He did not recover until several months later, and remembered nothing of what had happened inside the Shrine. Despite his undeniable genius, the future Dr. Strangelove, was never again of sound mind.

In the first quarter of 1942, the Red Army, commanded by Generals Zhukov and Vlassov, stopped the German army a few miles from Moscow.

As for the Standard of the Teutonic Knights, it was recovered by Soviet soldiers in 1945 in a railcar transporting some of the treasures stolen by the Reichsmarshall.

*In this story, Emmanuel Gorlier ponders the fate of the Nycta-
lope's most trusted friend and advisor, the Japanese diplomat
Gno Mitang during World War II and how a good man faces
the moral challenge of being on the losing side...*

## Emmanuel Gorlier: *Twilight*

The road was slightly lit by the weak headlamps. Gno Mitang
and his chauffeur sat in darkness inside the car. Gno was lost
in his thoughts.

*They say that the American planes are able to strike at
the heart of the Empire now. In a few hours we'll be in
Tokyo... All is not lost, we might be able to strike back. For
three years now, we've gone from defeat to defeat. I was
forced to leave France and my friend Leo to personally take
charge of the Emperor's Privy Council. If only I'd stayed in
Japan! What an awful idea my successors had while I was
gone to attack the United States! And since my return I've had
to manage everything. Saving time! Hoping for the situation to
turn around! I really think this is our last hope. If the project
doesn't succeed, the only thing we'll have left is dying with
honor, like our ancestors.*

Just then, his thoughts were interrupted. The chauffeur
had turned around and was speaking to him:

"Your Excellency; should we stop at the Imperial Palace
or do you want to go directly to the factory?"

"The factory," responded Gno without hesitation.
"There's not much time."

The large military vehicle was already crossing the outskirts of the capital. If it had been daylight, Gno could have
seen endless neighborhoods where there were hardly any adult
males; the wooden houses now held only the sounds of children, the elderly and women talking about their daily chores...

*If only a quick victory could return everything to normal,* thought Gno. He wondered if he had been wrong to have supported those who believed that Japan should spread its influence to the mainland. But as his French friends said, "once the wine is poured, you might as well drink it.

Ahead of them, after a cleared area, were the three strands of barbed wire that protected the factory's perimeter. The chauffeur stopped the car at the sentry booth and a guard approached and asked to see their papers before allowing them to pass through the barrier. The driver handed over the documents and said:

"His Excellency Gno Mitang is in a hurry."

The guard saluted smartly and quickly opened the gate.

The vehicle entered and parked in front of the entrance of a large, four-story high wooden building. Gno went inside, walked down a corridor and opened the door to a laboratory that took up almost the entire square footage of the building, as well as its entire height.

In the center, supported by straps, was an enormous creature. Describing it wasn't easy; it resembled a sort of stone-colored tyrannosaur. It was lying down, otherwise it wouldn't have fit inside the room, as its size was far greater than the dinosaurs which had once walked the Earth.

Gno approached a scientist in a white coat who bowed to him and said:

"Your Excellency, we have not been able to find the energy necessary to awaken Godzilla from his thousands of years' long sleep. But I believe there is hope. I have just heard from one of owe European contacts that the work of an Italian physicist is showing promise."

"And where is this Italian scientist?" asked Gno.

"I believe he has emigrated to the United States to escape the Fascists."

"Too bad. He must have made even more progress since the work you've heard about. We need to do something quickly; we're losing the war and the only reason that I am even considering using this ancient horror that we're not even sure we can control, it's because I really don't think we have any other choice.

"I'm going to let the Emperor know where we stand tomorrow. Don't fail me!"

Gno was preoccupied as he left the laboratory. He got back into his car and told the driver to head to the Imperial Palace.

The Emperor was still awake and he requested an audience. Gno had had a trusted relationship with Emperor Hirohito for many years that allowed him to see him easily; a very rare privilege. Hirohito, who normally wasn't particularly involved in day to day matters of State, had been attentively following the events that bothered more and more.

A chamberlain came to tell Gno that he was awaited, and as he walked towards the imperial office a deafening roar pierced the night. Air raid sirens began to scream.

*Another American attack,* he thought. *And we are no longer able to stop them.*

He entered the Emperor's office and was bowing deeply when the first bombs were heard exploding in the distance. The Emperor stood and went to the window. Part of the city was already engulfed in flames as the incendiary bombs continued to fall.

Gno stood next to him and, together, they silently watched for long minutes as the city was destroyed by fire. The wooden buildings were burned almost instantly. At one point, the intensity was so great that an unstoppable firestorm was created.

The minutes became hours. Their faces were fixed into masks of horror as they watched the autodafé of the capital city. As the light of dawn broke over the devastation, where some flames still burned here and there, the Emperor broke his silence:

"I must leave the palace and share the pain of my people!"

Several hours later, Gno was at the calcified ruins of the factory. The scientist, his white coat covered soot, approached him and said:

"We took refuge in no man's land and we all survived. Unfortunately, the factory was completely destroyed; only Godzilla made it. He'll truly be an unstoppable weapon!"

"We need to give up. It's too late. When the Emperor returned to the palace after visiting what's left of Tokyo, his face in disbelief and shock, his eyes had a look of determination that has been missing for months. I doubt that the conflict will go on for much longer. Have Godzilla thrown into the ocean. We need to spare our children the potential risk. We've made enough mistakes.

"But maybe we can find the energy source that we need quickly...?"

Gno Mitang remained silent. He looked around at the razed Tokyo and thought of the thousands of deaths that had occurred during the night; women, children, the elderly... He answered in a grave voice:

"I have the feeling that when that energy is discovered, Japan will no longer be the same. If the Emperor wants it, we will be better off concerning ourselves with rebuilding her, than with continuing to battle for imaginary results."

*Roman Leary has made it his mission to chronicle the Nycta-lope's post-World War II adventures, concentrating on the moral rebirth of the character, and exploring the theme of his immortality. In this story, which takes place soon after* The Children of Heracles, *he throws a new light on the events chronicled by La Hire in* Enter the Nyctalope...

## Roman Leary: *A Moment of Perfect Happiness*

*Saigon 1951*

*Dear Jenny,*

    *I am so glad that you enjoyed my last letter. You have no idea how flattering it is for an old guy like me to get praise from such a bright and beautiful young lady. Of course, it could be argued that you're biased, being my grand-daughter and all, but I'm going to take it at face-value and assume you mean every word of it.*

    *The pictures that you sent are very, very good. I have to admit, you've succeeded in changing my mind about digital photography. I may be a stubborn geezer when it comes to computers and e-mail, but I'm not so much of a Luddite that I can't recognize a great innovation when I see it. Just don't let yourself become so reliant on the technology that you start letting it do the work for you. Remember, you can buy a million dollars' worth of paint and brushes, but that won't make you Rembrandt. Talent, patience, and practice make an artist. You've got plenty of the first. Stick to the other two and it won't be long before I'm not the only Kovac with a Pulitzer.*

    *I've been thinking a lot about the question you asked me, about whether or not I had a favorite picture. My gut response was to name the old prize-winner, but the plain fact is that I've never liked that image. Can you believe it? Oh, it's a great photograph all right, but you know it was taken just a few*

*hours before my Pop died. I can never look at it without think-*
*ing I should have been in New York with him, instead of ad-*
*venturing on the other side of the world. That's why I never*
*look at it at all.*

*Then, of course, there's the old line about how it's like*
*asking which of your kids you like the most. You know,* they're
all my favorites ha-ha. *But that's just a lazy cop-out and you*
*deserve better than that.*

*So, I went in the attic, got out the archives and started*
*going through them one by one. I've got to say, a lot of my*
*stuff was pretty good, better even than I remembered. It was*
*nice to come back to it with a little distance, a little detach-*
*ment, and see that it really is a nice body of work. Maybe I*
*should do a show at the local library.*

*Anyway,* Get to the point Grandpa, *I hear you saying, so*
*I will. I was in the third box when I found it. As soon as I saw*
*it, I said to myself,* Mike, this is it.

*Just to be sure, I went through all the others, but that*
*was the one I kept coming back to. That was* the one, *no ques-*
*tion.*

*Well, there's a copy of it with this letter. What do you*
*think?*

*I won't be surprised if you're not too impressed. I sup-*
*pose there are others which are more dramatic, more fraught*
*with meaning. But remember your question: You didn't ask*
*what my best picture was, you asked which one was my favo-*
*rite, and now you're looking at it. Let me tell you why...*

Dr. Adrien de Villiers-Pagan, the immortal, admired the wom-
en as they strolled down the Rue Catinat. He had come to believe that Vietnamese women were the most beautiful in the
world, and he gazed upon them with an appreciation that bor-
dered on reverence.

He was sitting at a table beside a milk bar, savoring a
chocolate malt which, by some miracle, remained cool in the
glass despite the sultry Saigon heat. Occasionally, a familiar
face would walk by—a French soldier or a child he had helped

at the clinic—and there would be a wave or a nod of acknowledgement. He enjoyed these brief moments of familiarity. They were friendly reminders that he was still a participant in the human experience, even if, strictly speaking, he was no longer fully human.

He was taking a final, noisy sip at the straw when he noticed the man staring at him. He was a tall man, lean and muscular in his tan summer suit. He stood apart, still as a stone in the drift of humanity along the crowded street. At first, the doctor wasn't completely certain he was object of the fellow's gaze. The man was wearing sunglasses, and his blank expression could have betokened merely a preoccupied mind rather than ominous scrutiny. Then the man began to walk toward him.

Villiers-Pagan felt uneasy at the man's implacable approach, but he was also curious. There was something familiar about the man, something about the way he moved…

The doctor smiled. *Of course*, he thought. *He was bound to seek me out eventually. I'm actually surprised it took this long.*

He stood up to greet the man as he drew near. "I'm so glad to see you," he said. He gestured to the chair opposite his own.

The man seemed slightly taken aback. "Do you recognize me so easily, after all this time?"

"Oh, the beard and the glasses are fine distractions," the doctor said. "But I literally know you inside-out. Won't you please join me? I will buy you a chocolate malt."

A hint of a smile crossed the tall man's features. "I think I would prefer something with a little more bite."

Villiers-Pagan laughed. "Come now, old friend," he said. "It is early yet. I promise you will be refreshed by this treat. Me, I can't imagine a morning without it."

The man sat down with a sigh. "Very well," he said. "I must say, your tastes have changed since we last met."

"A great many things have changed, few for the better."

"This is true for me as well," the tall man said. He removed his glasses, revealing striking greenish-brown eyes of an almost metallic hue. "I suppose you are aware of the turn my life has taken."

"I am," said the doctor.

"Then we won't have to waste time talking about me. You, on the other hand…"

"I suppose you have a great many questions."

"Indeed I do," said Leo Saint-Clair, once better known as the Nyctalope. "For example, how is it that I am carrying on such a pleasant conversation with a man who has been dead for nearly fifty years?"

*To a kid like you, Vietnam is probably synonymous with movies like* Rambo *and* Platoon. *Well, I actually spent a lot of time there in the early fifties, and I can tell you that there's a lot more to the place than jungles and rice paddies.*

*In those days it was the French, not us, that were caught up in a war that had turned into a seemingly endless slog through the muck. I went over there with the intention of staying a couple of weeks at the most, but that turned into a couple of months. If you wanted blood and hell, there was plenty to photograph out in the bush, but Saigon, that was another story. The place was…addictive. To me, Saigon in '51 was like being lost in a strange and pleasant fever dream while a storm rages outside. You can hear the thunder, and you see the lightning from the corner of your eye, but the beauty and the heat keep pulling you down into sleep. You just want to the dream to last as long as possible.*

*I never lacked for company, that's for sure. There were plenty of Brits and Americans over there to pass the time with, not to mention lots of pretty ladies. Don't worry, I won't tell you anything embarrassing, but you should remember that your Grandpa wasn't always a wrinkly old coot.*

*Anyway, there was this one reporter that I occasionally shared drinks with named Thomas Fowler. He worked for a London paper, the* Times *maybe. He was kind of a jerk, to tell the truth. One of those cynical Limey snobs who thinks you're too dumb to know when he's being ironic. That being said, he was smart as hell and I enjoyed his conversation, as long as it was in small doses.*

*This Fowler, he had a connection with a young American named Pyle. I can't really remember his first name, something like Aldo. I only met him once or twice. He was a quiet guy, earnest to the point of being laughable. Incredibly, it was an open secret all over Saigon that Pyle was involved in some kind of espionage. Nobody knew exactly, precisely what he was up to, but it was* something. *I remember one of the few times I talked to him, he wouldn't shut up about how Vietnam needed a "Third Force" to come in and set things right. He might have been talking about the U.S., or maybe he meant himself. Who knows? He seemed like a nice enough guy, but of the two I preferred Fowler...*

"...And that's how I made everyone believe I had drowned in the ocean."

Leo slowly shook his head. "A remarkable story," he said. "The people who call me ruthless should spend some time with you. Didn't you think about what this would do to your family?"

"I thought about them a great deal," said Villiers-Pagan. "I have never stopped thinking about them. I never will."

"And yet you are here, hiding under an assumed identity..."

"Not making a very good job of it, apparently. How did you find me?"

Leo reached into his breast pocket and produced a folded piece of paper that he passed over the table. The doctor opened it to see a clipping from a magazine, possibly *Life*. On the page was a picture of a smiling nun watching over a group of Vietnamese children at play. In the background, looking on in bemusement was himself, the very image of a benevolent physician.

The doctor laughed. "Incredible," he said. "One can barely make out my features in these shadows. How could you be so sure it was me?"

"I am not likely to forget the man who saved my life. I was assisted considerably by the fact that, to all appearances, you haven't aged a day since the last time I saw you."

"Yes, that is remarkable, isn't it?"

"Very."

Silence fell between them. The sounds of the street— chattering voices, bicycle bells, buzzing engines—merged almost into a melody. The doctor closed his eyes and listened to it for a moment. In the distance, there was a percussive crack that may have been a simple backfire, or a grenade.

"You have told me how you came to be here," Leo said, "but not why."

Villiers-Pagan smiled. "If I simply say, *that is none of your business, my good fellow*, will you accept that as an answer? Will you move on to another subject? Perhaps even no longer be here when I open my eyes?"

"I am afraid not."

The doctor sighed.

"Please look at me," Leo said. "I am not here to do you an ill turn, but I have come very far to find you, and I will not leave until you have told me what I wish to know."

"Why are you so adamant?" Villiers-Pagan asked, asperity creeping into his tone. "You of all people should know that some things are better left alone."

Leo shrugged. "Call it the habit of a lifetime," he said. "I was once a detective as well as a warrior. I suppose I'm simply no good at leaving a puzzle unsolved."

"I do not think you will like what you hear."

"I seldom do."

The doctor nodded. "So be it," he said. "If anyone has a right to know, it is certainly you. It began the night of your operation, the night that I placed in your chest a heart made of plastic and steel..."

*One morning, out of the blue, I got a call from Pyle. I was surfaced to hear from him, but I didn't want to ask him point blank what he wanted because I figured that would be rude. So I let him waste time talking to me about a girl he was in love with named Phuong. "It means* phoenix," *I remember him saying. "Isn't that beautiful?"*

*I told him it was absolutely gorgeous and that I'd be glad to take pictures of his wedding, if he would meet my price.*

*"You're joking," he said. "I don't know if I like that, but I understand that you don't mean any harm. Actually, it's photographs that I want to talk to you about. I'd like to give you a tip, some information about where you might get some good pictures."*

*I told him that I was interested, and he said that I should be near the square by the Continental at around eleven twenty-five.*

*"What happens then?" I asked.*

*"A demonstration," says he.*

*"Of what?"*

*"It would be best if would just go and see for yourself."*

*I went back and forth with him for a few minutes, but he refused to give anything more. All he would do was emphasize that I should be* near *the square, not* in *it. Looking back, I can't believe that I didn't see any danger in that particular distinction, especially considering the rumors about him. It just never occurred to me, not even once, that an overgrown little boy like Pyle could be involved in anything where people might actually get hurt...*

Adrien finished his story, then smiled as he waited for his listener's inevitable protest of disbelief. The man did not disappoint.

"That's ridiculous," Leo said. His lip was curled in disdain, but his voice lacked conviction.

*In his soul, he knows it is true*, Villiers-Pagan thought. *Perhaps he has known all along, but never dared to openly consider it, to absorb its full implications.*

"You're familiar with the written account," the doctor said. "The facts were very well-publicized by your biographer…"

"And dismissed by anyone with a modicum of common sense. He was prone to the wildest exaggerations, which was something I frankly encouraged. It was safer for everyone involved."

"There is something in what you say, but he told the plain truth more often than I think you would like to admit. Or, in this case, even realize. When you were stabbed by Grigoryi Alexandrovitch, your heart suffered a mortal wound. You were clinically dead for at least five minutes before I got to you, and you didn't register a pulse until after the heart transplant was completed several hours after that."

Leo gave a dismissive wave of his hand. "If that's correct, then I would have suffered catastrophic brain damage. I would be a complete vegetable, and I flatter myself that that is obviously not the case."

"You would have under normal circumstances," Villiers-Pagan said. "In fact, that is exactly what I expected to happen."

"I beg your pardon?"

"Though I proclaimed otherwise at the time, I truly did not believe I could restore you to any semblance of health and vitality. When I was brought to you, I saw immediately that your wound was fatal, and that there was no hope of implanting the artificial heart before brain death. But I decided to go forward because you were an ideal test subject for the heart."

"But…you would have been sentencing me to a living death," Leo said, more amazed than angry. "I would have been nothing but a soulless husk kept alive by your machine."

"Not for long. Your mother, if no one else, would have certainly intervened and demanded that you be allowed to die with dignity. By that point, however, the thing would have been accomplished. You would have died a hero, a martyr to one of the greatest advancements in the history of medical science."

Leo gave a smile that was glacial in its coldness. "Well," he said, "maybe it would have been better for everyone if that is what had happened. But it did not. Why?"

"An unexpected side effect."

"From what?"

"When I was initially brought to you, I injected you with a serum I created to preserve tissue in cases exactly like the one I was then facing. Theoretically, it would place the body in a state of temporary suspended animation until the successful completion of a life-saving procedure. In your case, it was done purely as a matter of form. I never expected the formula to work for more than an hour, ninety minutes at the very most."

"Clearly it succeeded far beyond your expectations," Leo said.

"Far, *far* beyond," the doctor replied. " As with the heart, you were my alpha patient. The serum had never before been tested on a human subject. When it became clear that not only were you going to survive, but survive in a state of perfect health…"

Villiers-Pagan shook his head, as if still reeling from the astonishment he had felt, and so skillfully hidden, on that long ago night. *The patient will make a full recovery*, he had announced with a suave air of professional satisfaction. But inside, he had been fairly screaming. *This is impossible! Impossible! What in God's name have I done here?*

*You have conquered death,* replied a voice from the darkest part of his soul. *You hold the greatest dream of mankind in the palm of your hand.*

"I became obsessed," the doctor continued. "I felt as if I had been elevated to godhood. I had visions of entire nations bending their knee to beg for my secret. I lost all semblance of detachment, objectivity. And in a moment of weakness, I did something incredibly foolish…"

"You couldn't resist trying it on yourself."

"No. I could not."

"And the result?"

"You see it before you. I am over one hundred years old, but I have the body I possessed at fifty! Oh, I have a few more gray hairs, some lines around the eyes, but I have not suffered so much as a common cold since the turn of the century."

Leo nodded. "Yes, yes, I can see all that. But that doesn't explain why you abandoned your family and position. As you have said, you could have had the world. Why did you run away?"

"I came to my senses, and thank God for it! Think of the lengths that some would go in order to possess this power, to have it all for their own. Once my secret became known, what would my life have been worth? I may have been safe from the depredations of age and disease, but not murder or impri-sonment. How could I ever be safe with such deadly know-ledge? How could my family?"

"And so you fled."

"I saw no other choice."

"Faked your death and disappeared."

"It was the only way to be sure my family would be safe."

"No."

"I beg your pardon?"

"It was not the only way. You could have come to me."

"Oh, good God! You forget that you were barely more than a boy then!"

"Did that stop you from making me the subject of your experiments?"

Villiers-Pagan fell silent.

"Did it ever occur to you," Leo said, "that I had the right to be taken in to your confidence?"

"I was too focused on myself," the doctor said softly. "I am sorry, Leo. I am sorry, but I never gave you a second thought."

Leo nodded. He looked down at his hands, and his brow furrowed. His hands curled into fists.

Villiers-Pagan felt his pulse pick up. He was, after all, facing a man who was no stranger to violence. What was

266

going through the Nyctalope's mind? The doctor decided to venture a guess. "You've never really thought about it, have you?"

Leo did not move or speak.

"Yes," Villiers-Pagan said, "I can see. I understand. You were so accustomed to your health… your energy… your strength… You never considered how strange it was that they never ebbed, never faded."

Leo looked up. "Will we ever die?" he asked quietly.

"Eventually," the doctor said, "but not before everything we have ever known or loved has fallen away."

*I showed up in front of the Continental about twenty minutes ahead of schedule. I had my eyes peeled for anything out of the ordinary, but it was just like any other day. It wasn't long before I got impatient and started wandering around the square. After a moment or two, I found myself standing near a milk bar (yes, there are really are such things). My eye fell on of a couple on a couple of somber-looking guys who appeared to be in some kind of deep philosophical discussion. One of them struck me as familiar, but I couldn't place where I had seen him before. I was really working my brain, trying to fig-ure out how I knew him, when he looked up and made eye con-tact with me. I was pretty embarrassed, because I realized I had been staring. He said something to me in French, and I just shook my head. I was about to head back into the street, when his friend turned around and looked at me. He was younger than the other guy and, by the looks of him, a hell of a lot meaner.*

*"British?" he said.*

*"American," I said.*

*He pointed at his buddy. "Do you have business with this man?"*

*"No. I didn't mean to be rude. It's just… I thought he might be someone I knew."*

*"That is quite impossible," he said. Then he smiled. "No one knows him, or me. We are strangers even to ourselves."*

*Now, I tend to be really annoyed by people who make cryptic remarks like that, and I usually pay them back in their own smart-assed coin. But, in this case, I decided to let the guy have his little joke, or whatever it was. After all, I had been the one doing the gawking. I just said, "Sorry to interrupt," and turned to walk away.*

*I had gone about thirty feet when the world exploded...*

"You know," Adrien said, "I believe I do know that fellow. In fact..."

His sentence, never to be completed, was lost in a deafening thunderclap that slammed Leo sprawling into the street. For a moment, he was too stunned to move. Then his mind, trained to ways of battle, recovered itself. *Bomb*, he thought, *and a big one too. Am I injured? I can't hear a damned thing, but that's no surprise...*

He forced himself to his knees, and winced as a sharp pain registered in his left shoulder. He looked down to see a large shard of glass, probably part of a windowpane, embedded in his flesh. He thought of Adrien, and cast his eyes about for the old doctor.

A moment later, he found him.

*The shockwave sent me rolling ass over teakettle, and I'm pretty sure I blacked out for at least a few seconds. I got knocked around pretty good, but mostly just bruises and scrapes. I'm embarrassed to say that, when I started to recover myself, the first thing I was concerned about was my camera. Can you believe it? I had just been in the middle of a bombing and all I could think about was my damn Kodak. All I can say is, I was still pretty young and maybe entitled to being a little stupid and selfish. Anyway, it turned out the camera was busted all to hell. Grace of God that it wasn't my head that got cracked open instead.*

*Looking back now, my strongest impression of those first few minutes after the blast is the silence. I was surrounded by people who were weeping and screaming, covered with blood* and dirt. But I couldn't hear them. I was temporarily deafened by the blast, so I couldn't hear their cries. I could just see their twisted up faces, their tears making lines through the gore on their cheeks.

I got to my feet and started to stumble around. I hadn't completely got my act together, and I wasn't sure exactly what to do. None of it seemed real. Even after my hearing started to come back, and all that death and horror started ringing in my ears, it all still felt like something that I was experiencing through someone else's senses. Then I heard a familiar voice, and I was suddenly myself again. The voice was desperate and not at all laced with the usual arrogance, but there was still no mistaking that it was Thomas Fowler, my buddy from the Times. He was standing on the other side of a hastily erected cordon, waving his hands and shouting at a policeman, demanding to be let through. For some reason I fixated on him as my true north, and headed straight for him through the smoke and the milling throng. I tried to call his name, but all that came out was a nasty-sounding cough and some blood. It was no big deal, just a cut inside my mouth, but it probably looked terrible to anyone who happened to notice.

I was about to try again when I saw another acquaintance step up and grab his attention.

"Pyle," Fowler said. "For Christ's sake where's your Legation pass. We've got to get across. Phuong's in the milk bar."

By now I was standing right behind the officer who had blocked Fowler. My mouth was open to say something to them, but something kept me silent. Neither of them noticed me. They were completely absorbed in one another, and if I was in the corner of their eye it was as just another of the dusty red walking wounded.

"No, no," Pyle said.

"Pyle, she is. She always goes there. At eleven-thirty. We've got to find her."

"She isn't there, Thomas."

"How do you know? Where's your card?"

"I warned her not to go."

*Fowler turned away as if to resume his argument with the policeman, then froze as the significance of what Pyle had said struck home. It hit him about a tenth of a second after it registered with me.*

"Warn?" *he said.* "What do you mean warn?"

*That was an asinine question, since he knew exactly what he meant, as did I. This stupid, pointless exercise in mass murder was the "demonstration" that I had been scheduled to photograph. Pyle had certainly known about it, probably even orchestrated it. God only knew why. I never asked.*

*Later, I became consumed with a killing rage that I thought was going to eat me alive, but not then. At that moment, all I felt was shock and an incredible wave of sadness for all the maimed and killed that surrounded me in the square.*

*Pyle and Fowler kept jabbering at one another, but I have no idea what they said. I couldn't stand the sight of them anymore. I turned and walked back into the chaos, determined to see if there was someone I could help. By that time policemen and paramedics with stretchers were already swarming through the destruction. I almost tripped over a priest who was giving last rites to a man whose legs had been blown off.*

*Then, by the ruins of what was left of the milk bar, I spotted my two new pals, the Frenchmen who didn't even know themselves. The older guy was flat on the ground and younger one, the hardcase, was kneeling beside him. Nobody was helping them, so I decided to see what I could do.*

*When I came to them, it was clear that the old guy was a goner. A piece of shrapnel had gone through his neck and the blood was just gushing out of his carotid artery. The hardcase was trying to staunch the flow with his bare hands, but it wasn't working. I knew it was futile, but I knelt and ripped off my shirt and held it out to him. He gave me a curt nod and pressed it to the man's wound. It was sodden in a matter of seconds.*

*Then the older fellow's eyes fluttered open and looked at me, then at this friend...*

"Death has caught up with me," Villiers-Pagan said.

"Not yet," Leo said. "Do not try to speak."

"Don't be absurd. I can feel it. I can feel..."

"Quiet, I say! There is still time..."

"No, please listen. I need to know...I need...you..."

"What?"

"I...need...you...to...forgive..."

*They said some things to each other in French. I'm glad I couldn't understand, because I've always felt that, whatever they exchanged, it would have been wrong for me to hear it. It's bad enough having to live with what I heard pass between Fowler and Pyle. I will tell you this much. At the very end, the old man seemed to be asking his friend something. The younger man leaned over and whispered something in his ear, and whatever it was, it must have been something the guy needed to hear. He gave a kind of weak sob, lifted his arm, and gently placed his hand on the young man's neck. It was so much like the way my own dad hugged me. The tenderness of the gesture, and the shock of its familiarity, moved me in a way that's difficult to describe.*

*I saw the life go out of the old man's eyes. The young man rose up and turned to me. "Thank you," he said, "for trying to help."*

*"I'm sorry about your father," I said.*

*He looked confused for a second, and I could hardly blame him. After all, he had never identified the dead man as his dad, but he didn't have to. I knew that he was.*

*"It is all right," he said after a moment. "He lived a very full life. Let us honor his memory by helping some of these others."*

*I suppose we did just that, but the rest of that day is just a miserable blur. I got separated from my friend at some point, and I never saw him again.*

*I tried to catch up with Pyle later, but without success. I had every intention of pounding the bastard within an inch of his life, but it turned out someone else got to him first. Unfortunately for Pyle, they didn't allow him even the inch. He was stabbed and left to drown in the mud one night by the bridge to Dakow.*

*I thought about attempting to talk to Fowler about it, but decided not to. What would have been the point? I saw him a few times at the Continental with an attractive young woman I'm pretty sure was the Phoenix they were both so consumed with. Fowler, gentleman that he was, had apparently elected himself to take care of the bereaved would-be Mrs. Pyle. Rather sporting of the old chap, I thought.*

*One evening, a few months after the bombing, I was shuffling through some of my photos when I came across an image that startled me with the force of an electric shock.*

*It was the picture, Jenny. The very one I have sent to you. Pick it up and take another look at it. As you can see, the focus of the image is the nun and the little children. But if you take a look in the shadows there on the right, you will see a portly but stylish-looking fellow looking on them with what I have always believed was a smile of genuine affection.*

*It's him, of course. That was how I recognized him that day, just before he was killed.*

*The fact of the poor man's death is not what makes this picture so important to me. I had seen people die before, and Lord knows I've seen plenty since. I treasure it because of the joy I caught there. See how the nun and the kids are all smiling and laughing? They weren't doing that for the camera. I'm not sure if they even noticed me. They were simply enjoying a moment of perfect happiness, and I believe the man in the shadows felt happy for them.*

*I used to hope that somehow, some day I would be able to give the picture to the man's son, but I finally gave up on that. I'll let you have it, along with the story. Maybe you can pass it on to your own grandkids one day.*

*Write back soon, and send some more pictures. Believe me when I say you've got a great eye. I'm expecting great things from you.*

*I love you, Jenny.*

*Yours,*

*Grandpa Mike*

*David Vineyard's contribution to this collection is an exciting adventure romp, featuring the Nyctalope (rehabilitated since Emmanuel Gorlier's* The Three Sisters*) fighting alongside a colorful cast of heroes and villains, reminiscent of an action movie of the 1960s. It finds its* raison d'être *in one of Jules Verne's lesser-known novels,* Mathias Sandorf, *which he wrote as a variation on the theme of* The Count of Monte-Cristo— *Verne greatly admired Dumas—while adding super-science to the mix. Like Edmond Dantes, Sandorf is unjustly imprisoned and returns as a Captain Nemo-like science pirate named "Dr. Antekirtt," whose lair is the prodigious island where the story takes place...*

## David L. Vineyard: *The Mysterious Island of Dr. Antekirtt*

*Antekirtta, 1954*

The Captain swore steadily through teeth clamped on the blackened stem of his pipe as he fought the helm of the fishing boat. His breath, indeed everything about him, reeked of alcohol, and his eyes had the far-away, unfocused look of a man lost in drink. He was a burly black bearded man in a dark blue sweater and pea coat wearing a peaked cap pulled low over his red-rimmed eyes. Outside the wind howled at near gale force as the small craft fought through the rough waters of the Eastern Mediterranean.

Leo Saint-Clair stood in the shadows of the deck house, his keen, strangely colored eyes seeing through the darkness, picking out the details of the ship's bow as it plunged into the rough sea through the slanting wall of rain that whipped them. The tires roped to the bow as a guard were thrown like so many pillows by wind and sea. He studied the Captain du-

274

biously, and thought about taking over the helm before they all drowned.

The Boy came through the hatch just then. He wore a slicker over an absurd outfit of plus fours and a blue sweater over a white shirt. His fair hair stood up in a cowlick in front, even in the downpour; the small white terrier that always accompanied him stood by his leg, shaking the excess moisture from his fur. Ordinarily neither the Boy nor the Dog should be on this voyage, much less the sodden sailor at the helm, but it was the Boy who had initiated this desperate adventure, and he was, after all, no ordinary youth, no more than Leo Saint-Clair, sometimes known as the Nyctalope, was an ordinary man.

"Good dog," the Boy chided as the dog shook off the last of the rain. He looked up apologetically at Saint-Clair, but the broad-chested man only glared on. He didn't mind the Dog or the Captain half as much as the Boy's obvious hero worship. Perhaps there had been a time when he would have welcomed that look—indeed had welcomed it from all comers, but now... Things had changed. Mistakes were made; men made them and lived with the consequences, even heroes, and the more public the mistakes, the more painful the consequences.

"You shouldn't be up on deck in this blow," Saint-Clair said.

"Mr. Prince and Mr. Morane asked me to fetch you. Anyway, my dog and I are pretty fair sailors; you can ask the Captain..."

"What do they want below?"

"They have the charts out. They thought that, perhaps, a council of war..."

The Captain had begun to sing a vaguely obscene sea shanty of dubious origins in a low voice. He looked as if he would pass out any moment.

The Boy sensed the Nyctalope's concern. "I'll stay with the Captain," he boy volunteered. "We've weathered much worse storms than this. Anyway, this is practically sober—for him."

Saint-Clair nodded. He was less than reassured, but he had all of the drunken sailor he could stomach. He turned the collar of his coat up and pulled a cloth cap down over his hair. He stepped out in the storm, fought to close the hatch, and fell into the natural rolling walk of the sailor as he rode the storm. Even though his eyes could pierce the darkest night, the slanting rain meant he had to keep a keen watch.

Below, the cabin was lit by a yellow light, wan and sallow. Two men sat around a crude table. One was tall, lean, well muscled, with dark hair, steel-grey eyes and a pleasantly chiseled face. He wore a campaign shirt with epaulets and buttoned down pockets, the sleeves rolled up to reveal lean bronzed forearms. He looked up as Saint-Clair entered.

"Morane, Prince," Saint-Clair said, acknowledging his companions with a nod.

The second man was younger, not a great deal older than the Boy above. He was bronzed and weathered, with thick, near white hair and sharp blue eyes. He wore a blue pullover shirt and white denims. He was smaller than Morane, just below Saint-Clair's medium height. Despite his youth, he was a trusted agent of Interpol.

As Saint-Clair entered and shucked off his cap and coat in the close cabin, the younger man stood and took a blackened pot off the stove.

"Coffee?"

Saint-Clair nodded and straddled a chair resting his arms on the back. His chefs at home would be horrified by this foul steaming mixture, but the Nyctalope had drunk worse during his adventurous life. He thought of the foul tea served by his Nepalese guides at the roof of the world, or the potent Arab coffee served to him in Algeria, or even the black tea so popular in Chile, served in a covered metal cup…

Prince handed him a cup of foul-looking, thick black mud, and took his own seat. This was even worse than the tea he had drunk during the curiously formal ceremony of the caravan-sari along the Silk Road on the way to ancient, blue-domed Samarkand.

They had picked up Prince in Tripoli 15 hours earlier. The American Bonisseur de La Bath had suggested Prince to them when Morane's Scot friend, Ballantine, had been sidelined by a twisted ankle. So far, it seemed a good choice, though one could never be certain until the crucible of fire tested a man's flesh as well as his will. Saint-Clair would have preferred to have had the ex-OSS man with them, but the American had assignments for his CIA to worry about, and no time for what might prove a fruitless adventure.

"How's it look up top?" Bernard Prince asked.

Saint-Clair sipped the foul brew and shrugged. "Bad. We'll be lucky if the drunk doesn't run us aground."

Prince smiled. "I know he doesn't seem like much, but we're in good hands. He's a damn fine sailor."

"So everyone keeps telling me."

"Well," said Morane, "in any case, we have him. We might as well hope he's as good as they say—drunk or sober."

"A damn sight better drunk, I'd wager," Prince said, "than most sober. Anyway, this is a lucky little boat. I like her name, the *Cormorant*. Wouldn't mind having a ship of my own with that name someday."

"The Boy said something about a council of war," Saint-Clair said. He was feeling old in this company. Even the Captain was younger than he was, though he looked no older than Morane. Physiologically, he might be 30ish, but mentally... It was the heart, not the mind, that was artificial, and nearly immortal.

"Yes," Morane said. "I—we, were wondering if our 'friends' were very far ahead of us."

"They have half a day on us," Prince said, obviously a point he had made before Saint-Clair came down.

"And the same weather," Morane added. "And I can assure you that, whatever his other skills, the Yellow Shadow is no sailor."

"Nor that half-German-Chinese with him, I'll wager," Prince added.

"You're both forgetting Largo," Saint-Clair said. "He may sail a desk now, but he made his fortune running waters as rough as these as a smuggler, black marketeer, and running refugees—the ones he didn't drown whenever the authorities got too close. No, he's every bit as good as our drunken friend at the helm. Still, we can move faster in this fishing vessel than the freighter they're taking, and we can get in much closer. We should beat them to it, but not by much."

Prince seemed relieved. *More hero worship*, Saint-Clair thought. He would feel more secure if Prince and the Boy had more of Morane's reserve. He had had too many lives depend on his actions, and there had been too many dead in his wake. There was a time that didn't worry him, but now... His return to France from semi-self-imposed exile had been done quietly, as discreetly as a celebrity as he had once been could manage. Things changed, but governments still had needs. Malraux, a friend who had become an enemy, was now a friend again--of sorts. Others had been forgiven, so why not a man as useful as the Nyctalope? Hadn't he saved countless lives during the war while seeming to collaborate? He was, after all, a legend, and the current government dealt in legends. The useful ones, at least. One advantage of being nearly immortal was the ability to outlive the tides of fortune. If he was no longer the living symbol of the old Imperial France that he once was, he still had his uses. A flag too old to be waved in public could still prove useful as a shroud for the Republic's enemies. And there were always enemies. Old and new.

"What do you think we'll find on Dr. Antekirtt's island?" Bernard Prince asked.

"Probably nothing," Morane said. "Nothing but legends."

"I don't know," Saint-Clair said. "There have always been rumors. Locals say the place is haunted. They won't even fish in its waters. Though you'd think all those pirate warships sunk back in 1884 would make for good fishing grounds. An artificial reef." He didn't add that he had been born only a few years before the great battle. He wondered what these men

278

would say if they realized he had been at this game since 1897...

Prince leaned back. "I've heard the stories, but I never really believed them. Who was this Dr. Antekirtt?"

"A genius," Saint-Clair said. "He was originally a Hungarian patriot, Count Mathias Sandorf. He and his allies were betrayed when they tried to drive the Austro-Hungarian rule out of power back in 1867. They were sentenced to an inescapable prison, the Donjon at Pisino, a dreadful place above a deep cataract and a rushing river. They were left for dead, but they escaped. Of the three, only Sandorf made it to safety. Over the next 15 years, he became Dr. Antekirtt and created his fantastic island fortress of Antekirtta. Apparently, he was a genius of the first class, inventing many remarkable weapons, the likes of which are only now common. His fast little submarines, *Electric 1* and *2*, were said to be far ahead of their time, and his yacht, the *Ferrato*, a wonder. My father, a sailor himself, told me of both.

"Over the years, there have been attempts to visit the island and liberate its secrets, but they've always met with disaster. The last I know of was during the war. Himmler, that fantastic foul troll, followed one of his visions and sent an SS team to raid it... Skorzeny's men, though not led by Skorzeny himself, but by a man named Drax..."

"Hugo Drax?" Morane spoke up.

"Yes. That one. The one in the papers a couple of years ago over that rocket business in England. Those famous scars of his were from his visit to Antekirtta. He was the only one to escape alive, and barely at that. Anyway, since then, the place has had an even worse reputation, and it doesn't help that the currents are tricky and the natural harbors treacherous. Antekirtt no doubt knew a secret way in, but if he did, he didn't leave the secret with anyone."

"Tell me, Saint-Clair," Morane asked, "what do you think we'll find on Antekirtta?"

Saint-Clair shook his head. "I wish I knew, but I can almost promise that, at the very least, we'll find..."

"...Death," the Yellow Shadow said. "I think we can be certain that the island is a deadly trap."

Julius No, the strange half-German-Chinese, tapped his fingers on the top of the teak table in Largo's luxurious cabin. "I knew Drax. A fool, but a dangerous one. He spoke of terrors, and he was not a man given to such things. Those burns of his, he attributed to a fire-breathing dragon..."

"Ha!" Emilio Largo barked a sharp unpleasant laugh. "Booby traps perhaps, even wild animals. But dragons? Really, my dear Doctor!" Largo's dark eyes flashed with contempt.

"Dragons come in many forms," Dr. No said. Though he showed no anger, it was clear he disliked Largo and his manner.

The Yellow Shadow showed nothing, but inside he seethed. Why must he be plagued with such incompetent lieutenants? It was bad enough that devil Morane was involved in this, but to have to deal with these two... And that fool Tadeus who had tipped that damn Boy Reporter... He should have known better than to consult that brilliant mad Professor, who was one of the Boy's closest friends. Well, he had paid for his mistake with his life, though not at Monsieur Ming's hand, but too late to benefit him. By the time he had learned of the leak, the Boy had already approached French Intelligence, and they, in turn, Bob Morane; and the former air force Commandant had brought in the Nyctalope, and now Interpol in the form of the young but already formidable Bernard Prince. What a mess! What an unholy mess! Still, if the island held the secret he suspected... That was why he had brought Dr. No was along—and Largo, for his ships and his knowledge of the sea.

Bob Morane, that upstart Prince from Interpol, the Boy Reporter, and... Leo Saint-Clair... That was the wild card—Saint-Clair.

A light on the phone at Largo's left hand flashed red. The sailor picked it up. He spoke quickly in Greek, then hung up.

"We're there," he said. "No sign of anyone else, though in this storm... The Captain says we seem to be in a brief calm. I suggest we go ashore now before it blows up again."

The Yellow Shadow nodded, and rose. So far things were going well. Still, he felt a certain unease. He'd feel more at ease if he knew what was going on in the mind of...

...The Nyctalope leaped from the bow of the dory into the water and took the line to pull it toward shore. Prince dropped in the water on the other side and grabbed the line to help. In the boat Morane sat with a British-made Sten gun, silenced like the ones used by the commandos during the war. The Boy held his dog under his coat in the stern, by the motor.

The storm had let up briefly, and they had taken advantage of that to come ashore. They had left the Captain back on the fishing boat, snoring raucously. Saint-Clair would have preferred to leave the Boy and the Dog with him, both to keep them out of the way and to watch the old souse. He was by no means sure the old reprobate would still be there when they returned. But he had been outvoted. It was the Boy who had brought them here, Morane pointed out, and Prince agreed.

Fools! This was deadly business, and no place for sentiment or adventure. Men might well die tonight—even boys.

They secured the dory and gathered their gear. Saint-Clair wore his silenced Browning in a shoulder rig under his pea coat and carried a silenced Sten gun like Morane. Prince was carrying a big Browning Automatic Rifle, the BAR, a gun that could shoot concrete to pieces. Even the Boy carried a 9mm automatic that he seemed quite familiar with. Only the Dog went unarmed, but even he was subdued, as if he, too, knew the danger that surrounded them. Both Saint-Clair and Morane carried heavy packs on their back, and Prince had one slung over his shoulder with extra ammo for the BAR.

They were ready for a fight.

They had landed on the northwest corner of Antekirtta. Monsieur Ming and Largo would have to utilize the natural inlet called Kencraf on the southwest side of the island, where the old lighthouse stood and the remnants of the pirate armada lay under the sea. Saint-Clair and Morane had opted for the route Drax and his men had taken after a U-boat had landed them ashore. The added bonus, in Saint-Clair's view, was a grizzly one. The Drax expedition had not been so long ago that there would be no signs of it. And, even if time had largely erased some of those signs, the Nyctalope's eyes would spot them. The trail of Drax's dead would warn them of any booby traps planted on the island, which might still be active and deadly, even after all these years.

They walked in the footsteps of ghosts, damned phantoms whose restless souls were lost to the winds of Antekirtta. Both parties were avoiding the small city Dr. Antekirtt had built and lived in. Their goal was the laboratory located near the center of the island, a Moslem fortress converted by Sandorf for his experiments.

Saint-Clair took the point. The island was almost certainly loaded with lethal traps. His uncanny eyes were vital to their chances. If anyone could spot a trap... Morane had explained it succinctly: "The Nyctalope's eyes are our secret weapon. Whatever devices the Yellow Shadow may have with him, he and his associates will move slower—or risk a quick, violent death. We can beat them to it."

"To what?" Prince had asked. "I'm still not sure what it is that we're looking for."

"Power." It was the Boy who had spoken. "The Professor—well, as best as I could make out, he's not always clear, the original absent-minded genius—but he said that the man who came to him was asking about power sources. That's the real secret of Dr. Antekirtt, the power he harnessed. That's what we're looking for, I think, what Monsieur Ming and Dr. No are here for—the secret of Antekirtta."

"Power," Saint-Clair had said. "That's always what it's all about ultimately. Power to create—or destroy, pure unadulterated...

"...Power," the Yellow Shadow said.

Dr. No looked at Monsieur Ming, but said nothing. He knew what the Mongol was thinking. Antekirtta held secrets, perhaps one especially dear.

They had come ashore in a fast boat lowered from Largo's ship, with a team of 12 armed and dangerous men recruited from the armies of minions at Ming's command. Hard men, cold-blooded, ruthless killers, every one. A match for most men—but for Morane—or the Nyctalope? Even in Hong Kong, Dr. No had read of the man Saint-Clair's exploits, and even if they had been exaggerated by the popular press—and they almost certainly were—he was still a dangerous foe. And while he knew nothing of the Boy, other than that he was a well known journalist despite his youth, and only had Ming's judgment of the man Morane, it was clear that this was unlikely to be an easy expedition.

The storm had laid while they came ashore—a good omen—but now the wind was freshening and the cold rain was beginning to whip up. A few minutes earlier, they could see the ruins of the old lighthouse on the point above the Kencraf inlet, but now it was growing darker. Dr. No, who despised the cold, regretted being here. Still, if Ming were right...

Largo was busy getting their gear ashore. He might be a greedy and dangerous ruffian, but he was a useful one. A tool, but a clever and useful one. When Blofeld had suggested him for the mission, the initial reaction had been doubt, but it was clear now he had been the best man for the job.

"We must move quickly," Dr. No said to the Yellow Shadow.

"But with care. I have no illusion that we are alone on the island. We cannot afford to imagine ourselves as ahead in this race. I will post men well ahead as scouts. They will gladly sacrifice themselves to any surprises the island has for us."

Dr. No nodded. It was a wise policy. Such men were only good for the fodder of these dangerous operations. In ordinary circumstances, neither he nor Ming would even be here—but this was no ordinary circumstance.

Largo was coming toward them. "We're ready." He carried a German Mauser on his hip in its wooden holster-stock, and, slung across his shoulder, an American Thompson machine gun with a drum, like the gangster he was. Ming carried a Walther P-38 in a holster under his coat, and Dr. No was unarmed. He considered his hands delicate tools and had no intention of harming them by carrying anything so crude as a gun.

The Yellow Shadow lifted his hand and waved three fingers. Three of his men split off from the others and moved ahead. The rain was now falling steadily and beginning to slant, as it had earlier. The wind off the sea was stiffer, picking up. Already, it was impossible to see their ship anchored in the inlet.

Largo took up a position behind the Yellow Shadow's three men. Another man, similarly armed, filed behind him, then Ming and then Dr. No and the rest of the men. There was a sort of overgrown trail leading up off the beach, and they took to that, rather than the rough country on either side. Even this was overgrown and rough going.

But, Dr. No could not help wondering, were they really...

"...alone?" Bob Morane was saying. "I don't think so."

The Boy had asked when they had stopped to rest. The white dog was in his lap, getting his ears scratched; Prince was squatting on a rock, checking the BAR. The rain was worse, but they had found an overhang of rock to the lea of the wind and were relatively sheltered. Morane reached out and tousled the Dog's wet head, and the grateful animal shivered playfully. "In any case, Saint-Clair is right. We must proceed as if Ming and the others are already on the island."

As if on cue, the Nyctalope appeared to the accompaniment of a flash of lightning and a clap of thunder. His hair was wild and wind-blown, and his features leaner and more drawn than on the photos and illustrations the Boy had seen from the hero's heyday. He was such a strange figure. According to rumors, he was virtually immortal, possessing an artificial heart, and had traveled to the four corners of the world—and beyond. If only half the stories than the man La Hire had written in the newspaper had some basis in reality, Leo Saint-Clair was nothing less than a Nietzschean *ubermensch*, a super-man, as much of the American comic-book variety as the intellectual one.

As he ducked to enter the shelter, he tossed something at their feet. Prince lay aside his rifle and picked the object up. It was an insignia, one with the distinctive lightning markings of the SS.

"We're on the right trail, at least," Saint-Clair said. "I found that about 20 yards ahead. There was more, but no sense disturbing the dead."

The Boy's head jerked up. The little white dog softly yelped as if he understood.

"A trap?" Morane asked, as Prince handed him the grim souvenir.

Saint-Clair nodded. "An old hunter's trick. Nothing extraordinary, save from what I can tell, it was activated by a crude electronic eye. Just a heavy log suspended from rope and the electronic tripwire. Spikes had been driven into the log and sharpened—perhaps even poisoned. This fellow..." he nodded to the insignia the Boy now held, "...was still hanging there after all this time—at least what was left of him. I saw signs that another man may have been injured. I can't imagine a man like Drax wasting much time on the wounded, so the body is likely close."

The Boy Reporter offered the insignia back to Saint-Clai, who shook his head. "Keep it. I've seen enough of them to last me a lifetime. From here on, we'll have to be doubly careful."

Prince nodded, again picking up the BAR. "Hadn't we better...?"

Morane nodded. "No sign it's letting up. I don't suppose Ming and his group are letting up either though. Once more into the breach, *mes amis*."

The Boy and Prince both laughed. To them, it was an adventure. A grand adventure. Saint-Clair shrugged. He had spent a lifetime in search of, and living adventure—more than one lifetime. It was never like the books. It was always earnest, and always good, and bad men and women died. The Boy's youth, Morane's courage, Prince's toughness, none of them were armor against the cold finger of death that waited for them at every turn on this island. He had killed, and he had survived. He had watched friends die, and he had taken vengeance. He knew the true face of adventure. A skull. A grinning, leering, humorless skull. He would be much happier if he knew where the Yellow Shadow and his party were. It was always safer to have the enemy in...

"...view," Emilio Largo was saying. "In my view, we're moving far too slowly. Perhaps you and the Doctor should stay back while I go ahead with a few of your men?"

The Yellow Shadow was not used to having his orders questioned. He didn't care for this Largo. He was a bully and a sadist, and there was more than a touch of cheap melodrama about him. Not that Dr. No was any better, but he, at least, had the restraint of his Asian blood. Largo was a vulgarian, a self-made man of the worst sort. Even if one admired his ruthlessness, there was a twisted quality about him, a perversion. Only Monsieur Ming's sternest command had kept the fool from bringing a woman along with them. Really, a woman on an expedition like this!

"We'll stay together," the Yellow Shadow said sharply. "Morane and Saint-Clair are both capable of lying in ambush for us, and picking us off silently. Morane may be a boy scout, but he's an efficient one, and the Nyctalope..."

"The Nyctalope," Largo virtually spat the word out. "A man who some say has an artificial heart and can see in the dark. What nonsense! Perhaps he was good—once. But he hasn't done anything since the war, that I know of. He's a has-been. And, anyway, if anyone believe those absurd stories, they would have to believe that the man is close to 80..."

Ming ignored the rant. He knew secrets that would leave the boastful Largo shivering in a corner, sucking his thumb like a cowering child. How could a man like Largo even imagine a man like the Nyctalope?

Though his mind was distracted, the Yellow Shadow was always aware of his surroundings. They had made their way about half a mile inland along the overgrown trails, and as yet encountered nothing that slowed them more than debris that had to be climbed over or gone around. There were few animals about, but the storm would have seen to that. Such creatures would take shelter and ride out the wild night. They had more sense than men.

There had once been a thriving village on the island, home to scientists and artists, but it had largely died out by the time of the Great War, and been largely destroyed by German bombers during the WWII, when they had carpet-bombed the island before the Drax expedition. No one seemed to know what had brought about the end of Dr. Antekirtt's little Eden, but Ming suspected that it was as simple as human nature. The good Doctor might have been a beneficent despot, but he was still a despot, and whatever pretense to democracy he had set up on the island, it was first and foremost his experiment, his dream. And when the dreamer dies—what becomes of the dream?

They had come to a fork in the trail. Seeking respite under an overhang of foliage, they studied the divergent paths.

"The question is," Dr. No said softly, "which is the road less taken?"

Largo snorted. "One way to find out." He signaled one of Ming's men toward the path on the left, and he took up his machine gun and boldly stepped toward the path on the right.

Ming started to stop him, then stopped. Let the reckless fool find out for himself. With a nod, the Mongol sent his own man to follow Largo's order. Largo was already halfway up the right path, sweeping the barrel of the Thompson ahead of him like a soldier on point.

"A brave man, our Signore Largo," Dr. No said with quiet sarcasm.

Largo disappeared first. It seemed quite a long time that he was gone. After a moment, they saw his figure reemerging, still swaggering, a nasty smile on his lips, a cigar clamped between his thick lips.

He stopped.

The Yellow Shadow tensed. Dr. No rested his delicate hands on the Mongol's arm.

Largo turned his head. He cocked it to one side, like a dog at an unexpected sound. In this storm, it was hard to hear anything. He turned back toward the main party. He took a step.

Paused.

Turned again...

"No!" It was Ming's sharp voice.

There was a flash of light. It was too weak for lightning.

Largo had half-turned as Ming had shouted at him. That saved his life. Almost.

He fell to the ground, screaming.

"Now we know the road forward," Dr. No said.

Largo was writhing on the ground, his hands to his face, still...

"...Screaming. I heard a human scream."

Saint-Clair froze, and behind him so did Morane, Prince, the Boy, and even the Dog.

Prince unslung his rifle and worked the action, Morane, like Saint-Clair, had recognized that the scream came from a distance. "Another of Antekirtta's traps," said the airforce hero as he relaxed.

"At least, we know we're not alone," Prince said, relaxing, a little teased by his reaction.

The little dog began a howl, but the Boy hushed him. "I'm sorry," the Boy began to say..."

"Don't be," Saint-Clair said. "I doubt they heard it, and even if they did, they already suspect we're here. And you can hardly blame the animal. That scream was almost inhuman. Either way, the pup is an advantage for us. His hearing and

sense of smell are keener than my eyesight. He sensed something a few seconds before we actually heard the scream. I
saw his hair bristle." It was the most human moment the Nyctalope had shown. Morane half expected to see him tousle the
Dog's ears.

"Well," Prince said, "At least they're down a man. One
more to our side."

The Boy was unexpectedly smiling. "I hope the Captain
didn't hear that. He'll think he's having the terrors."

Even Saint-Clair chuckled. Then he turned serious. "I
make them closer to shore than I would have thought," he
said. "If the charts we have are accurate, we should be a few
klicks from the villa and fortifications. I suspect we'll find
more of Drax's party as we get closer, but we're ahead, and a
wounded man will slow our adversaries a little more."

"Not for long. Ming is far from sentimental," Morane
said, "but I agree, I think that scream will slow their pace if
nothing else. God knows what the poor devil ran into."

Saint-Clair nodded. Ever since they had landed, he had
felt a presence, as if they were being watched, and he was not
given to hysterics or unease. This island had an uncanny effect
on him, and he didn't like it. He didn't believe in demons,
ghosts, or the whole pantheon of the supernatural, but he had
seen more than his fair share of the odd and the unnatural, and
this whole place stank of it. No wonder sailors avoided it. For
the first time, he began to wonder if there might be something
worthwhile to salvage from Antekirtta after all. Something
still powered the electric eye that had killed Drax's man, at
least as far back as the war, and, though he hadn't said anything to the others, the trap hadn't looked as if it dated from
the last century when he had examined it. Antekirtta had supported some population longer than history suggested.

The storm had let up a little again, but if he was any
judge, it was only another respite. Storms in this part of the
world were notoriously fickle and likely to swirl around in
complex currents, striking again and again until they blew
themselves out. And this place was odd to begin with. Strange

currents in the sea, and stranger ones in the sky. That was why they had abandoned Morane's original idea to use a helicopter, seeing as he was an ex-fighter pilot—why Ming and the others had come by sea too. Even a sea plane would have never navigated a landing in these waters, at the best of times. It was as if Antekirtta had been chosen to be as uninviting as possible to any intruder.

Taking the point, he swept the darkness, checking the little dog as they moved ahead. The animal's nerves were good. Fear kept you alive. For too many years, Saint-Clair hadn't known that feeling. It made him dangerous to himself and others. Since the war... Well, even an immortal had to grow up sometime...

They had been moving vaguely uphill for a while when, suddenly, he stopped. He raised a hand, but the others had already halted. They had seen the dead SS he had found and passed his remains quietly, keeping their thoughts to themselves, but since then, they had been a more sober crew.

The Nyctalope signaled the others to wait, and went forward. He slung the Sten gun under his arm and drew his Browning with the specially designed suppressor. He thumbed the safety off and went ahead on cat feet.

Then, he froze.

Slowly, he knelt down. He carefully moved some brush aside with his free hand.

There, in the brush, carefully hidden, was another electronic eye. He had come within a centimeter of tripping it. Noting its position, he stepped back several feet, then searched for a stone. Picking a good size one, he hefted it, waited a beat, then tossed it. It broke the beam from the electronic eye.

There was a flash of light.

The object up in the tree looked like a dragon's head in the darkness, even to his eyes. A beam of light like a flame leaped from it, and, directly across from its path, cut a swath though the side of a large tree. Smoke rose from the green trunk where the beam had struck. Had Saint-Clair broken that electronic eye beam, the "dragon's eye" would have cut him in two.

And it would have, if he hadn't noticed a bit of yellowed white in the dirt where the electronic eye had been.

It was another of Drax's unlucky crew—his half-buried skull to be exact.

The beam of light had decapitated the SS. Probably even cauterized the wound with its heat. Nasty.

Morane had come up quickly when he had heard the sizzling noise of the tree burning. "My God," he whispered.

"Yes," the Nyctalope said. "My sentiments exactly. Perhaps we should post a sign."

Morane whistled. "What in God's name?..."

The Nyctalope smiled. "Here be..."

"...dragons," Dr. No said. "As I warned Signore Largo, dragons." He was examining the device that had fired the beam of light and wounded Largo. It resembled nothing so much as a dragon's head until it was uncovered.

The Yellow Shadow had just sent Largo back on a stretcher made from some branches and his men's jackets. They were losing time, and Largo's scream had surely alerted the others. Normally, he would have killed the fool if for no other reason than his arrogance, and raising an alarm, but he wasn't sure if they could trust Largo's crew if word got back to them that he had murdered their leader. "He'll live, but he might lose that eye. Not so terrible a fate for a pirate I suppose."

Dr. No nodded. "This weapon is quite remarkable," he said, as if discussing a new specimen. "An electronic eye set it off. Largo must have tripped it. When you called out, he turned, and only caught a glancing blow along the edge of the optical nerve. If not, he might well have been decapitated. I've read of certain experiments, but nothing this advanced. The amplification of light through a jewel, usually a ruby I believe, to create such an intense beam that it can cut through the strongest metal—or flesh. You noticed the wound was cauterized..."

Ming was after bigger fish than weapons of light, but he made a note to have one of his men take the "dragon" back to the ship. Dr. No was still studying the weapon. The half-German-Chinese had recently run afoul of several tongs and only Ming's own Shin Tan had protected him from the vengeance of the Si Fan and others. With the money he had embezzled from the tongs, and what Ming was paying him, Dr. No had claimed to have purchased an island, a small key near Jamaica, where he planned to mine bat guano while indulging in his scientific curiosity—a brutal but clinical curiosity. Frankly the cold-blooded devil gave even the Yellow Shadow a chill. Still, the irony of Dr. No's planned self-imposed exile and this island fortress did not escape him.

"You think our competition is ahead of us?" Dr. No asked, as he reluctantly turned from the dragon weapon.

"Yes," replied Ming. "But I doubt they know what they are looking for. They have some vague idea I imagine... The man Saint-Clair is no fool, but since Tadeus knew little, he could give little away, and I doubt the eccentric Professor could tell them much, even if he wanted to. The man can't remember to match his stockings."

Dr. No shrugged. He, too, had been a victim of society's disdain for the pure intellect. One would think a man such as Ming, a scientist himself, would have more tolerance, but— Well, it hardly mattered. Soon enough, he would have his own little island fortress on Crab Key, well guarded by the mixed blood Chinese, crudely called 'chigroes,' whom he had carefully groomed as his servants with rewards weighed against harsh punishment. Once there, he was assured of his privacy. He couldn't imagine the British would be a problem—they seldom were in Hong Kong. So far, the only drawback involved birds. Birds! The Audubon society thought of Crab Key as some sort of private sanctuary. What nonsense, birds. In any case, he was confident that he could handle any British policeman they might persuade to look into his business. Perhaps, he would build his own "dragon" to keep the bird watchers and nosy policemen at bay. One more mobile and less clinical than this one. He was a traditionalist in many ways. Dragons should breathe fire, not beams of light, however deadly.

The rain had let up, though lightning still danced in the sky. More men had joined them from the shore, and the mood was nervous and tentative. Being willing to die for the Yellow Shadow and actually doing it were two different things. Largo's wound had cast a pall over the expedition.

"It has struck you of course that there is a conundrum here," Dr. No said

"A conundrum?" Ming replied.

"Yes. This—this weapon. It is not merely that it is advanced—Einstein didn't predict the electric eye until just before his work on relativity—indeed, it was that, and not his more famous work, that won his Nobel..."

"Your point?"

Dr. No paused, held his anger. "While Dr. Antekirtt was obviously a genius, and well ahead of his time, we must ask ourselves if he discovered some kind of self-replicating energy source... My dear Monsieur Ming, this Antekirtt—Count Sandorf—was last heard of before the beginning of the 20th century, but his weapons are still operational, and the electric eye is still connected to a source of power..."

Ming's bright dark eyes sparked. Yes! Fool that he was! Largo had distracted him. It was obvious. But that left one question: if the island's defenses were maintained—by who... or...

"What is it?" the Boy asked, watching as Morane carefully dug the earth out around the electronic eye Saint-Clair had found.

The Nyctalope shrugged. Morane had slapped his forehead, then, taking a hunting knife from his boot, had dropped to the ground near the electronic eye. Meanwhile, Prince was

293

studying the "dragon" after taking it down from its hiding place.

"There are no wires" Prince observed. "So what powered it? I can understand the electronic eye tripping and firing it, but what powered it—or for that matter..."

Morane had finished digging out the electronic eye mechanism. He lifted it from the ground. It was no larger than a stake a surveyor might use, with the glass encased "eye" like a flashlight.

"No wires," Saint-Clair observed. Something stirred in his memory. He had encountered something similar once; power transmitted through the ether without wires, like radio or television signals

"Of course," said the Boy. "The Professor talked about this, but I thought he was babbling. Now it all makes sense." Even his pup was wagging his tail excitedly, as if he, too, sensed a mystery being solved. "Before I left, the Professor kept saying something about power through the air. I thought he was talking about airplanes or rockets or some such, but now..."

"Power through the air," Saint-Clair said.

Morane was examining the "dragon" now. "Here, see this small recess. It's a lens. A receptor. The eye activated it and also powered it. And there's another on the other side... Prince, put the weapon back, as close to exactly as it was as you can."

Prince did as Morane asked. Then the Commandant placed the eye back in the ground and waved them all back. He used his hand to break the unseen beam from the eye to the weapon. There was a flash and the tree was again scorched.

Prince removed the weapon again while Morane was careful to turn the eye away from the weapon. But it was Saint-Clair who had grasped the obvious. He moved quickly off the trail and thrashed in the bushes. The Dog barked excitedly until the Boy hushed him, but by then Morane, too, was thrashing in the brush.

"Here," said Saint-Clair. "About five feet away..."

"And another," Moraine said. "About six more feet in."

"I don't see..." began Prince.

"The Professor experimented with this once," said the Boy. "He nearly burned down the Diva's villa, but the idea was sound enough. Power, electrical power transmitted through the air without wires. The eyes act as transmission stations and focus the power. They don't look big enough to store it, so they carry the current from eye to eye and, when the beam is interrupted, it activates the weapon. They must be planted all over the island like this..."

It was Prince who saw the most obvious advantage first. "Then, if we follow them..."

"Back to the source," Morane said. "Of course, it will be rough going, but better than stumbling along looking for traps."

"Then, we had best move quickly," Saint-Clair said. "Ming and No aren't fools. They will think of the same thing before long."

"No doubt," said Prince, but he was laughing. He had seen the one thing the others had missed.

Morane and Saint-Clair looked at him as if he were mad, but the Boy suddenly began to laugh too. Even the little dog pranced as if he had gotten the jest.

"I don't get the joke," Morane said.

"Neither do I," added Saint-Clair.

But then Morane smiled broadly too. And to think, it had been his idea in the first place. Simpleton. And even as he smiled, he saw the same thought break on Saint-Clair's features.

They had an advantage the others could not duplicate. The Nyctalope's...

"...eyes," swore the Yellow Shadow. "Damn their eyes!"

His men crashed through the rough on either side of the path like so many elephants. Ordinarily, as stealthy as ninjitsu, the fear of the "dragons" had made them nervous, and nervous men were never stealthy. Still, even with that disadvantage, their pace had increased once they began to follow the path of the electric eyes.

Dr. No seemed to find it all amusing. The idea of power sent directly through the air had fired his mind.

"Of course, it was the great dream of the Slav genius, Tesla, to transmit power through the air, but while it is theoretically possible, the probability of overcoming the numerous problems and drawbacks stopped even his great intellect. Our Dr. Antekirtt must have indeed been a genius to not only conceive of the idea when Edison was still toying with filaments for his light globes, but to harness the power and overcome it. The potential as a weapon alone... Imagine..."

But the Yellow Shadow needed no lesser imagination to fire his vision. If the power could be used to trigger a simple light amplification weapon, then imagine if it was used directly. Not powering a toy, but directly used against an enemy. Already, he was considering the electronic eyes which were used to carry the invisible current. Was a few feet their limit, or could that be extended with a greater generation source? What if a nuclear reactor was available? He saw visions of entire cities in flames and the world on its knees—to him— alone. When Dr. No would no longer be needed... Antekirtt's laboratory was such a dangerous place...

He closed the fist of his artificial right hand. He imagined Dr. No's skull crushed with that grip. Power, and his alone to wield. But in the shadows. Let others stand in the limelight. He preferred to manipulate his puppets from the darkness of anonymity. Vanity had been the downfall of others with the same dream. It would not be his.

An excited shout.

Another eye had been found.

He already knew the trail was leading to the fortress at the center of the island. That much was obvious. Where else would Antekirtt have built his generator but in the fortress of Antekirtta? And now, they had a safe path to that generator.

Only one thing concerned him. A small thing. A dangerous thing.

The man Morane was a fool, but one blessed with luck and remarkable cunning. Indeed he seemed to lead a charmed life, and now with this team of his... The Boy was nothing. The sailor? A mere drunk. The Interpol agent? A policeman, nothing more. But the other...

He knew the stories about the Nyctalope. An almost inhuman hero; the embodiment of Colonial France, a sort of living emblem. A ruthless soldier and adventurer, a legend in the flesh. They had never met, but once before, a long time ago, in China, there had been a remarkable Triad of which the Yellow Shadow was one arm. Saint-Clair had almost single handedly smashed their plans. Ming had been forced to flee, to go underground. Saint-Clair had only been hours from not only destroying the Shin Tan and his plans, but from destroying him. That made him a deadly enemy. An enemy to be respected. Feared. Destroyed.

He would not rest until he stood over the body of the Frenchman, and cut out his artificial...

"...heart," Saint-Clair was saying. "This is the heart of the island."

They stood on a rise and looked down on the fortress of Antekirtta. It was a large structure, first built by Crusaders during the Second Crusade, and later conquered by the Seljuk Turks, who had made many improvements to the place, including a low outer wall that surrounded the main grounds. Inside, there was a courtyard with stalls and other small buildings around the inner walls, and to the southeast, a barracks— it couldn't be anything else—a building about three stories tall. There were other structures of equally obvious origin: a stable, downwind from the other buildings; an adjoining smith; what looked to be a munitions dump that apparently went underground; and the main structure or castle, a curious mix of Western and Eastern architecture, given a strange even Gothic appearance by the scuttling clouds above.

All of it deserted and quiet.

They made their way down the steep hill slowly. There was no sign of the Yellow Shadow, so they were ahead of the game. As they neared the ruins—there was no other name for them—the three men grew more cautious, and even the little dog seemed to sense the danger, keeping close to the Boy. No one spoke, but Saint-Clair could see the determination in Morane's face and the heightened awareness in Prince's eyes.

But there were no more traps. None they could see anyway.

The great gate was open, a heavy Moorish style door that now hung shattered by an explosion.

Again, no one spoke, but they all thought the same thing. Drax. He had made it this far, if no farther.

Saint-Clair entered first, the Sten gun unslung, moving through the center of the courtyard. It was overgrown and unkempt, full of shadows and pools of deeper darkness, gray even to his eyes. Behind him, Morane entered to the right, and Prince to the left, the Boy and the Dog behind them, the young reporter keeping an eye on their rear.

Nothing happened.

Saint-Clair spotted several electronic eyes, but they were inactive. Had Drax, and his SS, getting this far, deactivated them?

No.

Not Drax. And not Ming either.

And yet, one thing was clear. The electronic eyes within the fortress were as well cared for as those outside. They weren't alone. Eyes were watching them. Eyes that had chosen to allow them inside the fortress unassaulted.

So far.

Saint-Clair felt the hair on the nape of his neck stand up. The mystery of Antekirtta had long intrigued him. It had once been a sort of paradise, a haven for political refugees, artists, artisans, and scientists, then... Something had happened. Those who knew kept quiet. Antekirtt had died not too long after the great pirate battle that had ended his quest for revenge, and the island seemed to die with him. By the end of the Great War, it was known to be deserted, and by the Second World War, it was thought to be haunted. The fate of Drax and his men had only added to that myth. But was it a myth? What did hide on Antekirtta. Or who?

From the corner of his eye, he saw the Dog stop, sniff the air, stiffen. The animal's hair bristled as it had earlier.

Saint-Clair raised a hand. Morane stopped. Prince followed suit, using a hand to signal the Boy to stay back.

The party was at the great stone steps that led up to the main structure of the fortress, the original Crusader building. Like the rest of the place, it was overgrown and crumbling, and yet wasn't that a path well worn up and down the steps?

He scanned the shadows of the old building, seeking some movement, a hint of life, an ambush...

Slowly he began the ascent of the stone steps.

One.

So far no trap. Two.

He reminded himself to breathe. He could almost hear his heart beating. If someone had coughed, it would have sounded like a gunshot. Three.

Another two steps and he would reach a wide landing of sorts, then another half dozen steps to the main entrance.

And so far...

The figure came out of shadows so deep that even the Nyctalope's uncanny eyes hadn't seen him. One instant, there was nothing, then a flash of distant lightning and...

All three men swung their weapons toward the figure. The little dog barked once sharply.

The man seemed unaware of their weapons. He merely raised his hand, and spoke a single word...

"...Welcome," Dr. No said. "We should expect an unpleasant one."

That seemed obvious, but Ming nodded. Their progress had been exponentially faster once they left the main trail and followed the electric eyes, but it was still slow going, and the Mongol could not help but feel they were losing more than time. Experience had taught him the folly of arrogance, and he knew that men such as Bob Morane and Saint-Clair had not survived as long as they had by luck alone. The Yellow Shadow had known others who had crossed the Nyctalope's path and lived to regret it. That old business in China still stung, and if Dr. Natas held no grudges, and the one known as the Blue Scorpion had met final defeat at the hands of a brazen American engineer, Monsieur Ming had a long memory and desired pay back.

Perhaps this would afford him that opportunity. It was pleasant to think of Saint-Clair and Morane at this mercy...

One of his men came toward them swiftly. He spoke softly to the Mongol, his eyes cast down as was proper.

Ming turned to Dr. No.

"Just ahead. The fortress..." '

They moved quickly, but still with care. They were above the fortress in a copse of wood and well concealed, though they kept well back mindful of the Nyctalope's eyes.

The fortress lay in the shadows. It was still and seemed abandoned. They watched for several minutes, but saw no sign of movement. Flashes of distant lightning illuminated the courtyard. Low scuttling clouds created fantastic images. But nothing living moved.

Neither Dr. No nor Monsieur Ming dared to think they were ahead of the others. From here on the danger was only greater. One question remained in the forefront. What danger lay ahead? What lay unseen in the...

"...shadows," their host said. "For too many years, I have lived among the shadows of the dead."

He was a small man and, despite his age, obviously still fit. There was something of the athlete about his carriage, and a sense of tremendous energy and wit about him. His eyes were quick and saw more than they revealed. He had given them a queer name, but one Saint-Clair suspected was his own: Point Pescade.

His greeting had been perfectly designed to gain their attention:

"We must hurry, gentlemen. There is little time and we're all in grave danger..." Instinctively, Saint-Clair had turned to the direction the enemy was advancing from. "No, no, not them. There's far greater danger and little time. I have put this off too long, and now... Pray that there is still time. Come with me, gentlemen, and I will explain everything as quickly as possible."

He had told them about the mysterious "Dr. Antekirtt" and his war of revenge for the way he had been wronged, how Mathias Sandorf had used his genius, and the gifts of the island, to build a sort of scientific utopia after defeating his enemies, and then had been struck down by an enemy he could not have imagined.

As they talked, Point Pescade led them down a narrow stair into the catacombs located beneath the main building. Prince and the Boy agreed to keep watch while Saint-Clair and Morane followed the old man deeper into the darkness.

"How could he have known? How could he have guessed? Madame Curie was years away and Röntgen had yet to make his discoveries... How could the Doctor have begun to guess..."

Saint-Clair looked sharply at Morane. There was an unspoken agreement to let the old man tell his tale in whatever rambling way he chose. Obviously, the fellow was a bit dotty with age and loneliness.

As they moved deeper, they heard a curious hum, like some sort of giant generator, and they began to notice a radiant light emanating ahead of them. Before they could comment on it, they came upon a great room lined with giant machinery that resembled in many ways a generator, the source to the hum of power and light. Passing the giant generators, they came to a wall lined with panels and gauges, obviously monitoring the source of the power.

"And there, gentlemen, is the source of Antekirtta's power. You can't imagine how many hours the Doctor worked down here, how often I assisted him... Do you see, gentlemen, do you begin to comprehend? I myself installed that monitor after the last war... too late, too late..."

Saint-Clair followed the old man's pointing finger to the monitor in question and, suddenly, a chill ran up his spine.

"Marie Curie," Morane said, "Wilhelm Röntgen. The invisible enemy..."

"Radiation," Saint-Clair said.

"Aye," Point Pescade said sadly. "How could the good Doctor have known? Have guessed? He thought he had found the greatest boon to mankind since Prometheus gave us fire, and instead... At first, there were mysterious illnesses on the island, cancers, blood diseases, strange burns—we couldn't have known. Soon, people began to leave, and the Doctor's health began to fail as he wore himself out, down here, trying to discover the secret, all the time exposing himself to certain death—a slow, lingering death, that first claimed all he had loved, then his own life."

"My God!" Moraine said. "He built a nuclear reactor in the 19th century."

"No," Pescade said sharply. "No, gentlemen, not built one—found one. The entire island is a natural nuclear reactor, a volcanic wonder. That is what the Doctor found, but he could not have guessed..."

"...The price of the gift."

As they spoke, Morane had moved closer to a wall dominated by a large switch with bright red handles. It was quite big and would need two hands to pull it down. He reached out to touch it...

"No!"

Morane froze.

"Forgive me, but should you throw that switch without protective gloves and before I throw this switch..." Pescade indicated a large red button on the low panel before him... "You would receive a massive radiation burn to your hands, possibly fatal. You must remember this place may be a work of genius, but by modern standards... I fear I lacked the genius of my friend and mentor. It has been all I could do merely to maintain the island safely, and not even that..." He turned to Saint-Clair, locking his eyes with the man's uncanny orbs. "That was why I sent for you."

"Sent?"

"Indirectly, of course, but the bait was laid, and who else would be chosen for such a mission? No, there's no time for modesty. I needed a man of your caliber, even knowing that it would also draw other, more ruthless men. I needed to give you this."

The old man moved toward a closed cabinet which he opened. Inside was a large old book, stuffed with papers and wrapped in oil cloth.

"Doctor Antekirtt's journals, gentlemen. All his discoveries, all his wisdom. It's time to let the world be reminded of his genius, and time to carry these secrets away from this place before they're buried forever."

"Buried?" Saint-Clair asked.

"Buried," the Yellow Shadow repeated. He was smiling, his weapon aimed at the Nyctalope's chest. Behind him was Dr. No and several of his men, two of them closely covering Prince and the Boy. The little dog was nowhere to be seen.

"Don't tell me that you have failed to understand what this doddering fool was trying to tell you," Ming gloated. "My God, man, think. A natural nuclear reactor. These great generators... Perhaps you would care to tell them, Doctor?"

The Chinese glided forward like a great snake. He moved toward the switch where Morane had been standing. "No doubt you know the island is a natural nuclear reactor. To some extent, the entire planet is, but what you cannot comprehend is the simple fact that, in tampering with nature, Dr. Antekirtt upset the balance. Are you familiar with the term 'China Syndrome?'"

Morane had gone white. "Meltdown."

"Exactly," Ming said. "Meltdown. The entire island collapsing on its core, a tremendous explosion and a release of

303

radioactive gasses. No doubt, the island will cease to exist. The geologists who monitor such things will put it down to a volcanic eruption, but... Tell me, how long do you estimate?" he had spoken to Point Pescade.

"Should I fail to throw that switch? A few hours. It controls the rods which help to cool the reactor which the volcano powers. They're failing, but should hold out a little longer..."

"So that you have time to give our friend Saint-Clair here Antekirtt's notebook?. Such a waste. For the greater glory of France? What a joke. No, no the good Doctor and I have better things to do with this gift." Ming was gloating.

The Nyctalope was seemingly at ease, but beneath the exterior, every muscle was tense. He could feel the tension build, and knew that his moment, the moment of action, was near. From the corner of his eye, he had seen the Boy's little dog in the shadows. He might be small, but could provide a diversion, and all Saint-Clair needed was one moment. If only the animal waited for the right moment.

Dr. No was standing by the switch now. "So this decides all our fates? Throw the switch and the island lives for another few hours, leave it and..." He smiled thinly and reached out for the switch.

*Let the old man keep silent*, Saint-Clair thought.

Dr. No put both hands on the switch.

Point Pescade moved a single step, hiding the red button with his body.

Dr. No threw the switch.

Then, everything happened at once.

The Chinese-German scientist was jolted; his body became an arc of light and fire, his hands almost ablaze. An inhuman scream escaped his lips. For a moment, he hung there before his body broke contact. Then, still screaming, he ran from the room, holding his burning hands in front of him.

The little dog leaped forward and sank his teeth into the ankle of the guard behind the Boy.

Bernard Prince ducked and drove his elbow back into the breast bone of the man guarding him. The fellow folded like cardboard as the Interpol agent's hand chopped down on his exposed neck.

The Nyctalope drew one of his Brownings and calmly shot the guard who was screaming at the little dog between the eyes.

Bob Morane leaped and knocked aside Monsieur Ming's gun as it fired. There was a momentous struggle, then the bigger man forced Morane off. Moving faster than he would seem capable of, the Yellow Shadow was off through the catacombs, following Dr. No. The Nyctalope lunged to follow him.

"Saint-Clair!"

It was Prince. He was pointing at the control panel.

Point Pescade was slumped against it. A red stain ran down the front of his shirt. Saint-Clair recognized the dark color of heart's blood.

He and Morane kneeled by the fallen figure. While the aviator checked the wound, Saint-Clair cradled the old man's head.

"Take it easy. We'll get you to help... Prince, press this red button and throw that switch..."

"No," Point Pescade said, his voice curiously strong. "No. It's better this way. Don't bother, son, I know a fatal wound when I... Promise me that you will get the Doctor's papers away. You must decide what to do with them. I'm too close. That's why I chose you. Please, promise me you will..."

But that was the last thing he said—in this world.

Ming and his men gave them no more trouble. With the island's protection cut off, they made quick work of returning to their boat, and much to Saint-Clair's surprise, when they reached the *Cormorant*, the Captain was halfway sober and the engines warm. They were underway in a matter of minutes.

The first pink tint of dawn was teasing the horizon in the east when, to their south, the Sun rose with a vengeance. There was a flash of light so bright that, for an instant, they could see through the flesh of their hands to the very bone, and then the sky was filled with fire and rubble as the island disintegrated as if it had never existed.

At Saint-Clair's command, they grabbed the gunwale. In the next moments, a roar like the Heavens themselves had opened hit them, and then a wind, hot as the Devil's breath, sent the boat rocking and the waves rolling under them.

It would be a near thing, the Captain had told them, but they could outrun the worst of the tsunami that would follow the island's destruction.

The Boy and the Dog went below first. It had been a long day. Prince went next, a single finger raised in salute as he did. Morane lingered for a moment. The diary of Doctor Antekirtt lay on the engine housing. He looked at it for a long time, then at Saint-Clair.

"Coming below?"

"In a minute." Saint-Clair watched as Morane went below.

The island, at least the place where it had been, was dark once more. In the east, the Sun was now a promise rather than a hope.

He lifted Antekirtt's notebook. In this journal were answers that men had sought for centuries. And it would soon be in the hands of his own beloved France, perhaps heralding the dawn of a new century of French power and greatness…

But at what price?

Slowly and with deliberation, he tore the pages from the notebook. He tossed them to the seven winds and watched as they fell to the surface of the still roiling sea.

And when he was done, he went below. For the first time in a long time, he felt human, he felt part of something. There was such a thing as redemption, even for men who could not die in the ordinary way of mortals.

For the Nyctalope, the dawn had come again after too long a darkness.

*In his novel* Belzebuth, *the eponymous villain captures the Nyctalope's wife, Sylvie, and their son, Little Pierre, and using a technique of suspended animation, takes them to the year 2100. Leo, Gno Mitang, and his two assistants follow, also using suspended animation. La Hire then chronicles Leo's battle against Belzebuth in the future, but ends the book by having Leo waking up in bed, as if the entire story had been nothing but a dream. This explanation fails to account for the fact that Sylvie, Gno, etc., all shared the same dream! More likely, it is as if some unknown time traveling entity rescued the Nyctalope and his family and tampered with their memories. In this story, Emmanuel Gorlier finally resolves that puzzle.*

## Emmanuel Gorlier: *Out of Time*

*July 15, 2103. 10:30 p.m.*

Leo Saint-Clair stood before the great glass window that occupied a section of his office aboard his sail boat *Stella*, presently cruising off the coasts of Douardenez in Brittany, watching the storm unleashing its fury over the Atlantic. The night was pitch black, except for the powerful swathes of lightning that occasionally burst from the sky like angry bolts thrown by the old gods of this ancient Celtic land. To most people, the darkness outside would have been impenetrable. But to the Nyctalope, it was clear as daylight, and he could see each gigantic wave pummel his unsinkable floating citadel. The irresistible force of the storm striking his unmovable ship was the perfect analogy for the thoughts that currently occupied his mind: could a single man, even him, withstand the repeated assaults of Fate?

Leo looked grimly at a folder on his dark mahogany desk. Perhaps the answer to his question lay inside? It contained the diary of his arch-foe Hughes Mezarek, a.k.a. "Belzebuth," the progeny of two of his ancient enemies, the mad scientist Maur Korrides and the vengeful Diana Ivanovna Krasnoview, the Red Princess, better known as Titania, whom he had defeated 176 years ago—although it was only four years ago in his personal timeline.

Leo would never forget that fateful night when he had learned that a man calling himself "Belzebuth" and claiming to be Korrides and Titania's son had kidnapped, in the name of revenge, his wife Sylvie and his young son Pierre, then used a novel process of hibernation which he had designed to take them to the year 2100. Of course, he had followed the madman, using the same methods, and defeated him. Belzebuth had died a miserable death, shot by one of his own victims, leaving Leo virtual master of this future world. How could it have been otherwise? Wasn't he the Nyctalope, after all?

But in death, Hugues Mezarek had taken all his secrets with him. How could he, a man in his 30s, whom Leo had never before met, be the child of Korrides and Titania. How could an unknown enemy have dedicated his entire life to the destruction of the Nyctalope?

Leo despaired of ever learning the truth—until Mezarek's diary had been miraculously found in a hidden safe kept by the arch-villain.

It had, of course, been sent immediately to the Nyctalope for study. And now, it lay on his desk, waiting to reveal the secrets of a man born out of time…

*The Diary of Hughes Mezarek*
Tonight, May 31, 1928, I am both one-year-old and 35-year-old.

I am not one man, but two!

My plans are complete at last!

Tomorrow, June 1, 1928, I shall embark on an irrevocable course of action that will result in the destruction of Leo Saint-Clair, the Nyctalope, the man responsible for the deaths of my dear parents.

I shall use this diary to chronicle the tale of my revenge. I dedicate it to the great Maur Korrides, my father, and the beautiful Diana, my mother, to show that nothing can withstand the will of a truly superior man—not even the hated Nyctalope!

Because of him, I never knew the love of my mother and the wise guidance of my father. I was denied the tender comforts of a true family when they both perished in an ignominious Spanish jail a year ago, soon after the birth of my younger self.

I was raised instead by their followers, who had dedicated their lives to fight the King of Spain. My education was entrusted to my uncle, Prosper Korrides. He had lost the use of his legs a few years prior, in the crash of a spaceship of his own design with which he had explored our Solar System. Thanks to his science, I quickly mastered the arcane arts of physics, biology and chemistry. My uncle had developed various processes to help Men adapt to extraterrestrial environments. I became the beneficiary of some of these, which increased considerably my physical strength and mental prowess. When I was 10, I was told I already looked like a 15-year-old...

My parents' followers eventually succeeded in bringing down the Spanish Monarchy in 1931 when King Alfonso XIII fled Spain to find refuse in Rome. But, unfortunately, they failed to grab power and build the scientific dictatorship of which my father had dreamed. Instead, a bloody civil war broke out.

I shall never forget the night of January 1939 when General Franco's troops burst into our last refuge and massacred all our men. A commando of the sinister Condor Legion, comprised of "volunteers" from the German Lutwaffe, burst into our underground quarters where my uncle and I had been hiding, hoping to escape our enemies. The commando was headed by a German scientist named Zemo who had heard of my uncle's scientific discoveries and had been dispatched especially by their Führer to capture him and put his talents to the service of the Third Reich.

Colonel Zemo was delighted to find not one genius—but two! My uncle and I, now the sole survivors of Titania's men, were quickly packed into a plane and flown to Germany. There, I was separated from my uncle, and assigned to work at Castle Zemo in Bavaria, creating an array of super-weapons meant to ensure the Reich's ultimate victory.

I was all too happy to collaborate with Zemo—a brilliant scientist himself—knowing that the labors of my genius would be used to bring down Saint-Clair's beloved France, and perhaps the Nyctalope himself! How dearly I wanted to take a more active part in my hated enemy's downfall! How often I begged Zemo to release me! But the Nazi never trusted me. After the horrible accident that condemned him to have a hideous hood permanently attached to his face, Zemo trusted no one. That grim fate had tipped him over the edge and he, like his masters in Berlin, began to succumb to total madness. I clearly understood then that the Reich was doomed to fail.

Wishing to escape the *Götterdämmerung* that that ranting madman Hitler had in mind, I secretly plotted my escape. In April 1945, as Zemo vanished in the fog of the war, I managed at last to flee from his castle. Using my status as his prisoner, and posing as a German resistant from the virtually extinct White Rose movement, I managed to cross the invading Allied lines and, eventually, reach France.

But fate had managed to thwart my most cherished ambition: it turned out that, blinded by his patriotic fervor, the Nyctalope had collaborated with the Vichy regime! Just as I had finished settling comfortably in new surroundings, under the new identity of "Hughes Mezarek", I found that Saint-Clair had been discreetly asked by the French authorities to leave the country and had relocated in ignominious exile in Argentina! Was I to be deprived of my revenge?

No! For a most ingenious plan then formed in my mind. Where Zemo and his Nazi cohorts had failed, I, Hughes Mezarek would triumph! I would become the Master of the World—and still destroy my Great Enemy in the process!

During the War, the Nazis had been very thorough in collecting all scientific papers published by allied scientists. That is how I had come across an article published in 1939 in the *Revue de Mathématiques* by one Noël Essaillon, a crippled French scientist who claimed to understand the mechanics of time travel. There were a few errors in the paper, but they could be easily fixed, and I had filed it away in my eidetic memory for future use.

The time had now come to put Essaillon's discovery to good use! I immediately tracked down the reclusive scientist who lived alone with his daughter. I found that Essaillon had perfected his process, with the help of a fellow mathematician, Pierre Saint-Menoux, who had since disappeared.

It was child's play for me to gain Essaillon's trust and, offering to go looking for Saint-Menoux, I used my considerable financial resources to help the old scientist, who was by then on the verge of financial ruin, manufacture a second "timesuit."

Fully dressed in the green "Noëlite" suit, I, Hugues Mezarek, became a full-fledged time traveler on June 1, 1948! I was then 21, although anyone looking at me would have deemed me to be in my mid-30s.

I had, of course, lied to Essaillon. I had no intention of looking for the careless Saint-Menoux. My ambitions lay elsewhere!

I should, however, have been more careful in heeding the old scientist's advice, for like my predecessor, I, too, almost became a casualty of time travel. Instead of rematerializing at the safehouse I had planned to use, I rematerialized at Neuve Chapelle near the Belgium border. It was October 28, 1914, and the German Army had dumped 3000 shells of poison gas upon the French and British trenches.

My Noëlite suit proved to be my salvation, as it protected me from the deadly gases, but, in the process, became irrevocably ruined. As the complex compounds used to manufacture Noëlite could not be made until at least the late 1930s, the pathways of time were forever closed to me!

But if I had just suffered a serious blow, my plans were nevertheless still intact. I was in the era that I had chosen. I had work to do! In the chaotic turmoil of the Great War, I easily found a way to travel to the United States where Hughes Mezarek, a refugee from the bloodiest conflict in all human history, quickly managed to acquire doctorates in medicine, physics and chemistry.

After the War, I became a famous professor at the universities of Boston and Leipzig.

From a distance, I kept an eye on my dear parents. My father, Maur Korrides, had just returned from Mars, after the death of his wife, Marguerite, at the hands of the Martians. My mother, Diana Ivanovna Krasnoview, was now becoming famously known in the West as the "Red Princess."

My frustration was immense, for I knew from Saint-Menoux's journals that to interfere in their lives might have caused me *to never have been born*! So I remained a powerless observer from afar, condemned to a worse torture that even Dante could have imagined: to watch my parents die again as a result of the ignoble intervention of the Nyctalope!

My thirst for revenge on the accursed Saint-Clair only grew more intense. He had robbed me of my family; I would take his!

My tool would be a revolutionary hibernation technique developed by Zemo to allow the Nazi leaders to survive the war and someday return to crush their enemies.

My plan is simple: tomorrow, I am going to steal Saint-Clair's wife and child. Together, we will "travel" to the 22nd century in the three impregnable hibernation capsules that I have built. There, I shall easily become Master of the World, enslaving Saint-Clair's kin, bending them to my will, knowing that in the past, my powerless enemy will be doomed to age and die, deprived forever of his loved ones!

A slow agony! A long life of pain and endless suffering—just as he visited upon me! I can envision no better revenge!

*July 2103.*

Leo slammed the diary shut.

He had, in fact, managed to follow Mezarek to the 22nd century, using an alternate hibernation technology; there, he had quickly crushed the villain and been reunited with Sylvie and their son, little Pierre. Contrary to Belzebuth's mad hopes, it was now the Nyctalope who was Master of this world...A world in which they expected to spend the rest of their lives...

It wasn't Mezarek's insane schemes which disturbed Leo and kept him awake, looking at the storm outside, but what the madman had written about him, in that "other life" that had been his—might yet be his?—in 1928.

Could it be true that noble Germany had again fallen victim to the madness of war? Worse yet, that it had surrendered its greatness into the clutches of a lunatic Antichrist named Adolf Hitler? That the same Antichrist, whom Leo thought he had once defeated in the person of the arch-fiend Leonid Zattan, had subjugated, utterly humiliated Eternal France? And, worse of all, that he, Leo Saint-Clair, had... collaborated... with such evil? And been forced into exile?

No! That was unthinkable!

And yet, there was Mezarek's diary, casually referring to a sequence of events that was a living abomination to him!

Such a thing could not be! Never!

*October 10, 2103. 10:30 p.m.*

Chief Scientist Oxus—a descendent of the once-leader of the XV—rose as Leo entered the Great Hall of Science which occupied the space where the city of Puteaux had once stood.

"I take it you have good news for me?" said the Nyctalope in a French which sounded oddly accented to his contemporaries, just as that of a man of the 18th century would have been to him.

"Yes, Great Nyctalope," replied Oxus. "Thanks to Mezarek's diary, we were able to duplicate the substance he called 'Noëlite.' The mathematics were child's play to our supercomputers. Time travel is now achievable."

"Has anyone tried it?" said Leo.

"No, no one. I knew your desire to be the first."

"Very well. I'm ready."

"Follow me!"

*November 7, 1923. 10:10 p.m. Munich.*

Leo had been in Munich for two days, enough time to do a thorough recon and select the best possible spot for the job. Now, he sat at the window of this empty house in complete darkness—which was like daylight to him—Mauser in hand—no anachronisms left behind!—waiting for the little man with the funny mustache to come out of the beer hall.

The next day, the same little man—the Antichrist!—inspired by Mussolini's March on Rome, was planning a putsch at the notorious *Bürgerbräukeller* beer hall, the first move in a surprising ascent which, in the space of 10 years, according to the history books of the future, would see him rule Germany, crush France, and ally with the accursed Bolsheviks who destroyed Leo's father!

Leo adjusted his sight. He was ready. The man would die. Here and now!

The beer hall opened. The little man came out, surrounded by some of his associates, Alfred Rosenberg, Hermann Göring, Rudolf Hess, and few others Leo doesn't recognize.

His finger softly squeezed the trigger...

"I've got him," said Bob Morane, putting the needle gun back into its holster. "He's completely paralyzed."

"It's pitch dark in here," said Manse Everard. "Only another nyctalope like yourself could have made that shot!"

"I still don't like it," said Bob. "To save Hitler's life... You don't think he might have had the right idea?"

"The Time Patrol's job is to preserve history, Bob, not to rewrite it. Besides, Colonel Graigh showed you the alternate timelines. Without World War II, it's either the Nuclear Wars

314

of the 1970s or the Eugenic Wars of the 1990s—not an improvement!"

"I guess you're right… What will become of the Nyctalope?"

"We'll pick up him and his family," said Everard, "erase their memories and put them back in 1928, before he traveled to the future. This entire adventure will be like a dream to him…"

*June 19, 1928. 11 p.m. Chateau de Blingy.*

Leo Saint-Clair woke up suddenly, and sat up in bed. Sylvie was sleeping peacefully beside him.

*What an amazing dream*, he thought. *So… precise, so detailed…*

With his extraordinarily keen senses, he listened to the silence of the night, but could not detect anything out of the ordinary.

Shrugging, he fluffed his pillow and went back to sleep.

# *Timeline*

## by Emmanuel Gorlier

*(translated by Jean-Marc Lofficier)*

1337 B.C.: *Fiat Lux!* During the reign of Pharaoh Akhenaton, a priest of Aton known by the nickname of "Eyes of Aton" receives the power to see through darkness to defend good and justice from the God. This power will reappear in his descendents when these values are threatened.

May 1337 B.C.: *The Three Sisters*. The "Eyes of Aton" prevents the assassination of Pharaoh Akhenaton, plotted by the sorceress Hecate using an extraterrestrial gem nicknamed the Egg of Set. The gem emits an all-destroying ray of energy when placed in conjunction with its sister gem located on the Moon. Following these events, the deadly gem is entrusted to his safekeeping. It will be passed on from father to son throughout the ages.

December 1639: *Fiat Lux!* Henri-Jean de Sainte-Claire, a lieutenant in the guards of Cardinal de Richelieu, a distant descendant of the "Eyes of Aton," is injured by Cyrano de Bergerac in a duel and, as a result, suddenly acquires the ancestral power of nyctalopia.

December 1641: *Fiat Lux!* While investigating the conspiracy of Cinq-Mars, Henri-Jean discovers that it is secretly masterminded by alien Invaders who have the power to mimic human form. Henri-Jean thwarts their first attempt, but is distracted by a pretty girl.

September-October 1642: *The Three Sisters*. Henri-Jean discovers that his would-be girl-friend is one of the alien Invaders sent to distract him from his investigation. He pursues her and her accomplices, and destroys their flying saucer using the Egg of Set. He is then shocked by its raw power and decides it is too dangerous to ever be employed again.

1657: *The Three Sisters*. Using one of Cyrano's inventions, Henri-Jean travels to the Moon in order to neutralize the power of the Egg of Set by moving its sister gem to another location on the lunar surface.

1834: Birth of the Nyctalope's grandfather in Banyuls-sur-Mer, in the Roussillon region of Southern France.

1852: Birth of Princess Alouh T'Hô, daughter of a Hindu prince and Chinese Empress Tseu-Hi, in Nanking, China.

1855: Birth of Jean-Pierre Saint-Clair, the Nyctalope's father, in Collioures, France. Jean Pierre is raised by his mother while his father manages a farm.

1862: *Passions Ardentes*. The Nyctalope's grandfather joins the notorious Catalan smuggler Salbadou in an expedition to Morocco to free a young girl prisoner of a desert tribe.

1877: Birth of Maur Korrides.

7 May 1877: Birth of Léon Saint-Clair, the Nyctalope, in Banyuls-sur-Mer. (The name of his mother was never mentioned by Jean de La Hire.)

28 January 1878: Birth of Comte Adolphe Célestin d'Espie de La Hire, the Nyctalope's biographer, in Banyuls-sur-Mer.

1877-1888: The Nyctalope spends his childhood at his grandfather's house. His father, a sailor in the French Navy, is often away from home. Circa 1882, the Saint-Clairs move to Bourg-la-Reine, near Paris, to live near Leo's mother's family.

February-May 1885: *L'Homme qui peut vivre dans l'eau*. Jean Pierre Saint-Clair is now an Ensign in the French Navy and second-in-command to Louis de Ciserat aboard the *Cyclone*. Meanwhile, scientist Oxus and his brother-in-law, the mad monk Fulbert, plot to use the powers of the "Hictaner," a water-breathing man which they created through surgery and radium rays, to become masters of the world. They are defeated when the Hictaner and his father, Charles Severac, turn against them, with the help of Ciserat and Saint-Clair. Oxus and Fulbert disappear. The Hictaner marries Moisette, Oxus' daughter, and together they retire to Tahiti to live in peace.

1886: The Hictaner and Moisette have a daughter, Christiane.
    Birth of Glo Von Warteck at Hollow Rock in the Bermudas.

1888-1891: Leo studies at a high school near Paris. There, he meets Gaëtan de Mirbonne, whose path he will cross again during his military service and in 1913, when Gaëtan is French Consul in Naples, Italy.

1892: Death of Leo's grandfather.

1892-1894: Leo spends a few years in Russia where his father has been sent as part of a diplomatic mission.

1894: Birth of Diana Ivanovna Kaline in Russia.

1895-1897: Leo goes to university; he earns a masters in sciences; he is also captain of the Bourg la Reine rugby team, where he plays with his childhood friends Robert Champeau, Jean Degains and René Croqui (his future companions in a tragic 1898 adventure).

1895: *The Season of the Shark*. In Tahiti, the Hictaner is slowly mutating into a shark-like creature. He discovers that Fulbert has allied himself with the Dagon worshippers of Tobias Marsh and is intent on creating an army of "Deep Ones" to take over the world. The two villains clash and Marsh releases Dagon. The Hictaner sacrifices himself to save Tahiti, but he and his wife Moisette die in the cataclysm (which will be blamed on a tropical storm). Their daughter, Christiane, is adopted by the Saint-Clair family.

Early 1898: Death of Leo's maternal grandmother.

March 1898: *L'Assassinat du Nyctalope* (tr. as *Enter the Nyctalope*). The spy Sadi Khan attacks Jean-Pierre Saint-Clair to steal his Radiant Z invention and gravely wounds him. Leo and his three friends pursue him to Geneva. Leo is wounded in the head and acquires his powers of nyctalopia. He then infiltrates the terrorist cell of Dr. Serge Ivanof, but is exposed by the beautiful Katia Garcheff. He is tortured to death and dies on March 21. He is resuscitated by Dr. Adrien de Villiers-Pagan who transplants an artificial heart into him. The terrorists are exposed and defeated, but Sadi Khan manages to escape; Katia commits suicide.
*The Three Sisters*. It is later revealed that Sadi Khan also stole the Egg of Set which was in the possession of Jean Pierre Saint-Clair.

1898: Attempted Martian invasion of Earth, as described by H.G. Wells in his account, *The War of the Worlds*.

1898-1901: Leo fulfills his military obligations at the Saint-Cyr Military Academy.

1900: Death of Jean Pierre Saint-Clair, Leo's father, who never fully recovered from his wounds.

1902: Engineer Korrides succeeds in synthesizing "Heliose" but overwork leads to a nervous breakdown and his wife has him temporarily committed.

1902-07: At some point, Korrides' first wife passes away while he is still in the hospital.

1902: Glô von Warteck is a student at the Paris University; thanks to a secret inscription in the gardens of the Cluny Museum, he manages to find the long-lost secrets of alchemist Nicholas Flamel hidden in a Benedictine Abbey in Saône et Loire.

1902-1905: First trip of Leo to Tibet, where he meets ancient lamas who teach him some of their occult knowledge.

1902-1912: Glô von Warteck travels around the world, discovering more occult secrets: he visits the Synagogue of Amsterdam, the Synod of Dordrecht, the libraries of Saint Mark in Venice and the Vatican in Rome, the Mosque of Saint Sophia in Constantinople, and learns from the Copts of Egypt, the Maronites of Lebanon, the Monks of Mount Carmel, ands various wise men in Arabia, Isfahan, Kandahar, Delhi, Agra and, finally, the Brahmins of Benares.

1906: Leo is in India with Pilou where he continues his education in the esoteric arts.

1907: *Le Trésor dans l'Abîme*. Korrides is released from the hospital to help build a revolutionary, heliose-powered submarine in order to recover a treasure from a sunken ship. Unfortunately, heliose interacts with gold in a catastrophic fashion and the treasure is destroyed. Korrides manages to escape and marries a member of the salvage crew, Marguerite Dormach.
*La Captive du Démon*. Mathias Lumen purchases his estate in the island of Ouessant off the coast of Brittany.

1907-1908: At some point, Leo spends at least four months in China.

1907-1914: The Korrides, presumed dead, live in obscurity in America under the name of Mr. & Mrs. James Norton.

1909-August 1910: Leo explores Central Africa, assisted by Corsat and Pilou. He triumphs several times over a rival explorer named Koynos, who will later become one of the XV.

September 1910-March 1911: *Le Mystère des XV* (tr. as *The Nyctalope on Mars*). Leo pursues the kidnappers of his fiancée, Xavière de Ciserat, captured with 14 other girls, including Christiane, the Hictaner's daughter. He discovers the culprits: a mysterious organization dubbed the XV, led by Oxus. They have built a base on Mars and are seeking ideal wives in order to create a perfect society. The XV are at war with the Martians who attacked Earth earlier, and plan to eventually conquer it.

Leo invades the XV's base in Congo and manages to reach Mars, although Xavière's father is killed during the journey. Thanks to the help of his rival Koynos, whom Xavière has seduced, and who is later executed, the Nyctalope succeeds in taking Oxus prisoner and becomes the XV's new leader. He then leads a French commando which has arrived on Mars to attack the Martians. Thanks to Camille Flammarion, Leo learns to communicate with the aliens and strikes an alliance with some and defeats the others. Having secured a beachhead on Mars, Leo marries Xavière.

October 1911: On Mars, Leo and Xavière have twins.

1912: In Schwarzrock in Germany, Glô von Warteck begins work on the teledyname.

June 1912: Leo spends some time in Turkey.

July 1912: Back on Mars, Xavière gives birth to a third child: Pierre, but dies in childbirth. Pierre is sent to Earth to be with his father; the twins stay on Mars to be raised by Christiane and her husband.

Fall 1912: *Le Corsaire Sous-marin*. The Black Corsair steals a revolutionary submarine from the French Navy and uses it to attack the United States and Venezuela, seeking revenge for harm done to his family by those two countries. Leo joins the forces fighting him and manages to acquire the secret scientific "testament" of Engineer Korrides for France.

Then, Leo first encounters the German agent Wanda Steilman, who has been encouraging local tribes to rebel against the French, and becomes his lover. She is captured and sentenced to die, but manages to escape.

At the end of the year, Leo publishes his book, *Exploration du Tibet Perdu*, which will be translated into several languages and bring him a steady income.

June-July 1913: *La Croisière du Nyctalope*. Leo and Wanda Steilman meet again during a cruise on the Mediterranean. Leo then thwarts Wanda's schemes aiming to steal the fortune of Russian Princess Irena Zahidof. Leo pursues Wanda to the Caucasus, where she is killed by her own men. Leo considers marrying Irena, but she dies too, probably poisoned by the Russian secret police, the Okrana.

September 1913-February 1914: Leo, Pilou and Corsat travel in across the Pacific. In Viet-Nam, Leo meets Doctor Yeslun.

1914: Korrides and his wife leave Earth and travel to Mars on a heliose-powered spaceship.

August 1914-November 1918: First World War.

August 1914-June 1917: The Nyctalope takes part in the battles of Champagne, Verdun and Ypres. He earns the rank of "Commandant." He meets Captain d'Harmont (see *La Croix de Sang*, 1925) and the soldiers Vitto and Soca, who will later become his assistants (see 1924).

October 1914: Hugues Korrides arrives from 1948 in a time suit, which is irremediably destroyed by the War. Forced to stay in that time period, he takes the name of Hugues Mezarek.

February 1916: *The Lesson of Captain Danrit.* The Nyctalope meets Lieutenant-Colonel Driant (a.k.a. Captain Danrit) during a secret mission and exposes a German invasion force hidden behind Dr. Krueger's invisibility field. Driant will be killed in the ensuing offensive.

July 1917: *The Hunters of Mars.* Leo returns to Mars seeking new and better weapons against Germany. He helps John Carter defeat an alien Predator plaguing Helium. The Predator's destruction inadvertently activates an ancient Martian capsule dug up by Oxus.

*The Children of Heracles*: The Martian capsule awakens an ancient genetic compulsion buried deep within the men who are descended from Martians, causing then to go mad and kill each other. The French colony does not survive. Oxus and everyone else dies; Leo kills his twins and only survives himself because of his artificial heart. Leo then returns to Earth, having buried his all too painful memories deep within his subconscious.

Summer 1917: Korrides returns to Earth alone, without his wife, aged and bitter. It is possible that he, too, was a victim of the destruction of the Martian colony, which would explain his wife's disappearance and his lingering hatred towards Leo. Korrides ends up selling his services to the Bolsheviks.

September 1917-November 1918: The Nyctalope goes on a variety of secret missions for the Allies, possibly assisted by Vitto and Soca. During one of these, he meets and collaborates with Mathias Lumen and Captain Marc Ayrol of the French Navy. From Lumen, he learns of the existence of Leonid Zattan. (La Hire states that Leo was promoted to the rank of Colonel, but it seems he was only a Commandant (equivalent of Major).)

1919-20: Hugues Mezarek becomes Professor of physics and chemistry in Leipzig then goes to teach in Boston.

January 1919: *Black and Bold.* The Nyctalope thwarts the plans of Doctor Fisturn who was using a plague germ to kill the survivors of the Black Corsair's organization in order to secure the secret of transmutation of base metals into gold.

February-April 1919: The Nyctalope goes to Southern Morocco to subdue a rebel chieftain.

May 1919: The Nyctalope frees Alphonse XIII, King of Spain, who had been kidnapped by anarchists. He also saves the honor of Duke Petro d'Arendar who was threatened by a woman.

June-August 1919: Leo meets singer Laurence Païli in Antibes and spends some time with her. He also meets Helen Parsons (later to be known as Djinn) and spurns her advances.

September-October 1919: The Nyctalope travels to China and defeats an evil triumvirate comprised of Monsieur Ming (aka The Yellow Shadow), Doctor Natas (aka Fu Manchu) and the Blue Scorpion, who were trying to take over the country.

October 1919: In Morocco, while vacationing, Helen Parsons is captured by a rebel Berber tribe and becomes the wife of their leader, Ou-Skounti.
Until 1925, she sends several death threats to Leo. She also organizes a gun smuggling ring to arm the rebels.

February 1920: Leo's mother dies from pneumonia.

February 1920-April 1921: A grief-stricken Leo travels alone in the Sudan.

May-June 1921: *The Nyctalope vs. Lucifer.* Baron Glô von Warteck, a.k.a. Lucifer, uses his formidable occult powers to place Hélène Ciserat (wife of Raymond Ciserat, one of Leo's friends) under a spell. He also tries to steal a millionaire's fortune, Laurence Païli's affections, and seeks to plunge France in political chaos. Finally, he schemes to enslave the world with his teledyname, a machine that will amplify his hypnotic powers.

The Nyctalope, assisted by Corsat and Pilou, invades his foe's German fortress of Schwarzrock. Then, with the help of Grysil, a former slave of the Warteck family, he destroys their underground lair in the Bermudas. Finally, he attacks Glô's North Pole base and kills Lucifer.

Leo marries Laurence Païli. They have three boys, born between 1922 and 1924.

September-December 1921: Leo returns to Morocco and meets his friend Rached Ben Atia, as well as several mystics based in Fez.

January-February 1922: The Nyctalope goes on a secret mission to South Africa with Baron Jean de Ciserat and Comte Hubert de Pibriac. Together, they defeat the Mexican adventurer Matalpa and his Spanish associate, Guiroun.

March-June 1922: Leo helps Jean de La Hire write the story of his fight against Lucifer.

1923: Leo travels to London several times to prepare his expedition to Mount Everest.

July-October 1923: Great motorized trip through Central Africa with Pilou. Corsat retires from his life of adventure.

November 1923: *Out of Time.* The Nyctalope, back from the year 2103, tries to kill Adolf Hitler in Munich during the Beer Hall Putsch but is thwarted by the Time Patrol which erases his memory and takes him back to 1928 (see *Belzébuth*).

January-June 1924: *L'Amazone du Mont Everest.* The Nyctalope embarks on an expedition to Mount Everest, accompanied by Jean de Ciserat, his wife Gaëlle, Hubert de Pibriac, Pilou and (unknowingly) his old enemies, Matalpa and Guiroun. In Tibet, they discover a secret kingdom inhabited by amazons ruled by Queen Mizzeïa Khali VII, who falls in love with Leo and, after an aborted revolution, eventually follows him back to France.

It is possible that Leo's affair with Mizzeïa caused his divorce with Laurence, who is never mentioned again. Laurence probably got custody of their three children.

December 1924: After spending some time in India, and with Pilou wanting to retire, Leo goes to Corsica to recruit two new assistants, Vitto and Soca.

January 1925: *La Croix de Sang.* Leo's friend, Comte d'Harmont, asks Leo for his help: a strange curse killed his wife and now threatens him, his sister and his daughter. Leo travels to d'Harmont's castle in Touraine and, with Vitto and Soca's help, exposes the villain Armand Logreux d'Albury, aka The Master of the Seven Lights, a dark magician who seeks to steal the d'Harmont's fortune. Leo, adopting the guise of Romani leader Pedro del Campo, uses the young sybil Nèves first to seduce, then destroy his enemy who is left alive but paralyzed.

October 1925: Helen Parsons take part in the rebellion of Adl el Krim. After her husband's death, she vanishes into the desert with her two children. Some believe she was killed by a stray bullet.

January 1926: The Nyctalope goes on a secret mission to Siberia, working alongside the British Intelligence Service and an agent from the Soviet Government. The purpose of this mission is unknown, but it might have had something to do with either Leonid Zattan or Fu Manchu. Leo meets Dominique de Soto, whose identity he learns from his British colleague.

February 1926: In Spain, the Nyctalope infiltrates Leonid Zattan's criminal organization, using the alias of Pedro del Campo.

March-May 1926: *La Captive du Démon/La Princesse Rouge.* The Nyctalope discovers the truth behind the battle between the forces of Mathias Lumen and those of Leonid Zattan. A Nostradamus prophecy states that the future husband of the "Golden Virgin" will play a decisive role in the forthcoming battle against the Antichrist. The "Virgin" turns out to be Sylvie MacDhul, the daughter of billionaire Gregor MacDhul, a friend of Lumen. Zattan has Sylvie kidnapped and taken to his fortress of Issyk-Koul, in China. The Nyctalope joins forces with Gno Mitang, Lumen's assistant, and Marc Ayrol. Together, they invade the fortress, capture and defeat Zattan.

Meanwhile, Lumen has been killed by Diana Ivanovna Krasnoview, a.k.a. the Red Princess. Zattan is nevertheless sent in exile and dies soon after. Diana is captured by her enemy, the Kiewicz family, but manages to escape.

1926: Diana marries Korrides and together, they start a new criminal organization, the Haschischins. She adopts the nickname of "Titania."

May 1926-March 1927: Leo and Sylvie get married; then, they go on a cruise around the world.

February 1927: Birth of "Little" Pierre, the son of Leo and Sylvie. (Not to be confused with the older Pierre, whose mother was Xavière de Ciserat, born in 1912.)

March 1927: Maur Korrides and Diana Ivanovna Krasnoview have a son, Hugues, the future Hugues Mezarek a.k.a. Belzebuth.

May-June 1927: *Titania/Ecrase la Vipère!* The Nyctalope witnesses the assassination of a member of the Kiewicz family by Maur Korrides, avenging his wife, Diana Ivanovna Krasnoview. This in turn leads to Diana and her Haschischins kidnapping Sylvie and Little Pierre from the house of Pedro d'Arandar in Spain, and taking them to their island fortress in the Mediterranean. Leo, Gno Mitang, Vitto and Soca, invade the island and capture Diana, but with Korrides' help, she escapes with her captives. Leo pursues her to Abyssinia where he finally succeeds in freeing Sylvie and defeating Diana. The Red Princess is murdered in her cell by a gypsy girl. When he learns the news, Korrides commits suicide.

June 1927-January 1939: *Out of Time.* Hugues, the son of Korrides and Diana, is raised by his uncle, Prosper Korrides, who subjects him to an experimental treatment that accelerates his physical growth and intellectual capacities.

November 1927-May 1928: Leo, Sylvie and Little Pierre travel through Africa.

June 1928: *Belzébuth/L'Ile d'Épouvante.* Sylvie and Little Pierre are kidnapped by the grown-up Hugues Mezarek, a.k.a. Belzébuth, who returned from 1948 to 1914 and has been waiting for the right time to avenge his parents. He places them in a state of suspended animation until the Year 2100. The Nyctalope and his friends follow him, using the same method. But the next day, Leo wakes up in bed with Sylvie as if nothing had happened and it had all been a dream...

*Out of Time*. We now know that Leo and his family and friends were returned to their own time by the Time Patrol, with their memories erased.

1928: Death of the Black Corsair.

October 1929: *Death to the Heretic!* The Nyctalope is in Egypt and helps Indiana Jones and the young American millionaire Bruce Wayne stop the Gang of Anubis who was trying to destroy the tomb of Akhenaton.

Late 1929: Death of Little Pierre in unknown circumstances.

December 1929: Moved by his son's death, Leo uses his wife's fortune to create the CID, Comité d'Information et de Défense, a secret organization that takes over from the remnants of Mathias Lumen's organization, to defend France and her European allies.

March-April 1930: *Gorillard!/Le Mystère Jaune*. The Nyctalope and the CID protect French inventor Yves le Moal against a mysterious organization whose leader is nicknamed "Gorillard" or the "Mastodon." Leo discovers that the secret leaders of that evil empire are the Seven Living Buddhas of Urga, in Mongolia, who seek to destroy western civilization. Their agent, "Gorillard," is none other than Dominique de Soto, a Frenchman whose family carries a feud against the Saint-Clair since the 17th century. Leo captures two of the Living Buddhas and finally defeats de Soto, who is later executed.

June-August 1931: *Les Mystères de Lyon/Les Adorateurs du Sang*. The Nyctalope and the CID fight the sect of the Blood Worshippers led by the Chinese princess Alouh T'Hô, which steals the life force of young victims to prolong their own lives. With the help of his older son, Pierre, Leo discovers Alouh T'Hô's lair, but is captured and taken to her citadel in

Southern China. Alouh T'Hô eventually falls in love with the Nyctalope and agrees to no longer operate in France.

1931: Death of Sylvie, also in unknown circumstances.

September 1931-March 1934: Alouh T'Hô tries to become Empress of Chinas but is thwarted by Gno Mitang who supports her rival, Pou Hi. On March 1, 1934, Pou Hi becomes Emperor of Manchukuo. The Japanese have won this battle.

1932-1936: After Sylvie's death, the CID begins to fall apart and is ultimately disbanded.

1932-Early 1934: *Les Chasseurs de Mystères*. The Nyctalope returns to Mars. The official reason for his visit is to study the possibility of a new colony, but what he actually does there remains unknown. This appears to be his last visit to the Red Planet.

February-March 1934: *Le Sphinx du Maroc*. The Nyctalope goes on a secret mission to Morocco to fight another rebellion, led by the desert chief Merebbi Rebbo and Helen Parsons, who now goes under the name of "Djinn," secretly supported by Otto Von Kubitz' Nazis. Leo is helped by his friends Rached Ben Atia and Xavier de Pibrac, who has invented a device that can broadcast sound and images in a 3000 km radius. The French Army wins the battle. Djinn is killed in a psychic attack by Moroccan mystics. The Nyctalope has recovered from Sylvie's death and has a romance with Naïma, a young local girl.

May 1934: *The Nyctalope's New York Adventure*. The Nyctalope travels to New York, where he meets Nero Wolfe and the Shadow.

June 1934-December 1935: *Le Roi de la Nuit*. The Nyctalope, Gno Mitang, Vitto and Soca, travel to the wandering planet

Rhea in a rocketship invented by Professor Maxime d'Olbans, using an anti-gravitational metal called Z-4. (It might be a synthetic form of heliose or cavorite.) On Rhea, Leo stops a war between the Daysiders, a peaceful winged race, and the Nightsiders, a race of man-beasts who live in darkness, and makes peace between the two. Three months after his return to Earth, Leo marries Veronique, the Professor's daughter.

Before May 1936: Leo and Veronique separate.

June-October 1936: The Nyctalope fights Princess Alouh T'Hô in Morocco. Leo captures the Princess, who manages to escape. He pursues her but finally loses her trail in Lhasa in Tibet.

November 1936: The Nyctalope travels to French Indochina and there, befriends Monsieur Levillard of the Deuxième Bureau. (He will meet him again in *La Sorcière Nue*.)

1937-1938: Leo travels with Gno Mitang in India, Morocco and Spain, meeting powerful mystics and occult masters to improve their knowledge and powers.

May 1937: *L'Énigme du Squelette.* A scientist friend of Leo's is murdered by a weapon which disintegrates his flesh, leaving only his skeleton behind. Leo and Gno Mitang investigate and discover the identity of the murderer, Maya de la Cruz. Behind her is her sinister uncle, Comte Albert de la Cruz Tanguy, the inventor of the death-ray used by his niece. Maya commits suicide after being exposed.

January-March 1939: With the help of a few friends left over from the CID, Leo sets up a secret base in the Moroccan deserts, where he stores some on the extraordinary inventions and weapons in his possession in the event of a new world war.

January 1939: In Spain., Prosper Korrides and young Hugues are captured by the Nazis and taken to Baron Zemo's castle in Germany.

September 1939: World War II starts.

September 1939-April 1945: Hugues works designing weapons for the Third Reich.

June 1940 : *L'Enfant Perdu*. The Nyctalope and Gno Mitang witness the kidnapping of a child and the death of the woman who was his guardian.

July 1940 : The Nyctalope allies himself with the Vichy regime.
*The Lesson of Captain Danrit*. Meanwhile, his elder son, Pierre, joins General de Gaulle in England and becomes alienated from his father.

January 1941: *Rien qu'une Nuit*. The Nyctalope and Gno Mitang witness the kidnapping of young Madeleine d'Evires. They unmask and defeat the villain, dark magician Godfrey Cultnom, and free the girl.

1941: *A Present for Hitler*. Göring dispatches the Nyctalope, Maciste and Dr. Strangelove on a secret mission to Russia to find the remains of the teledyname.

1941: *Marguerite*. Near Lyon, Leo saves a French aviator from the clutches of the Vichy Milice.

June 1942: *L'Enfant Perdu*. Leo and Gno Mitang find the child who had been kidnapped and kept prisoner by gypsies and free him.

March 1945: *Twilight*. Back in Japan since late 1942, Gno Mitang decides it is better to not revive Godzilla than continue the war.

April 1945-June 1948: During the fall of the Third Reich, Hugues escapes and comes to France. He meets and befriends scientist Noël Essaillon and his assistant Saint-Ménoux who are working on a method to travel through time.

May 1946 : *La Sorcière Nue*. Monsieur Levillard, now an important official in the Ministry of the Interior, asks Leo to help solve a series of mysterious disappearances in Southern France. Leo, Vitto and Soca discover that the guilty party is none other than Princess Alouh T'Hô and her Blood Worshippers who once again are stealing the life force of their victims. The Nyctalope defeats the evil sect and frees its victims; Alouh T'Hô commits suicide.

January 1947: *The Heart of a Man*. To avoid being arrested for having collaborated with the Nazis, the Nyctalope leaves France and goes to Argentina. There, he avenges the death of a former girlfriend by killing the man responsible for her death. He also meets former Sûreté Inspector Giraud (a rival of Hercule Poirot's) and is almost recruited by Ernst Stavro Blofeld.

February 1947: The Nyctalope is sentenced to ten years' imprisonment in absentia by the French Courts.

June 1948: After Saint-Ménoux, Hugues uses Professor Essaillon's invention to travel back in time. (He will arrive in October 1914.).

1949: *The Children of Heracles*. In the American Southwest, the Nyctalope teams up with Professor Quatermass and the OSI to destroy an ancient Martian Capsule of the same type that caused the death of the French Colony in 1917. He finally comes to realize and accept what he did on Mars.

1951: *A Moment of Perfect Happiness*. In Saigon, the Nycta-lope locates Doctor de Villiers-Pagan who operated on him and saved his life in 1898. He learns that, at the same time that he was transplanted with an artificial heart, he was injected with a serum that has extended his life and stopped the aging process. Villiers-Pagan also injected himself with the serum, but dies in a terrorist explosion. Leo forgives him for having used him as a guinea pig.

1954: *The Mysterious Island of Doctor Antekirtt*. The Nycta-lope agrees to go on n unofficial secret mission for the French Government. He teams up with Bob Morane, Bernard Prince and Tintin to prevent Monsieur Ming, Doctor No and Emilio Largo (both agents of SPECTRE) to steal the nuclear secrets of Mathias Sandorf, a.k.a. Doctor Anterkirtt, on the island of Antekirtta. In the end, the island blows up and the Nyctalope destroys Antekirtt's secrets which he deems too dangerous.

August 1957-February 1958 : *The Three Sisters*. Tipped by OSS 117, the Nyctalope learns that the Soviets are preparing to send a satellite to the Moon to exploit the Ioun Stone hidden there by his ancestor. (They have the third stone stolen by Sadi Khan in 1898.) To stop them, Leo officially surrenders to the French Authorities, negotiates a pardon from President Coty (granted on November 15, 1957) with Geo Paquet and SNIF, and finally goes to his secret base in the Morocco desert. There, he uses Professor d'Olbans' rocket to go to the moon, destroy the Soviet satellite, and move the stone to the Sea of Tranquility. (His actions, however, have been monitored by the Americans.)

1969: Neil Armstrong picks up the second Ioun Stone on the Moon.

1972: *A Day in the Life of Madame Atomos*. Alouh T'hô is mentioned in passing as still being alive.

June 2100: *Belzébuth/L'Île d'Épouvante*. Hugues Mezarek a.k.a. Belzebuth and the Nyctalope come out of suspended animation and battle for the control of Earth. Hugues is ultimately betrayed by his own men and defeated.

July 2100-October 2103: *Out of Time*. The Nyctalope eventually learns of his past as a collaborator and decides to travel back to 1923 and assassinate Hitler.

## The Nyctalope novels by Jean de La Hire

*(bibliography compiled by*
*Jean-Marc Lofficier & Emmanuel Gorlier)*

### Primary novels:

*Le Mystère des XV* (1911) (tr. as *The Nyctalope on Mars*)
*Lucifer* (1922) (tr. as *The Nyctalope vs. Lucifer*)
*L'Amazone du Mont Everest* (1925)
*La Captive du Démon* (1927)
*Titania* (1929)
*Belzébuth* (1930)
*Gorillard* (1931)
*Les Mystères de Lyon* (1933)
*L'Assassinat du Nyctalope* (1933) (tr. as *Enter the Nyctalope*)
*Le Sphinx du Maroc* (1934)
*La Croisière du Nyctalope* (1936)
*La Croix de Sang* (1941)
*L'Enfant Perdu* (1942) (tr. as *The Nyctalope Steps In*)
*Le Roi de la Nuit* (1943)
*Rien qu'une nuit* (1944)
*La Sorcière Nue* (1954)
*L'Énigme du Squelette* (1955)

### Related Novels:

*La Chair et l'Esprit* (1898) (Jean de Sainte-Claire, cousin)
*L'Enfer du Soldat* (1903) (Jean de Sainte-Claire, cousin)
*Régiment d'Irma* (1904) (Jean de Sainte-Claire, cousin)
*Les Vipères* (1905) (Jean de Sainte-Claire, cousin)
*Le Trésor dans l'Abîme* (1907) (Maur Korrides)
*L'Homme qui peut vivre dans l'eau* (1908) (Jean-Pierre Saint-Clair, Oxus, Fulbert, The Hictaner)
*Le Corsaire Sous-Marin* (1913) (Maur Korrides + cameo by Leo)

*Les Trois Mignons* (1913) (Jean de Sainte-Claire, ancestor)
*Passions Ardentes* (1919) (Leo's paternal grandfather)
*Les Dompteurs de Forces* (1925) (Hubert de Pibriac)
*Les Grandes Aventures d'un Boy-Scout* (1926) (Prosper Kor-rides)
*Le Roi de la Sierra* (1927) (Paul de Saint-Clair, cousin)
*Les Chasseurs de Mystères* (1933) (cameo by Leo)

JEAN DE LA HIRE
L'Enigme du Squelette
FANTASTIC
Editions d'Hauteville

# Credits and Sources

## Fiat Lux!

| **Starring:** | **Created by:** |
|---|---|
| Quentin Travers | David Fury |
| Cyrano de Bergerac | *Historical* |
| Henri-Jean de Sainte-Claire | based on Jean de La Hire |
| Rochefort | Alexandre Dumas |
| Pardaillan | Michel Zévaco |
| Richelieu | *Historical* |
| Cinq-Mars | *Historical* |
| François de Thou | *Historical* |
| The Invaders | Larry Cohen |
| Manethon | *Historical* |
| Akhenaton | *Historical* |
| Merira | *Historical* |
| **And:** | |
| The Watchers | Joss Whedon |
| The Chamber of Horus | Edgar P. Jacobs |

Original title: *Fiat Lux!*
English adaptation by Jean-Marc & Randy Lofficier
© 2011, Emmanuel Gorlier
Previously published in *Tales of the Shadowmen N°7*, 2011

## The Three Sisters

| **Starring:** | **Created by:** |
|---|---|
| Rhialto | Jack Vance |
| Imhotep | *Historical* |
| Hecate | Emmanuel Gorlier |
| Akhenaton | *Historical* |
| Merira | *Historical* |

| | |
|---|---|
| Henri-Jean de Sainte-Claire | based on Jean de La Hire |
| The Invaders | Larry Cohen |
| Cyrano de Bergerac | *Historical* |
| Géo Paquet (The Gorilla) | Antoine-Louis Dominique |
| Roger Noël | Vladimir Volkoff |
| Commissaire Ferret | Henri Vernes |
| Hubert Bonisseur de La Bath (OSS 117) | Jean Bruce |
| Engineer Korrides | Jean de La Hire |
| Professor d'Olbans | Jean de La Hire |
| Sadi Khan | Jean de La Hire |
| Neil Armstrong | *Historical* |
| *And:* | |
| The Ioun Stones | Jack Vance |
| Acheron | Robert E. Howard |
| Z-4 | Jean de La Hire |
| Planet Rhwa | Jean de La Hire |

Original title: *Les Trois Soeurs*
English adaptation by Jean-Marc & Randy Lofficier
© 2011, Emmanuel Gorlier

## *The Season of the Shark*

| *Starring:* | *Created by:* |
|---|---|
| The Hictaner | Jean de La Hire |
| Paul Gauguin | *Historical* |
| Tobias Marsh | based on H.P. Lovecraft |
| Fulbert | Jean de la Hire |
| Dagon | H.P. Lovecraft |

Original title: *L'Heure du Squale*
English adaptation by Jean-Marc & Randy Lofficier
© 2011, Julien Heylbroeck

# The Lesson of Captain Danrit

**Also Starring:**
Pierre Saint-Clair
Captain Danrit (Colonel Driant)
Doctor Krueger

**Created by:**
Jean de La Hire
*Historical*
Robert J. Hogan

Original title: *La Leçon du Capitaine Danrit*
English adaptation by Jean-Marc & Randy Lofficier
© 2011, Emmanuel Gorlier

# The Hunters of Mars

**Also Starring:**
Oxus
John Carter
Dejah Thoris
Tars Tarkas
Norman of Torn
Phra
Kantos Kan
The Predator
Alan Quatermain
John Roxton
Sola
*And:*
The Tharks
The Sorn
The Cephales
The Hither
The Hross
The Thern
Ancient Martian Capsule

**Created by:**
Jean de La Hire
Edgar Rice Burroughs
Edgar Rice Burroughs
Edgar Rice Burroughs
Edgar Rice Burroughs
Edwin Arnold
Edgar Rice Burroughs
Jim & John Thomas
H. Rider Haggard
Arthur Conan Doyle
Edgar Rice Burroughs

Edgar Rice Burroughs
C.S. Lewis
H.G. Wells / Jean de La Hire
Edwin Arnold
C.S. Lewis
Edgar Rice Burroughs
Nigel Kneale

© 2011, Matthew Dennion

## The Children of Heracles

**Also Starring:**
Bernard Quatermass
Steven Karnes
Jeffrey Stuart
Anthony Vincenzo
Agent Lord (The Master)

Big Bad John
Nicholas Flynn
Lt. Col. Jack Evans

Office of Scientific Investigation
Piedmont, AZ
Evans City, PA
Snowfield, CA
Desperation, NV
The Martian Capsule

**Created by:**
Nigel Kneale
Robert Abel & Alan J. Adler
Curt Siodmak & Ivan Tors
Jeff Rice
Barry Letts, Terrance Dicks
& Robert Holmes
Jimmy Deal
Roman Leary
Lou Morheim
& Fred Freiberger*
Martin Caidin
& Kenneth Johnson
Michael Crichton
George Romero
Dean R. Koontz
Stephen King
Nigel Kneale

Previously published in *Tales of the Shadowmen N°6*, 2010

## The English Gentleman's Ball

**Also Starring:**
The Phantom Angel (Beauty)

Gregor Mac Duhl
Simone Desroches (Belphegor)
Sylvie Mac Duhl
Jeeves
Bertie Wooster

**Created by:**
Randy Lofficier based
on Charles Perrault
Jean de La Hire
Arthur Bernède
Jean de La Hire
P.G. Wodehouse
P.G. Wodehouse

Previously published in *Tales of the Shadowmen N°5*, 2009

## Death to the Heretic!

| Also Starring: | Created by: |
|---|---|
| Bruce Wayne | Bob Kane & Bill Finger |
| Alfred Pennyworth | Bob Kane |
| | & Jerry Robinson |
| Indiana Jones | George Lucas, |
| | Philip Kaufman |
| | & Lawrence Kasdan |
| Prof. William Omaha McElroy | Earl Barret, |
| (King Tut) | Robert C. Dennis |
| | & Charles R. Rondeau |
| Amelia Peabody Emerson | Elizabeth Peters |
| Radcliffe Emerson | Elizabeth Peters |
| Dr. Hugo Strange | Bob Kane & Bill Finger |
| Ted Grant | Bill Finger & Irwin Hasen |
| Dr. Francis Ardan | Guy d'Armen |

Previously published in *Tales of the Shadowmen N°7*, 2011

## The Nyctalope's New York Adventure

| Also Starring: | Created by: |
|---|---|
| Henry Arnaud / Lamont Cranston / The Shadow | William Gibson |
| Ivor "Ikey" Llewellyn | P.G. Wodehouse |
| Jacob Z. Schnellenhamer | P.G. Wodehouse |
| F.X. Weinberg | Anthony Boucher |
| Jacques Butcher | Ellery Queen |
| Dr. Orestes Preson | F. & R. Lockridge |
| Judge Ernest Coméliau | Georges Simenon |
| Zigomar | Léon Sazie |
| Paulin Broquet | Léon Sazie |
| Moe Shrevnitz | William Gibson |

| | |
|---|---|
| Sebastian Tombs / Simon Templar / The Saint | Leslie Charteris |
| Nero Wolfe | Rex Stout |
| Archie Goodwin | Rex Stout |
| Monsieur Anatole | P.G. Wodehouse |
| Tom & Dahlia Travers | P.G. Wodehouse |
| Inspector Cramer | Rex Stout |
| Sergeant Stebbins | Rex Stout |
| Colonel Dubois | Pierre Nord |
| Saul Panzer | Rex Stout |
| Prosper Lepicq | Pierre Véry |
| Fritz Brenner | Rex Stout |
| Harry the Horse | Damon Runyon |
| Little Isadore | Damon Runyon |
| Spanish John | Damon Runyon |
| DA Skinner | Rex Stout |
| Anthony Quinn | G. Wayman Jones |
| Alexandre Prillant | Jean de La Hire |
| William Valcross (Big Fellow) | Leslie Charteris |
| Inspector Fernack | Leslie Charteris |
| *And*: | |
| The Churchill Hotel | Rex Stout |
| The Panther Pilsner Brewery | Clyde Bruckman |

## *A Present for Hitler*

| ***Also Starring:*** | ***Created by:*** |
|---|---|
| Nina Boucher | Roman Leary |
| Otto Von Kubitz | Jean de La Hire |
| Herman Göring | *Historique* |
| Maciste | Giovanni Pastrone |
| | & Gabriele d' Annunzio |
| Dr. Merkwürdigliebe | Stanley Kubrick & |
| | Terry Southern |

Original title: *Un Cadeau pour le Führer*
English adaptation by Jean-Marc & Randy Lofficier
© 2011, Emmanuel Gorlier

## *Twilight*

| *Also Starring:* | *Created by:* |
|---|---|
| Gno Mitang | Jean de La Hire |
| Godzilla | Ishiro Honda, Takeo Murata |
| | & Shigeru Kayama |

Original title: *Crépuscule*
English adaptation by Jean-Marc & Randy Lofficier
© 2011, Emmanuel Gorlier

## *A Moment of Perfect Happiness*

| *Also Starring:* | *Created by:* |
|---|---|
| Mike Kovac | Don W. Sharp & Warren Lewis |
| Adrien de Villiers-Pagan | Jean de La Hire |
| Thomas Fowler | Graham Greene |
| Alden Pyle | Graham Greene |
| Phuong | Graham Greene |
| Jenny | Roman Leary |

© 2011, Roman Leary

## *The Mysterious Island of Dr. Antekirtt*

| *Also Starring:* | *Created by:* |
|---|---|
| The Captain | Hergé |
| The Boy Reporter | Hergé |
| His Little White Dog | Hergé |
| Bob Morane | Henri Vernes |
| Bernard Prince | Michel Greg |
| | & Hermann Huppen |

| M. Ming (The Yellow Shadow) | Henri Vernes |
| Dr. Julius No | Ian Fleming |
| Emilio Largo | Ian Fleming |
| Hubert Bonisseur de La Bath (OSS 117) | Jean Bruce |
| Bill Ballantine | Henri Vernes |
| Mathias Sandorf (Dr. Antekirtt) | Jules Verne |
| Hugo Drax | Ian Fleming |
| The Professeur | Hergé |
| Ernst Stavro Blofeld | Ian Fleming |
| Dr. Natas | Guy d'Armen |
| The Blue Scorpion | George F. Worts |
| Pointe Pescade | Jules Verne |
| André Malraux | *Historical* |
| Heinrich Himmler | *Historical* |
| ***And:*** | |
| Antekirtta | Jules Verne |
| The Si Fan | Sax Rohmer |
| The Shin Tan | Henri Vernes |

Previously published in *Tales of the Shadowmen N°7*, 2011

## *Out of Time*

| ***Also Starring:*** | ***Created by:*** |
| Hughes Korrides (Belzebuth) | Jean de La Hire |
| Maur Korrides | Jean de La Hire |
| Diana Ivanovna Krasnoview | Jean de La Hire |
| Prosper Korrides | Jean de La Hire |
| Heinrich Zemo | Stan Lee & Jack Kirby |
| Noël Essaillon | René Barjavel |
| Pierre Saint-Menoux | René Barjavel |
| Sylvie Saint-Clair *née* MacDuhl | Jean de La Hire |
| Pierre Saint-Clair | Jean de La Hire |
| Oxus | Jean de La Hire |
| Bob Morane | Henri Vernes |

| Manse Everard | Poul Anderson |
| Colonel Graigh | Henri Vernes |
| The Time Patrol | Poul Anderson |
| | & Henri Vernes |
| Adolf Hitler | *Historical* |
| Alfred Rosenberg | *Historical* |
| Hermann Göring | *Historical* |
| Rudolf Hess | *Historical* |

Original title: *Nyctalope, si tu savais...*
English adaptation by Jean-Marc & Randy Lofficier
© 2010, Emmanuel Gorlier
Previously published in *Tales of the Shadowmen N°6*, 2010

## SF & FANTASY

Henri Allorge. *The Great Cataclysm*
Guy d'Armen. *Doc Ardan: The City of Gold and Lepers*
G.-J. Arnaud. *The Ice Company*
Cyprien Bérard. *The Vampire Lord Ruthwen*
Aloysius Bertrand. *Gaspard de la Nuit*
Richard Bessière. *The Gardens of the Apocalypse*
Albert Bleunard. *Ever Smaller*
Félix Bodin. *The Novel of the Future*
Alphonse Brown. *City of Glass*
André Caroff. *The Terror of Madame Atomos; Miss Atomos; The Return of Madame Atomos*
Félicien Champsaur. *The Human Arrow*
Didier de Chousy. *Ignis*
Captain Danrit. *Undersea Odyssey*
C. I. Defontenay. *Star (Psi Cassiopeia)*
Charles Derennes. *The People of the Pole*
Georges Dodds (anthologist). *The Missing Link*
Harry Dickson. *The Heir of Dracula*
Jules Dornay. *Lord Ruthven Begins*
Sâr Dubnotal *vs. Jack the Ripper*
Alexandre Dumas. *The Return of Lord Ruthven*
Renée Dunan. *Baal*
J.-C. Dunyach. *The Night Orchid; The Thieves of Silence*
Henri Duvernois. *The Man Who Found Himself*
Achille Eyraud. *Voyage to Venus*
Henri Falk. *The Age of Lead*
Paul Féval. *Anne of the Isles; Knightshade; Revenants; Vampire City; The Vampire Countess; The Wandering Jew's Daughter*
Paul Féval, *fils. Felifax, the Tiger-Man*
Charles de Fieux. *Lamékis*
Arnould Galopin. *Doctor Omega; Doctor Omega & The Shadowmen*
G.L. Gick. *Harry Dickson and the Werewolf of Rutherford Grange*
Nathalie Henneberg. *The Green Gods*
V. Hugo, P. Foucher & P. Meurice. *The Hunchback of Notre-Dame*
Michel Jeury. *Chronolysis*
Octave Joncquel & Théo Varlet. *The Martian Epic*
Gérard Klein. *The Mote in Time's Eye*
Jean de La Hire. *Enter the Nyctalope; The Nyctalope on Mars; The Nyctalope vs. Lucifer; The Nyctalope Steps In*

Etienne-Léon de Lamothe-Langon. *The Virgin Vampire*
André Laurie. *Spiridon*
Gabriel de Lautrec. *The Vengeance of the Oval Portrait*
Georges Le Faure & Henri de Graffigny. *The Extraordinary Adventures of a Russian Scientist Across the Solar System* (2 vols.)
Gustave Le Rouge. *The Vampires of Mars*
Jules Lermina. *Mysteryville; Panic in Paris; To-Ho and the Gold Destroyers; The Secret of Zippelius*
Jean-Marc & Randy Lofficier. *Edgar Allan Poe on Mars; The Katrina Protocol; Pacifica; Robonocchio; Tales of the Shadowmen 1-7*
Xavier Mauméjean. *The League of Heroes*
José Moselli. *Illa's End*
John-Antoine Nau. *Enemy Force*
Marie Nizet. *Captain Vampire*
C. Nodier, A. Beraud & Toussaint-Merle. *Frankenstein*
Henri de Parville. *An Inhabitant of the Planet Mars*
J. Polidori, C. Nodier, E. Scribe. *Lord Ruthven the Vampire*
P.-A. Ponson du Terrail. *The Vampire and the Devil's Son*
Maurice Renard. *The Blue Peril; Doctor Lerne; The Doctored Man; A Man Among the Microbes; The Master of Light*
Jean Richepin. *The Wing*
Albert Robida. *The Adventures of Saturnin Farandoul; The Clock of the Centuries; Chalet in the Sky*
J.-H. Rosny Aîné. *Helgvor of the Blue River; The Givreuse Enigma; The Mysterious Force; The Navigators of Space; Vamireh; The World of the Variants; The Young Vampire*
Marcel Rouff. *Journey to the Inverted World*
Han Ryner. *The Superhumans*
Brian Stableford. *The New Faust at the Tragicomique;The Empire of the Necromancers (The Shadow of Frankenstein; Frankenstein and the Vampire Countess; Frankenstein in London); Sherlock Holmes & The Vampires of Eternity; The Stones of Camelot; The Wayward Muse.* (anthologist) *The Germans on Venus; News from the Moon; The Supreme Progress; The World Above the World*
Jacques Spitz. *The Eye of Purgatory*
Kurt Steiner. *Ortog*
Eugène Thébault. *Radio-Terror*
C.-F. Tiphaigne de La Roche. *Amilec*
Théo Varlet. *The Xenobiotic Invasion*
Paul Vibert. *The Mysterious Fluid*
Villiers de l'Isle-Adam. *The Scaffold; The Vampire Soul*

Philippe Ward. *Artahe*
Philippe Ward & Sylvie Miller. *The Song of Montségur*

## MYSTERIES & THRILLERS

M. Allain & P. Souvestre. *The Daughter of Fantômas*
A. Anicet-Bourgeois, Lucien Dabril. *Rocambole*
A. Bisson & G. Livet. *Nick Carter vs. Fantômas*
V. Darlay & H. de Gorsse. *Lupin vs. Holmes: The Stage Play*
Paul Féval. *Gentlemen of the Night; John Devil; The Black Coats
('Salem Street; The Invisible Weapon; The Parisian Jungle; The
Companions of the Treasure; Heart of Steel; The Cadet Gang; The
Sword-Swallower)*
Emile Gaboriau. *Monsieur Lecoq*
Steve Leadley. *Sherlock Holmes: The Circle of Blood*
Maurice Leblanc. *Arsène Lupin vs. Countess Cagliostro; Lupin vs.
Holmes (The Blonde Phantom; The Hollow Needle)*
Gaston Leroux. *Chéri-Bibi; The Phantom of the Opera; Rouletabille
& the Mystery of the Yellow Room*
William Patrick Maynard. *The Terror of Fu Manchu*
Frank J. Morlock. *Sherlock Holmes: The Grand Horizontals; Sher-
lock Holmes vs Jack the Ripper*
P. de Wattyne & Y. Walter. *Sherlock Holmes vs. Fantômas*
David White. *Fantômas in America*

## SCREENPLAYS

Mike Baron. *The Iron Triangle*
Emma Bull & Will Shetterly. *Nightspeeder; War for the Oaks*
Gerry Conway & Roy Thomas. *Doc Dynamo*
Steve Englehart. *Majorca*
James Hudnall. *The Devastator*
Jean-Marc & Randy Lofficier. *Royal Flush*
J.-M. & R. Lofficier & Marc Agapit. *Despair*
Andrew Paquette. *Peripheral Vision*
R. Thomas, J. Hendler & L. Sprague de Camp. *Rivers of Time*

## NON-FICTION

Stephen R. Bissette. *Blur 1-5; Green Mountain Cinema 1; Teen An-
gels & New Mutants*

Win Scott Eckert. *Crossovers* (2 vols.)
Jean-Marc & Randy Lofficier. *Shadowmen* (2 vols.)
Randy Lofficier. *Over Here*

## HEXAGON COMICS

Franco Frescura & Luciano Bernasconi. *Wampus*
Franco Frescura & Giorgio Trevisan. *CLASH*
L. Bernasconi, J.-M. Lofficier & Juan Roncagliolo Berger. *Phenix*
Claude Legrand, J.-M. Lofficier & L. Bernasconi. *Kabur*
Franco Oneta. *Zembla*
L. Buffolente, Lofficier & J.-J. Dzialowski. *Strangers: Homicron*
Danilo Grossi. *Strangers: Jaydee*
Claude Legrand & Luciano Bernasconi. *Strangers: Starlock*

## ART BOOKS

Jean-Pierre Normand. *Science Fiction Illustrations*
Raven Okeefe. *Raven's L'il Critters*
Randy Lofficier & Raven OKeefe. *If Your Possum Go Daylight...*
Daniele Serra. *Illusions*